The Architect's Manifesto©

The Architect's Manifesto

A Political Thriller

Steve Jaffe

A Weaver of Tales Press

www.aweaveroftalespress.com

A Weaver of Tales Press

Palm Desert, Ca. 92211

This book is a work of fiction. Names, characters, places, and incidents either are products of the author's imagination or are used factiously. Any resemblance to actual events or locales or persons living, or dead is entirely coincidental.

 ISBN 978-0-9819410-5-9

 For information about this book or A Weaver of Tales Press email: sjaffe822@gmail.com or visit website at www.aweaveroftalespress.com

Dedication

To my wife Nancy, my best friend and biggest supporter, without your love, collaboration, and encouragement, I would not be a writer today.

Other Novels by Steve Jaffe

The Haven House Chronicles, The Conspiracy
ISBN:978-0-9819410-0-4

Children With Invisible Faces
ISBN:978-09819410-4-2

God's Looking Glass
ISBN: 978-0-9819410-2-8

The Stranger I Came To Love
ISBN:978-0-9819410-3-5

The Invisible Enemy
ISBN:978-09819410-4-2

Review all books at: www.aweaveroftalespress.com

1

A Year and a Half Before the Presidential Election

President Chesterfield paced around the situation room like a caged tiger. He was awaiting word if his forty-billion-dollar top-secret satellite launch had booted up and was ready to protect the entire cyber-infrastructure of the United States. He had made a campaign promise to protect his country from its enemies who continued to hack the information infrastructure every citizen trusted. No more will Americans be influenced and manipulated by countries that hate democracy.

His predecessor, who was convicted of treason, had fled the country and was under the protection of Russia. He had lost all his business holdings and was paying Russia millions of dollars to live there the rest of his life with his daughter and two sons, draining his wealth. What would happen to him when his funds ran out was anyone's guess.

The entire room was filled with the president's closest advisors. They all sat silent their eyes riveted on the eighty-inch monitor.

They had live coverage of their new weapon and were waiting for confirmation that the satellite had booted up.

Chesterfield stopped pacing. He was positioned behind his NSA director Douglas Babcock's chair. His hands were squeezing his director's shoulders tightly. "How long will it take for you to confirm that my weapon has been activated and ready to do its job?"

"Anytime now, sir. I've had one of our weather satellites positioned so we can witness this magnificent event live from one of their high-resolution cameras. This will be historic, sir," he said.

President Chesterfield flopped down in his chair, riveted on every twitch on his NSA Director's face. His presidency and re-election were riding on this satellite's software to allow the United States to disable any enemy's cyber threats. The tax dollars he had spent he justified was for national security. He had inherited a mess from the previous president, who had refused to allocate enough money to counter Russian and Chinese cyber-attacks into America's election systems and power grids. He had made a commitment to every citizen that he'd defend the country from all threats, and within minutes, his promise was about to be kept.

Chesterfield made bold promises during his campaign run within his first term restore the security systems the United States needed to thwart any cyber attack by any foreign enemy. It had not been easy selling his current idea to Congress. It had been voted down four times. The House of Representatives had a memory loss about their failures with the last administration, blaming him and his administration for not adequately protecting the security of the country he swore to protect and defend. He realized he had to take matters into his own hands and declared a National Emergency, re-allocating funds from the military budget.

Inside the situation room with him and the NSA Director, where his Joint Chiefs, the Secretary of Defense, the CIA Director and his Chief of Staff. Congress did not know about this secret project. Failure was not an option he could afford a year and a half before his re-election bid, which every national poll was showing him not doing well. For the president, this would be a game-changer.

He watched the large digital wall clock ticking down. He had two more minutes until his weapon was fully functional. He'd have the ace up his sleeve to help him get re-elected and overcome the impeachment inquiry that had started.

Babcock was rocking back and forth in his chair. He was rubbing his hands together nervously. "Mr. President, this project will be huge for this country. Your administration's war on terrorism will be a big victory for you," he said.

"Not just the war of terrorism," president Chesterfield said, "but our ability to disable weapon testing around the world by our enemies, especially North Korea," he said, his voice calm and resolute. "The NSA will, once again, be this country's eyes and ears, keeping us safe again."

The digital clock continued to tick down...three, two, one. Then, the large monitor went black for a few seconds, as the weather satellite's cameras stopped recording, and the new communications satellite attempted to boot up and become operational.

Babcock was pressing his earbud, listening to a response from Houston. His face turned bedsheet white. He looked at the president and shook his head.

Chesterfield did not know what to make of his reaction. "Speak up. What's happening?"

Babcock's words sputtered out of his mouth. "Sir, we've lost our communication signal. NASA is trying to reboot again, but nothing was happening. Right now, we have a satellite spinning around the earth, and we do not have any control over it," he said, blotting his forehead with a napkin.

"What the fuck does this mean? What just happened? If we don't have control, who does?" He was rubbing his temples, his chin resting on his chest, a vacant stare at the monitor.

"Sir, I doubt anyone could have hacked into this system. It was top secret-with firewalls that are impenetrable. Only the people in this room knew about what we were doing. We'd be in a whole lot of trouble if our enemies got a hold of this weapon," Babcock said.

Chesterfield leaned back in his high-back leather chair, his hands squeezing his cheeks. "If we've lost control, then it needs to be destroyed," he ordered.

Babcock bit his lips, drawing blood. "Sir that might be a problem. We have no communication with the satellite. Our missiles cannot reach the high orbit we had placed this satellite in. It was, if you remember, your fail-safe scenario."

"Shit. So, we watch and wait. Maybe pray that a foreign hacker group has not gotten control of our most powerful weapon? I feel this will be the final nail, in my already decomposing coffin," he sighed.

2

Twenty-four months before the Presidential Election

The crisp February wind whipped through the open window of the Black Ford LTD, as it sped down 10th avenue heading toward the Lincoln Tunnel. Brian Russell sensed he was heading toward New Jersey to some secluded spot where the mob buries the men they want to disappear. His heart sank as a familiar voice from the front passenger seat spoke.

"You should not have done this, Brian. Ellison and the council are pissed. You're a traitor. You could have spoiled all our plans. You realize there will be consequences," his friend Todd Mathews said. His voice was cold and stern.

Brian Russell just shrugged his shoulders. He smiled at the man he once called a friend. "What happened to you Todd? I thought ...well, it doesn't matter now, does it?" he said, his voice trembling.

"It does matter that we, the council's inner circle, the Architect's most trusted members, must meet all of our timetables. President Chesterfield is trying to disrupt the status quo and disrupt our ability to grow our wealth. You once believed in our manifesto and that our plan is for the good of our country and every American," Mathews said, his tone calm and unemotional. "You signed an oath to transform America. Instead, you've attempted to tank the world economies, threating the Architects strategy...must I go on listing your stupidity?"

"Maybe what I've done was needed to reset our country and the world from people like you and the Architect," said Russell, an air of confidence in his voice. "You know that copies of the files detailing all of your plans are set to go out to all the major news organizations," he said smugly. "What the council is planning for NSA's new communications satellite, the chip you had me create, is going too far and I won't let it happen. I created the software, and only I can disable it," he bragged, then realizing he had just signed his death warrant.

"You're very foolish. We have too many proxies on our side at NASA and the NSA. And, we knew about your little scheme. It almost bypassed our security, but you failed. We now know you're our enemy. All the emails, with your attachments, have been intercepted and deleted. Our loyalists at the NSA believe what you were doing was against the Architect's Manifesto and jumped at the chance to help us. Our country and the world, need a major reset and we are the men that can do it," Mathews said smugly. "We tried with the previous president, but failed. Not this time."

"You're all mad. This country will never let this happen," Russell said defiantly.

Mathews was losing his patience with him. "Soon, we'll have full control, and no one will be able to stop us. Just know that your wife and children will be well taken care of once they file a death claim. It was very naive of you to think we do not know every move our employees take," Mathews said, his calm tone evaporating into one of arrogance. "We had such high hopes for you. We have all been tested during our probation. Some, like you, have failed, and have paid the price. We need men and women loyal to The Architect's inner circle and who believe in his vision. Loyalty is paramount to our success."

Brian was surprised by the overreaching power of the group, but he prayed that they did not know about the two friends to whom he had sent the thumb drive files. He was sure those two people were beyond the reach of the Architect. If not, all that Russell had risked would have been in vain. He knew the packages would be received later today. They were untraceable, as the return address had a fictitious business name and bogus address. The note inside would reveal who sent the package. He leaned his head back, feeling a deep sense of relief. He knew it was all going to be over soon.

3

Brian's eyes were empty as his forehead pressed hard against the car door window. He struggled to recognize any landmarks, as the car sped to some unknown location. His mind was on overdrive remembering the day; his crazy decision had changed his life. It happened during a briefing with the Architect and his most trusted advisors.

That meeting had taken a scary turn for Russell. What he had heard from the Architect and Frederick Ellison, who he worked for, gave him the chills. For the first time, he fully understood what his role within Architect's council had been. Thoughts of treason exploded like a mushroom cloud inside his head, muffling the chatter within the conference room.

The one thing that scared him the most was the computer chip he and his team of software analysts had been asked to create. When he heard that it was going to be inserted within the motherboard of an upcoming NSA satellite launch of a new and powerful NSA cyberweapons satellite Russell knew the Architect was up to no good. He knew if it worked, he would be tried as a traitor to the country he loved, and the Architect would finally have his greatest wish, unstoppable power.

During the meeting, everyone had to renew their allegiance to this project, and the Architect's Manifesto. There was no wiggle room.

A few days after the meeting, Russell had been asked to update Frederick Ellison's computer with a new virus protection software. He was the only person allowed inside his boss's office and to have access to his laptop. He knew that The Architect and Ellison were like brothers.

He had tried to forget about the meeting earlier that week, except it was bothering him too much. Ellison's screen had accidentally remained opened, revealing files of the Architect's

Manifesto. He quickly glanced at the thirty plus folders and their titles. At first, the headings seemed innocent enough. "What's in a silly title?" he muttered. Then, he read one file large file that piqued his curiosity: *"The Architect's Manifesto."* Once inside the folder, he could not stop reading all the entries that had been made. It was like reading a suspense thriller. As it turned out, these files were the entries from four generations of Architects.

At first, he thought Ellison had helped write some of the current entries, but after reading more and more of the actual plans and its hundred and fifty-year timeline to create a wealthy family dynasty, he suspected it had to be Dunham. He quickly scanned the other file folders and found them to contain other encrypted files that he could not readily open.

What frightened Russell the most was the endgame the current Architect had planned. He was alarmed at what this man and his family had accomplished since the late eighteen-hundreds at the expense of so many lives. What Russell realized he had created with his computer chip was the grand finale. Stage Five would not happen until a lot of domestic and foreign distractions took place. They were designed to distract the president so the Architect's Manifesto could be implemented unnoticed by the NSA and CIA.

The files had notations of conspiracies, deceptions, murders, as well as bribes that involved men in high places. Not just within the United States, but throughout Europe and the Middle East, building a network of hundreds of thousands of loyal conspirators to the Architect's plan.

The first entry in the journal went back to eighteen hundred and ninety-five. While some files were encrypted, Russell knew he could break the code once he was home. Some of the folders were open and easy to read and understand, which seemed a little too arrogant for a man of such secrecy.

Russell realized that what he had in his possession was more significant than that. The Manifesto had detailed dates and events they had created to build their wealthy family dynasty. The Architect's current wealth recorded in his file had grown to trillions of dollars. His family was into every industry in the United States and around the world.

These Architects were geniuses, Russell thought. Each completed playbook was passed down to each first-born male heir with instructions to begin their manifesto and build upon the creator's blueprint. He knew he could not live with himself if he did not expose the current Architect's Manifesto.

The Architect's inner circle believed that they were the chosen ones who had the responsibility to take care of everyone. They were instructed to keep a precise balance and order among the poor, middle-class, and the rich.

The group was more than just wealthy; they were the men and women who controlled everything from behind the scenes. They were implanted within governments, intelligence agencies, conglomerates, and law enforcement agencies within the United States and around the world. They were also embedded within news organizations so their message could be spread as fact. They had the power to influence public opinions and financial markets, as well as conflicts between countries in every region on the face of the Earth. Enemies of the Architect would quickly disappear, and the case would be buried by one of his proxies.

While Russell was not from the original inner circle, he came into it for the innovative new computer systems he created that helped bring the group and their plans into the twenty-first century. Little did he know he was assisting the architect with his final step to becoming the political power he so wanted.

The sound of Mathew's voice triggered the moment he had been captured at Clancy's, a small tavern near the Hoboken ferry. He had been waiting for his friend, the CEO of York Industries, to arrive. His friend sat on the financial regulatory board that controlled the stock exchange. At Harvard Business

School, they both had been idealists back then, believing they could make a better world for the average Joe.

Mathews was thirty minutes late. His tardiness only put Brian's nerves on overdrive. Russell's eyes grew wide with fear when he detected three men enter the tavern wearing trench coats.

He watched the first man his eyes riveted on him, pressing his finger to his ear, and talking into his watch. These men were out of place, and he knew what it meant. The man talking had seen Russell and signaled his partners to approach the bar, cutting off any means of escape.

Russell's heart pounded loudly, drowning out the chatter inside his head and in the tavern. He took one final gulp of his third Martini. He whispered a sad goodbye to his only friend now...Hendricks Gin. He felt the firm hand clamp on the back of his neck.

"Mr. Russell, you need to stand up, remain calm and come with us quietly," he said flashing his FBI Shield.

4

The TV personality and investigative reporter Paige Turner had signed off from her Sunday broadcast. Her boss, Clay Thomas, had signaled her a two-thumbs up.

Her show *"Corrupted Intelligence: The Manipulation of the American People"* had become one of Sunday's most-watched TV shows since the previous president was tried and convicted of treason. She believed the wealthy still controlled the daily lives of every American, as well as the catastrophic events that seemed to manipulate the financial markets every week. Like her boss, she was beginning to think one wealthy family was the puppet master. She just did not who this person was. At one point, she believed it was the previous president, but it turned out he was not as wealthy as he had made himself out to be. He was just a puppet who was put into office to line the pockets of the wealthy. She needed a break, and it was not coming fast enough.

Clay did not seem happy today. She knew he had pressure from his sponsors and backers to make her show live up to its promise to expose the real shadow government that controlled everything.

"Your show was great as usual. I love what you're doing," said Clay, with a 'but' coming. "We need to narrow it down and expose someone. The sponsors are beginning to get nervous your audience is going to go elsewhere to find something to hate about their country. We need someone to blame for all our problems, and the anger everyone is feeling. While we can blame President Chesterfield, we both know he's not the cause. He inherited a mess."

Paige said. "I can't make up something that's not there. You know me. If everyone is unhappy with my show, then cancel it," she growled.

Clay raised both hands, his palms facing toward Paige. "Whoa. Nobody is saying to cancel your show. We need a better direction to get the ratings a bit higher."

Paige shook her head, showing her frustration with her boss. "I'm getting close. The problem we have is that there are too many billionaires and none of them want to be interviewed. I don't have a magic wand, that I can snap it in the air, and presto, we have our villain. I'm good at what I do, but not that good."

"Forget about what I said. I will handle the sponsors and the board of directors. You do your job, and it will all work out. I'm sure of it. You've always been able to expose the story at the right time."

Paige stood and gave Clay a warm hug. "You're a good friend. I'll push my team to see if we can rattle some cages before the next show."

Her hand-picked team of reporters consisted of a group of seasoned men and women who loved the non-partisan independence the network and show had granted them. Whatever they worked on, they acted for all Americans. "Red or Blue" played no part in their investigations or recommendations to the Turner. Nothing was politically slanted. Paige did not take sides, not even with the current president.

Her team was spread out around the United States and in all corners of the globe. Their mission, to uncover and report about powerful, influential men and women who affected the lives of average Americans and ordinary people in and around the countries that were America's allies. Then Paige would give their stories her *Corrupted Intelligence* test during her Sunday broadcasts.

Paige was a real kick-ass reporter who was embedded in the Iraq and Afghanistan wars early on in her career. She had been the first female to follow into action a SEAL team, reporting the news from both points of view in the Middle East.

For a reporter, a female reporter, there was nothing she could not do. She never used her beauty and charm to manipulate the men she had to interview. Unfortunately, for those men, it was a distraction, and she took full advantage of it.

She had just turned forty-five and was in the best shape of her life. Her five-foot-ten, a hundred forty pounds of lean muscle, with a face of a model, long black silky hair, and almond-shaped hazel eyes, was an asset for her. She did not present herself as a tough, get under your skin type of journalist. She never thought of herself as competitive but losing was not an option for her. Each story would not be aired unless she was one hundred percent sure it was truthful and most importantly, accurate.

On her drive home to Malibu, her briefing with Clay Thomas had her concerned. He needed her to find some real links to her *Corrupted Intelligence* theory. She believed something was happening inside the United States. She felt it. The problem for her was she could not put her finger on it. Like 9/11, the warning signs were there; they did not know where or when it would be happening. And, Paige believed that something huge was coming. Her gut told her it was coming sooner, rather than later.

There was new information she had been briefed on, about a wealthy businessman, Albert Dunham. He had her concerned. He had refused her numerous requests for an interview. He was one of the most philanthropic men in the world. She wondered if most Americans loved him, and most countries around the world respected him, so what was he hiding?

She needed to clear her mind. She was having her horrible flashbacks about the death of her husband. He too, had been an investigative journalist. He shot and killed while reporting about the formation of a shadow government hidden deep inside the beltway of Washington. The police called it a random shooting, but Paige believed he had been ambushed and murdered. She needed a comfortable ten mile run on the beach and Highway One to clear her mind.

* * * * *

Paige had returned from her run, slowing down as she approached the driveway leading up to her beachfront house. Breathing heavily, she decelerated to a fast walking pace. It was her cool-down routine. She moved her head from left to right, sighing as her eyes panned her prized hundred eighty-degree views of the Pacific Ocean. She paused for a few stretches briefly lifting her head, so her eyes could switch to the crystal blue sky, dotted with white puffy clouds.

Paige took a deep cleansing breath, *"Boy I'm blessed,"* she whispered. She always reminded herself how lucky she and her husband Rick had been to snatch up this property. That happy thought evaporated, as she bit her lower lip, the reality sinking in that her husband was not alive to appreciate their home.

Turner's mind never stopped second-guessing her decisions. It was her curse. Her head never emptied from the "What if's" that plagued her every day since Rick was murdered. It was the same loop over-and-over again: *"what if I had not allowed Rick to go alone? What if I'd said no and had another reporter go in his place?* Then reality set in and she realized there was nothing anyone could have done to prevent what happened to her husband. He was assassinated because he was getting too close to the men that were part of his investigation. If it hadn't happened then, it would have happened another time.

Paige understood Rick was a professional, and he did what he was trained to do. She had to live with the pain of her husband's death by burying herself in her work 24/7. She knew she'd never stop looking for her husband's killer or killers believing it was purposely done by some homegrown Second Amendment fanatics that were manipulated by some powerful politicians. She had made a promise at his gravesite that she would find his killers.

Paige let out a deep sigh, trying to erase those bad memories and focus on her upcoming show next Sunday. After stretching and finishing her cool down in front of her double stained-glass doors that hid her expansive living room with floor to ceiling double-paned windows that faced the beautiful pounding surf, she noticed a small package at her front door. Before opening the door, she lifted the FedEx package that had been resting on the left side of her entryway.

She was surprised to receive any packages at her home. Only close friends and Clay Thomas had her address. All media business was sent to the station, care of Paige Turner. She did not recognize the return address or the business name. Then, she remembered a disturbing phone message she had received from her friend Brian Russell.

They had remained close friends when they first met at Stanford. He was a guest speaker at her investigative reporting classes. She had received his message a few days earlier. She did not pay much attention to it. He had told her he was sending her a package with something that would help her with her corrupted intelligence theory.

She put the package down at her desk and decided to jump into a shower. Before she sat down to relax and review her notes for her next show, she needed to steam off the dirt and grime from her run.

After drying off and slipping on her sweatpants and hooded Stanford sweatshirt, she opened the FedEx box and shook out a tiny thumb drive. What fell out next was a folded sheet of paper showing a family tree that dated back to the late 1800s. Brian had included a handwritten note that made Paige very nervous.

"*Paige, I am sorry to get you involved with this. You're the only person I believe can expose this man. Please read all the files. They tell a scary story about this family and the current heir. You will need to find someone to open the encrypted files. I believe they contain the specifics of this Architect's entire game plan, his manifesto for our country. I might not be around to help you with this. I did something...well...I'm running for my life right now. Please help."*

Paige was stunned by the note, her eyes wide with concern as she popped the thumb drive into her computer. She began reading files about one man's dream for his family's future who had the title *The Architect,* and how he planned to be wealthy and control the United States. Paige did not at first think much of what was inside the files, except when she read about what this person had mapped out with his Five Stage Plan, she could not stop reading. Also, on the thumb drive were fifty additional files that were encrypted.

Paige knew that if all of what she read in these files were true, the upcoming election was about to change America forever. The current president would not survive his first term.

What Turner knew as a reporter was that she had to tread very lightly, with stolen property. Brian had just put her in the middle of an ethical conundrum. She wanted to talk to him first before she began investigating this *Architect.*

5

Albert Dunham hung up the phone; his mood was hyper, ready to explode. His enforcer assured him that the stolen files would be back in his possession, once again hidden from the world.

He was upset that he misjudged Russell's loyalty. "*What did I not see with Russell?* Dunham questioned himself. "*I thought he believed in my vision.*"

He had no time for this Russell problem. He was meeting with the Israeli, Palestinian and Hamas leaders tomorrow and then with Greece, Italy and Spain's finance ministers the following day. They were part of his Stage One and Stage Two inside his Manifesto.

It did not matter that his plan might be exposed. What mattered more to Dunham was the encrypted files Russell stole. They were critical to his fifth stage inside his manifesto. He prayed that those files were not in the wrong hands.

His manifesto's first phase was set to begin in a few days, with the final stage implemented no later than ten months from today. His plan was flexible and knew his schedule could be moved up if needed. What he was planning was not precisely his great-grandfather's plan, but one that had an excellent vision for every American, including himself.

Capturing all copies of his files was his only priority now. He could not afford delays or setbacks. It would start a domino effect putting him too far behind on his plans. The timing was everything to the Architect. His network of loyal men and women within the United States government, military and intelligence communities and in over seventy-five key countries, were all on high alert ready to carry out their agreed-upon missions at his signal. He just needed to know if Ellison had contained the leak.

Leaning back in his chair, his arms locked behind his neck, he stared at the ceiling. A fan circulated slowly, matching the crazy thoughts spinning inside his mind.

"This country grew to be a superpower because of my great-grandpa," he whispered. "If it weren't for him, the United States would be a third world country, relying on Europe for its economic stability. It's my turn to fix America's problems once and for all." His voice grew louder as each thought consumed him. His phone buzzed, startling him.

"Albert, are you alright?" his wife Maggie asked.

He leaned forward his voice cracked into the speaker on his desk. "Just fine. Too much on my mind, sweetheart."

"Well, if you need anything, just let me know," she said lovingly.

He massaged his scalp falling back into his chair deep in thought. *Everything will be okay. I hope* he told himself.

His eyes squeezed tight. A shiver shuddered over his body at the thought he was going to be responsible for Russell's death. He could not understand why he felt panic about killing someone. He had ordered other traitors eliminated before. Members of Congress, senators, journalists, even a Supreme Court judge had felt his power.

He pondered why this Russell's failure upset him so much? He thought for a moment and realized he was the driving force for the computer chip that was going to be added to the motherboard of a new NSA satellite. "Shit, Brian, look what you've done," he whispered, glancing at his watch.

He had delegated the interrogation of Russell to Ellison. His men were the best he had and would get what they needed from their traitor.

However, today, the Architect would rest, and his all too familiar role as a philanthropist would come to life. He would be receiving an award this afternoon for the charity work his foundation was doing for the poor and homeless. Then, tomorrow, another award for all the inner-city projects he supported, and then an essential trip to the Middle East and Europe that would be part of his upcoming two stages. Rumor had it that he was in line for Fortune Magazine's Man of the Year award. His Image was the most important thing to him, and nothing was going to shame him in the eyes of the world.

6

Brian Russell, battered and bloodied, was surprised he was still alive on a crazy Friday afternoon after the beating he had experienced. Ellison's tormentor was screaming at him. His words were drowned out by the burning pain radiating over his entire body.

Russell's nerve endings were on fire with each breath he took. He knew he had ribs broken. He didn't know how many. The swelling on both of his eyes prevented him from seeing who was yelling profanities at him.

He had told them everything they had asked. Their methods of torture were on par with what was suspected the CIA used for years. Nevertheless, he suspected they were not satisfied with his answers, as they continued punching his face and alternating to his broken ribcage.

Occupying the damp, humid room were members from the Architect's inner circle. They were all shouting out questions at him. They were there to witness what happens to traitors, as well as to show their loyalty to a man who controlled every breath they took.

While he could not see clearly, he could sense he was in some metal storage container, the angry voices were echoing off the walls, while a bright floodlight directed at his face hid his interrogator identity from his view.

What he heard spewing from his tormentor's lips was very satisfying. It gave him some pleasure that he had made the Architect nervous. He tried to smile with the thought that he had everyone worried that their little secret was floating out there ready to expose them, and their corrupted plan for every American to see.

Russell tried to open his swollen eyelids to see who was approaching his chair. But the white beam of light made it impossible. He sucked in a painful breath.

A familiar voice leaned in close and calmly whispered another question for him to answer. By the Irish accent, he knew it was Frasier Montgomery, the Architect's enforcer. At that moment, Russell fully understood that the pain would continue until they were satisfied with his answers. Another forceful slap to the back of his already throbbing head knocked him forward on the metal chair he was strapped to, knocking him over to the cement floor and landing on his broken ribs, with his face resting on the warm bloody floor.

Fraiser Montgomery yanked him up by the collar of his shirt. "Brian, my good friend, I hate having to do this to you, but you have not been truthful with us, right?" he said in a soft melodic voice, his Irish accent reflecting his displeasure.

Brian shook his head violently, trying to spit, but he was so dehydrated, his lips caked with dried saliva, and blood, that he had nothing left, but a loud moan, as it fell from his tongue.

"I've told you everything," he pleaded, his voice raspy and barely audible. "Please stop and let me die."

Frasier just laughed. "Brian that will happen when we believe you have told us everything. So, make it easy on yourself, and you can die quickly and painlessly". Montgomery was interrupted by another familiar voice. Brian tried to smile as Albert Ellison began speaking.

"Brian, I am so disappointed with you. You had so much promise. We let you into our world, groomed you for great things, and gave you enough wealth to last a hundred lifetimes. And..." he paused, yanking Brian's head back by the nape of his hair, "you violated your loyalty oath. You have not convinced me that we've intercepted all of the copies you made." He twisted his head abruptly to his left, exposing his wife and young son strapped to two chairs, duck-tape covering their mouths.

"Now, you little ungrateful shit, tell me the truth or your wife dies first."

Brian, with what little eyes sight he had left, could see the fear on his wife's and son's face. "You didn't you say my family would be okay?" his voice trembling. "I've told you everything," he coughed out. Seeing the look on Montgomery's face told him that no matter what he told them his family was going to die with him.

Frederick Ellison bent over and looked Russell in the face. "We lied. Traitors and their family are always eliminated," he said without any emotion.

Russell spat in his boss's face. "Ellison you're an evil man that will get what's coming to you, you bastard," he barked.

Ellison turned, pointed his gun at Brian's wife, and put a bullet in the middle of her forehead. He leaned down his face directly in front of Russell's. "Your son will be next if you do not tell me what I want to hear. I promise you I can have this unnecessary torture stopped right now if you tell us who else has copies of our files?"

Russell mouthed he was sorry to his son, who was crying uncontrollably and shaking in his chair after witnessing what just happened to his mother. "I have nothing else to say," he said, his voice cracking. He watched Ellison turn from him and put his gun up to the side of his son's temple and blow half his head off.

With no feeling on his face, Ellison came over to Russell with one final question. "What surprises me is that you did not send copies of your little conspiracy to the reporter bitch Paige Turner." Ellison grinned when he saw the tell on Russell's face. Right then he knew Turner had a copy. He turned to Frasier and signaled him to end it. Ellison turned toward the live video feed and gave the Architect two thumbs up.

"We are done here. Dispose of the bodies and let's all meet back at my office at nine this evening. We have one loose end that needs to handled delicately." Ellison turned his head and saw Montgomery press his revolver to Russell's temple. He walked away, just shaking his head in disgust.

Brian knew it was finally going to be over. What he had witnessed had given him a sense of relief, not that the pain would soon be over, and not that Ellison had any idea who the second person was that received the copied thumb drive, but knowing his wife and son would not be subjected to Frederick Ellison's sadistic inhuman personality anymore.

7

Later that evening, after Russell and his family's brutal murders, the Architect's council of five remained silent, waiting for Ellison to appear. They were loyal for many reasons: Money, power, and mostly fear that kept them in line and obedient. Today, they witnessed the Architect's and Ellison's cold and ruthless punishment to a traitor.

What the Architect stood for, what he believed in, had been handed down to him from his great grandfather. It was more than a religion to him; it was a way of life that grew the economy in a way that benefited everyone within their circle. There was the one percent that commanded absolute respect within their secret world that only the wealthy knew and understood. One thing of utmost importance was loyalty to the Architect's Manifesto and their secret shadow government.

The Architect's current wealth far exceeded the GDP of the United States. He knew he was the wealthiest man in the world. With his allies in every country and throughout the United States, he was set to rule the United States and do what other dictators dreamed of accomplishing.

It was the Architect who had the power to dictate when the GDP grew or shrunk. It was part of the playbook that had been put in motion when the United States was in its infant stages and continuing to the present day. How America's democracy functioned was controlled by an engraved formula inside the brain of each of the Architects.

Many years ago, the current Architect believed that the United States and the ignorant voter needed to have their politics tribal. There would be no middle ground. He understood how uninformed and complacent the American voters were and how easily manipulated they could be, always wanting to vote for the person who represented their tribal beliefs. For his plan to succeed, fear and uncertainty had to be stuffed down every American's throat every day.

The Architect dictated everything through his thousands of surrogates. Those deputies had hundreds of loyal followers. He estimated that over fifty million people supported his surrogates in business and Congress.

Now the Architect had a few months to get the final chapter of his great grandfather's plan put into action. Then he would have the United States entirely under his control, generating hundreds of trillions of dollars for the next hundred years for his legacy, while he controlled all the superpowers with President Chesterfield's new communications satellite.

As he watched Ellison enter the conference room from his video screen, he saw his five board members sitting stoically, waiting for direction of what they needed to do to get his plan back on track.

The Architect cleared his throat. He leaned into his microphone. "Gentlemen," he said. "I am not sure if we still have a problem. I do not know if any more copies are out there. Our reach is far and wide, and our friends will keep me in the loop of every decision or investigation that might interfere with my...he corrected himself. I mean our plan. My one concern right now is Paige Turner. We have to monitor her from a safe distance. Ellison, it will be your job to see that we do not show our hand too soon," he said, his face blacked out on the TV Monitor, his identity hidden.

Ellison nodded and pointed to everyone in the room to acknowledge their agreement. The Architect was happy to see his inner circle seemed onboard.

"Now, work with your closest contacts and keep Frederick up-to-date. Be aware Turner and her staff of reporters have good instincts and will know if you are not telling the truth, especially if she does have a copy of my files. If she gets wind she's being watched she will not hesitate to try to expose our plans. Don't fuck up."

The Architect paused, his hands locked behind his back as he paced around his office on his estate. "Right now, Turner is working on her pet project of *Corrupted Intelligence*, which I am sure you all agree, is ridiculous. All we want is to make this country wealthy and take our fair share of it. We should allow her theory to fester. Assist her if you can. If she wants to interview any of you, do it. Don't get in her way. She needs to remain distracted and off my trail for the next nine months. I want to see all your heads nodding in agreement," the Architect demanded, his mechanical voice sounding like Darth Vader. "Any violation of my wishes will be dealt with harshly. You are all dismissed," he said, his tone threatening.

The Architect knew it would be a waiting game; one Turner was very good at too. He understood the reporter's investigative style was to pursue her leads first, keep all findings under wraps until she felt she could speak the truth with substantiated evidence on her TV show. He had to bait her with false leads. He needed the computer chip installed and then nothing she reported would matter.

What the Architect had in his favor was that he was well-respected in the United States and around the world. His only flaw was that he was an impatient man. Like any person in power, he had weaknesses. His drive for control blinded him, while at the same time drove his need to be loved by everyone. Unlike president Chesterfield's predecessor's foolish need to use Twitter to promote his thousands of lies, the unmasked Architect decided to project himself as an honest and patriotic American. He could not eliminate all of his faults. He needed to micro-manage everything, which drove his inner circle crazy.

This Paige Turner problem had him edgy. He knew he had to watch his surrogates from a distance. He understood the first move would have to come from her. He had his attornies ready to pounce on her if she tried to expose the files on the thumb drive.

He checked his watch and realized he was running an hour behind. "Off to those fucking awards," he cursed.

He had his private plane fueled, ready to take him to the Middle East tomorrow. Then, if the first meeting went well, he'd be off to Italy for the last of his two critical discussions that would put Stage One and Two in motion.

8

Clay sat at the patio table on Paige's deck at her Malibu house. He could not take his eyes off her, as she chewed on her rare piece of steak. She was not a voracious eater, but he could tell something was on her mind, as she ripped into her food, cutting, not chewing, just swallowing.

Clay was happy to have been invited to dinner to discuss a new story Paige wanted to run by him. He was feeling uncomfortable with her nervous behavior. "Paige put your fork down and talk to me. I can see you're troubled about something," he said in a fatherly tone.

She seemed startled as she dropped her fork on her plate. Paige tried to paint her captivating smile on her face, but she could see by the look in Clay's eyes, it was not working.

Paige strained a smile. "I've been sent stolen digital files from a friend. It has damaging evidence on one of America's family dynasties. Inside the files, it points to someone going by the title *The Architect*. I have some thoughts of who it might be, but I am baffled as to what to do about all of it?"

Clay put his fork down; his face turned serious. "Stolen property. I don't want to know. You have to turn it over to the FBI immediately," he ordered.

Paige looked down at her plate of food, unable to look at her boss, shaking her head. "I can't do this. It's from a reliable source, and until I can confirm what he sent me, I will have to investigate and see where it leads me."

"I've been down this road with you before, and it almost closed down our news organization," Clay replied nervously.

Paige could see that she had not prepared Clay properly. She raised her hand in the air. "I will talk to you after we finish dinner. I promise to eat a little less gluttonously," she said, picking up her fork and cutting another slice of her steak and slowly putting the meat in her mouth. She exaggerated her chewing, smiling, exposing her food on her teeth. They both laughed.

* * * * *

After dinner, Paige plopped down on her husband's leather recliner; it hugged her as Rick would. Her laptop rested on her bent legs. She was unsure how or what she was going to say, as she scrolled through the files. "I don't know what I have right now. Some of it seems unreal and farfetched, while there are parts that are worth investigating..."

Clay interrupted. "What are you talking about? What are you reading? What are you referring to? Who sent them to you? Just start at the beginning," he said, frustrated.

Paige told her boss about her friend Brian Russell, and his working relationship, with Frederick Ellison and Albert Dunham.

"Before the package came, I had received a disturbing and unsettling voice message from Brian, which by itself was confusing. Russell had always been a doom-laden individual. I just shrugged the message off before I tried to call him back. Then, his package came, and his message seemed more shocking. I am not sure what any of it means?" she said, shrugging her shoulders, a puzzled look on her face. "I want to talk to Brian and ask him some questions first before I take any of this seriously. It was just how he sounded on the voice message about a man he called The Architect. It was what this Architect has planned for the United States that had him upset," she paused, sucking in a deep breath. "Everything in the files I could open sounds like a coup is being set in motion."

Clay was scratching his scalp, deep in thought. "How do you even know where these digital files came from? Can anything inside these files get authenticated?"

Paige raised her eyebrows and said. "I just got them and will be working on connecting some dots, but right now, I do not know the origin of those files yet. All I have are a group of files written by a man and his family that tells a chilling story. When I hook up with Brian, I hope to have some of those questions answered. Right now, he's the only person who can help me."

Clay understood the signs when Paige, whom he trusted, was tormented. "Sweetie read me some of the things in the files, and let us try to make some sense of it. What does your gut tell you about this Architect?"

Paige bit her lower lip. "The Architect might be one of a dozen billionaires, however, a lot of what I've already read points to Albert Dunham. His family tree matches up with what I've read so far."

She let her boss listen to the phone message she had received, and then read the note inside the package Russell sent her. Clay seemed noticeably surprised by her friend's handwritten words.

Clay stood and walked over to Paige, kissing her on the top of her head in a fatherly manner. "What do you think he means by tanking the markets'? How can one person do that?" he asked puzzled.

"I am not sure," Paige replied, shaking her head. "I've suspected that for some time investigating my Corrupted Intelligence theory. I need some more time to figure it all out. Based on what I've read so far, I am not sure I'll have that luxury. If these file notes are correct, phase one and two are ready to be put into motion."

"Then, talk to me when you have spoken to Brian," said Clay. "Go do what you do and deal with this. If it turns out to be a worthy story, then we'll report it."

"If you don't have to go right now, let's try to relax and watch 60 Minutes," Paige said.

*****

Thirty minutes into the *nightly news*, there was a news flash, which brought them both to the edge of their seats. The news reporter was brief:

"Brian Russell, the head of Cyber Security, for Ellison Industries Inc. was found murdered at a Newark warehouse late Friday afternoon," the reporter pressed her finger to her earpiece, her eyes growing wide. *"We had just received more details from the police that Brian Russell had been tortured hours before he was executed. Tied to two chairs were his wife and son,"* the reporter sucking in a nervous breath. *"Both were shot at close range. Execution style,"* she said, wiping a tear from her cheek.

Paige clicked the TV off and just stared at Clay. "Shit. This thing is bigger than it looks. The Architect must want these files back. To execute Russell and his family for stealing his goddamn files, must mean they are critical to his plan?" she said, getting up and heading to her desk. "I need my entire team working on this. We need to get all the encrypted files opened. This guy is a monster," she shouted.

Clay, the color drained from his face spoke. "Fuck, executing his wife and kid for what your friend stole? It's now apparent to me that Russell died because of these files. We might need to alert the FBI about what Russell sent you. We can't be seen holding back evidence in an active investigation," Clay said.

"I don't know. What if this Architect, as he says, has most of the law enforcement in his back pocket? Let's dig a little deeper and wait and see what the FBI and local law enforcement do about these murders?"

9

Paige had gotten to her office at ten-thirty that night. She needed some secluded time to work uninterrupted and use the media agency's new AI software that might help decipher all the information inside the thumb drive.

She had begun spreading out the papers she had printed out from the thumb drive. She had pinned the Architect's family timeline spreadsheet to a corkboard on the wall next to her desk. She figured she had to use broad strokes now to visualize the threat her friend Brain was frightened by inside the Architect Manifesto.

She entered all the titles of each file, including the encrypted ones. She entered key subjects into each folder and pressed the sort key to see what pattern if any the computer would find. She knew she had to open the encrypted folders so her artificial intelligence software could come up with some answers or leads for her to pursue.

She wanted to delve into Albert Dunham, and Frederick Ellison with the hope her software would connect the dots and point them to the Architect, as well as who was his surrogates. She knew she would be opening a can of worms for herself and her media organization.

Dunham was a beloved American without any known scandals and possessing stolen files that were evidence in the Russell murder was a whole different ballgame.

Paige had a knack of seeing the big picture inside a good story. She knew with this hot potato she had to figure out a way to investigate it without leaving a trail back to her.

While she madly entered as much data as she could, her hands could not stop trembling from the picture in her mind of how Brian and his family had died because of this stolen thumb drive. She finished inputting the first round of information and waited for the computer to spit out its first analysis.

"What's so threatening to this Architect that murder was his only solution," Paige muttered. There were essential secrets she knew she had to uncover.

Paige kept asking herself the same questions as she dug deeper and deeper into the Architect files. She did not fully comprehend what she had in front of her; however, she knew she would be in the middle of something dangerous, once she probed more in-depth into the encrypted files.

Finally, her computer spat out its report. Paige began reading the first printed records from the creator of this family's blueprint for America. The first entry date was May 10, 1889. After she had finished the first fifteen pages, she thought she was reading about current events.

Paige, sipped on her cold coffee, scanning back a few pages and realized this person, who called himself *The Creator*, the first Architect, had started to set in motion, a new economy, and a new political system, years before the turn of the twentieth century. The Creator worked behind the scenes letting his vast amounts of money help him get his way with the political powers at that time. The list of legislative leaders assisting this man in was shocking. What the first Architect put in motion was so very far removed from what the founding fathers had envisioned or even imagined would happen to their idealistic experiment in democracy they had spilled blood for a century earlier.

"Damn, this Creator was building a shadow government based solely on money and wealth-building that loosely followed the Constitution," she babbled under her breath. What appalled her, even more, was the judges in the Supreme Court favored this creator and his long-range plan.

Paige was now taking notes, jotting down ideas she needed to pursue, as well as making a list of who she would talk to and who she could trust.

"This first Architect was brilliant," Paige muttered. "Damn, he was laying the foundation for the wealthy to control everything that affected America's economy. Holy cow!" she spat out. "What he knew back then, his vision for a form of a capitalistic democracy that favored the very rich, was visionary."

Paige was now talking to herself as she continued reading what the computer printed out. "Shit, this creator bragged about setting in motion the great depression. He even made a fortune from it," She stuttered, after reading another entry.

Taking a break to digest what she had just read, she combed both her hands through her long black hair. "Crap, Great Grandpa confessed in writing about his role in starting *World War I.*

She rubbed her eyes and stretched her toned arms over her head. When she got back to reading more of the files, she was mesmerized as she turned over each page. The current Architect had detailed steps on how to control politicians and make a fortune for their family and heirs." Paige stammered. "They are the perfect definition of my *Corrupted Intelligence* theory.

She read the criteria for becoming the next Architect. The first choice was the eldest son. He was well tested and then groomed over his other siblings to take over the Creator's dream. What was confusing Paige was that there were over fifty families that fit the description of the Architect and his family lineage. She decided to continue digging more in-depth and began to narrow down the families based on the timeline she had in front of her.

Within an hour, she had narrowed it down to three families that fit the Architect's profile. Only one family stood out more than the other two. It was her first suspicion; the Dunham family. They had gained prominence in the late nineteenth century, competing with the Rockefellers and Morgans. As she compared each point in time from the entries in the files, more and more of them again matched up with the Dunham family accomplishments.

Her lips were moving, but no sound was escaping from her mouth. "*So, would anyone even care about how this family made their fortune?"* Paige was smart enough to know that people without wealth admired those who had it, not caring too much how they built their wealth. *"So, where's the story?"*

She closed the last folder from the current Architect making a notation on the record: *Albert Dunham*, to help her stay focused on her research. Paige leaned back in her high-back chair, stretching her arms high above her head; her spine was painfully stiff. She was exhausted after three painful hours of reading and note-taking.

She was anxious about what the current heir kept referring to a *"Stage One"* he was ready to be put it into motion. What he stressed over-and-over again was getting full control of the United States. *"What the hell does he mean full control?"* she typed in those words into the computer and pressed sort. "What does he mean, *MarketTurmoil?* Paige scratched her left arm. She wondered if she had enough time to figure it out, alert the authorities before the next seven days were up. But what could she tell anyone? Who would believe her?

Paige said softly. *"What would I say to the authorities? I have some information, from files that a dead friend of mine stole. That some man is going to manipulate the markets and take full control of the United States?"* Just saying it out loud, sounded crazy.

As if a light bulb turned on inside her head, Paige slammed her fist on her desk. "It is not about what I can read, but the important facts that are inside those encrypted files. That's what has the Architect scared," she barked.

She returned the printed papers to a large envelope and placed the thumb drive in her office safe. She had made a few duplicates of the thumb drive for her safe deposit box, just in case the same people who murdered her friend came to her home or office looking for what Russell had stolen. She knew she needed the encrypted files opened before she could report on any of this.

What Brian Russell had given her had a few flaws. While the thumb drive contained a lot of information and appeared to have come from this Architect's family, the encrypted folders could not be connected to them the way her friend had sent them. For all she knew, they had come from another source, and with Russell dead, she would be unable to corroborate.

She was tired and decided that tomorrow she would start her investigation and her feather-ruffling. If she had learned anything from her years of experience investigating stories, it was getting to the right people fast, and asking the pointed questions that would begin to make the cockroaches scurry for the darkness.

First, she needed her team to get on board. She sent out a group text, knowing it was the fastest way to get everyone to drop what they were doing and meet with her tomorrow.

10

Sean Adams and Bradley Stevens had arrived promptly at Paige's Malibu house at seven in the morning. They were two of her most trusted reporters. They all knew that Paige liked to keep explosive investigations on the down-low, so they did not question her or the fact that they had to drop everything on a Sunday and get to her house.

Paige had begun the meeting by bringing her team up to date on what had happened to Brian Russell. She then, methodically, gave a recap of what she had read inside the Architect's Manifesto files and the analysis her computer gave her. She kept the meeting somber, stressing the potential dangers they all could face if they opted-in to help her.

"Brian had stolen these files from his boss and chose to become a whistleblower. Shit...he's dead because of what's on this thumb drive," she held up. "I believe the encrypted folders are the key to all of this. The other dossiers are just the notes from a family of egomaniacs," Paige paused to regain her composure.

"Russell's murder, as well as the savage killing of his wife and son, are no coincidence. I owe it to him to find the man or men responsible for his death and expose this Architect's Manifesto. She was not letting on that she believed Albert Dunham was this person. She wanted her team to come to their conclusions on their own. They were great investigative reporters, and she had faith they would confirm her suspicions.

Bradley was first to speak. "Paige, you're too vague. Give us something to fire us up about this guy's badass plan," he asked.

Paige realized she had been leaving out many of the pieces to the puzzle she had on the thumb drive. She nodded, pursed her lips, and responded. "What I have read so far..." she said, as she began passing out copies of the current Architect's five-stage plan... "is that this man has a prearranged scheme with many detailed stages that are inside his encrypted files. What scared me the most is this guy believes he will be the next Emperor of the United States...*EOTUS* that is if he can implement his game plan on schedule," said Paige, holding back her chuckle.

Paige struggled not to laugh and said. "His endgame is to make himself more than just the president of our country, but its ruler. He has numerous quotes about Julius Caesar, a leader he admirers. One quote scares me. Let me read it to you:

"I am...no, I want to be like Caesar. I want to give little trouble to my opponents, then, after they have been overpowered and had accepted it, they will see that my tyranny was only in name and appearance and that my first acts were not so cruel, but the requirement that was needed for my monarchy to work smoothly as a gentle physician. That my acts of cruelty would seem to be assigned by Heaven itself. Then and only then will the American citizens have a terrible yearning for me and accept everything I have done to rule them."

"I know this sounds ridiculous, even crazy, however, how he plans on going about it, could work. His great grandfather was just as crazy, but a financial genius. If his notations were accurate in the original playbook of the creator, a lot of shit happened to our country that was instigated by the first Architect."

Bradley had to stop Paige. He did everything to hold back a big laugh. "Are you listening to what you've been saying here? Whatever you've got, sounds like the rantings of a lunatic. Do you believe that one man will be able to insert himself inside our lives, and make us believe Heaven sent him to rescue us? We do have a constitution...remember?"

"No, I don't believe it either," Paige said emphatically. "Sadly, I do remember the previous president, who I can't say his name, or I'll become sick, had thought himself above the law and lied about everything and his followers loved him. You do remember that the Evangelicals thought God had sent him to recuse the United States. He kept his entire base during his entire first term. I am not so sure our country would be against another president like the one the Architect wants to be."

Sean Adams interrupted the conversation. "I don't believe any American citizen would want to go back to where this country was six and a half years ago."

"I hope you're right. Nevertheless, as we've seen, money, billions of it, has the power to change our world as we know it. If the Architect gets control of the House, the Senate, and the Supreme Court, as well as many lower Federal courts, what is there to stop him, especially if he had the people behind him one hundred percent? This family fits my *Corrupted Intelligence* theory perfectly, and that's what scares me the most. Men like this have been controlling the masses for centuries. Hitler is another good example of it."

Bradley could not hold back his remarks. "Everything you've read so far sounds like someone who is taking credit for events that had already happened."

Paige shook her head. "At first, I thought that too. I believe this guy is the real deal, shit his family was the real deal. We need to investigate what I have, what all of you now have, and ease my mind that this is not the blustering of a crazy man. Right now, all I know is that this investigation will be very dangerous. I won't hold it against any of you if you decline to help," she said her voice cracking. "Brian and his family were brutally murdered for what is inside these files."

Both reporters sat up straight, their butts on the edge of their seats. Bradley and Sean were nodding their support. Bradley was first to respond.

"Okay. If your suspicions are correct, and I do trust your gut, we will need to bring in more investigators. We will need to do a lot of digging and double-checking of the facts," he said.

Paige looked Bradley in the eye, nodding her head. "Not too many. We need to keep a tight lid on any investigation into this Architect. If we begin to touch upon any portion of his plan, his surrogates will know. I believe by what I've read so far; he's too well like and respected. He knows his files have were stolen. It won't take him long to figure out Brian, and I were friends. If he believes our news organization has Russell's stolen files, then I don't have to tell you the shitstorm of trouble we'd be in," said Paige, her voice cracking.

Bradley looked Paige in the eye. "After everything you've told us, I'd bet this Architect is Albert Dunham."

Paige was shocked. He had gone right to her theory. "What makes you think it's him?

Bradley could see that he nailed it. "I've been reporting on him for the last ten years, and he does have the ego and balls to be this Architect. My priority will be to find out how the investigation is going on who killed your friend. That will help me know who and what we are dealing with," Bradley said, his facial muscles tense and flexed tight, exposing a 'Y-shaped blood vessel on this forehead that was ready to pop.

"Do your investigation into Russell's murder the same as you'd do any murder investigation. Let's leave Dunham out of this for now. If our research goes well, if Albert Dunham is the Architect, it would be revealed as we gather more information."

"Got it, boss," said Bradly.

Paige looked at Sean, who had remained quiet, listening as he had always done when starting an investigation. "Sean, I need you to look into Brian Russell's job duties with Ellison Industries. I need a list of who he worked for and with. Check on people he recently had contacted or met. Do a complete workup. Companies he worked for in the past, their origins and especially all their affiliates. I want to see if there is a common denominator. Maybe Dunham is pulling all the strings. One other thing, the Architect's father has a notation about PM10 and how that helped build a pharmaceutical company he owns. Do you know what PM10 is?"

Sean was scratching his scalp, deep in thought. "If I remember it correctly, it is Particle Matter 10. It's the fine dust that is blown around from high winds. It's suspected to be one of the causes for many respiratory illnesses, as well as cancer," Sean replied. "Paige, I know Dean Miller, the cybersecurity billionaire guy. He's a software genius who might be able to help put some of these puzzle pieces together and open the encrypted files. Can I give him a call and set up a meeting?"

Paige smiled. "He's a good friend. Met him at Stanford. Tell him I say hi." She flipped a page on her yellow legal notepad and addressed Bradley. " I need you to do something more for me. I made copies of the first fifty years from Great Grandpa's notes. I need you to research those years and bring me a list of all major businesses that had a lot of influence on our country back then, as well as our politicians. I have dates and specific notations, at first glance correspond to the time of the Great Depression and the beginning of World War One. I found two notations with dates: August 21, 1913, and November 4, 1928. Both dates correspond to entries that mention WWI and The Great Depression. Look for any scandals, families that were building wealth at the expense of the working man and who had close ties to mayors, governors, congressmen, and senators, as well as foreign dignitaries. I am not sure if there were any records kept back then about campaign donations or scandals of politicians taking bribes, but if there is something to find I know you'll find it," Paige said flipping another page and reading her notes. She did not tell Bradley or Sean what she was reading.

She saw the curious looks on both the reporter's faces, especially Bradley. He had become her big brother after Rick died. Paige said. "I have some personal investigations I have to do first..." before she could continue, Bradley interrupted.

Bradley scowled, deep in thought. "Paige, this Stage One sounds very important to the Architect's plan. Without it, it seems that he cannot move forward. If that's the case, then something big is about to happen, and you need to proceed with caution," he said, biting his lower lip.

11

The Architect had just finished his briefing with Ellison and was furious. "I understood why Russell had to be eliminated, but, his wife and son?" he screamed. "This is not who we are. The family was supposed to be off-limits."

Ellison did not hesitate to respond. "Albert, we could not take the chance Russell did not tell his wife about the satellite or any of your upcoming plans. She was an emotional loose end. It was something that needed to be handled," he said coldly. "Maybe he hid a copy in his home? I couldn't take that chance."

"Not smart. Russell's murder we could have buried within our network in law enforcement. Now, the FBI and Homeland Security are looking at this as a terrorist threat."

Ellison was shaking his head. "I have it all contained. FBI director Roberts and two deputy directors at Homeland are going to close the case as a drug deal gone bad. We've already planted enough evidence to show that Russell had a big cocaine problem and owed some drug dealers a lot of money. Trust me it will all die down in a few days," Ellison said.

"Drugs? Not enough money? Are you shitting me? He was wealthy beyond imagination. We saw to it."

"Albert, stop worrying. I've got it under control."

"Then explain why investigative reporters working for Paige Turner are beginning to crawl up our asses with tons of questions about his murder investigation? I'll bet Turner has copies of my files."

Ellison did not seem too concerned. "I know...I know. They are just simple fishing questions. They are just trying to shake some bushes to see what scurries out. If we stay calm and proceed with Stage One, this Russell matter will soon be forgotten as yesterday's news."

The Architect shook his head, throwing his arms in the air, frustrated with his friend. "I hope you're, right? Do you know my meetings in the Middle East and Italy are next week? I've put everything in motion for Stage One to start then. Every contractor has been paid in advance."

Ellison could tell his friend was coming unglued. "Look, all of your stock investments have been sold, and re-allocated to circumvent the Stock Market adjustments that will happen once Stage One is triggered. Your short positions on over twenty stocks are in place. Everything will go off without a hitch. The SEC won't find a trail back to you. Right now, let Turner's investigation continue. She's too far behind to catch up with us," he said confidently.

* * * * *

After his meeting with Ellison, Dunham called his enforcer, Frasier Montgomery. "We're you onboard with Ellison's decision to eliminate Russell's family?"

"It was something that needed to be handled. We did not believe Russell's wife would have kept her mouth shut after her husband was murdered. Remember, no loose ends," he said coldly.

Dunham held his tongue. He knew Frasier was a hothead. "I'm concerned about Paige Turner's last three interviews with CEOs within Russell's network. There could be some defectors loyal to him," he complained.

"We are monitoring all her reporters. We have it all under control, Albert. So, calm down and let us do our job," Frasier said.

The Architect was now screaming into his phone. "I will not calm down," he yelled, staring at his phone. "Turner's getting too close. It needs to stop," he said, his voice had dialed down to a warm simmer.

Frasier took a deep breath before he spoke. He had felt his friend's rage for over a quarter-century. "We can slow down Turner with a little accident. She's always running on Coast Highway near her home," Montgomery said, his tone cold and biting.

Dunham pounded his fist on his desk. "Fuck no, you idiot. We need to keep watching and observing. If we get linked to any attempt to murder her, especially with her being a close friend to Russell, and my files turn up...shit, then we'd all be screwed."

"I think you're too cautious right now. No one so far knows it was us that killed Brian Russell or his family. Frederick has it tied to a drug deal gone bad. I've learned from my past mistakes. Trust me, Turner's demise will be reported as some hit and run accident."

The Architect was scratching his scalp, thinking. He needed Turner distracted, so in a year and a half, his dream of becoming the Emperor of the United States, a modern Julius Caesar, would make his world perfect. There were many bricks he still had to lay and let the cement dry. Dunham knew he did not need Paige Turner to interfere with his plans. He had to get his files back, especially the one that detailed the computer chip Russell created.

The Architect snapped back to his conversation. "You only know one way to solve problems...murder. So, listen to me. It's not going to happen that way. I have bigger plans for Turner. Now, get her reporters to follow some details inside my files. Those reporters will not impair my plan. Don't hamper their investigation. Expose those areas so Turner and her reporters will be chasing their tails. Tell our people if they are questioned, be cooperative, so whatever investigation ensues it will stay far away from the upcoming satellite launch."

Frasier sighed loudly. "Just an accident while Turner is doing her morning jog or late afternoon bike ride would solve all of our problems faster," Frasier said unemotionally.

"Shit. You're like a two-year-old whining to get his way. No! I want her, and her reporters distracted, not harmed. Brian Russell's death is being investigated by them, and any more suspicious murders or accidents connected to Turner will hinder my plans. Just give her something to sink her teeth into that she'll believe is the story.

Frasier shrugged his shoulders. "Maybe a little scare?" he suggested.

The Architect was ready to strangle his friend. "Fuck. You never give up, do you? What part of *NO* don't you understand? Are we clear?" Dunham scolded his friend without it requiring an answer. "It would be the icing on the cake when I see Paige Turner's expression when I become President. No *EOTUS*."

Frasier sucked in a deep frustrated breath before responding. "As you wish. I will begin leaving the breadcrumbs today. But, mind my words. If this does not work, Turner will have to be eliminated if she and her people get too close. "

There was a long silence on the other end of the phone. "Just make the distractions work," Dunham said before slamming his phone onto its cradle.

* * * * *

Taking in a deep cleansing breath, Dunham's mind filled with one immediate concern. One of Turner's reporters was asking questions about PM10. It was his father's plan he had kept active. He searched his memory, trying to justify if it was worth keeping the PM10 plan viable? The answer was obvious. It was what helped build five of his pharmaceutical companies into multi-billion-dollar businesses. He just prayed that Turner would not pursue that avenue of the family plan.

He sunk into his high-back desk chair, his head pressed hard into the headrest. He could not stop thinking about his father's PM10 plan. "If Turner figures that out before the election, it will ruin me. Shit, I'd be put in Federal prison," he said, his voice barely audible.

He immediately called his chemical company. When the line picked up, and he heard the familiar voice at the other end, he said. "Don't speak; just listen. We need to modify the formula on the retardant effective immediately. Stop all production, as well as distribution." He could sense by the heavy breathing his brother, who ran this company, wanted to comment. "This is not open to discussion," he said coldly.

"Albert, I got it," his older brother said.

Dunham was furious his brother used his first name, especially over the phone. He knew the cyber division of the FBI had been monitoring a group of billionaires. He had tried very hard to remain off the grid at this facility so there would be no connections to him and his brother's business dealings. However, he knew Teddy still resented him for being the chosen one. Not wanting to engage with him, he ended the call without even a good-bye.

12

Dean Miller, a forty-eight-year-old billionaire from Silicon Valley, was trying to finish up his lecture at UCLA. He had created, *Symtec Systems*, a cybersecurity software company, to the National Security Agency. This most popular lecture was about hacking and penetrating firewalls.

His class an off-shoot from the successful hacking tests he performed at his company to expose how vulnerability the United States infrastructure, especially the election systems had become. He finally had to sell his multi-billion software company to the government after the constant harassment, and raids on his business by the NSA, FBI, Homeland Security, and CIA. They kept closing down his testing lab after each of his successful hacks.

After numerous congressional hearings and attempts by the Justice Department to get him to cooperate, he relented and sold them his patents for a hefty price, with an offer to work for the government. Miller was a patriot, down to his inner core. His moral compass would not allow him to work for or with the government.

The way the world had been changing, the way the internet was being used to recruit young men and women to become Jihadists against the United States, the way foreign governments were quickly hacking government agencies, Miller's software systems had become the best defense against the cyber wars that were threatening America.

Dean Miller's decision to retire did not last long. He was offered a professorship at UCLA, teaching coding and cybersecurity to eager students that wanted to have a new and long-lasting career in the internet's new frontier: defending against cyber-attacks. He had been provided a private lab to work on his new ideas.

At UCLA, he developed new software that could tag politicians and corporate executives, similar to how Facebook used their software. Only his program was more powerful.

Miller's ultimate goal was to hold politicians accountable for what they said and did, especially those who influenced them. He was a computer genius, able to see the future of what computers and data storage could do for America and the world. He also knew that his cyber world was evolving, but not in the right way.

His unique expertise had helped develop the way every government around the world was collecting data, tagging data, and building libraries of information about every person around the world. Unfortunately, what he helped create, also created power and the infringement on personal privacy. This new power was being used to divide and manipulate Americans. It allowed wealthy people in business faster ways to control markets, change buying habits, control the dollar's value, instantly create a volatile news event, and build vast amounts of wealth for themselves.

Being part of the future had turned out to be a curse for Miller. He persistently offered up safeguards to protect the public, but once the NSA had taken control of Symtec Systems, they would not listen. They now had the patents on all the cybersecurity programs they had bought, and they now controlled the sphere of how and where that software worked.

Miller knew that the NSA had, with the help of a few of Miller's ex-employees, developed a new cybersecurity weapon that was going to be part of a new communications satellite. He did not approve the concept of this new cyber weapon, but he had been warned by President Chesterfield, that he could not speak of this project to anyone.

Dean did not believe in Science Fiction, but he was seeing what every American feared, *Big Brother* taking away everyone's freedom. The daily monitoring of targeted classes of American citizens, legal and illegal immigrants, as well as companies doing business around the world, had gotten a strong foothold in everything everyone was doing. In the name of National Security was the government's answer. Miller had realized he needed to build new countermeasures that would be able to monitor how his old programs were intruding on America's citizens.

Dean was wrapping up his lecture. It had been a long semester. His students were the best group he had had in many years. His course on "Analytics and Patterns in Data" was a big hit with the young men and women and the university board at UCLA. His lecture theatre had one-hundred-fifty eager and hyper students, who listened, recorded, jotted down notes on every word professor Miller said. His students loved him. His course was a distraction so he could finalize the new software he was developing to build detailed resumes of politicians, so registered voters would understand the real platform of their favorite candidate.

If they said it, and it was on the internet, his software could capture it, tag it to the individual's name, and sort it into a detailed report making it difficult for any congressman or senator to deny what they had said or promised. Miller had hoped he would be able to root out the politicians who were bought and paid for by lobbyist groups, and help find worthy people who wanted to do something good for their country.

He had started a new PAC, *"We the People,"* injecting the first billion dollars into the fund. To his surprise, his movement had become so popular, that he had over a hundred million followers and fifty-million donors, with each donation averaging $50 per year.

Dean was on schedule to revamp with his software how politicians would be looked at with real facts and words that they had spoken while in office or while running for office. Voters would have a clear picture of what the politician voted for, or did not vote for. He did not favor democrats or republicans; he just wanted to change over the House and Senate with moderates that wanted to get things done for all Americans.

For the first time after a lecture, he rushed out of the stadium, not taking any questions so that he could get on the road to his home in Playa Del Rey overlooking the Pacific Ocean. He rushed into his office, tossed his briefcase on his desk. It landed on a FedEx package. He glanced at the return address. It was from a name he did not at first recognize. He wanted to open it up but decided he could do when he got home. It was 2:45 PM, and if he did not get on the Harbor Freeway in ten minutes, he would be stuck in horrible traffic.

He knew his wife and two children were anxiously waiting for him to take them on a long four-day getaway to Catalina Island. His eighty-four-meter hybrid propulsion yacht moored out of Long Beach was fully crewed and ready for the crossing of the channel. This boat was equipped and stocked like a mini cruise ship. His children and wife loved the luxury of their new yacht. Dean had it fully equipped with computers that rivaled any government agency.

He stuffed his laptop inside his briefcase, along with the FedEx package and ran to his car in the faculty garage. He threw his attache case onto the passenger seat, fasten his seatbelt and pressed the ignition button. Nothing happened. He tried again. The car would not start. His dashboard lights were flashing.

"Shit," he cursed, pounding the steering wheel with his fist. He remembered during his last car service, his mechanic. He had told him he would need a new battery. "Stupid, stupid," he scolded himself. He took out his cell phone and called the garage.

"Jerry, it's Dean. You were right. I need a new battery, like now." He could hear his mechanic giggling. "Can you get over to the university garage right now and replace it? I need to get on the road. I am taking my family on vacation, and we need to get to Long Beach at 7:15 PM. Can you help?"

"Mr. Miller, I can be there in twenty minutes and have you on the road with no problem." The connection was cut off, and Dean was now calling his wife, Allison.

He did not want to go back to his office. He decided to sit in his car. He turned Pandora on his phone and inserted his earbuds to listen to "Love Songs Radio," which played his and Allison's favorite songs.

Looking over at this briefcase, he remembered about the FedEx package and decided to look at the contents. As he pulled out the thumb drive, an envelope with his name handwritten on it fell on the passenger seat. He unfolded the letter to discover it was from Brian Russell. His heart began to pound; sweat began to pour off his forehead. He recalled his friend's very alarming phone message he had received from him yesterday. Now he was staring at a piece of paper that was labeled: "The Architect's Manifesto," and a thumb drive.

He had never heard that title before. "Shit," he held up the drive. "Is this stolen property?" he muttered. He knew the law very well, especially on intellectual property. He shrugged his shoulders. His curiosity got the best of him. He inserted the thumb drive into the USB port on his laptop.

Brian Russell, a brilliant computer analyst, first came into Dean's life two years ago when he audited a lecture titled: "Computer Analytics and How the Wealthy Are Stealing Your Money." Russell was very interested in Miller's ideas. Over the weeks that followed, they became good friends.

Russell, on his own, was helping fund Miller's new project. Dean remembered how upset Brian had become with his work, especially with the direction his boss, Frederick Ellison, was taking his company. "Shit, did he steal this from his workplace?" he asked himself.

He started reading what Russell had sent him and became enthralled by what the files revealed about this Architect and his family, especially what he was planning on doing. He tried calling Brian, but his phone was not in service, which he found very strange. Looking at his smartphone for the first time all day made him gasp. On his screen was an AP News Alert that shocked Dean.

"Brian's dead? He was murdered and tortured?" he said his voice quivering. "His wife and child too?" Dean did not believe in happenstances and continued reading the files on his computer. He was startled by a loud knocking on his door window. His mechanic Jerry was standing holding his new battery.

His mechanic, both his arms filled with military tattoos, always had a charming, friendly smile and signaled Dean to pop the hood. "Mr. Miller, I will have you on the road in fifteen minutes."

"Thanks, Jerry," he said nervously. He ejected the thumb drive and put it in his briefcase. A million thoughts spun inside his head, and none of them made any sense. He did not know why Russell sent him this package. The recorded message, his brutal death, and now these mysterious files from maybe one of America's wealthiest and respected men, only made Miller more curious.

* * * * *

Dean pulled into his driveway only an hour behind schedule. Allison and his son Allan and daughter Sandra were waiting by the front of the garage door. Their bags were all lined up. They were ready, but Dean was not.

Dean kissed his wife's cheek, putting his briefcase on the hallway floor. "Sorry I am so late, but we have plenty of time and will be out of Long Beach harbor and sailing to Catalina with plenty of time to spare," he said forcing a big smile on his face.

Sandra, a cordial young woman of fourteen, was showing her displeasure with her father's remarks. With her arms crossed, she said, "You promised we'd go out to a nice dinner before we boarded our boat. We need to leave now, or we will be eating on our new yacht, and you know how I get sick eating while we are sailing," her tone biting.

"Sandra, I had a rough day, and promise I will get us out of here with enough time to enjoy a good dinner. Our chef is preparing your favorite meal, and we won't leave Long Beach until you're finished. Now, you and Allan start loading the car with your bags, and your mother and I will be out shortly," he said sweetly. He motioned for Allison to follow him into the house.

"Do I not get a hug and kiss," Allison pouted. "You look stressed? Everything alright? You've got that look of yours.

Dean took a deep breath and stopped on the porch, turned around, and put his arms around his wife. "Sorry, with the battery going dead, that was not the worst thing to happen. He kissed her gently on the lips, then squeezed her a little tighter, burying his head in the pocket of her neck. "We need to talk before we hit the road," he said his face turned serious.

Allison stepped back and walked inside with her husband. "I've not seen you like this since you sold Symtec. What's going on?"

"You remember Brian Russell," he saw her nodding her head. "Well, Brian, his wife, and child were found murdered today. I had received a disturbing voice message from him yesterday, then just now got a package delivered from him. He played the voice message for her. Then they both sat down on the living room couch. He quickly popped the thumb drive into his desk computer.

Allison was not just his wife, but his partner, and co-creator of their new cyber software. They had met at Symtec twenty-five years ago, and it was love at first sight. They had so much in common and shared the same concerns about what they saw was a troubled future, as the internet became more powerful.

"What do you want to do with all of this?" she asked.

"I am not sure," he said nervously. "But I think I have to do something. Brian's dead. I believe it had something to do with these files he took. I think this might be a good way for us to test our new software and see if we can piece together a logical roadmap of what these files have inside them and see who might be connected? What I know is that I want to try. Brian was a nice guy that might have gotten caught up in something bigger than he could handle."

"Are you sure his murder was about this Architect's plan? Do you think we...our family could be in danger since he sent this to you?" she said nervously?

"I don't know. What I do know is that Brian trusted me with this mess, and I need to check it out. Maybe figure out why Brian had to die for just stealing these files?" he noticed Allison's worried look. "First, I have to decrypt some additional files on the thumb drive to have a clearer picture of what was scaring Brian." He sucked in a deep breath before continuing. "If I discover something, I promise I will turn it over to the authorities. Let's go on vacation, relax and then I can come back to this problem in four days." He knew it was a little white lie. He knew by what he read inside the Manifesto, he had only seven days or maybe less to figure things out before Stage One wad implemented.

13

Dean had finally flopped down on his lounge chair, his feet leaving the warm white sand at Descanso Beach. He and his family were relaxing at the new upscale playground down from the historic Casino on Catalina Island. He looked over at Allison, who was on her stomach, her novel resting on the sand below her head. He admired how she could turn-off everything around her, and truly relax. He wished he had that ability, but it was not going to happen after what he had received from Brian Russell.

He could not get his friend's nervous voice out of his head, after re-listening to his message. It was making him sick thinking about they had died. *"What did he expect me to do with the thumb drive?"* he asked himself. He wished he had brought the package so he could begin to use his new software to help figure things out.

He shrugged his shoulders and scolded himself for not giving it a rest. "You're on vacation," he whispered. "It can wait."

Dean was ready to open his Pandora app when his phone began to ring. The number was blocked, and he let it go to a voice message. When he heard the ping, he noticed he had a message waiting. He could not resist, so he opened the app. He looked at Allison and again wished he could veg out and forget the outside world, just twenty-six miles away.

With his earbuds still in, he listened to the call. It was a reporter, Sean Adams. The reporter introduced himself explaining he was calling on behalf of Paige Turner. His message made him sit up straight, startling Allison.

"What's wrong now, Dean?" she asked, a little testy.

"Nothing. Go back and continue reading," Dean said, patting her shoulder. "I need to take a little walk. I'll be back in thirty minutes."

Allison was frowning. "Whatever," she replied a little put-off. She gave him one of her disapproving looks he hated.

Back on his yacht, he grabbed a cold beer from the mini-bar refrigerator and listened again to the reporter's message. What puzzled him is that this reporter wanted his help in investigating a story he's doing on Brian Russell. He asked if Dean's software was ready to be tested? The reporter thought it might help him connect the dots on Russell's murder.

"Paige Turner? Sean Adam? He knew Paige. They had met years ago while at Stanford. What does she have to do with Brian Russell?" he mumbled. Dean knew all about Turner and what she was doing with her *Corrupted Intelligence* theory.

She had turned out to be a great investigative reporter, and Adam's call was no accident. "*Does Paige know about the thumb drive too?"* he wondered.

There was nothing he could or would do while on vacation. He texted the reporter and told him they could talk when he returned from his vacation. He did not want to mention his whereabouts, so he put his phone on *Do Not Disturb* for the duration of his holiday. He grabbed a fresh beer, took his small motorboat back to the beach, and walked back to his chaise lounge next to Allison.

14

Paige could not understand all the ramifications of what she was reading. She found something very peculiar about what Great-Grandpa Architect had written. “*This man believed the federal government was supposed to be the babysitter of every American citizen,”* she said silently.

"This guy was a corrupted intellectual, but a genius nevertheless," Paige’s voice barely above a whisper.

As she kept reading, she realized that the foundation had been laid down over a hundred-fifty years ago to allow the wealthy to put into power the elected officials they needed to help build many family dynasties. With Citizens United and the TV media, the United States had been remolded almost a hundred and eighty degrees from where the founding fathers had envisioned their new democracy to be. She slapped her forehead, realizing what she had told herself did not make sense.

When her TV show first came on the air, she began it with an analysis of the founding fathers. She tried to lay out the foundation of her *corrupted intelligence* theory. She recognized the founding fathers were very wealthy white men, who owned slaves. The only citizen who could vote were men of their class and stature. Their slaves or wives were unable to vote. What she was reading inside the Architect's Manifesto, scared her.

"Shit, if a billionaire like Dunham or Ellison pulls something like this off, the United States, as we now know it, will return to the time of our independence," Paige moaned.

Her initial investigation had pointed to these two men. They were childhood friends, and their lives fit the model inside the diaries.

Turner knew Americans were ignorant about current events, some believing what their leaders told them, others oblivious to what was going on around them. After hundreds of interviews, she had concluded the average citizen could be easily fooled with lies by the moderators they listened to on TV, radio, or their opinionated newspapers.

She was frustrated with the tribal warfare that was shaking up the country she loved. Once they picked their side, nothing a politician or businessman would say would be questioned. Now with Facebook, Twitter, and other social media outlets, they had become the new News Media of the Twenty-First Century.

Paige knew that instead of unifying every American, the powerful with their *Corrupted Intelligence* had created two opposite factions of voters, who only voted for their favorite team. She knew she was making small inroads with her viewing public, but with what she was now investigating could jeopardize her reputation if she could not find definitive proof about who the Architect was.

She felt she was in a catch-22. Either devote all her time and effort to exposing the Architect, and his vast web of co-conspirators and end up stirring up enough trouble for herself and her struggling news organization. She prided herself that her show had not yet been labeled *"Fake News"* by the people she investigated. However, a rush to judgment about Dunham or Ellison could bury her and her network.

She knew the public was de-sensitized from years of economic struggles to make ends meet. People were getting by and were angry. Dunham and Ellison seemed to be helping the struggling masses. Blue-collar workers, the middle-class were believing those men's promises and lies, with the hope for a better life.

Paige understood why the average person just stopped listening and only focused on their lives. America had no more heroes taking up important causes.

Paige opened the current Architect's file to the page that had her nerves on edge. She re-read the most current entry and was once again trembling at the thought of what this madman had in store for the United States.

She knew she needed more help than her staff of reporters could provide. But, at this point, she did not know who she could trust. She decided to call her late husband's friend Scott Rogers.

Rick had met Scott at college. Paige had met Rogers a few times, with the last time being at her husband's funeral. She followed his career after her husband died. He was now working for a new cyber division inside the U.S. Marshalls office. If anyone could help her understand the Manifesto she had in her possession, he could.

15

It had been three days since Brian Russell's murder, and the NYPD and FBI had no leads or motive. Dunham was pleased that his surrogates were hindering the investigation. He knew he could not afford any scandals or inquiries that would involve him or Ellison. He had enough to worry about with Paige Turner and her probing.

He still was not a hundred percent sure if the reporter had a copy of his files, or if she did that she'd be able to decrypt the critical files Russell stole. All he was sure of was that Turner was getting too close for comfort. Dunham just prayed Frasier kept a cool head and followed his orders just to observe and advise.

He left his home in Bethesda to his secret board meeting at his ranch in a remote area near the Baltimore/Pennsylvania border. Over fifty of his closest surrogates would be in attendance. They ranged from the current FBI and CIA directors to Senators and Congressmen. The group was rounded out with ministers from Spain, Italy, and Greece, as well as the finance ministers from Egypt, Saudi Arabia, Yemen, and South Africa.

Stage One had finally had all its components in place to implement seamlessly. What Russell had stolen was not showing signs Turner, and her reporters knew about their meeting or Stage One. Today, Dunham needed an update from everyone in attendance and to know that everything would go smoothly.

Dunham, a control freak knew that timing was crucial. If any of his co-conspirators failed to meet their timetable, Stage One would not work. They all knew the consequences if they failed.

Before he left for this meeting, he picked up the original bound file his great grandfather wrote. He held it like it was a sacred bible. He opened it to the first section, bookmarked with a red ribbon. It was his favorite motivating piece to his overall plan. The appropriate notations and insights the creator had put into the first manifesto for every Architect to read and learn from gave him goosebumps.

Dunham whispered, "Your idea for World War I was genius," he said. "You've helped us figure out how to accomplish your greatest wish," he muttered, talking to the old tattered pages. He brought two fingers to his lips and then planted them on the file. With respect and grace, he closed the sacred words, returning it to his safe.

* * * * *

Albert loved the half-mile serpentine driveway that led to his ranch. It was his own secured Camp David. As a young boy, he would ride his bike up and down the drive imagining himself as a motor cross racer. Tightness gripped his heart, as his emotions took over, wishing he could recapture that particular time he once enjoyed. Hearing the squeal of the massive brass gate open, snapped him back to the present.

The cobblestone driveway was lined with tall eucalyptus trees that hugged the road to the main house. Two security guards, holding AK-47's, patrolled the grounds. His butler walked briskly to his car door and opened it.

"Sir, everyone has arrived. They are waiting for you inside. The Ballroom has been prepared and made ready for you," the butler said.

Dunham thanked him. "Please let everyone know that we'll be starting the meeting in ten minutes," he said.

The large room was filled with fifty men who had no choice but to share in the vision of the Architect. These men influenced over ten thousand loyal followers of the Architect's dream. Those followers had thousands of their own faithful men and women who believed in their vision for America.

The Architect had numerous compromising files, with hard evidence, on each member. If leaked to the authorities, it could put them away for decades. They all knew they were trapped inside his complicated web of destruction.

Each surrogate was transported to the ranch in large buses with blacked-out windows. As an added precaution, they were all instructed to wear black hoods while on their bus ride. They did not know where they were or who's home they were in.

There were congressmen, senators, FBI, CIA, and State Department personnel. Included were CEOs from ten of the largest conglomerates controlled by Dunham. The ministers from the countries that the Architect needed to make Stage One work perfectly were also in attendance. It was a perfect mix of leaders with the power to re-shape the United States and the world in his image. For now, he had the beginnings of a shadow government that would do his bidding.

Dunham never attended his meetings in person. He had himself broadcasting from another location at his ranch. His face and voice masked to keep his identity hidden for the time being. Today he was just the Architect.

"Gentlemen, we are finally on the verge of seeing all of our hard work succeed. Unfortunately, as you know, my plan, our plan, has been compromised. While I believe we've contained the leak, we need to tread lightly until it has been confirmed that all copies of my files are back in my possession." He was able to look at his monitor and watch the expressions on everyone's faces. He did not like what he saw.

"I hope each of you takes this seriously?" he said threateningly. "We've come too far for us to fail."

The meeting lasted another twenty minutes, with each person given an assignment to finalize Stage One in three days. He told everyone about his successful trip to Europe and the Middle-East and to watch the news that was about to explode across the country. He told everyone that events had been set in motion to distract President Chesterfield and the American public.

"I want all of the congressmen and senators to stay behind. We have more to discuss." Frasier Montgomery directed the others out a side door, where they were escorted to two minibusses, handed their black hoods, on their way back to their personal transportation.

Dunham was proud of his little band of congressmen and senators. He had them in his back pocket. He had nicknamed their group "The Dirty Dozen" a mix of conservative Democrats and Republicans, right centered in their political philosophy. Their name had stuck and was being used by every media source.

They were brought together after the failure of Citizen United and the other Super Pacs that failed to defeat President Chesterfield in the last election. The loss was terrible, especially after all the money they had spent, but not unmanageable. There were enough congressmen and senators who could stifle a too progressive president, giving them enough time to regroup and get ready for the next presidential election and the final assault Dunham would need to become President or as he saw it EOTUS.

He knew that the most important thing that the Republicans needed to accomplish was to keep control of the Senate and to keep the House with their slim majority which they got back after the turmoil the democrats created to impeach the previous president.

The Dirty Dozen had a job to do, as well as the NSA, and they had to do it fast. The words from Dunham were clear and concise.

He needed the Dirty Dozen to distract Paige Turner. Frasier handed members of Congress instructions that needed to be followed. "I want the reporter chasing a story that would have her thinking she was investigating specific entries inside my stolen files. If she falls for the lead and bites, I will know she has a duplicate thumb drive", he said, pausing to sip some water. He continued. "Then she would be dealt with," he said coldly.

He tried to continue, but Congressman Parsons raised his hand. He was reading the instructions and had a puzzled expression on his face. "It is highly irregular to bring in a reporter to a congressional hearing room to give any testimony," he said.

Dunham drew in a deep breath. "You're smart enough to figure out a logical way to ask her to speak before your committee. Just get it done. Do your fucking job." He continued his briefing with the others.

"Stage One will be triggered by events in Europe, the Middle-East and in the United States in three days. The timing needs to be perfect. This is crucial," Dunham said. "This will be one of the cornerstones of my playbook."

He knew this first move on his chessboard would lay the foundation for him to win over the American voters. Only he understood the final endgame that the NSA was helping him accomplish. It was critical that Paige Turner not have a chance to open one of his critical encrypted files. That was why he needed her distracted and chasing her tail.

The Architect needed to keep his distractions moving at light speed, keeping the president and all his men running in circles. Dunham would soon have all the power, while the government supported and acted on all his desires. If he wanted his health care companies to improve their bottom line with rate increases, or the financial markets to rise or fall at the most convenient time, his wishes would be made with just a snap of his fingers, or there would be hell to pay.

It was his dream now, and nothing, not even Paige Turner would get in the way. The pain-in-the-ass reporter just needed to be sent on a few wild goose chases.

After talking with the Dirty Dozen and satisfied they understood his wishes, he met Todd Mathews, his financial money planner.

"Have you sold a majority of my investments?" Dunham asked his tone calm.

Todd was always nervous around Dunham. "The final transactions are being completed as we speak. I had to do them in small increments and at various times throughout the afternoon sessions in Europe and then in the New York Stock Exchange," he replied with confidence. He was looking at his watch. He pointed to the dial. "It's done," he said with a smile.

Dunham was now staring, his eyes little slits. "If this works, then the fuck up with Russell will be irrelevant," he said. He noticed Mathews puff his cheeks out and let out a long breath.

"You can go now," Dunham said, pointing to the door. "Tell Gregory Wilbanks I am ready to see him now."

Wilbanks strode in with confidence. He was Dunham's super geek and in charge of his cybersecurity team.

Without a hello, Dunham said. "Update me on my cybersecurity."

"Just the normal European hackers are trying to get in, but my security software's firewalls are working. You're safe to proceed with Stage One," he said. "There is just one minor glitch I noticed, but it is being taken care of as we speak. Nothing to worry about. Some students at UCLA are trying to get into one of our systems."

"Are you handling it?" He watched Gregory nod. "Very good," he said, rubbing his hands together. "Timing is everything," he kept repeating nervously. "I believe this time it will all work," he said.

16

The FBI's investigation into Brian Russell's family's brutal murder was now yesterday's news. Like every story in the Capitol, someone having a cold was enough to distract the reporters that scurried around the halls of Congress looking for a juicy story.

Now the news cycle had turned to Paige Turner. She had been summoned to Washington, DC, to meet with the Congressional Committee on Political Corruption. All she understood was they desired her input, from an investigative reporter's viewpoint, and current expert on corruption. They only told her they were interested in hearing who she believed were the hidden men behind the Super Pacs and the powerful lobbyists. She was skeptical about their request because she already knew that most of the congressmen on the committee were all bought and paid for by those said lobbyists.

At first, she decided not to answer any questions from reporters that covered DC politics. She wanted her colleagues, before her meeting, to speculate on why she was there. On her way up the Capital steps, she turned abruptly and stopped. She was surprised what spewed out from her lips

"I know all of you are very curious as to why I am speaking today to Congressman Parson's Intelligence Committee. So am I. As all of you know, my close friend, Brian Russell and his family were brutally murdered three days ago, and already all of you are on to another scandal here in our

Capitol. All I know is that the FBI is burying this story. Why Director Roberts is not pursuing this investigation baffles me and should make all of you curious? First reports, inaccurately given were that Russell was in debt to a large Mexican drug cartel and was found to be hiding two kilos of heroin in his home." Paige had become emotional while she spoke, part of it true and part of it an act.

She leaned in closer to the cameras and microphones that were pointed at her face. "Maybe some of you can help figure out what happened? My friend and his wife and son were executed. My gut tells me he knew something about some powerful people. It would be a shame if his death became unsolved murder and another listing in the obituary section of the newspaper," said Paige. She turned and bolted up the steps to her meeting.

"Nice going," she muttered to herself. "I know tonight's news cycle will have Russell, his wife, and son plastered on every channel across the nation." She hoped her little show would upset the men she was about to speak with. She had always been a pain-in-backside of every Capitol Hill politician, and this visit was starting off to be perfect.

When she was first called by Parsons, he tried to flatter her, telling her how much he appreciated what she was doing to expose all leaders in the country that fit her *Corrupted Intelligence* theory. He had told her his committee had some questions for her regarding her progress. He said they were determined to bring the country back to the people and felt she was the most unbiased reporter they knew who could be objective and help them.

It seemed strange to Paige that this group would talk to her. They had been the loudest critics of her weekly show, and everyone on the committee had refused to be a guest.

With her antennae on full alert, she agreed to meet with them. She was a journalist who went toward the story. She thought that maybe this meeting could shed some light on the

Architect and possibly Russell's murder. She needed help and was willing to see what this group of politicians had to offer.

* * * * *

Before Paige was called into the congressional chamber. She raised her finger at the congressional aid, signaling she needed one more minute.

Paige was wrapping up her conversation with Bradley Stevens. She was giving him specific instructions on what she needed him to do next. "Be sure you dig deep into this "Dirty Dozen" group. I have a sense that while they talk about giving the average American a voice, the only words I've ever heard from these politicians is the voice from the people paying their bills," she said, her sarcasm coming across loud and clear to Stevens.

Bradley interrupted. "I can already tell you that six Republicans still have ties to huge lobbyist groups, even though they say they don't," he said. "The others are another story. "Three of the Democrats have a long history of siding with Republican issues. The other three...well, all I can say, the jury is still out on them. I should have some answers for you when you return. Now, go have some fun." Paige saw one of the committee aides waving her in.

"Bradley I'm being called in right now..." she tried to end the call, but not before Bradley could get in the last word.

"Don't let your guard down. My gut tells me they have an agenda, but not about what you are there for. That's all I have to say for now," Bradley said.

Paige just grinned. She knew how he thought, and she trusted her friend's instincts better than anyone. "One last thought. If Brian Russell turned on Frederick Ellison and Albert Dunham, there might be other employees who need a little coaxing to come forward. Let's discuss when we meet up after this congressional shit show," she said.

Paige slipped her cell phone into her sport coat pocket, pressed the record button, and briskly walked over to the large double doors that opened into the conference room chambers.

17

The committee room was not large by congressional standards, but it was set up like a hearing room. Only eight members out of the twelve were in attendance on an elevated stage secured behind an oak-paneled pony wall. Paige smiled. "*First Red Flag,*" she told herself. She was directed to sit at the conference table with one solo microphone, a glass, and a pitcher of water that was already sweating.

Paige's mind was spinning out of control. *If they wanted my help, why all the formalities, and where are the other four members?* she thought. Her question was immediately answered before she could even speak.

First, Ms. Turner, on behalf of our committee, we all want to thank you for agreeing to come and help us. I apologize for all the formality, said Congressman Lloyd Parsons, "but, as a committee doing government work, on the taxpayer's dollars, we need to put everything we will talk about today on the record. You were one of the voices during the previous administration complaining about the back-door meetings that president conducted, as well as this committee," the congressman said, his Southern drawl pronounced. "I presume you know everyone in the room. So, for the record, let me introduce all of our members."

Congressman Parson proceeded to point to each member, as he named them, and they all nodded back a polite hello to Paige.

Turner did not know a few of the members, but it did not matter. She was sure Bradley would have some dossiers on them that would be very enlightening.

Paige smiled back at the congressmen. She made a friendly nod to Congressman Alan Sessions, Democrat from Arizona. Then another nod and wink to Theodore Burke, a Republican from Louisiana. She gave Jerome Williams the Democrat from North Carolina a wave with her right hand, and to the rest of the panel, she just mouthed hello as their names were called. Thaddeus Hooper, a Republican from Georgia, Harry Thorpe a Republican from Ohio, Timothy Randall a Republican from Texas and Clark Allen a Democrat from Arkansas all said hello back to her. She found it interesting that the eight in attendance were the most conservative congressmen in Washington. What it all meant or why four of the least conservative members were absent at this time seemed unusual, to say the least.

A light bulb went off in her head. *Maybe just these men are part of the Architect's group?* She told herself. Paige leaned forward, speaking softly into the microphone. "I am honored to be here. As a member of the news media, I am a bit puzzled as to what I can do for this committee. Nevertheless, I am all ears," she said, cupping both her ears with her hands.

Congressman Parsons responded. "Ms. Turner, I first want to send all of our condolences to you for the tragic loss of your friend, Brian Russell and his family. I know that the FBI and local police are working on solving this horrendous crime," he said, his voice a cold monotone.

"I'm astonished by what you just said. If the FBI director is hard at work trying to solve the Russell family murders, it's being kept very quiet," she said, letting her emotions show.

The congressman seemed taken aback by her direct question. He sucked in a nervous breath. "Had you spoken to or had any contact with Mr. Russell recently? I mean before his death?" Parsons asked. The question took Turner by surprised.

Why was he asking me that question? Paige thought. *Did he already know the answer and was testing me? How did Parsons even know Brian was my friend? Did he want to know about the phone message? Or was he fishing?* It was a tricky question, which she knew she had to tread lightly with her answer.

Paige knew what she had received from her friend was stolen property. She also understood that since Brian's murder, what she had in her possession was evidence. By not being forthcoming to the FBI, it could bring a whole bunch of trouble for her and her team.

Being a reporter, she also knew that what she had been given by a source did not have to be revealed until the authorities presented her with a warrant. And, even at that, freedom of the press afforded her some latitude.

Paige's wheels were now churning faster and faster as she thought about how to respond to the congressman's question. She decided she wanted them to show their hand first.

"Not recently. Brian Russell had left me a brief voice message trying to hook up for lunch and catch up," Paige said, a hint of sadness etched on his face.

Parsons jumped at his response. "What did he say on the message?" he asked.

Paige furrowed her brow before she responded. "Just what I told you," she replied, showing her agitation with the question. "I'm feeling very guilty he was murdered before I could get back with him. He was a good friend," she said, eyeing each congressman to see if they bought her little lie. She knew she had made her first mistake. The committee with the information she had revealed could ask the FBI to get a FISA warrant and tap into her answering machine and hear what Russell had said to her.

Paige could see that a stenographer was recording all she had said, but since she was not sworn in, she knew her lie could not be held against her. She was now more worried about the voice message being intercepted.

The meeting went on for a little over an hour. Most of the questions kept coming back to Russell and any communications she might have had with him before his death. Paige was starting to believe this meeting was more of a fact-gathering hunt for someone else. Were these men working with the Architect? Maybe Bradley would have those answers when he met up with her tomorrow?

Paige, being the investigative reporter she was had to ask the obvious question. She panned each member and then looked Congressman Parsons straight in the eye. "I find today's meeting a little peculiar. I thought I was here to try to help you with your committee's current investigation, but it seems to me you are doing an investigation for the FBI about my murdered friend. Don't you think your questions should be directed to Director Roberts and local Police?" she said curtly.

Congressman Parson blushed. With the politest southern manners, he responded. "I am so sorry. I have a habit of getting off-topic a lot. We do apologize for anything we have said or asked that would have made you think you were connected to the investigation of your friend's murder. I knew Mr. Russell too, and am still in shock," he said apologetically.

Paige made a mental note of what Parsons had just said. *Bradley should check out his connection to Russell.* Then she remembered she was taping this meeting anyway.

The congressman sucked in a deep breath and sat up straight in his high back chair. "What we need your help on is to investigate where all the money had come from during the last election. While I originally supported what the Supreme Court had upheld allowing big donors to fund campaigns under the radar was good for the American Democratic process, I now have a different opinion," he said taking a sip of water.

Turner raised her eyebrows; a surprised look appeared on her face. "What you just said is a little perplexing," she said her tone biting. "You already know I am investigating this problem, but your committee has been stonewalling my reporters and me for months. When can I get all of you on my show? Why the big turnaround?" she said sarcastically.

Parsons began looking at his fellow congressman for some help, but no one was stepping up to the plate. He cleared his throat before he spoke.

"I know it might appear hard to believe that a conservative Republican like myself can change his point of view. I mean my political point of view. The questions you've tried to get answers to in the past has stirred up some doubt of what I allowed to become law," Parsons paused and could see that Turner was not buying what he was saying.

Before the congressman could continue, Paige interrupted him. "Okay. Okay," she said. "If you cooperate and agree to come on my show, I might be able to help you with your investigation," she said, her expression serious.

Parsons appeared uncomfortable with her request. Nevertheless, he agreed to be interviewed down the road. "What we, this committee would like you to do, under the radar, is find out who is pulling all the purse strings with all of the Super Pacs. We already know who the big donors are, but we do not know who is controlling them. You will have this committee's full cooperation".

Turner looked confused. "I am still not sure how I can help you? Are you saying that one person is controlling all of the Super Pacs and all the major donors for his personal gain?" she asked suspiciously. *Are they trying to distract me?*

The question took Parsons by surprised. "Precisely, we believe there is one man or maybe a secret group that is working against what the United States of America stands for. This committee does not know who they can trust out there, and with your reputation and influence, we believe if there is someone or some group trying to disrupt our economy, as well as control our way of life, you're the person who can find it. If we investigate, then those people we seek will go into hiding."

Paige knew when she was being bull-shitted, and this was one of those times. Nevertheless, she wanted to know more about these politicians and acted like she wanted to help them. Maybe they could lead her in the right direction and nail the Architect.

Paige was nodding her head, as a big smile cracked on her face. "I would love to help you and my country. I am at a loss as to where to begin?" she said sincerely, trying not to reveal she was lying. She wanted to ask more questions, remembering Bradley's advice and ended her question.

Parson's voice cracked as he replied. "It's all speculation on this committee's part, Ms. Turner. We just thought..." he paused, gathering his thoughts. He had realized he might have said too much already with his clumsy approach to probing what Turner might already know. "Just do the best you can do." He bit his lower lip, waved his hand at the reporter signaling her the meeting was over. He no longer could look at Paige.

Turner could see how uncomfortable Parson had become. Her gut instincts told her that the congressman's actions were a weak attempt to test the waters to see if she knew anything about the stolen files. She slid her chair back and stood facing the committee. "I can report back to you in thirty days. Will, that work?"

Paige noticed the congressman's relief when she said thirty days. Another mistake you son-of-a-bitch. Parson's had given Paige a significant lead. Now more than ever, she had to figure out what was going to happen before Stage One took place in three days.

Congressman Parsons nodded his approval and banged his gavel, signaling the end of their meeting. He stood up abruptly and stormed out of the chamber.

Outside in the hall, Paige called Bradley. She got him on the first ring. "You were right. They were testing me. I think we've got a lot of people shaking in their boots. There were too many questions about what I might know about Brian and what he might have said to me or sent me? I need you to go to my house and erase Brian's voice message ASAP. I made a mistake inside and said too much."

"Will do boss. I will make a copy first," he said.

"I am starting to believe what Brian had died for was more serious than I imagined. The Architect's "Stage-One" plan he wants to begin in three days has everyone on the committee on edge. Not sure what they might be nervous about? I can't talk here. I am flying home in four hours. I will fill you in tomorrow at my home.

Paige made a mental note to re-look at the files on the thumb drive. Other than the Playbooks, there were some odd named folders. She thought it was not just exposing the Five Stages that had the Architect nervous, but what might be in those other encrypted files.

18

Dean Miller was still restless after two days on Catalina Island. He popped up from his recliner, standing over his wife. He told Allison he was going to take a nap on the boat. He could not get Brian Russell out of his head and wanted to test his new software. If it worked, he would instantly see everyone Russell had associated with, and who he had contact with during the last six months. It was essential for him to build a flowchart to have an accurate timeline before his friend's murder.

He clicked on keyword criteria and began typing in: Brian Russell, his employer, and current known address. He uploaded a recent photo of Brian's face. Miller then pressed enter. A small hourglass began revolving clockwise on his screen. The software was now accumulating all tags associated with Russell's photo, as well as the other search criteria. If the program worked properly, which he knew it would, it would show all the people connected to his friend in the last six months. This process he knew would take around forty-five minutes.

Next, he called two of his aids who helped developed his new software. They were employees from his old company, and he needed something more from them that he could not do from Catalina. Seth Alexander was the brightest and most committed young man he had ever met. He was very idealistic, dedicated to exposing the government and all its corruption. He wanted a country that was for the people and not one that benefited large corporations or powerful politicians over American citizens.

Miller now needed his interns to create an ancestry type family tree from the search results he was doing on Brian Russell. If this worked, he would have enough data when he got back home to give him a clear picture of how everyone in his friend's life might be connected, including all the business dealings he had.

He knew his software had some bugs in it that needed some re-coding, but once it was fixed this software program would be able to access enough data on the internet highway to fill 60,000 Libraries of Congress. It would also latch onto all geospatial and location intelligence sites, without breaking any hacking laws.

Dean understood, better than anyone, that the internet highway was a constant and ever-moving artery of data flowing freely at high speed. His new software was coded precisely to capture the data like a fisherman's net and interpret it. No personal records were revealed; it was not part of the search capabilities within his new tagging program, preventing identity thieves from using the information. However, once the data was snagged, it would be mapped and sorted, creating a detailed summary of the person and persons associated with that individual. It was the new future geared toward investigative reporting.

Dean's original objective with his software was to create a working organism for his *We the People* movement. He wanted what he built to layout a detailed resume of every politician and everything they ever said, voted on, as well as the people they associated with. He believed this would be a powerful tool to educate the American voters on their favorite candidates. He wished he had created it during the previous president's time in office.

The concept seemed logical. The software could be intrusive and in some circles a violation of the constitution. However, Dean was sure by not invading an individual's private data, and just organizing the multitude of data already streaming on the internet, would be perfectly legal. Google and Facebook were already doing something similar with their software, so he believed he was in safe territory.

Dean knew that using this data would upset the establishment who controlled the political system. Nevertheless, he felt he had a civic duty, as an American, to go forward with his plans.

Miller was hoping this initial search on Brian Russell would begin to put together a clear picture of what he had to do with this Architect and his Five Stages. The big question was what was so damaging to the Architect that he had to murder Russell and his family?

What he had already read, did not make sense. He at first did not understand Brian Russell's concerns. The encrypted notes, the vague references still needed to be decoded before he could make a judgment. He hoped that Stage One that was going to be implemented in a few days would not be something horrible for the United States.

After Stage One happened, he believed, with his software, it would provide him with enough proof to hand over to the authorities who were investigating his friend's murder.

Dean closed his laptop and returned to the beach to join his wife and children. He wanted to continue to relax, but Russell and the thumb drive were keeping a tornado of thoughts spinning inside his mind. "One or two umbrella drinks might help," he said out loud.

19

FBI Director Chad Roberts was anxiously waiting to hear from Congressman Lloyd Parsons on how the meeting had gone with Paige Turner. He disliked the reporter, her weekly show, and her goddamn *Corrupted Intelligence* theory.

It wasn't that long ago when she went after the previous president, while he was the FBI director. While he knew firsthand all the lies and misrepresentations, his president always made, director Roberts felt he should have been given the benefit of the doubt, since he was a businessman swimming in the cesspool of the Washington swamp.

Paige Turner had seen it differently and exposed his scandals, lies, and corruption that was rampant within his cabinet and administration. Her followers began believing all the stories, the fake news, and voted him out of office after four years. When Congress tried the president as a private citizen on treason charges, he fled to Russia. He hated Turner and was hoping he'd get the go-ahead to make her disappear.

Sitting at his desk daydreaming of better times, he was interrupted when his cellphone rang. He read on the display that it was Parsons.

"Be brief and concise. None of your drawn-out southern bull-shit," Roberts said rudely. "Short, concise remarks are all I want."

Parsons disliked Roberts. While he had every right to talk frequently with the FBI director, he would have enjoyed keeping his distance and not have to deal with him.

The Congressman knew Roberts felt the same and did not hold back showing the same attitude toward him. Unfortunately, Parsons had no choice but to be the director's puppet. The FBI Director had too much compromising crap on him and knew that at any time he could have him arrested.

Congressman Parson drew in a deep breath before speaking. "The meeting went as expected. Turner was elusive. She gave us no indication she knew anything about the theft of the files or what her friend wanted to talk to her about," the Congressman said, his voice cracking from the tension he felt at the other end of the line.

FBI Director Roberts let out a long-disgusted sigh. "Your assignment was to determine if she knew anything. Well, does she, or doesn't she?" the director barked.

"We could see she was skeptical about why she was at our meeting. She did say she had gotten a voice message from Russell before he died. She said it was just to get caught up."

"Did you press her on the message?"

"She did not get specific. We had to tread lightly with our questions since she was there on the pretense to help us with our ongoing investigation into undisclosed money coming into Washington. She's smart and seemed to be reading all of us. What I gathered from the meeting was that she did not know anything, but my gut tells me we piqued her interest in our committee. We have not seen the last of this pain-in-the-ass reporter. I would expect she will start investigating all of us and seeing if we are really doing anything meaningful or just a front for something else. I told you this meeting was the wrong thing to do," Parsons said, his tone testy.

"I'm not interested in your fucking opinion. Just tell me if you feel we can proceed on without any disruptions?"

Parson cleared his throat before replying. "I guess that you can proceed on. Turner said she would be getting back to us in thirty days with what we asked her to do for us, which would be too late for her to stop or investigate your group or Stage One," the congressman said. Then he heard his phone go dead.

Parsons held his phone in his outstretched arm, staring at it, his hands shaking. He knew he was one of those on the inside of Dunham's shadow government who was expendable. "Bastard," he said into the mouthpiece.

20

Dunham listened to FBI Director Roberts for ten minutes, as he was brought up to date about Turner. He was not pleased with the uncertainty, and not happy with what Roberts wanted to do to the reporter.

"I need to check out her voice messages on her phone. She told Parsons Russell had left her a message two days before we captured him," Roberts said, breathing hard. "If she has any indication her friend was scared or had stolen files to give her, she might already know too much. She has to go," he said.

"You and Montgomery never give up, do you? Let me make myself perfectly clear. You will not harm or go near Turner or any of her reporters. We are in the process of beginning Stage One that will be the first of many distractions I need to happen before the satellite launch," Dunham screamed into his phone. “I have someone monitoring Turner and need you two to focus on your current job duties and the tasks I need you to complete.”

“Copy that,” Roberts acknowledged.

Dunham wasn’t finished showing his frustration at the FBI director. “Keep the Russell investigation going, moving it along slowly. Erase any sign your men picked him up at Clancy's Tavern. I can't begin to tell you what would happen if it got out that the day Russell died he had been picked up by the FBI. And, you stay the fuck away from Turner. You understand?" Dunham commanded. "We can't afford the heat right now."

Roberts rolled his eyes. "My opinion is the same as Frasier's. I think Turner should be eliminated. You should trust our judgment. Let us do what we do best.

"The two of you thought you knew best when you murdered her husband. It put us behind on my plans. We had the right president in our back pocket then. Your actions got Turner to turn up the screws, and now we have a new president to deal with," Dunham said. "Now stop telling me you know what you're doing."

"Then, I need to check out her voice mail, and if it shows Russell told her enough, then I can have my men in California dispose of Turner without it coming back to us. A simple car accident on one of the many curves to or from her home would appear to be another accident on Coast Highway. Shit, accidents happen every day in Southern California," he said, his tone composed.

Dunham threw his arms in the air, frustrated with how his meeting was going. "Opinions...opinions are like ass-holes, everyone has them, but some are shittier than others," Dunham replied. I am not concerned that she knows about my manifesto. Who will believe her? My only wish is that the stolen encrypted files will not get opened before I implement Stage Five. I can't afford to have anyone know about the new satellite chip."

"If she does have your files, wouldn't it be better to get her out of the way, so the other stages are not revealed?" Roberts asked. "If the FBI or Homeland investigates her death, it would be just another distraction so you could move forward unnoticed."

Dunham let out a disgusted breath. "Think about what she has to go on now. If we can keep her guessing and come to dead ends with any investigation she starts, it would be better than killing her. The encrypted files have a failsafe built into them. After five failures to open them, they will self-destruct. I want her chasing her tail. We have most of the people in authority on our side. Let's give her some room to paint a picture so we can paint her as an alarmist. It will work better for us," said Dunham, his voice stern. "And...if I want her dead, you will not be the person I will go to have it done. If you and Frasier are talking to each other, you're creating a trail."

Roberts flipped him the bird, holding up his phone in front of his face. "As you wish, sir. But, as soon as I feel she's a threat to me, she's gone.

"No," screamed the Dunham into his phone. "When I say she's a threat, not you, then she's gone. Just do your fucking job, and all will be right with our new America. Don't force me to do something about you," he said, ending the call abruptly.

Nothing fazed Roberts when Dunham's abusive attitude toward came to the surface. He knew he was more bluster than action.

Roberts reviewed the report from his field agent who he had assigned to monitor Turner. When he read about Bradley Stevens and Sean Adams, and who they were already looking into, he was steaming. He knew those reporters were bulldogs. "Not this time," he said.

21

Everyone on Turner's team arrived on time. They could see Paige was in a serious mood. Bradley Stevens was the first to speak.

"This thing is bigger than we think. It has tentacles that reach into almost every government agency. We're talking the military, especially Special Ops." Bradley could see Paige's eyes grow wide. So, he continued. "Between the hawkish lobbyist groups and our Generals who do not like President Chesterfield's peace-loving agenda, rumors are floating about a secret strike on Iran's nuclear facilities and weapons stockpiles. It has Israel's full support from its conservative wing. What scares me the most is that this covert action does not have the approval of the Israeli parliament and or our government. It's possible that someone independent from the government, like a Dunham or one of his surrogates, like Frederick Ellison, might be pulling strings?" Bradley said, his tone seemed calm, but the tension in his facial muscles reflected differently. "Again, this is all speculation. I am not one hundred percent sure if some of the notations in these Architect files are referring to this attack. I'm unsure if it will be one attack," Bradley said. "I am not sure that the most beloved American, Albert Dunham, could be this diabolical man, going by the title *The Architect*?"

Paige was already on the edge of her seat. "What's your best estimate of when this secret strike might happen?"

Bradley shrugged his shoulders. "I can't say for sure. Maybe a week, a month, but no more than six months. By all appearances, it seems that one of our government contractors with their Black Ops teams is already in Israel doing some secretive field exercises. Another strange coincidence, it's being done without CIA Director Hood's support or President Chesterfield's knowledge. I had to call in a few favors to get some hint of this operation."

"How reliable are those sources?" Paige asked.

"Very. I can't believe that the CIA director and the president are being left out of the loop until I heard it from my source," Bradley said, his tone somber.

Paige was shaking her head, unable to comprehend the ramifications of a secretive strike on Iran. "Do you believe we, I mean our government, would do this?"

Bradley shrugged his shoulders. "Israel has gone so far-right in their thinking they do have the ears of our hawkish generals and politicians. Maybe it wasn't a coincidence that their Prime Minister came a month ago to talk to the House of Representatives. The Prime Minister is very good at using guilt to get us to do their bidding in the Middle East. Maybe president Chesterfield is looking the other way for deniability purposes if the attack goes south. He does have a re-election bid coming up. All of this scares the hell out of me," Bradley said, folding his notes and slipping them back into his inside jacket pocket. "This could be one of the distractions noted inside the manifesto, so the *Stage One* scenario can happen without us knowing it."

Paige cupped her mouth with her hand and let go of a big sigh. "Or this is his Stage One or part of it? Maybe I should break this piece of news on my upcoming Sunday show?"

"Not a good idea. If you're right, then this hidden group will know you have their files. If you're wrong, you'll damage your creditability or worse end up like Russell," said Bradley.

"Then what's our next course of action on this? We need to know more, especially the non-government influence on this," Paige said, while she jotted down some notes for herself.

"Already on it. I have two international reporter friends in Israel as we speak. I'll have eyes on the ground in a few hours. You'll have an update by eleven this evening," Bradley told her. "Also, if this is going to happen, what's the downside of setting Iran back a few decades?"

"Maybe it would create another vacuum in another strategic country in the Middle-East that would let another terrorist group get a foothold? Just get me some more updates on the situation," Paige said. She then turned her attention to Sean Adams; her finger pointed at the young man. "You're next," she said.

"Right," said Sean. "I've got a lot of confusing stuff which I am still investigating and sorting out. There's a lot of backdoor dealings going on with some of America's largest corporations, from some key sectors. A group of congressmen and senators are in the mix. Even staff from the FBI and Justice Department. My source had witnessed them all boarding a chartered bus heading toward the Pennsylvania border," said Sean.

"Do you know where they were going?" Paige asked.

"Not really. I researched that area and found out that the Dunham family has owned a secluded ranch in that area, something like a Camp David. A very secret place. I'm checking it out to be sure."

Paige had a confused look on her face. "Are you saying that a busload of corporate leaders, congressmen, and senators, as well as FBI and CIA personnel, were traveling together? That makes no sense," she said. "I'm not even sure it's legal?"

Sean puffed out his chest, proud of what he was about to say. "My source was able to track them on traffic cams for the first fifty miles. He lost them before they left Maryland. About five hours later that same bus appeared back on the traffic cameras coming back to DC. As far as the corporations meeting together, I'm not sure if there were any Sherman Anti-trust violations. But, right now, that's beside the point. What I do not know is the *What*, *Why* or *Where* they had gone or if they had a sanctioned government-sponsored meeting that day. There is nothing on the congressional schedule referencing a conference or whatever, outside of the capital."

Paige was twirling a lock of her hair with her index finger, deep in thought. "Do we know what businesses were represented on the bus?"

"There were leaders from our top financial institutions, military weapons, oil and gas industry, health companies, and the most disconcerting of them all, our telecommunication industry meeting secretly with government officials in an off-sight location, behind the back of the president. You know that whoever can control those four industries, can control the United States and possibly the world...that's if they can get control of the major oil reserves in the Middle-East," Sean said, his voice sounding exhausted. "I know I sound like an alarmist. What might be going on is a coup, by a shadow government most likely in the forming stages for years."

Paige was rubbing her cheeks with both hands, looking overwhelmed. "That's crazy. Everything nowadays is controlled by computers. It would take something remarkable to be able to coordinate oil wells, financial markets, telecommunications, shit it's impossible. There must be another reason for this meeting? Is there any way we can get Pennsylvania to let us see their traffic cams?" she asked.

"I've already tried. It seems they do not like reporters too much and told me to put my request where the sun don't shine. I did get one important piece of information. The chairman of the board for all of Ellison Industries, Frederick Ellison was there too. It's known that he's a close friend of Albert Dunham. I am still investigating his background and when they became connected. It is challenging getting any information. It's like we have been blacklisted. Their people won't talk to anyone from your show. I had to lie to get what I just told you."

"Good work," Paige said. "Keep digging and lying when you have to." Paige looked at Bradley again. "Do you have more to add to all of this?" she asked with a silly grin on her face.

Bradley nodded. "Yup. What I found might tie all this together. First, let me clarify that. I had a little help from a computer geek at UCLA." He thumbed through his notes. "Oh, yes, there it is. His name is Seth Alexander. He works for Dean Miller as an intern. You know the billionaire cyber software king. The one who sold his company to the government for a huge sum of cash."

Paige had to cut Bradley off and stop him from rambling off track, which he did a lot. "He's a friend. I've known him since Stanford. Now, get to the point, Bradley."

"It seems that Dean Miller is investigating the same thing we are investigating. Seth could not confirm, but I am beginning to believe that Russell sent out more thumb drives containing those Architect files."

"Why aren't we talking to Miller instead of his employee?" asked Paige.

"He's on vacation with his family. He'll be back in a few days. I'm planning on going to see him when he gets back."

Paige shook her head. "I should talk to him. I'll text him. He might feel more comfortable discussing things with me."

"Fine," Bradley replied, acting a little hurt.

"Don't get upset. I need you and Sean working on what's going to happen with this Stage One. I think we're done here," she said.

She was immediately on her cellphone, texting Dean Miller's mobile number. "*Call me when you return home. We need to talk about Brian Russell and the thumb drive you received. Say hi to Allison and the kids.*

22

Dean had just gotten dressed when his cell phone pinged. It was Seth Alexander. The text reads, *"CALL ME-IMPORTANT"!* Then a second text popped on his screen. This one sent chills up his back. *What does Paige know about Russell and the thumb drive? Does she have a copy too?* He ignored her message. He had one more day to worry about her.

He heard Allison singing in the shower and knew it would take her at least an hour to get ready. His two kids were already downstairs relaxing by the pool, waiting for their parents to take them to their celebration dinner. It was a family tradition to pick a unique restaurant and recap everything they could remember about their vacation.

He thought about calling his intern Seth, but then again decided to wait. He promised Allison no work on vacation, and he needed to keep his promise, even if it's just for a few hours. He shut down his phone.

He peeked his head inside the bathroom to tell his wife he'd be downstairs with the kids. He could not stop staring at his wife, naked in the shower. They had been married over twenty-five years, and she was still the sexiest woman he had ever laid eyes on. He slipped off his clothes, stepped into the bathroom and whistled at her, his body begging to be invited in.

She opened the clear glass door and stood there wet and soapy, her hands on her slim hips. "What are you looking at, my handsome, at attention, pervert," she said playfully. "I could use some help soaping down the rest of my dirty, dirty body. Can you help a poor girl get cleaned up?" she teased playfully.

Dean looked at his watch, looked at his pouting wife. It was a no brainer. Whatever tension he had been feeling about Brian Russell was being washed away, as his wife's wet and soapy body rubbed up against his.

"Let's remember we have dinner reservations with the kids at seven this evening," he said while Allison massaged his already aroused body.

Allison looked deep into his eyes and whispered with a sultry voice, "I will have you ready on time. Now shut up and soap me down."

* * * * *

Seth had waited almost two hours and realized that the professor was not going to call him. He stared at the preliminary search he had done on Brian Russell and was surprised at all the people who were connected to him.

It was a who's who of very influential men around the United States and the world. What he found even more interesting is that the search had automatically expanded its sphere of influence and created a massive flow chart showing the depth of Russell's influence around the globe. There were too many common denominators that painted a fascinating picture of a large organization that had their fingers into every aspect of the American economy and the federal government. "Ah, ha," he shouted in his small studio apartment off Gayley Avenue, in Westwood Village, four blocks from the UCLA laboratory. "Just what we have thought all along. There is a shadow government out there. Is this Architect the real ringleader?"

He decided to test Dean's software a little bit more and see what would turn up before he returned from his vacation. What he did not know was that Miller was the only one who knew how to use his software, so the cyber infiltrations he generated would go undetected. Seth did not imagine what he'd be triggering before he pressed the next search button.

With a broad proud smile, Seth hit the search key and watched the computer screen begin to do its job.

23

Albert Dunham had just read over the meeting notes Frederick Ellison prepared for him. "So, you think we're ready to proceed with Stage One?"

Ellison nodded. "We're ready. Just one fly in the ointment sir. Paige Turner's reporter, Sean Adams, knows about our conference. He has communicated it with Paige Turner. I don't think the reporter knows the location, or that you were involved, but the meeting is now on the record. My biggest concern is he will figure out you have a ranch in that area.

"How did you get this information?" Dunham asked.

"Our NSA friends were monitoring a staff meeting Turner was having with her reporters, and this bit of information popped up. Not sure what they will do with it, but I will bet Paige Turner is looking for a story. What they heard, confirms that Turner's entire team know about the Architect's Manifesto and have the thumb drive Russell stole from you."

Dunham shrugged his shoulders. "What's the big deal? My encrypted files, the most critical part of my plan cannot be opened. She doesn't have anyone on her staff who is cyber smart. So, let her, and everyone read my files and all the other manifestos. And, about our meeting, it means nothing. We, like most businesses, have meetings and get-togethers. It's perfectly legal, and if it wasn't, no one, either in the house or senate, will investigate. If she wasn't at the meeting, or if one of your bartenders, like what happened to Romney, did not record the meeting, we should be safe to proceed."

"I agree," Ellison said with caution. "There was no staff at the meeting— just members. However, with what the NSA recorded, it seems that your suspicions about more copies being sent might have been confirmed. Dean Miller, the billionaire software genius, who helped build the satellite's software the NSA is using for their upcoming launch, might have a copy of your files too. What has me more concerned is that he's the only person capable of decrypting all of your files."

Dunham massaged his scalp, a nervous habit he had when he was upset. "Even if Miller has a copy of my files, he won't be able to decrypt them until it's too late. And, for Turner, it won't matter if she has a copy. She needs to do her due diligence before she can release it in a story. Let's not worry so much. Once Stage One is on the books, the pain-in-the-ass reporter will be chasing her tail on that story, along with President Chesterfield. Then, we'll be onto Phase Two and Three."

Ellison just shook his head, biting his lower lip, thinking of the right words to say. "Then I think we should have Director Roberts increase his monitoring of the situation. I, for one, want to know for sure that Turner isn't digging deeper into our business. If she is, then we'll have no choice but to start eliminating the threat whether you like it or not," he said. "There are too many other members under the umbrella of your Playbook who have a lot to lose like you."

"I do not want Director Roberts anywhere near Turner and her people. He's a hothead and can screw things up. I have someone who can get a better fix on what might be going on," he said.

"If they leak a story about our secret meeting it might raise some eyebrows," Ellison remarked.

"Dunham was now rubbing his chin, lost in thought. "Okay. I'll handle it. My guy will control the situation. He knows I do not want anything on this meeting out there until Stage Two is initiated."

"Got it. So, Stage One can proceed next week?" Ellison asked.

"It's a go," Dunham said with a smile.

* * * * *

Later that day Frederick Ellison was having a face-to-face with FBI director Roberts. "Albert does not want you near Turner or her people. He wants you to pull your men back immediately. Dunham says he has a guy who can watch the reporter." Ellison seemed dismayed. "If it's the person I think it is, he's ruthless and cannot be trusted. Can you, without being noticed, keep some of your men on Turner and her people? Then report back to me. I will feel better knowing what's going on. Our boss is smart but too emotional about his satellite launch.

Roberts' face lit up with an evil smile. "How close can I get?" he asked, cracking his knuckles.

Ellison knew that look and lashed out. "What part of what I just said did you not understand? If Albert finds out you or your men where anywhere near Turner and her reporters, he'll...well let's not go there just yet."

"Albert would not have the audacity to hurt me. He knows me too well and what I am capable of," said Roberts smugly.

"You are doing this for me and me only. So, keep your fucking distance. Just get close enough to listen and not be seen," Ellison said sternly. "I want a report within a week. The sooner, the better," he said.

"What if I find Turner is too close, you know if she knows of our plans and is getting ready to expose what's coming down about Stage One or Stage Two?" Roberts asked. "Can I then stop her?"

"Report back to me on your findings. Albert and I will decide what to do. You are to stay back and gather the information, understand?" Ellison said. Roberts felt the threat but just smiled at the man.

"I am still the FBI Director and will do whatever it takes to keep America and our interests protected." He got up and directed Ellison out of his office.

24

Albert Dunham was talking to a large group of African Americans in downtown Detroit. He had been asked there to discuss infrastructure and his ideas on how billionaires can help rebuild struggling inner cities.

"Thank you for having me," he said, smiling. "After spending a good part of the morning with your mayor, I am shocked at how rundown your city has become. I can pass blame. I can tell you who is at fault, but those words won't get things fixed. I, for one, am tired of seeing our politicians using the same old finger-pointing and blaming the other side to distract from what's needed in America," Dunham said, pausing to sip from his glass of water. He was calm, confident, and not using a teleprompter.

"I am not ashamed of the resources my family, and I have accumulated over the last one hundred and fifty years. That's the American way. Sadly, I am ashamed of some of my billionaire friends who brag about not paying their fair share of taxes or even paying any. With the amount of wealth I have amassed, it would be immoral on my part to not want to give back to this great country that has made it all possible for my family to succeed. Taxes are the easy way to do it, but I do not trust our politicians to spend our tax dollars wisely. So, I am proposing that men like me make a formal commitment to inject at least a billion dollars each into America's infrastructure development. I am also proposing that our crumbling schools be brought into the modern era with computers, textbooks and with teachers trained to get every American child ready to be a productive citizen and realize the American dream," he said, stopping to let the cheers and applause die down.

He spoke for another thirty minutes. He waved to his audience and walked away from the podium to a standing ovation. As he sat down in his limo, he placed a phone call. All the national news outlets were reporting on Dunham's speech. Everyone was praising you for even considering something of this magnitude.

One reporter at the auditorium where Dunham had just finished his speech was talking into her microphone.

"*Albert Dunham is the real deal. He wants to give back some of his wealth to the country he says he loves. I hope more billionaires jump on his bandwagon?*"

* * * * *

"Frederick, has Stage One started?" What he heard made him happy.

As Ellison kept bringing Dunham up to date, then he was interrupted with a breaking news alert coming from the Middle East.

25

Bradley Stevens had discovered a secret operation activated in the desert of Israel. He had just finished his briefing about the Special Ops groups camping near the border of Israel and Jordan with Paige and her team. What he had uncovered was frightening.

Paige and the others looked stunned. "Does President Chesterfield know?" she asked.

Bradley checked his notes. "I could not get any confirmation from the White House Press Secretary. I asked Carolyn Waterfall, our Secretary of State, and she had no comment. I came away from our call, believing she did not know anything about this exercise."

"Have you uncovered who these men are?" Paige asked.

"All I've found out is that these men are a fringe group outside the US military and Israeli military. Operational exercises are going on right now within Israel's borders. If my informant is correct, there will be an attack on Iran within the next few hours. Also, if President Chesterfield is in the loop, he's staying away from the situation room, which is unusual for a president when a covert military exercise is happening. The president's in Virginia giving a speech to a group of teachers, promoting his new education plan. Obama did do something similar during another covert op, except he knew it was going on. He was giving a speech at a Press Corp dinner then. So, it's nothing too out of the ordinary." Stevens said, while still fumbling with his notes when Paige interrupted. "One other interesting item. Dunham had given a speech to a group of teachers, promoting his plan for America's schools at the same time as the president. If he's the Architect, this does not make any sense."

Paige appeared confused. "We'll deal with the Dunham problem another time. I need to address the Iran problem. Could this be Iraq all over again?" she asked, her voice cracking with concern. "If what you have said is true, then we might have a military event happening without congress or our president's knowledge."

Sean jumped into the conversation, a shocked look on his face. "We're too late. I just got tweeted that four large explosions at Iran's major nuclear facilities have leveled each plant. Also, three of Iran's biggest weapon facilities simultaneously have been destroyed. It appears to be a well-timed and coordinated attack. Oh, shit, two of their biggest oil refineries are on fire," he said, trying to catch his breath.

Bradley slumped back in his chair; frustration stamped on his face. "I guess my source was right. Just a little off on his timing."

"Could this have been part of the Architect's Stage One action?" Paige asked.

"I need to get back out there and find out. It's possible. Maybe something else is getting ready to happen too. We could have a full-scale uprising on our hands in the Middle-East."

Paige was turning on the sixty-inch TV monitor in the conference room. Every news channel was reporting about the attack. CBS News was saying it was believed to be an Israeli mission. She switched to ABC, and they were saying it was thought to be a CIA operation. With each channel surfed, Paige and her team kept hearing conflicting reports. Not one news agency had anything concrete or definitive about the attack. No group was claiming credit for the attack.

Bradley was getting off his cell and snapping his fingers at the group. "My friend at the CIA has confirmed it was not one of their operations. He said President Chesterfield had no clue who was behind this operation. Israel is not speaking to anyone.

They have their military on full alert," Stevens said. "President Chesterfield denies this was a joint operation with Israel. My contact says they suspect that an outside group, working with a conservative faction within Israel's Mossad, is responsible. The CIA had been monitoring these groups for some time and then lost their visual on a small band who disappeared during the exercises around ten days ago. That's all he has for now. My source is going into lockdown any minute. I will be blind for a while," he said, his voice had a nervous edge to it.

Paige was stunned. Her eyes were wide with concern, wondering what the impact of this attack was going to have on the Middle East. She needed to know. She wanted more facts. Just something more than what Bradley had just told her. Then it hit her. Was this tied to the recent secret meeting in the woods in Pennsylvania? She began questioning if she had interpreted the notations correctly. She started wondering if this could be a diversion of something bigger that was going to happen. But, how would this give the Architect the power he wants?

Paige's mind was spinning out of control. Then, the other news flashed on the monitor. "Shit, the stock market is tanking," she cursed. "Bradley, can you find out if there had been any large sell-offs in the last few days? Can we tie the meeting that had happened the other day at Dunham's ranch into all of this?"

Stevens was immediately jotting down something in his notebook. "I should have those answers later today. I have a good source at the Security and Exchange agency that can help," he said, as he rushed out of the room.

Paige was now nervously pacing around the room, talking to herself. Her color had drained from her face. "My gut tells me that we're in for something bigger and more destructive here in the United States. We need to do a better job interpreting what's written is these goddamn files. We have to get ahead of these Stages," Paige said, her words gave her the chills.

Sean said. "Maybe we should show the president what we have? He must have people that can interpret these files better than us?"

"Yeah, and what should we show him? Stolen files by a man who's dead. From maybe, and I do say maybe, a man who has given President Chesterfield tons of financial contributions to get him elected and probably more now to get him re-elected. Shit, Dunham just gave a beautiful speech in Detroit and made President Chesterfield look like an inept Commander and Chief. He's a damn hero now," she moaned, nervously combing her hair with her fingers.

"Shit, don't kill the messenger," said Sean throwing his arms up in the air. "If we have a playbook of a madman's dream for this country, then we owe it to all Americans to figure what will happen next."

Paige kept looking at some of the Architect's file notes. "What if we expose the data inside the files, without naming names? Maybe that would shake up Ellison or Dunham's plans? He might have second thoughts about moving forward with his other Stages?" she said.

Bradley was packing up his knapsack to leave, when he turned to face Paige, his head shaking his disapproval. "Let's think about that for a moment. If Russell's murder was for stealing the files, what do you think Ellison or Dunham would do to you if you expose some or all of the files inside of them?"

"We have to do something. We can't just sit back and watch?" Paige said, feeling sick to her stomach. "I can't believe Russell died for what we've all read. It has to be those encrypted files."

"I know you don't like the idea of talking to the president, then what about waiting for Dean Miller to return and see what he's working on?" Bradley said.

Paige was bobbing her head. "Yes. That a good plan. I hope nothing else happens before we meet with him."

Bradley was halfway out the door when he said, "let me and Sean dig a little deeper. Maybe something will turn up until we meet with Dean."

"Okay. Keep me posted," Paige said.

The minute her two reporters left, her cell rang. It was U.S. Marshall Scott Rogers. He worked inside the Marshall's new Cyber Domestic Terrorism Division.

"Scott, thanks for calling me back so quickly," she said. "Have you seen the shit storm in Iran?"

"Yes. Aren't you going to say hello first? Or, how have you been?" he asked.

Paige puffed out her cheeks, letting a long sigh slip out from her lips. "Sorry. I am up to my eyeballs in a shit story. So how have you been? We haven't seen each other since Rick's funeral, right?

"Damn. Sorry. I've been buried in my new job for the last few years. Rick was a great guy," Rogers said.

"I'm still dealing with it. He was the love of my life. But, right now, I'm buried in a breaking story that I could use your help. And, I apologize if I sound rude."

"Rick always talked about you. He loved you very much. He warned me about you that the story always came first. So, what can I help you with?" he asked cautiously. "I too have a shit load of crap to get to the president," he replied.

Paige never had any one-on-one time with Scott, but knew, from her husband, that he was a straight shooter. She wanted to trust him. But, chose to proceed with caution. "I'm sure you know about Brian Russell?"

"Yes. What a shame. Brian was a nice guy. I hadn't seen him in a while. We all dived into our careers after Stanford," said Scott, his tone filled with regret.

Paige wanted to tell Scott about the thumb-drive but thought better of it. "I received something from Brian that has me worried. It might tie into what just happened in Iran."

Scott was fast with his response. "If you have information about the attack, you need to turn it over to the FBI immediately," he said, his voice had turned harsh. "This attack has everyone scurrying around and if you have anything that can help the investigation...well...it's your patriotic duty, Paige, to give us what Brian sent you."

Paige knew he was right, but what she had was more than that. "I can't. I need to protect my source. Also, I am not so sure I can trust the FBI with what Russell had discovered. Someone at the bureau might be compromised. Can we first meet and discuss this in person?" she pleaded.

"I'm a U.S. Marshall. You can't trust me?" he said.

"I know. That's why I called you. What I have could implicate people high up in the FBI food chain who might have committed treason," she said. "That would be within the purvue of the Marshall's office?" Paige asked.

Scott let out a frustrating breath. "My office is in downtown Los Angeles on Spring St. Can we meet there later today?"

"No. Let's have dinner at Momed on Beverly. We can get a nice secluded table there and talk. One question. Have you heard of a man who goes by the title: The Architect?"

There was a long pause before he responded. "I don't think we should talk about this over the phone. I'll see you at six this evening, and we can discuss everything you have. Paige, please be careful," he said.

"Now you're scaring me," she said. "I hope you'll be able to help?"

26

President Patrick Chesterfield stormed into the Situation Room, looking like he wanted to kill someone. It was so quiet you could have heard a pin drop. The usually cool and calm leader of the free world was not so composed. Inside the room were his Joint Chiefs, the CIA director, the FBI director, the Secretary of State, the Secretary of Defense, Homeland Security, the NSA director, National Security Advisor, his Press Secretary and his Chief of Staff.

The Chief of Staff, Felix Wilson, was standing by the back door, checking everyone off a list or jotting down notes, no one knew for sure what he wrote in his infamous notebook. This habit drove President Chesterfield crazy, but he knew it annoyed everyone in the room more, and that was what he wanted.

"How could Iran be attacked, and not one of you in this room knew anything about it? Not even a hint from Israel?" he said sarcastically, his eyes glaring at his Chief of Staff and his CIA director Thomas Hood. He pointed at the director. "Have you anything to say for yourself?" Chesterfield said, his tone biting.

CIA Director Hood swallowed hard before he spat out his words. "I had briefed you three weeks ago. We all knew of the military contractor group that had been conducting training exercises with Israel's cooperation. We had taken our eyes off that group to follow the movement of a splinter group from Mossad. My team lost visual of them around ten days ago. At first, we didn't think much about it. Contractors move people around every day. They were all off the radar doing extreme exercises near the Israeli and Jordan border, but again it was not so unusual. Most of our military contractors train in different parts of the world, honing up on their skills," the CIA director paused.

Chesterfield, his eyes fire red said, "Where did you lose visual of this group?" he said, his tone biting.

Hood swallowed hard, gathering his thoughts. "We lost sight of them two days ago, somewhere near the Iranian border. I was going to brief you on that, but, well, I thought we would find them...we never thought anything like this was going to happen or was even in the planning stages. My agency was caught off-guard," the CIA director said, his voice cracking from nerves.

President Chesterfield could see all the stares in the room. He knew everyone there had recommended someone else for the CIA director's job, but he would not listen. He had paid back one of his largest donors, Frederick Ellison, for his support during the election. The donor had been a long-time family friend.

Hood was Ellison's nephew. Even though Chesterfield refused to honor other favors owed after his election as president, he had to accept this one. Ellison was hooked up to Albert Dunham, and they both were his biggest donors. He needed them for his re-election bid and did not want to piss them off. However, today, he was regretting that decision.

"Director Hood, are there any updates I need to know?" Chesterfield asked in a calmer voice. "Why hasn't the Prime Minister of Israel called me? Am I to believe he did not know about this too? He's always had his hand in everything happening in that part of the world."

"I haven't been contacted by anyone inside Mossad or anyone close the Prime Minister. All I know right now is that the damage to Iran is more severe than we had first determined.

The attack did not just focus on Iran's nuclear and weapons facilities.

While we still don't have confirmation, Iran's president and the Ayatollah were wounded. No word on their condition. One other thing, this group had destroyed was Iran's two primary oil-producing plants. If this intelligence is correct, this might just have been a coup, and a good thing for all of us," the CIA director said, a smile forming on his face. "This might have cut off Iran's main money-making machine and could prevent them from supporting or even sending weapons and money to all the terrorist groups they sponsor. Today's covert attack could be huge for us and the rest of the world's war of terrorism."

President Chesterfield was not buying any of this. "You believe we would not have known of a coup in this fucking Islamic country? Is your office so inept that no one, not one analyst knew anything? Heard any chatter? Anything?" he asked, his calm turning to rage. He saw the CIA Director trying to speak, but Chesterfield raised his hand like a traffic cop stopping oncoming traffic. "I've heard enough from you at this time."

"He looked around the room and began asking everyone in attendance for some opinions. No one volunteered, so he pointed to Admiral Hollingsworth, his chairman of the Joint Chiefs, to start.

"Mr. President, we have updated information. Unlike the CIA director, we have a clearer picture of what happened. Once we heard of the attack, I ordered our drones up to survey the affected areas. We are analyzing satellite data and should have a clearer picture of what had gone on. What we do know is that it was a well-planned and professional attack. We do not know the factions involved, but it smells like Mossad, led by Israel's conservative far-right hawkish politicians. If I might guess, it had the approval of the Prime Minister. I am surprised they would have done anything without warning you first. We know it was not ISIS. Iran has been giving them support, and it would be too foolish for them to spit in their faces."

Chesterfield interrupted the general. "I agree with your first assessment. I wouldn't put it past Israel to have orchestrated this attack. Their government has become so far right, so much like our old Tea Party fanatics and our hawkish right, that it might be possible they are supporting a group inside their country we know nothing about," the president said, his tone reflecting his exasperation.

General Hollingsworth took in a deep breath, trying to digest what Chesterfield had said. "If what you say has any plausible chance of being true, then I think we might be dealing with a compelling military group we have no information on or is affiliated with any specific country. What I do know from our intelligence on the ground in Iran is that even the Iranian government did not know this attack was even being organized," Admiral Hollingsworth pinched the bridge of his nose before he continued with his report, his annoyance written all over his face.

The president kicked the leg of his desk. "While I hate Iran, they do have one of the best intelligence agencies. It scares me that they would miss something this big unless the attack had some support within the Iranian government or military, maybe both," he said. "The Middle-East cannot tolerate another power shift with all the various jihadist groups looking for a new home base to build their army."

Admiral Hollingsworth was staring at the FBI director. He noticed a smirk on his face. "What concerns me the most, is that we might have an international faction of ex-military special ops from our country and some of our Western allies, financed by some very wealthy businessmen. I've suspected for a long time that some powerful men would have a big interest in manipulating the financial markets, and this would be one big way to do it. Every stock exchange is in free fall today. If this is so, then we might have a bigger problem on our hands.

Sir, we need to talk after this meeting, alone, if that's possible? I think we have some traitors..." he said, looking directly at FBI director Roberts.

Chesterfield felt the room chill from the Admiral's request. "Does anyone here have any more to add about this tragedy? If not, then you are all dismissed. Admiral, you can stay behind. He looked at this Chief of Staff, Felix Wilson. "Felix, you hang back also.

When the room cleared, the president looked at the Admiral signaling him to speak.

"We have a bigger problem sir, than this outside military faction. I believe our intelligence agency has been compromised. Hood, when he reorganized the CIA to make it more efficient, to allow a smoother flow of information between the military and Justice, ended up creating too many levels that are not reporting to each other. Once again, bureaucracy runs amuck, or there's a bigger scheme lurking inside your administration."

"I don't understand. I thought we had a well-oiled machine that was working better than ever." Chesterfield asked Hollingsworth.

"We did for a while, sir, but over the last eight or nine months, we have not been getting accurate information or able to talk to the right people in charge. It is not my job to gather intelligence; it's the CIA's. Their lack of cooperation has forced me to take other measures," Admiral Hollingsworth said, clenching his jaw.

"Are you accusing my CIA director of intentionally undermining our intelligence agencies? Are you saying we have traitors within my administration?" Chesterfield barked.

Admiral Hollingsworth did not seem rattled by the president's outburst. "Sir, what I am saying is that we have a serious problem when we cannot gather information from our own agencies that would have told us what was happening. No other country has the intelligence gathering apparatus we have.

No other country knows as much as we do about what's going on or going to happen around the world. And, yes, I am saying that someone, maybe not the CIA Director directly, but someone within his agency and maybe Justice, especially your FBI Director Roberts, is going around you to achieve something beyond my scope of understanding. I am not a lawyer, but my gut tells me treason is not out of the picture."

"Are you saying this started when I took this office?"

"No, sir. It began during the Bush years when we entered the Iraq war. Back then, the president gave his advisors too much leeway, especially his Vice-President, and you know what happened with the Iraqi war. I'm going to continue to work with my people who I trust to get to the bottom of this group. You need to look into cleaning house before it gets too late," the Admiral said cautiously. One other thing. A reporter from Paige Turner's media group seemed to know about this military action before we did. A Bradley Stevens had spoken to someone in your cabinet just an hour before the attack took place."

President Chesterfield looked shell shocked. He fell back in his chair, unable to speak. His chief of staff, Felix Wilson, stood and starting walking around the room. He picked up a grease pen and started writing on a White Board.

"Mr. President, you know how I feel about Hood. He was never qualified to handle such an important agency like the CIA. Now we are suffering because you owed a favor to Frederick Ellison and Albert Dunham." Wilson was the only person on the president's staff who could talk to him that way. "I need to find out how this Bradley Stevens character knew more about this operation before our incompetent CIA director."

"Felix, tone it down a bit. Don't you think I know that now? Plus, I've tried to change the influence money has on our government and have been doing a pretty good job trying to get legislation through the Senate and House to curb all of the influence the wealthy have on all of us. That's why I formed "The Dirty Dozen." They hopefully will come up with some concrete recommendations."

Felix laughed. "Sir, in the past five months, the committee has not moved one inch in any direction to solve the way the rich have taken control of our governmental process. Did you know that they asked the journalist and TV personality, Paige Turner, to speak the other day to their committee? They said they wanted her help to investigate all the Super Pacs and States where voter suppression had tried to take root? Strangely, all they focused on was the murder of Paige's friend, Brian Russell. You know the tech guy who worked high up in Ellison's organization. I had ears inside the meeting, and it seemed that Senator Parsons was more concerned with something Russell might have said to Turner before he was tortured and murdered," Wilson said. "I'm wondering if she has information about what is going on?"

"What does any of that have to do with what we are talking about today?" Chesterfield asked, scowling at his chief of staff.

"I am not sure, but your friends Dunham and Ellison seem to have their hands in some of this." Wilson had started drawing on the whiteboard in the situation room. "Let's put Dunham on top of this chart," he said. "Then let's put Hood to the left on your chart and the Dirty Dozen to the right." Like a corporate chart of a CEO's team of executives, Felix started painting a picture of his theory. "Your friend and largest contributor appears to be building a strong team to benefit his interests. Albert Dunham has influence with Hood and with Congressman Parsons and six other congressmen on the committee." The president interrupted.

"I still don't get how this relates to Iran and this secret military group?" Chesterfield said a puzzled, frustrated expression cracked on his face.

"I do not have all of those answers right now, but I have a theory that for a long time some of the most wealthy men in our country and especially someone like Albert Dunham, with all of his business interests will benefit the most from what had just gone down if he had advanced warning about it. I am not saying he's doing anything illegal at this point. I find it curious where his tentacles are latching onto. Right now, it's just my theory. Until I have more facts, I will leave it at that."

Chesterfield leaned back in his chair, his eyes looking up at the ceiling. "Should I replace Hood?" he asked.

The admiral raised his arms, reflecting he did not want to get involved with that decision, but Chesterfield's chief of staff did not hesitate with a response.

"Definitely, Mr. President. So we can get control of this situation, terminating him need to happen now. I've been sensing it for a while. Your re-election bid is being undermined. Hood is going to hurt you in the polls if you do not take action immediately. If more shit begins to pop up, it could end your second term bid and your presidential legacy. What you need right now is your own Black Ops group digging where no other agency or congressional committee can go. You need to find your enemies and purge your administration of them."

Chesterfield straightened up in his chair, his face serious, deep in thought. "I am not sure I want that. Just call Hood and tell him to be at the Oval Office in three hours. I want you to get me a few recommendations for his replacement before I fire him," he said somberly. "Also, get me any old files on past president's Black Ops teams. One other item. I want to talk with that reporter Paige Turner. I am interested in why the Dirty Dozen was so interested in the murder of her friend...you said, Brian Russell? Maybe Russell had something he gave her? Also, get me everything you have on Russell and his current murder investigation."

"When do you want to meet with Turner? She lives in California. She's not your biggest fan now," his Chief of Staff said.

Chesterfield waved off Felix's remarks. "Let's first deal with the CIA director and the Black Ops alternative. We still need to deal with the press and this Iran mess. My phone has been ringing all day from all our allies around the world. Then, I will call Turner myself and set it up."

27

Paige was meeting with Clay Thomas, her boss, at CMN regarding her upcoming show. "Before this Iran attack and the files Russell sent me, I thought I had found the man or men, who epitomize *Corrupted Intelligence*. With what I have inside these files paints a portrait of a man, living two lives at the expense of hard-working Americans," she said handing him a file with Albert Dunham's and Frederick Ellison's name on it. "Tell me I am wrong about these files predicting the attack in Iran?"

Clay looked at her, a befuddled expression on his face. "Anyone of us could have predicted one day a country like Israel would make a preemptive strike against Iran. They're mortal enemies."

Paige rolled her eyes. "What's inside these files is more than a coincidence or someone's far-reaching prediction."

Clay did not respond to her remarks. "You said, one man. You have two names on this report?"

Paige pursed her lips frustrated with her boss. "After researching timelines, and the details written inside these files point to Albert Dunham," she said.

"Are you crazy? Expose Dunham on national TV? Let the world know you have stolen files from the wealthiest man on the planet, that came to you from a murdered friend? Do you know how ridiculous you sound?" he said, his voice rising.

"Do you know what just happened in Iran? I believe the Architect had a hand in it."

"Based on what? Notations on a computer file. There has been lots of speculation that Israel would one-day bomb Iran. Maybe they did it? What you're reading could be the ranting from a crazy person, with lofty goals, but nothing I have read convinces me Dunham had anything to do with the Iran attack. You will not do your show on this subject. No...never," said Clay, noticeably upset with Paige. "The fallout for this station would be horrendous. Dunham and his army of lawyers would bury us."

She had never seen her boss so angry. "This story will be exposed. If not on my next show, but soon," she said. Before she could continue, her phone rang.

"President Chesterfield, yes this is Paige Turner," she answered nervously. "What can I do for you, sir?" She pointed to her phone, mouthing *"It's the president."*

"Sorry to call you on such short notice, but as you know we have a situation here in the Capital, I am hoping you might be able to shed some light on it. Can you meet me at the Oval Office tomorrow?"

Paige could not catch her breath. While she did not care for the president and his policies, she was curious about what he felt she had to offer him. "I will see if I can get a flight out tomorrow, but I am not sure?"

"I've already sent some transportation for you. Your ride will be ready at LAX, at the private air terminal. Be there in the morning at seven. I should have you back home by that evening," said Chesterfield.

Paige asked. "What's this all about, sir?"

"I'll bring you up to speed tomorrow. Have a good night's sleep young lady," the president said.

Paige looked at Clay, her eyes wide with disbelief. "The president wants to speak with me. Shit, what does he want? First the Dirty Dozen. Now, this?"

Clay just laughed. "Paige you're one of the most popular TV commentators. Maybe he wants you to interview him. He is running for re-election. Just go and listen. You'll do just fine. Don't screw it up with your righteous attitude; this could be great for our station," he said.

"It makes no sense, Clay. He's up to his eyeballs in the Iranian attack. What do I have to offer?" she said, taking in a deep breath. "Shit, does he know about Russell and the files he sent me?"

"Go and be yourself. It's probably nothing to worry about."

On her drive home to Malibu, her thoughts were spinning out of control. What she needed was a stiff drink so that she could get some sleep. Her earlier idea exploded into her head. "Does he know about Russell and the thumb drive? Shit, he's the president. He must have been briefed about my interrogation by the Dirty Dozen.

Then her phone rang. It was the restaurant in Beverly Hills she had made an appointment for her dinner with US Marshal Scott Rogers. "Yes, I'll be there," she said reluctantly.

28

She had arrived at the restaurant ten minutes early. The hostess told Paige that her friend was already at their table. She looked toward the back of Momed's and saw Scott, his arm raised.

He had not changed since Stanford. Maybe a little older, but still handsome with a chiseled face. Scott stood and gave her a big hug and soft kiss on the cheek.

"How long has it been?" he said.

Paige's smile evaporated from her face. "Not since Rick's funeral.

Scott did not seem to notice the sadness on her face. "What's it been five years? How are you doing?"

"Working twenty-four-seven. Just coping when I get home to an empty house. It's getting better day by day. One day I'll solve his murder and finally put his death behind me," she said, wiping a tear from her cheek.

"When I received your phone call, it brought back some fun times at Stanford," he said. "Rick, Dean Miller and, oh shit, Brian Russell. It's horrible what happened to him and his family."

Paige was nodding her head. "That's why I called you. I mentioned he had sent me some files he stole from his employer. He was going to be a whistleblower. I believe what he took has some connection to the attack on Iran and the tanking of the stock market. I wanted to go to the authorities.

But Brian said to not trust anyone at the FBI or CIA," Paige said.

Scott looked shocked. "What files are you talking about?"

"I mentioned the name The Architect, and you got serious?"

Scott just stared at Paige. "How do you know about this man?"

"I have his manifesto, as he calls it. I also have his family's previous manifestos. It appears for over a hundred and fifty years; this family of Architects had been planning to build enough wealth to take control of our country. The current heir, by his entries, believes he can become the next Emperor of the United States."

Without hesitation, Scott said the acronym "EOTUS. That's comical," he said. "But I have heard of this Architect before. My unit at the Marshal's office, about a year ago, was tracking a group of cyber hackers, and that name came up."

Paige was now curious. "What did you find out?"

"Nothing. FBI Director Chad Roberts, put our investigation on hold. He got my boss to give us a new assignment, which isn't going anywhere. Can I see your files?" he asked.

Paige shook her head. "If your boss gets ahold of this file, like your investigation, and shows the FBI director, I'm afraid it will be trashed. This guy has Five Stages to his plan with encrypted files I can't open up. That's why I wanted to see if you could help?"

Scott was rubbing his chin, deep in thought. "I can, but not at my office. I have a few loyal people from my cyber squad that sense something is going on at the Bureau and CIA that is not right. Let me make a few phone calls, and I can get back to you."

Paige let her smile return to her face and signaled their server to bring them some drinks. "It's time to forget business and enjoy and dinner," she said.

Seeing Paige's smile brought back memories of the crush he had on her back at Stanford. His friend Rick had won over her heart back then, so he backed off. It hurt, but he likes his friendship with Rick too much to let it become a problem. Scott remained close to his friend until they graduated and went their separate ways.

29

Dunham was sipping his Balvenie Single Malt Scotch Whisky, which he had proudly purchased for $47,000 per bottle, while Ellison gulped down his cheap Mexican beer. "All's gone well with Stage One," said Albert, an air of confidence in his voice.

"Only on the surface. Our contractors are scattering and going dark. Every intelligence agency in our country and around the world are on high alert. President Chesterfield would be a fool to keep Hood on as CIA director after this," said Ellison as he continued to down his beer. "My biggest concern right now is what Paige Turner is going to do with what she believes she has on you? We can't afford to have her open-up any of the encrypted files. It would ruin all your plans."

"Remember, all of those files have a self-destruct code that goes into effect after five attempts to break the code. That was one thing Russell did very well for us," he said calmly.

Ellison had a nervous expression growing on his face. "What if Russell didn't put in that code or gave them to Turner? Then, any two-bit computer geek could crack it."

"You worry too much. Russell is dead. All the distractions are working. Soon, I'll be in charge, and nothing they find out about me will matter," he said smugly.

"Then, let's hope that Chesterfield keeps Hood on as his CIA Director until after the launch," Ellison said.

"Let's stop worrying so much. All of this had been anticipated, and part of my plan." Dunham said. "The Playbook had been set up in such a way it reflected only my ideas, not specific actions. As for Hood, we knew all along that Chesterfield was nobody's fool."

"Yes, but it will be very tricky getting our replacement appointed before Stage Two and Three are implemented. We cannot start until we have the right CIA director in place. You need to speak with Chesterfield after the dust settles while he's looking for Hood's replacement. Now we need to just sit back and watch how Iran and the rest of the Middle East deal with this problem we dropped in their laps," Ellison said, with an air of smugness.

Dunham gave Ellison a puzzled look. "You think President Chesterfield will talk to me now? Let alone consider another recommendation from me for the CIA Director? You know Chesterfield is all consumed with his re-election bid. He might not want to remove Hood. Let's wait and see what he does."

Ellison smiled. "Yeah, he was honoring a campaign promise he had made to you. Maybe show some good faith and let him off the hook, apologize for my nephew, and then offer some advice. You two are still terrific friends. He did listen to your counsel when he formed the "Dirty Dozen at your suggestion."

"I'm not sure I should even get close to the White House now."

"I think you should. Right now, Chesterfield's probably looking for friends he can trust," Ellison said.

* * * * *

Albert was relaxing in his study, reading his playbook. He was focusing on his next Stage to build loyalty with more of the Homeland Security personnel. He had already gained more than he had ever expected inside the CIA and FBI, even without the help of Director's Hood and Roberts.

Dunham was reading a quote. "*Like Caesar, I too will garner the support from within Chesterfield's administration, and then move to bring the citizens closer to me as their leader,"* he said in a faint whisper, while he continued reading. "Phase Two and Three are coming," he said, his words floating inside the room for his ears only.

He closed down his computer screen, touching it with his two fingers that had just come from his lips.

30

All the news channels could not stop speculating about what had happened.

It had not been a full twenty-four hours, and the world was still reeling from the attack on Iran. The financial markets had a significant adjustment down, sending all exchanges to some of their lowest levels since the 2008 crash. Oil prices were escalating due to Iran's two main facilities being rendered non-functional. OPEC was blaming the United States and Israel for the attack. As a punishment, they cut their oil production in half, sending crude prices through the ceiling.

President Chesterfield was being pressured to open more areas in Alaska and light a fire under the slow-moving shale program that was being held up by environmentalists. Albert Dunham had locked in lease deals for fifty years up in Alaska's oil reserve basin. Then he got the contract for completing the new Greystone Pipeline and had snatched up stocks from twenty of the most solid United States Companies who were in free fall from the economic situation befalling Wall Street.

Dunham was especially proud of this move as his inner circle was going to see a capital gain on those investments upward in the tens of billions of dollars after the markets stabilized.

What Dunham and Ellison were able to do during this crisis was a bonus compared to the hundreds of billions of dollars they were about to make once Chesterfield's legislation passed to open up the oil fields in Alaska. It was going to be a prosperous time for Dunham and his followers. He was methodically solidifying his place as the wealthiest man alive. So far, Stage One had worked perfectly.

31

Ellison looked at Dunham, and with a forced smile said. "You do not have to do anything else in your lifetime, and you would have achieved your financial dream. Within a year, at the earliest, you will be the wealthiest and most powerful man in the world. Your wealth will be larger than the annual GDP of most of the countries in the European Union. We won't need Stage Two or any of the other Stages anymore," Ellison said happily. "We'll be safe and happy, as well as safe from prosecution."

Dunham just stared at his friend. "Are you crazy? Do you think I'm doing all of this for just the money? I already have more wealth than I ever dreamed I could have. I want the power. You know I want to be the Emperor of the United States. I want to control everything," he said. "My plan is following the same scheme Caesar had, which allowed him to become the legal dictator of the entire Roman Empire. We need the new chip installed unnoticed and on time. Then I will have control over what matters in the world and what matters to me," he said, gasping for air. "Understand, Caesar was not like any dictator. His citizens voted for him to become their leader, their emperor. You do know that the Roman Empire back then, had it written in their constitution they could if needed, elect a dictator for life. We almost had that here, before the ratification of the twenty-second amendment."

"Your plan is a longshot at best. The United States Constitution is a living organism. Changing its structure, to suit your whim, will be next to impossible. Nothing you can do will ever get a House and Senate to abolish that amendment. Let's say for a moment that you can pull it off. President Chesterfield would veto it in a heartbeat."

Albert started laughing. "You don't understand. When Stage Five gets implemented, every citizen, like every Roman back when Caesar took power, will welcome me with open arms as their dictator...no emperor. When I am EOTUS, Washington will jump when I say jump. If I want to start a war, it will happen at my command. Once I have control of the satellite, then my dreams will be fulfilled," he said, catching his breath. "Let's just stick to the playbook."

Ellison had a shocked look on his face. He had never seen his friend act so crazy about his stupid dream of being the new Julius Caesar. "Boss, can we take a more realistic look at what you are thinking about doing? It could be the death of all of us, and for what? Power? Respect?" he said. "No dictator in history ever had the respect or love of the people. Like Caesar, his reign was short-lived, murdered by his closest friend."

Albert, his eyes burned into his friend. "Is that a threat, Frederick?"

"No. Just reminding you of how history can be a great learning lesson."

"What I am doing is different. My plan will work. We will not stop now. I am so close," Dunham said, rubbing his hands together, while a big grin stretched on his face. "My family built this country, and now it needs to be in my hands so that I can make us the most feared nation, as well as the most respected nation on the face of the earth."

"I know what you want, but having all this wealth won't do that for you. You have to win over the hearts and minds of every American citizen...that's not going to be an easy task," Ellison said.

Dunham gave his friend a single-finger salute. "What does every American want in life? What are their true pathetic goals?" He saw his friend ready to answer him and put his hand up, signally him to not speak.

Dunham stood up and paced around the room, his hands locked behind his back. "No, let me answer that question. They want a comfortable living, their children going to good schools, and they want to look forward to a retirement that would keep them comfortable," Dunham said, an air of confidence in his voice. "What if we controlled most of America's jobs and controlled the financial markets as well as financial institutions around the world, so every American could see their tiny dreams come true. What if I can show them it can all be done without the type of government they've grown accustomed to or one which is so small that the taxes they pay will seem insignificant? What if they had free health insurance that was paid for by their government without higher taxes? If I get my five stages to go off without a hitch, then I can make it happen with just a touch of a button. Then, every politician, including the president, will be helpless. We are very close. So, don't put me in a downer with your righteous obnoxious moral attitude."

Ellison clapped his hands. "Excellent boss, but you forget one thing. You are not there yet, and Stage Two and Three will be a lot harder than Stage One was complete. You were lucky you got back most of your files. If they had gotten into the wrong hands, like president Chesterfield's with his resources, and it was brought out what you were planning, you'd be locked up for treason, and they'd throw away the key."

"Remember, right now; everyone loves me. To the average citizen, I am a great guy. My Manifesto's key stages are encrypted. It would take too long to decipher my codes. Then it would be too late. You are my frontman. All of this is on you right now. So, let's enjoy our victory today and start getting ready for the next two stages. Just remember the arrangement we made many years ago and do your fucking job."

* * * * *

Ellison was on the phone with FBI director Chad Roberts. He was curious about the meeting he had just attended. "Well, what went on? Was the president pissed?" he asked, unable to control his happy attitude.

"More than you can imagine," Roberts said, his tone serious. "I have to prepare my statement to the press. The CIA director's neck is on the chopping block. His statement to the press, well, it should be interesting hearing him explain why he had no word on the bombings. I wouldn't be surprised if Chesterfield replaces him immediately."

"That's was one of our contingencies. We need to get our man in as his replacement," Ellison said. "Can you make that happen without raising the president's suspicions?"

Roberts was not quick with his answer. "I am not so sure. He had a private meeting with Admiral Hollingsworth and Felix Wilson. Chesterfield's turning inward, looking like he's not trusting anyone in his administration, including me. You know I was not happy with Stage One, and felt it might affect what you have planned next," the FBI director said showing his contempt for Dunham's plan.

"Tell me how you really feel," Ellison shot back. "You know I don't give a rat's ass about your opinions. You're being paid a fortune of money to see that this works according to Dunham's timetable. No questions asked. You know there is no backing out now."

Roberts was a smart, astute man and understood the threat he had just received from Ellison. "All I am saying is that for us to, shit for Dunham to succeed, he cannot be so arrogant about the power he is building right now. While he has the money to buy whatever he wants, he still does not have the military to defeat this president. Chesterfield's nothing like the previous man in the Oval Office. He has a TNS attitude toward his job as president and the people around him," Roberts said with caution.

"I am not sure what you are trying to say to me?" Ellison asked his tone calmer.

"Stage Two needs to take a breather right now. There's too much investigation going on right now. We make our move too soon, and it could jeopardize all that we've been planning and working toward. Let me try to get close to Chesterfield and see if I can figure out what he's planning. It would be better for all of us if we know what his next move might be. I've been monitoring Turner as you wanted. She's on her way to meet with Chesterfield later today."

"Shit," Ellison said. "Do you think it's about Russell? He was her friend?"

Roberts responded quickly. "All I know is that Admiral Hollingsworth and Felix Wilson were locked behind closed doors when the president decided he wanted to meet with the bitch.'

Ellison sounded nervous. "You better have eyes and ears at that meeting. If she has the files and tells Chesterfield anything about Dunham, it could screw up everything."

"That's why I wanted to eliminate her after Russell."

"That might be what we have to do. Keep me posted," Ellison said, and then the phone went dead.

32

Paige was being escorted into the Oval Office for her first time. Even though she was nervous by the enormity of the room, she had convinced herself she was prepared to deal with this president. Bradley had given her a good briefing on what to expect.

Bradley had met Patrick Chesterfield when he was a CIA analyst working with an embedded Seal Team in Iraq. It was a dangerous and challenging time while he was there during the Gulf war. While they did not become close friends, they grew to respect each other. He understood Chesterfield's ambition back then. He could smell it on him. Like all up and coming politicians, ambition grows with their power.

Bradley's warning to Paige was simple: "*Listen, listen, listen...keep what you have in your back pocket. Leave Chesterfield in the dark for the time being. Remember, Dunham, is his friend and largest contributor.*"

He also told Paige that Chesterfield is a master interrogator and will know when you are lying even before you say a word. Wear your beauty queen smile, and everything should go smoothly.

Paige had been told to take a seat on the couch bordering the rug with the Seal of the President of the United States staring up at her. She tried to keep her open-toed three-inch heels off the beautiful carpet, but her long legs would not accommodate her desire. No matter how many times she tried to cross her legs, her shoe heel dug into the beautiful rug.

It was overwhelming being in the Oval Office, especially for a reporter. Her nerves were on edge during the flight out from Los Angeles. Those same feelings had her breathing nervously. Her palms were sweating; she had beads of perspiration on her forehead and upper lip, a first for her.

President Chesterfield had not even entered the room. *"Shit, I'm a mess,"* she scolded herself. *"Take a deep breath. You're a professional who has met with prime ministers, presidents, and other dignitaries around the world. You can do this..."* She had been muttering under her breath when Chesterfield entered the room abruptly, walking briskly over to the couch and sat down next to Paige. If she was nervous a minute ago, she was terrified now.

President Chesterfield did not extend his hand in a polite greeting. He just put his arm on top of the couch, stretching it out so he could touch Paige's shoulder, patting her gently. She was feeling her personal space invaded. She realized this was the president's trademark, his ability to keep people on edge. It was working.

"Ms. Turner I want to thank you for coming here on such short notice. First, my condolences on your friend's horrible murder. I want to assure you that the FBI is investigating this crime and I promise you we will have it resolved shortly," President Chesterfield said sincerely.

Paige did not know how to respond, making a feeble attempt. "Thank you, sir. He was a good friend. "If I may ask," she said with a bit of caution. "Why are the FBI and your office investigating Brian Russell's death. And, why would I be questioned by a Congressional Committee about it also? Isn't this a crime for the NYPD?" She thought that question would put Chesterfield on edge, but by the look on the president's face, it was not working.

"Good question. While I am not at liberty to discuss all the details of this investigation, it does fall under the Patriot Act. The method of torture, as well as the brutal murder of his wife and son, led us to believe it was not just a local crime. The autopsy revealed it was the work of professionals, with the signature of Al-Qaeda," the president said. "Besides, I have on good authority that he was first picked up by men posing as FBI agents when he was dragged out of Clancy's Tavern."

"Can I ask..." but, before Paige could get out her question, Chesterfield cut her off.

"No questions at this time. Also, what we talk about here today is confidential and cannot be repeated to anyone, especially your news organization or our fan base." Chesterfield noticed Paige's eyes grow wide with surprise at his comments.

"I know what I am saying is disturbing you, but you'll have to leave it at that. Once I find out more, you will be the first reporter to have the story," Chesterfield said, a little too condescending for Paige's liking.

Chesterfield did not hesitate to get right to the point as to why he called her to the Oval Office. "I assume you are aware of what had happened in Iran yesterday?"

"All I know is what I have read or heard on the news. I've tried to get more specific information from the FBI and Homeland Security, but no one is talking to the press at this time," Paige, without any indication she knew more than most responded. She saw the look on Chesterfield's face and could not tell if he believed her response. She now understood what Bradley was talking about how the president can rattle a person's cage.

"My question might have been a little simplistic. I know from the briefing I received a few of our congressmen were very curious about your relationship with your friend," Chesterfield paused, seeing Turner's surprise on her face. "We know from Russell's cellphone he had called you a day before his murder."

Paige was noticeably uncomfortable.

"Sir, are you spying on me and my friend?" she asked, her tone a bit angry. "What other calls are you monitoring. I am a reporter, a private citizen. Should I be worried that you and your NSA are spying on every American citizen again?" By her harsh tone, Chesterfield could see his guest was getting upset.

The president smiled. "I was not spying, just reading my briefing reports detailing how the FBI investigation is going. It's our new protocol since ISIS came on the scene. Now with the bombing in Iran, well, we need to take every precaution to protect American lives. Look, you are one of our country's most distinguished journalists, and well respected around the world. I just thought that maybe you and your friend would be able to shed some light on this situation. I do not like to admit it, but I am totally in the dark about the attack on Iran, and it concerns me."

Paige leaned back, relaxing her shoulders, feeling the president's hand tapping her shoulder before she responded. Paige was surprised the president would show a genuine weakness on his part. "I had not spoken personally with Brian. I had gotten a voice message on my phone, which maybe you already know what he had said? I had not spoken to him in almost a year and a half." Paige could see that Chesterfield was watching her facial expression closely.

In a more serious tone, Chesterfield responded. "That's interesting. I've was briefed that there was no message on your home phone. Where was this message you received? You do still have it, right?" It's evidence in the FBI's investigation."

Paige was now sliding away from Chesterfield, turning to face him. She remembered she had told Bradley to erase Russell's message. *Damn, I did delete the evidence.* She thought of trying to hide her guilt.

Chesterfield stood and walked over to a club chair across from the couch he had left Paige squirming on. "Ms. Turner, is there something you want to tell me about the message Russell left you?"

Paige, with a knee-jerk reaction, threw a question at the president. "Why would you, or your FBI tap into my home phone system? Are you monitoring me now? Aren't I protected under the constitution?"

"No, we are not monitoring your phone messages. Only Russell's, since he's a murder victim. Can you tell me exactly what Mr. Russell said on his message to you?"

Paige swallowed hard before she responded. "I'm not sure what you'd like to know. Brian sounded alarmed...maybe more terrified about something. We never got to speak after I received his message, so I don't know what was scaring him," she said, regretting she even said that much.

Chesterfield smiled with a little nod. "Have you received any packages from Russell before he died?"

Paige looked directly at Chesterfield, staring him down, just like Bradley told him to do. "You're monitoring my mail and deliveries too?"

Chesterfield could see he was irritating her. "I'm sorry. Again, my information was from my briefing with my Homeland Security Secretary and FBI director."

"FBI, Homeland Security, what's next, the IRS?" she mockingly laughed. "If and when I care to report what Brian sent to me in the mail or by FedEx, you'll be the first to know. Now, Mr. President, why did you ask me here? I do not think it was to talk about Brian Russell." Paige was now furious.

Chesterfield let loose a loud bellowing laugh. "Bradley taught you well. He was good at out staring me and putting me on the defensive with direct questions. Outstanding Ms. Turner. Here's the reason I wanted to talk to you." Before he could begin, his Chief of Staff, Felix Wilson, burst into the Oval Office, interrupting the meeting.

His face had trouble written all over it. "Sir, we need you in the Situation Room ASAP!" Wilson was a cold fish, his icy stare toward Paige brought a shiver all over her body.

Chesterfield looked at his Chief of Staff and then at Paige. "I am not sure how long this might take, but could you please wait here...I can get you some lunch. We still need to finish our talk. By the look on my Chief of Staff's face, what I have to say to you might be even more important now."

The president did not wait for a reply and was escorted out of the Oval Office, leaving Paige stunned and dumbfounded. "What the hell is going on?" she muttered, as the door slammed shut.

33

Dunham leaned back in his high-back leather chair, his eyes gazing at the ceiling. He knew his upcoming Stage Two kick-off was moving too fast. It was way ahead of his original schedule. The thought that his manifesto would be exposed, once Paige Turner met with president Chesterfield, he was in panic mode. All of this had started to derail his confidence. He knew he needed to settle down and refocus. He needed some immediate assurances from his closest advisor. He picked up his cellphone and dialed the one man who could calm him down.

He was using his secure line to speak to ex-Army General Tucker Phillips. He was the man who carried out a successful attack on Iran. He was the man who controlled the army of ex-special force veterans, as well as the disenfranchised rebels that were fighting to regain control of their countries. After five rings Phillips picked up, his voice unnervingly gruff.

"Glad you called sir. I have the update you requested," the General said, his tone serious.

"That can wait for now. What I've seen and heard so far was more than I expected. You and your men did a great job."

"Thank you, sir. I can sense you are not calling about our last mission."

"No. I need your help here in the United States. While I do not want to do this now, I must move up my plans. There's a slim chance that Brian Russell did compromise our mission. We need to begin to ruin President Chesterfield's re-election chances. I need him distracted. He's talking with a reporter, a

Paige Turner. I believe she has a copy of the files Russell stole," Dunham said.

"Sir, what do you have in mind?"

"I know your men need time to decompress from Iran, but can you put in motion those items we discussed at our last meeting that would begin Stage Two?" Dunham asked.

"Sir, everything has been in place and ready to go for some time. I need to activate the men I have in place. Give me the exact dates you want things to start, and I can have it activated before I return. Then, I can brief you on what we've accomplished so far. I have a few loose-ends to clean up here. I will be back in two days. I await your orders for Stage Two," Phillips said, his voice calm and controlled.

"Why wait. Shit, get the ball rolling now," Dunham said without a goodbye.

The General liked how cold-hearted his friend had turned out to be. Tucker was proud of how he had groomed the next leader of the Free World.

Dunham leaned back in his chair, a broad smile on his face, his hands interlocked behind his neck. No matter what he did, he was still nervous. Talking with General Phillips relaxed him. He thought about calling President Chesterfield to offer some counsel on the current events but thought it should wait until after Stage Two was completed.

"Chesterfield might not want to talk to me after Stage Two," he said, smiling. He looked at the photo of himself and Maggie, his wife, resting on his desk. He was wondering what his wife would think of him if she knew what he was putting into motion?

"*To achieve your goals requires some collateral damage,*" his father had drilled into him as he was growing up. *This is our world. Whatever it takes to complete our family manifesto is the only thing that matters."* Those words were the only thoughts he had swimming inside his head as he waited for the actual death toll to be reported.

34

Bradley Stevens was listening intently to Paige. He had some idea as to what President Chesterfield wanted to accomplish. He did not want to speculate at the moment.

"He's testing you. I wouldn't be surprised if they've videoed the meeting to analyze your facial gestures and voice inflections. He probably knows you are keeping something from him and when he gets back to your meeting...well, he'll use some tactic from his arsenal to get you to spill the beans," Bradley said. "I wouldn't doubt he's listening to our conversation, as we speak."

Paige started looking around the room for any sign of cameras or recording equipment. "You think Chesterfield's recording this meeting? Shit, listening to us talk?" Paige said, her voice quivering.

"It's been speculated every president since Nixon, records, and tapes everyone. The presidency believes it has the right, so they keep doing it. Don't worry about it. He'll never bring it up, especially to a reporter or he'll never get any dignitaries from other countries to meet with him. Most of the Senate and House Republicans can't stand him and would need another excuse to say no to everything he wants to accomplish. No matter what he comes back with when your meeting resumes, stick to what we discussed and get your butt back here, so we can keep moving with our investigation."

"It's easier said than done. Chesterfield's keeping me on edge and uneasy. I'll wait and see what he has up his sleeve and go from there. He's one scary son-of-a-bitch, but I have to believe he has the best interests of our country in his heart."

"Use your good judgment. That's one of your strengths," said Bradley. "I will," Paige replied. Chesterfield was walking back into the room, giving her a friendly smile. "Gotta go. Chesterfield's back."

* * * * *

The president did not go back to the couch where he was earlier. He waved Paige over by his desk and gestured for her to sit in the chair facing him. "Ms. Turner, I am sorry to have left you for so long, but we have something of a national emergency brewing, and our meeting is going to have to be cut short. I want to resume our talk soon. I want to get to know you better. You're a great American newsperson, who seems to have our nation's best interest at heart. Something I hope the American people see in me?" Chesterfield, for the first time, seemed stressed about something.

Paige, with her inquisitive nature, needed to ask a straightforward question. "Sir, does this pending situation have anything to do with the Iran attack?"

"I can't say right now. We are investigating all possible avenues to see if what is about to happen now has some connection to the Iran bombing or is going to be the work of a copycat group. We know we're about to be attacked on our soil. Just where and when is the question. The chatter is rampant. Shit, I cannot believe my intelligence community is in the dark on all this too. I need a break of some sort to put us on the right path," the president said, his tone very somber.

Paige was feeling guilty not telling the president about Russell's thumb drive and the Architect's Manifesto, but at the same time thought she was being set up to spill the beans. She elected to remain silent and listen, something Bradley drilled into her head.

Chesterfield, his lips pursed, said. "For so long this country of ours has been controlled by the wealthy, some of what they wanted was good for our country, but over the last twelve years, their power has taken us into new unchartered waters which has me very concerned. We have too many special interest groups influencing our political system, where no elected official trusts his colleagues, just their supporters. I never wanted to believe an American would try to cause harm to our country, but right now, I believe there is a group of wealthy individuals who want to promote terrorism for profit. They already have a group of congressmen and senators, as well as people within my cabinet, giving them the support they need."

Paige was wiping her sweaty palms on her dress. She sucked in a deep nervous breath. She could see the deep frustrated concern on Chesterfield's face. She knew she had some answers for her president, and like the good American she was about to expose her stolen thumb drive. She knew she got caught, hook, line, and sinker. There was something in the president's voice and expression that told her he was telling her the truth.

"Mr. President, I haven't been very open with you today. I do have something that might shed some light on all of this. It came to me the day Brian Russell was murdered. What I have confirms your worst fears. I don't know if I can reveal what I have since it's from a source, and I suspect Russell did not have permission to remove it from where it came. I don't know who to trust anymore. I need to check with my legal department and get back to you," she said dismayed.

Chesterfield stood and began pacing around the Oval Office deep in thought. "If you have something that might fall under national security, you need to hand it over immediately, he said, raising his voice.

"If I did that, who would you trust with it? Not your CIA or FBI? Right?" said Paige sensed she was coming across a little too snappy, bordering on disrespectful, by the look on Chesterfield's face.

The president nodded. "You're right. I do not know who to trust in my administration. Except for a few people I've known most of my life. Paige, please believe me. You can trust me. Just tell me what you have," the president said, sitting down next to her.

At that moment, Paige knew her life was about to change forever. "Let me first check with my boss and our legal department. I will stay in town so we can meet in a day or two from now," she said.

"I just hope you're not putting our country in danger by withholding important, timely information that could save lives," Chesterfield said, laying the guilt on her big time.

Paige was not worried about his comments. She knew what she had would not prevent anything, but maybe point toward Albert Dunham, the president's friend, and largest contributor. "I need twenty-four hours to think about what I need to do. I want you to answer one question. If one of your closest friends was responsible for what's been going on and what might be happening, what would you do as president?"

Chesterfield's eyes grew wide. "I am not sure what your hypothetical is, but any American, friend or relative who brings harm to our citizens or national security will be treated as a traitor and prosecuted to the fullest extent of the law," he said harshly.

"Good to hear. I will call you tomorrow with my answer," Paige said.

35

A day after the Iranian bombings shook the world, there were simultaneous explosions at three key subway stations located in Boston, Manhattan, and Chicago. Not since 9/11 had there been such a devastating attack on American soil. President Chesterfield was unable to relay confidence and assure every American they were safe.

Thousands of commuters were injured. The estimated death toll had reached over fifteen hundred, with another hundred struggling to survive. Each ER treating the bombing victims were in a Code Black scenario. While no one group had stepped up to take responsibility for the bombings, accusations feel on Iran's doorstep.

Commuter congestion at those key locations would last for months. In most cases, there were no logical alternate routes into those cities. Businesses were temporarily closed to let the people mourn the losses of their families.

The news media had gone into panic mode-speculation was running rampant. Iran had quickly denied they had a hand in the bombings. Every reporter was commenting on how fortunate it was that the organized attack did not happen during rush hour in each of the targeted cities.

While Homeland Security and the FBI were struggling to find answers to the subway bombings, four hours later, the runways at JFK International, O'Hare, and Los Angeles International Airports experience explosions that made craters the size of football fields, totally decimating every runway. All Planes were grounded.

The United States transportation mechanism had come to a drastic halt. President Chesterfield had declared a State of National Emergency, calling up every National Guard Unit.

With no group claiming responsibility for this attack, President Chesterfield began moving the Seventh Fleet into a strategic location near the Middle East and North Korea. If it were determined that Iran or North Korea was responsible, a swift and appropriate response would happen.

The media was demanding answers. Americans had taken to the streets protesting president Chesterfield. The House and Senate had begun to light a fire under the speculation that President Chesterfield was not doing enough to keep America safe.

* * * * *

The Situation Room was packed. The Secretary of Defense, Trent Hall, was shuffling his notes nervously. CIA Director Thomas Hood looked pale. He knew once again his department fucked up and his ass was on the line. The head of the Joint Chiefs, Admiral Hollingsworth stared blankly, biting his lower lip, looking like he wanted to kill someone in the room. FBI Director, Chad Roberts looked like he did not have a care in the world. However, Chief of Staff, Felix Wilson, was another story. He was pacing the room like a caged jaguar.

Everyone had been waiting for the Secretary of State and President to arrive. The last person to walk into the board room was Secretary of State Carolyn Waterfall, the first native American to hold a top position in the cabinet. She had just finished a briefing with President Chesterfield.

All eyes were focused on Secretary Waterfall as she entered alone. The president was not with her. She said. "The president will be along shortly. He asked that we begin our briefing, so we would be up-to-speed when he arrives.

Admiral Hollingsworth had already been instructed by Chesterfield on what he wanted him to do to get the meeting started.

36

It had been one day since Paige met with the president. She now had been sitting in the waiting room outside of the Oval Office for almost forty-five minutes. The Secret Service secured her cell phone. The entire White House appeared to be in lockdown.

Finally, she was escorted into the president's office, passing Secretary Waterfall who was standing by the couch she had sat on the other day.

"Ms. Turner," Chesterfield said, his tone calm and non-threatening. "Please sit. We have a lot of ground to cover. I'm sure you've heard about the attack on our subway systems and airports? Over fifteen hundred innocent American's are dead." The president could see the guilty look on Paige's face.

Paige, the color had drained from her face, was shaking her head in disbelief. "Sir, has any group claim responsibility?" she asked, her hands trembling. She already knew the answer.

Chesterfield was patting his forehead with a small washcloth. He looked stressed and ready to go postal. "My turn to ask questions. I want to know what the fuck you're not telling me. The bullshit you said you had to speak to your legal staff might have just cost American lives," he shouted. "We are now in a state of national emergency. If you can help us understand or can give me a clue who this Architect might be so I can see if he's the terrorist we are looking for, that would be helpful" the president said his face beet red.

Paige stood, a guilty sadness engulfing her entire body. She knew right then she had no choice but to trust her president. She reached into her purse and pulled out a copy of the thumb drive.

"Mr. President, this is what Brian Russell sent me. It contains some terrifying files written by an irrational man who wants to become Emperor of the United States," her voice cracking from nerves.

Chesterfield tried to refrain from laughing, understanding that Turner was not joking. "Emperor of America? Now that's a first. Not King or Dictator, just Emperor?"

"Sir, based on what I've read, this guy is serious about taking over our country. He has a very strategic plan called his Manifesto. Based on what he's written, he already controls a shadow government that his family had been forming for decades. If he accomplishes what he's written, it's just a matter of months before he takes over. It might be a farfetched dream of his, but with all, that's been happening, it all seems to fit. I don't believe in coincidences."

"Any suspicions as to who this person might be?" Secretary Waterfall asked.

Paige nodded. "You're not going to like what I have to say," she said cautiously. "Albert Dunham or Frederick Ellison. Or maybe the two of them working together."

"Are you fucking kidding me?" the president barked.

"No, sir. My research revealed that Brian Russell worked for both men. The files he stole I believe came from them. Brian was their main cybersecurity expert. He asked me to expose them to the world. Now he's dead, and I am in a dilemma. Without Brian to corroborate these files, there is not enough proof to convict either man for anything or proof these came from them. I have many encrypted files I've not been able to open. I am still working on them," she said.

"Then, why are you accusing them of any of this?"

"Simple. While inside the thumb drive, I found files that refer to these recent events and the man who calls himself the

Architect specifically references these last few events openly," she said.

President Chesterfield sucked in a deep breath and let it out slowly. "I guess I might have a serious problem with my two friends. I suppose it needs my attention. If what you're saying is true, then Dunham and Ellison have to be stopped immediately."

Paige was combing her fingers through her long wavy hair. "Mr. President, inside the current manifesto, the Architect brags about how many people in your administration are in his back pocket. He doesn't name them. I'm not sure who you can or should trust right now. For these events to have happened, and your top intelligence and law enforcement agencies to not have a clue, this should be a big red flag for you," Turner said. "If I did not know better, he has your people working for him right under your nose."

"Ms. Turner, I want to thank you for your help and insight with this matter," he said, holding up the thumb drive. "Is this mine to keep?" he asked.

Paige nodded. "I wasn't going to give it to you until I was sure you could be trusted," said Turner forcing a smile. "My only concern is that you now have in your possession stolen property from either Albert Dunham or Frederick Ellison. I am not sure how that will play out with the American people and your Attorney General?"

Chesterfield let out a big belly laugh. "I'm glad you're able to trust your president young lady, as well as speak frankly to me. It's refreshing. I hope I can find enough people in my administration I can trust with these files."

"I'm one person you can trust and should use to help you with this sir. I do have a little more freedom to dig into things without raising too many alarms," Paige said. "One thing your friend Dunham does mention is that he has Five Stages. I believe the Iranian affair, as well as the tanking of the global stock exchanges, were part of Stage One. And, now, with these new bombings, Stage Two is being initiated weeks earlier than planned. He must be nervous about my current investigation. If he's moving up his timetables, we do not have a lot of time to wait. I need to continue decoding his files.

Chesterfield stood and shook Paige's hand. "Right now, I might take you up on that offer. If you are correct, my friends fit your definition of *'Corrupted Intelligence,'* the president said. "Please continue doing what you do best, Ms. Turner, but keep me in the loop. I want briefings every day on your progress" He handed Turner back the thumb drive.

"I think for now you should keep your copy of the thumb drive." He handed it first to his Secretary of State and ordered her to download the files to her State Department laptop before Paige left.

Chesterfield said, "I'll digest this information and determine who I can use to decode those encrypted files."

Paige sucked in a deep breath before she replied. "Sir, I will do my best on that matter too. Sometimes my investigations begin moving so fast that I do not have time to rest, let alone eat. I will do my best to keep you informed. I do not want to tell you what to do. I would suggest you do not bring up Albert Dunham at this time. If he gets a hint, he's being investigated by you now, he could stop his next Stages or escalate them even faster, and we'd never catch him in the act. His endgame with Stage Five at this time is a mystery."

Chesterfield just nodded his head. "Paige, I can call you that?"

She smiled. "Yes. That's' my name. Am I now working for you?" Paige said, her tone somber.

"Not sure if I can hire a reporter to work for the United States Government? Let's keep your work between us for the time being."

"That's fine with me. I am not sure how my boss will feel about working with the enemy," she said jokingly.

The president let a big smile explode on his face. "Paige, from this point on you can advise me on anything and call me at any hour if you need my help with your investigation. Here's my card with a secure line on it." Then, without further discussion, he left for the Situation Room.

37

Before the president arrived, Chief of Staff Wilson had begun ripping everyone apart inside the Situation Room. "Where the fuck has the breakdown been? How in God's name could this happen on our soil without any warnings?" He took a deep, exhausted breath and kept going. "Hood, tell me you and your department wasn't asleep at the wheel again? Isn't our CIA supposed to know where and when radical groups are planning to destroy the United States?"

Wilson noticed a smirk on the FBI director's face and jumped on it. "Roberts, wipe that fuckin grin off your face. Over 1,500 innocent Americans are dead and more might be buried in the tunnels that collapsed on our subway systems. Both of you are useless," he was shouting when President Chesterfield entered the room.

Everyone stood when Chesterfield entered, and he waved them all to sit down. The president stared at everyone. He was noticeably upset.

"Let's forget about my upcoming election. It doesn't matter right now. Let's also forget about passing blame right now. I want answers without all the bull-shit every one of you has been giving me over the last few days."

Chesterfield never let his emotions show since taking office, but today, he allowed it to explode. "I have new damaging information about some of the people in my administration, some sitting right here, and it's not very pretty."

He could see some of his cabinet members squirming in their seats. He liked that.

"I was just briefed by a reliable source, that some of you might have allegiance to a very wealthy man— an American. Anyone want to comment about this?" he said, pursing his lips. "My faith in my cabinet is fading fast, so if any of you have something to contribute to what I just said, please do so immediately."

He directed his stare, filled with contempt, toward CIA director Hood, the nephew of Frederick Ellison, and FBI director Roberts. When he saw the others in the room relax their posture, he looked at them with cold, piercing eyes. "None of you are off the hook right now," he said, pointing his finger at everyone. "There have been massive breakdowns in our protocols which were put in place to protect our citizens. Homeland Security has told me they have not heard a peep from the CIA or FBI. No communication or intelligence briefings. Are we back to when each agency kept their intelligence to themselves and allowed the Twin Towers and Pentagon to be attacked without any warning? I know I have political enemies, but I would never believe they would stoop to killing innocent Americans, to punish me," he said, frustrated.

Chesterfield took a deep breath and continued. "I have new intelligence that some far-right American born fringe group, led by a man known as *The Architect...*" the president looked directly at Hood and Roberts. He noticed a surprised look on Roberts' face. "You've heard of this person?" he asked Roberts.

The FBI director, without any facial expression, replied. "No. Not really. Who is he?" he asked innocently.

Chesterfield knew when someone was lying. "What I know is he's been pulling strings on everything that has happened since the Iranian bombings." Chesterfield kept his eyes on Roberts. This time FBI director Roberts turned bedsheet white. Right then, he knew he had found at least one of his traitors.

Admiral Hollingsworth spoke up. "Sir, I've never heard of any wealthy man being called The Architect. Vice-president Cheney had that nickname for a while, but he's so ill he could not have pulled this off. Sir, are you sure he's an American?"

The president knew the answer. He wanted to keep it to himself for a while. "It's too soon to tell. I have a special team looking into finding him or at the least connect the dots that will lead us to him," Chesterfield said, not letting on he was working with Paige Turner and her team.

The president stood abruptly, interlocking his hands behind his back and started pacing the room. "We have another problem. I am surprised neither our FBI nor CIA directors knew about a hundred billion dollars of global arms sales we had thought went through France, Germany, Italy, Greece, and Jordon, are now floating somewhere inside Saudi Arabia and other parts of the Middle East. The thing that bothers me the most is that the Saudis do not know where the weapons are either. We're talking about attack helicopters, drones, missile launchers, and enough arms to stock a large military force. Like the one that attacked Iran." Chesterfield's face was beet red as he continued pacing the room, kicking the legs of chairs as he walked.

"What happened today was just the tip of the iceberg. We are under attack, and we do not know who our enemy is or when the next attack is going to take place." He could see Roberts trying to speak and waved him on to say something.

"Sir, this man...how did you discover him when we have never heard of him?"

"Here's my problem. I know one or two of you in this room know this Architect. Some of you might be on his payroll. I have the attorney general looking into this matter as we speak."

Roberts did not flinch. "I am offended you would even think I or anyone in this room would betray our country. I am going to rip apart my department and find out if anyone is helping this man. I have always been a loyal American and will get to the bottom of this."

Chesterfield was not going to dignify his remarks. "The bottom line is all of you are not doing your jobs. It seems the world is awash with money. Billions of dollars are being hidden away by a few global elites using shell companies and depositing their money in offshore bank accounts. Our tax laws condone this behavior, costing the United States treasury billions of dollars in tax revenue. The scariest part is that we have no records of or who they might be. We should have records, but some group inside my administration is hiding this information from the audit."

Felix Wilson interjected his thoughts. "We will be looking into the NSA. I can't believe they missed this attack," he said, pointing toward the NSA director.

Chesterfield waved for his Chief of Staff to sit. "My concern right now is this band of traitors has a military force, backed by billions of dollars, with what I believe is a stockpile of military arms we cannot find. We have been attacked by a paper country that is right now under our radar."

Admiral Hollingsworth stood. "Sir, with your permission I want to call up a special team I've worked with before that can give us some needed answers. They are ex-military but very loyal Americans."

The president began nodding his approval. He already knew the team the admiral was speaking about. He was happy to see the Admiral was one person he could trust.

Chesterfield looked at his CIA and FBI directors pointing to the door. "Hood and Roberts, you are dismissed. The rest of you, please stay back for a briefing on our current situation."

38

Dean Miller was happy to be home, looking forward to ripping into Russell's thumb drive. While he liked his family time, the bonding with his kids, and having a renewed intimacy with Allison, the recent events he had seen on the news while on Catalina Island had pointed to numerous notations in the Architect's files. He could not believe so much had happened in just a few days.

His last text from his intern, Seth Alexander, who had been working on the initial research into Brian Russell's murder, had uncovered something which appeared to be interwoven deep inside the Federal Government. Miller wasn't too excited about getting involved in a murder investigation; however, he was chomping at the bit to see what his software had turned up from his intern's initial search.

He still had the voice message from Paige Turner to return. He needed to first meet with Seth before he spoke with her.

Since listening to Paige's message, he could not believe that they had not spoken since her husband's death. Being forced to rekindle their friendship while investigating the murder of their mutual friend Brian Russell, seemed crazy since the last time they saw each other was at Rick's funeral.

After sending his text message to Paige, letting her know he would call her in a day or so, he went back to reviewing his notes he had received from Seth Alexander. The two men were going to meet a few blocks from the computer lab at UCLA. It was Elyse Bakery at Gayley and Kinross. Their meeting was scheduled that morning at seven. This place was a morning hangout for professors and students. The *Caprese Omelet* on their menu was Dean's favorite. With a few cups of coffee, he'd be ready for his morning lectures.

Today, was an atypical day in Westwood. Fifty-five degrees, sunny with clear blue skies, and very little traffic. Something in Miller's gut had him on edge. He couldn't figure it out and wrote it off to missing the easygoing lifestyle he enjoyed on the magical island twenty-six miles from Los Angeles.

Westwood was a Los Angeles suburb, densely populated with students. On many occasions before class would start, Dean would have his omelet, and take a three-mile meditative walk, around Westwood Village and the UCLA campus.

Unfortunately, today was not going to be meditative or typical for him. He had set up this meeting with Seth and was anxious to review what his intern had uncovered. He had tried to pull up Alexander's results the evening he had returned home, but for some reason, which concerned him, the results were not saved on any of the lab's computers that used his new software.

Seth had seemed very nervous, which was unlike him. He was a confident, assertive young man, who believed the truth will always prevail. Dean appreciated the insightful and innovative approach he inserted into every task he was given, and it seemed this time his student's unfailing drive had him worried.

Seth had revealed a side of himself that was making Dean nervous. His once spirited happy-go-lucky attitude had become despondent. His phone message came across as scared and very anxious about what his research had unveiled.

Seth was already fifteen minutes late. Again, this was uncharacteristic for his intern. Dean was sitting outside on the restaurant's patio, facing East, when he saw Seth on Kinross, trotting across Gayley, heading toward him. He was waving his arm, an excited expression on his face.

Dean must have heard it first, the loud engine roar and then the squealing tires. He looked right on Kinross and saw a black suburban speeding past where he was sitting. He then glanced at Seth, who was still running across Gayley.

In a panic, Miller stood up, waving both his hands. He was watching helplessly the black SUV speeding toward Seth. He tried desperately to signal his young intern to stop and look to his left, but his hyper signals did not alert him. His intern just continued to wave back at him. He never saw the black unmarked Suburban as it slammed into his helpless body, propelling him into the air, and launching him like a missile. When the young man landed, head-first on the hard roadway, his neck snapped like a twig.

The black SUV never stopped. The hit and run driver was speeding up Gayley and out of sight within seconds. Dean had no time to use his phone to record the accident. It had happened so fast. His heart was pounding, his hands shaking, as he stared powerlessly, his mind and body in shock.

Dean jumped over the patio railing and rushed to Seth's aid. He pushed the onlookers out of his way and felt for a pulse, but he knew the answer. He was horrified at what he saw. Seth's head laid at a ninety-degree angle.

Seth's eyes were stationary, wide with fear, only matched by his frozen opened mouth that was oozing blood. Miller wanted to throw up. He forced himself to be brave and composed.

He yelled out to the crowd of students who had gathered. "Someone call 911," he screamed. "Stop your goddam social media photos, and call fucking 911," he yelled again.

Seth was carrying his computer, and papers, in a messenger bag, twisted across his shoulders and torso. Dean wanted to rummage through it, maybe even take it to see what he was bringing him, but realized he'd be messing with a crime scene. He noticed his student had something tightly gripped in his left hand. He began asking the students if anyone had gotten a description of the car or a license plate number on their phones. No one responded. Some kept recording the twisted body of his friend on their phones.

Instinct took over, and he cradled Sean in his arms, his broken neck laying limply on his lap. While the students started conferring with each other, he gripped Sean's left hand as if he was comforting him and slid the object his intern had been holding tightly and palmed it. He didn't look at it, keeping his eyes focused on the witnesses all talking among themselves, others still recording the incident on their phones he assumed would be uploaded on Facebook or some other social media outlet. Just by the shape of the object, he knew what it was right away.

He gently laid Seth's head on the warm asphalt, stood up, and smoothly slipped the thumb drive into his pants pocket. He now could hear the police sirens. He wanted to leave, but out of respect to his friend, he stayed, not wanting him to be alone. He needed to tell the police what he witnessed.

While he waited, Dean texted Paige with the news of what just happened. *My intern, Seth Alexander who was working on the Architect investigation, is dead. It was a hit and run. I'm scared. We need to talk now!* He pressed send and waited for the police to arrive.

39

Frasier Montgomery was on his cell phone, as he sped east on Wayburn Ave until it became Le Conte Ave. He then turned right on Manning Ave, with a right on Wilshire until he was safely on the 405 freeway. "Sir, it's done. Seth Alexander is dead. He did not have a chance to talk with Dean Miller. I had hacked his laptop, and he had not backed up any of his research he had been doing on you and Ellison. It's a good thing our internal software can intercept any intruder. If it happens again, if Miller gets curious, I will know, and deal with it swiftly. Now, what's my next assignment?"

Dunham had not said a word. His silence was disconcerting. "Are you fucking crazy? I never told you to kill the young man. You were supposed to detain him, interrogate him as we did with Russell, get what he had, and report back to me. You're a stupid son-of-a-bitch," he screamed.

Frasier did not like being yelled at, let alone called names. "Albert, get control of yourself. The kid is dead. Nothing he had found out with his research had been saved on his computer. We're safe," Montgomery said confidently.

Dunham bit his lower lip, inhaling slowing through his nose, trying to calm his nerves. "What about the research he had found? Did you secure it? Did you even check if he had printed copies of it or maybe he put it on a thumb drive as

Brian Russell did?" Dunham's tone had become abrasive. "Didn't you think it would be important for us to know what he found?"

"No, I didn't, sir. I do know that he communicated with his professor. He did not want anything he had uncovered on his computer. He was scared and cautious."

"What does Dean Miller have to do with any of this?"

"Not sure. All I was able to find out about this, Seth Alexander is that he was finishing up his Doctorate program in Computer Science, and this professor was his advisor. If you remember, Miller was the founder of Symtec Industries, a computer geek that made billions selling his software patents and company to the NSA. The satellite you're so interested in incorporates a lot of Miller's microchips."

"Shit, I do remember him. He's a brilliant guy who should be working for us and not a University," Dunham said. "Didn't Russell take a course from him a few years back? Maybe he has a copy of my files too?" Dunham barked.

"Should I follow Miller now?" Montgomery asked.

Dunham was exasperated with his friend. "No. I need time to think. Shit, what if Miller had created a new tracking software that can track and tag what I am planning? Maybe that's what this Seth Alexander was using?" Dunham said nervously. "You idiot. Why couldn't you find another way to handle this?"

Montgomery was quick with his response. "I never thought of that," he said, his voice cracking.

"Frasier you never think of the big picture before you act. Kill, kill, and more kill is your only solution. You need to figure out a way to see if Miller has anything from his intern that can hurt me?"

"I'm sure he doesn't. The police were on the scene within minutes after the accident. The intern's satchel is in police custody. Right now, this country is reeling from the recent bombings, and this incident will be filed and forgotten until things cool down," Frasier said smugly. "One other thing. My friend at the LAPD is handling the case as we speak. He'll have the intern's bag ready for me to review."

Dunham was not happy again with Frasier's method of handling a problem. Now he had to rely on an LAPD detective he did not know. He knew he had no choice but to trust his fixer. "Okay. Let me know when you have the student's items. Then, monitor Dean Miller until you feel he's not a threat. I need you to stay close to Bradley Stevens one of Paige Turner's reporters. He had met with Alexander. I need to know if the intern gave him any information about us?"

"Will do, sir. Talk to you by the end of this week or sooner."

40

After Professor Miller gave his statement to the Los Angeles Detective, he briskly walked back to the restaurant, grabbed his briefcase, and rushed to his office at the university. He did not want to tell the detective anything about the investigation he had asked Seth to do, or that he believed his friend was intentionally murdered because of his research into the Architect Manifesto

"First, Brian Russell and now Seth," he moaned, shaking his head, as he picked up his pace to a brisk walk. "What is this Architect afraid of to revert to murder to protect his secret?"

His heart could not stop pounding. His anguish and grief-stricken emotions were overwhelming him. Should he look at the thumb drive first or should he call Allison?

He felt responsible for what happened to Seth. He was gripped with remorse from putting his employee's life in danger. But, how was he to know a simple search of Brian Russell's associates would result in such a horrific ending to his student's life.

Something on Russell's thumb drive has this Architect scared," he told himself. *If I guessed, it would be the encrypted files.*

He immediately dialed Paige Turner. He knew he was just a wealthy geek professor now, and not qualified to investigate any of the material he had in his possession. He wanted to help if he could, but he knew the safety of his family came first.

When his friend answered, he felt a warm relief coat his stressed body.

"So glad you picked up," he said nervously.

"Dean?" she asked, recognizing his voice. "By your voice, this is not a friendly call. I wasn't expecting your call so soon. Did something happen?" she said.

"You didn't read my text?" he replied nervously. "My intern, Seth Alexander, was just murdered. He was investigating the Architect and those damn files Brian Russell sent us," he said trying to catch his breath.

"Slow down, Dean. Murdered? What happened?"

"I was waiting to meet with him to review his findings. As he crossed Gayley...right in front of my eyes, this black Suburban sped up and intentionally ran him over. The guy never stopped to look at what he had done..."

Paige was now processing what her friend had just said. "Do you know what Seth had discovered?"

"No. Not currently. I have a thumb drive Seth was holding. I haven't looked at it yet, but the way he was talking, he had found something, something terrifying. Shit, it got him killed," Miller said, trying to catch his breath.

"I know one of my reporters had been in contact with him. Can I get a copy of the thumb drive?" she asked.

"Yes. I want you to do something with this. I do not know how to investigate this. I don't want to expose my family to this shit. Can you dig deeper into these files?" he said, sputtering out his remarks rapidly.

"Dean slow down. I know you're upset. I would be too, but you need to calm down now and think clearly," she said, trying to get him to settle down.

"Yeah. Thank you. What I was able to glean from my new computer software while on vacation is that that Albert Dunham and Frederick Ellison are connected to this Architect and must have something important, they want to be kept private," he whispered, as he continued walking to his office.

"I'm scared, Paige. I'm just a professor and family man. Not a crime fighter. I can help you with the encrypted files, but please nothing else," he pleaded.

"Where do you live now?" Paige asked, embarrassed she did not know.

"Playa Del Rey."

Paige sucked in a deep breath, mortified to discover he lived so close to her and they have not spoken for so many years. "I live in Malibu. Boy, I feel terrible we live so close and never connected."

Miller let a low giggle escape through his lips. "Nothing to be troubled about. Our lives have been complicated for a while. Let's try to rectify that," he said.

"Let's meet up in the next few days. Right now, I am up to my eyeballs in this Architect shit in D.C. If I can't see you, I will send my best investigator, Bradley Stevens. You can trust him. He was talking with Seth while you were gone. I'll call you by tomorrow. Can you send me a copy of your intern's thumb drive now?"

"Okay. The sooner I get this crap away from me, the better."

"What I need you to do right now is to make hard copies of what Seth had on his thumb drive. Is there a safe way for you to email it to me today?"

"Yes. Give me your email address. I have a new encrypted email program I can transmit data undetected."

"Perfect. Once I have it, my team will begin to decipher what Seth found. I'll do my best to keep you out of this investigation. Just don't speak to any police or government authorities about what Seth had been doing. Right now, I do not know who any of us can trust. Not the FBI or the local police." she told him ending the call.

Dean knew what Paige had said to him made sense, but he was now getting terrified. He was ready to insert the thumb drive into his laptop, when he paused, caution rushing over his body. "No. Not smart," he scolded himself. "Use your secured server and software dummy." He knew the software he had created, had a built-in firewall so his emails could not be hacked. He did not understand what Seth had on his thumb drive and did not need the same people who murdered him, knowing he was probing them too.

It was apparent to him what Brian Russell had stolen, what he had sent to him. He had this Architect, and the group working for him extremely nervous. "But, why turn to murder to prevent these files from going public?" Miller wondered. Again, he was thinking about the encrypted files. "That has to be the key," he muttered.

His curiosity got the best of him. On his secured server, he pressed send, and Seth's work was on its way to Turner. Miller had started looking over some of the files. After scrolling over the thumb drive data for four hours, he printed up the research results that Seth had downloaded on his thumb drive. He noticed that Seth did not use the lab's secure computer with the proper protective tags his software provided. That was the mistake that had exposed his young intern and made him a target.

His friend Paige Turner kept popping up on all of Seth's research, as well as a Bradley Stevens, an investigative reporter who worked with Paige. He was happy he had called her. Once he had finished his search, he downloaded the results onto another thumb drive. He then, using his secured software, emailed another large attachment to Paige.

He knew he had to call Allison. He did not know how to break the news to her as she adored Seth and treated him like a son. Within a matter of days, he had lost two very close friends, the United States had been attacked with multiple bombings, and the Middle East was once again on the verge of a major war. He did not believe in happenstances and needed to find out how all of this was related. He was now involved hook-line-and-sinker.

41

Dean was happy he and Paige could have a conversation over the phone. He was glad she had gotten all his attachments.

She still had her same businesslike demeanor he believed pushed most guys away from her at Stanford. It was something he liked about her, and they had become great friends. It brought back fun memories of when Brian Russell, Rick Turner, and Paige came into his life. He spoke first to break the ice.

"How long has it been Paige?" he asked.

"Not since Rick's funeral," she said, with sadness in her voice.

"Thank you for wanting to help," Dean said, his voice reflecting the stress he had been dealing with since Seth's murder.

"I am not sure how you are involved in this Architect story, but I am all ears. What type of package did Brian send you?" she asked cautiously. "I just need to know if you have anything different than what Brian sent me?"

Dean did not know how or where to begin. He was feeling overly paranoid that they were being watched and kept looking around nervously. "Without looking at your thumb drive, I can't say we have the same data, he replied. "I can't get Seth's murder out of my head. Yesterday, I sensed I was followed while I walked to my office yesterday after the accident. I'm not sure if those same people are monitoring me, us, right now?"

Paige wanted to tell her friend not to be so paranoid, but her experience told her if you feel someone is watching you, then someone is watching you. "I understand. I just got back from D.C. and getting caught up. I too feel there are a lot of eyes on me right now."

"Since I am a witness, the LAPD has asked if I would be available to offer them more details into what might have happened."

Paige wanted to ease her friend's mind and say everything will be all right, but she knew she couldn't. "I think I'll have a friend of mine Scott Rogers from the US Marshals office at our meeting tomorrow. He's trying to open the encrypted files Russell sent us. He knew Brian and Rick."

Dean hesitated before responding. "US Marshal? I thought we weren't trusting anyone at the Justice Department?"

"He's one I can trust. Maybe you know him?"

Dean was scratching his head. "Yes. Stanford Graduate. He's audited some of my lectures recently. Smart guy. I did not know he was with the Marshal's office."

They talked for over two hours. Paige was happy with the detailed description of what her friend had said Russell had sent him. Dean had notes on his drive that didn't exactly match up with what she had gotten.

"See you tomorrow. I'd like to see Allison soon," Paige said.

"I'm sure she'd like that. Again, thanks for wanting to help. I gotta go. Someone is knocking at my office door."

42

Frasier Montgomery flashed a fake LAPD badge at Dean. It wasn't fake; it just wasn't his. He had just gotten the interns satchel from his contact in the West Los Angeles Division and needed to question Miller.

Montgomery could not believe that Seth Alexander did not have inside his briefcase any research on the Architect after all of the probings he had done. He wanted to find out if the professor had in his possession of what he needed.

"Professor Miller, Detective Rourke," introducing himself. "I'm here to get some additional information regarding Seth Alexander's death yesterday, you remember, the hit-and-run accident?" he said his eyes focused like laser beams on the professor.

Dean slipped his cell phone into his pants pocket, his eyes focused on the detective and how he was dressed. Instead of a dark suit, white shirt, and tie, he was in a Dodger baseball cap, unshaven, a blue and green plaid long sleeve shirt, and faded denim jeans. When the detective spoke, he exposed a larger than usual space between his two front teeth. He had a slight Irish accent.

"Yes, I remember the accident. It's etched in my brain forever. Seth Alexander was murdered yesterday," Dean said, annoyed with the question. "It was no god-damn accident. I saw the car speed up and aim for my student. You're right about it being a hit-and-run, but it was plain old murder," replied the professor, his anger exploding from his lips.

Frasier kept his focus on the professor's eyes, looking for any tell-tale sign he was anything more than upset over the death of his student. "Can you tell me what you were doing at the Elyse Bakery at 7 A.M.?"

"I was meeting with my student and intern to review his doctoral thesis," Dean said, trying to keep his emotions controlled.

"Intern?" Frasier asked.

Dean was caught off-guard when the detective mentioned intern. He did not want to give away the actual connection he had with Seth and scrambled his thoughts to come up with a satisfactory response. "It's a paying position for some top students. They help me prepare my lectures, grade tests, and do some research for some of my classes."

Frasier was scratching his chin, deep in thought. "Research for what?" he asked, his eyes like little slits.

Miller had become extremely worried by the direction the detective's questions were going. He felt his face become flush. He blurted out the first thing that popped into his head. "What division are you out of?" he asked, noticing he finally put the detective on edge.

Frasier hesitated with his response, thinking fast about what division would be handling this case. He knew the name of only one division in the Los Angeles area and blurted out that answer. "Olympic Division. We are getting an overload of cases from other divisions. Since the recent bombings, every department is on edge and working twenty-four-seven to make sure LA's subway system security has no glitches. Now can you answer my question," he said testily.

"UCLA allocates for each professor a small budget to use for student interns. What Seth was helping me with was an advanced analytical course for next semester," he said with ease, his eyes focused on the detective to see if he was buying his little white lie.

"What's analytics?" he asked.

Dean was getting perturb with the line of questioning. "What does this have to do with Seth's murder? I do not have the time to give you a crash course on what I do or what my interns do for me," he replied, showing his frustration. "You can imagine I am distraught at what I witnessed yesterday and will answer any questions you have that might help find my interns murderer."

Frasier shrugged his shoulders. "Sorry for the off-topic questions. I've been a detective for almost twenty-years and found by asking a lot of questions I can better solve my cases. So, let's get back to the time of the accident..."

"Murder," Dean interrupted.

"Okay, murder," Frasier replied, his eyebrows raised reflecting his frustration. "What did you see?"

Dean gave the detective an exact account of what had happened. A full description of the vehicle, without the license plate. He told him the direction the car went.

"That's all that I remember," said Miller, looking at the detective to see any sign he believed his story. Detective Rourke had a great poker face. He blankly stared, his eyes fixed on Dean's lips.

"I do need some more information to determine if there was a motive too, as you say, the killing of Mr. Alexander. Can you tell me about your meeting? Please think hard about your answer, as it could be critical in determining a motive for your intern's death."

Dean's mind was a big blank canvass. "Seth's research project was about the NSA's new analytical facial recognition system and how it is invading and violating everyone's constitutional rights."

Frasier wasn't buying the story. He realized that any more questions would cause the professor to become more defensive and suspicious about everything that he was asking. "One last question," he said in a calming tone. "Was Seth researching specific individuals for his project?"

Dean shrugged his shoulders. "I cannot tell you. We never had our meeting, remember, he was murdered. I'm sorry I could not be a better witness."

"No problem. Thanks for your time. I hope, if I have more questions, you'll make yourself available to me again?"

Dean had met other detectives before, and this one seemed strange. "Detective Rourke, do you have a card with your name and phone number in case I remember something about the hit and run?" he noticed the detective getting nervous searching his pants pocket.

"I must have given my last one away. More on order. Just call the West Los Angeles Division and ask for Detective Rourke."

"You mean the Olympic? Right?"

"Um, yes I meant the Olympic," he replied, as he rushed out of the professor's office.

Dean watched the detective dash out of his office. He was wondering if he was a detective. He was on his computer searching for the West Los Angeles and Olympic Divisions to find a detective, Rourke. To his surprise, his search came up empty. Now he was scared and immediately called Paige.

43

Paige was happy to be home. DC politics made her crazy. With all that had been happening, she had become uneasy her friend Dean Miller was now caught up in the Architect mess. "Russell, what the hell have you gotten all of us into," she moaned.

Dean Miller was one of the good guys, with a beautiful family. He did not need to be risking his life or the safety of his family for this. She anticipated their upcoming meeting would ease his mind. She wanted him to get back to his perfect life.

She was preparing for her scheduled TV show. She had four guests slated to interview from the NSA, Homeland Security, DoD, and the FBI. She was trying to incorporate the Architect files into her *'Corrupted Intelligence'* theory and remembered what the president had asked her to do. She had not discussed this move with her boss Cliff Thomas either. She had a meeting with him in ten minutes to bring up to date on Dunham and Ellison. She still alleged they were linked to the Architect's plan.

She knew her boss would want hard, clear evidence. Sadly, the thumb drive files did not meet that test. She did not have enough time to investigate each notation to build a case to support her suspicions. She had nothing to pin the bombings or the attack on Iran on either Dunham or Ellison. It was just her gut leading her around.

As a reporter, with all the recent attacks that have happened and how they paralleled the entries the Architect had authored in his files, she was at a loss about pinning someone to the acts. Brian Russell, not being a professional investigator, made one significant error. He did not download verifiable proof from the files to prove they came from Albert Dunham's or Frederick Ellison's computer.

Paige felt what she had, as well as what had happened within the last ten days, was enough to raise the question there was an Architect, and he might have had some involvement or the mastermind of those terrorist attacks.

She saw Clay walking toward her office when her cellphone rang. Dean Miller's name popped on her cell screen.

"Dean, I can't talk now. I'm getting ready for a meeting..." before she could complete her sentence, Miller interrupted her in a panicked tone.

"I'll be quick. I just had a scary conversation with an LAPD detective," he said, in a nervous voice. "I do not believe he was who he said he was. I'm scared. I think whoever killed Seth, now believes I know something...shit, which I do. Should I call the police?"

Paige was thinking fast. "No. Don't call the police. Bradley is on his way to you. Tell him everything. Then we'll all talk tomorrow at my studio. I must go. Remember, don't talk to anyone, but Bradley," she said.

"What shit has Russell gotten us both into," Dean said nervously to Paige.

"I don't know. But trust me, I will be finding out," Paige said.

"I hope so. Seth Alexander lost his life because of what Russell sent us."

Paige saw Clay, his hands on his hips, looking anxious. "Dean, I have to go. I will call you later," she said in a huff and ended the call. She wrote on a yellow pad a reminder: *Call President Chesterfield. Protection for Dean Miller.*

44

Dunham, had a long, tedious briefing by Frasier Montgomery, concerning the interview with Professor Miller. His friend could not conclude beyond a reasonable doubt if the professor knew what his intern had uncovered. "I believe Miller was holding back something. He was very observant, as I questioned him. I believe he made me."

Like most of their meetings, Frasier believed extreme measures were the only solution to a problem. Dunham had first seen his friend in action when they first met in High School. It was not pretty, but it sure was effective.

Even though Dunham's plans were only known to a handful of his closest friends, he tried to hide his alarm about this new potential threat to his scheme. He could see Frasier was monitoring him closely. On the inside, he was boiling over, while on the outside, he tried to keep it hidden. He was not fooling his friend.

Dunham prided himself that he could look a person straight in the eye, and they would never see or sense his anger or deceitfulness. It was something he had perfected so that he could flow day-to-day, as one of the most respected and influential men in the United States. However, with all that had been happening these last ten days, he felt he was losing control, and he did not like that side of himself.

He tried to second guess how he could have been so wrong about Brian Russell. He had trusted him to keep his computer and Ellison's computer cyber safe, not become a thief. This error in judgment was becoming a nightmare for him. He knew he had to nip it in the bud quickly, and sadly, Frasier might be right in his assessment of the situation.

While Russell had been dealt with the only way he knew how, he was now dealing with multiple threats of maybe two or three additional people with copies of his files. All the stress and worry had put him in a no-win situation. It was times like this that nobody was safe, even the people closest to him.

Dunham was having flashbacks from his youth. He remembered how his father pushed him relentlessly to understand all the things needed to build wealth. His father was a brutal man who drilled into him that respect only came to those who were wealthy and used their power wisely.

In his early years, he did not understand why power warranted a degree of brutality so that respect would follow. Growing up as a Dunham, he learned that his family had been one of the most admired dynasties in the United States. They, by far, outranked the Carnegies, Rockefellers and the Morgans. It was his family's belief they needed to remain in the background, never allowing themselves to be in the spotlight.

As a young man, he loved the respect his family afforded him, and he pushed it down the throats of everyone he encountered. He did not see the value in how his family avoided the attention they deserved. He wanted everyone, even his schoolmates, to fear him more than respect him, as well as know that there would be consequences for not treating him with the reverence he felt he deserved.

His father had tried to control him. Unfortunately, his father had become frustrated with the path his son was choosing to take. His older brother Theodore, who should have been the heir to the Dunham legacy, was way too weak and slow to take over as the next Architect. So, the responsibility was placed on Albert at a very young age.

On numerous occasions, his father threatened to disown him and send him away with a modest allowance for the rest of his life if he did not change his ways. Fearing his father would come through with his threat, he learned how to adapt and make him happy. He was learning to love the taste of power.

While he flaunted his family's wealth, he was not a tough assertive teenager around other boys his age. Throughout High School, he was terrorized. Mostly because of how he looked. His overly pale skin, curly short blonde hair and being overweight, was all the class bully needed to name him: "The Fat Albino."

He would tell his father and beg for help. All his father would say: *"One gets bullied when you do not respect yourself. It shows, and people sense it. Look at yourself. You're overweight and need to be meticulous and scrupulous,"* he would preach while standing him in front of a mirror. *"Act proud of who you are and never show weakness,"* his father would always tell him. His father's constant lectures only made him more frustrated and angry. He knew his father did not like him or appreciate how he was maturing.

The young Dunham was the last heir to their family legacy. With it came more responsibility and pressure that at first did not mesh with who he wanted to be. He was smart, but not like the Dunham's before him. His father and his grandfather had a natural sense and understanding of what his great grandfather had envisioned for the family and America. They all understood the spirit of being an Architect. As Albert matured, he saw the original vision differently.

A big turning point had happened for him when he was in the tenth grade. It was a chilly spring day, and he was reading outside his classroom during recess. The class bully had begun his daily routine of picking on him and chanting the nickname he had coined: "Fat Albino." The young Dunham tried to keep his head buried in his book, but it never worked.

On previous days, he was able to ignore the painful reciting, but that day, ıt had gotten worse. Joining in were five other boys. Then before he knew it, all the students outside were gathering around and laughing. Even the teachers who were out in the yard, just stood there trying to hold back their laughter at the pain they saw on his face.

He had, on many occasions, complained to his teachers, but they, like his father, pressured him to learn to adjust and deal with what was going on. Like his father, the headmaster never offered to help him and turned a blind eye to all of it. As it turned out, the class bully was the son of one of the school's most prominent benefactors. That day it did not impress young Albert Dunham one bit. Why at that moment he chose to stand up for himself, he did understand, but it had proven to be the start of who he'd grow up to be.

He slowly put his book down on the bench he had been sitting on, took off his reading glasses, and slowly stood up. He had a fire in his eyes the bully had never seen before. It made him stop his chanting.

With the swiftness of a martial artist, he swung the instep of his foot between the bully's legs with such force he thought the large boy's testicles were going to fly out of his gaping mouth. He was hoping that would happen so that he could stomp on them. The powerful kick had the boy twisting wildly on the ground. Albert did not stop there. He began kicking him in the head until the crying boy was a bloody mess and unconscious.

When the bully's friends had tried to come to his rescue, a tall young muscular boy battered the other boys so severely and so quickly that by the time the three teachers who had been watching came over to break up the fight, all four boys were out cold and covered in blood.

The young Dunham and his new friend were marched off to the headmaster. Their punishment was swift and punitive. Both he and the other boy got expelled without even having their side of what had happened heard.

While waiting for their parents to arrive and escort them out of the school, Albert looked over at his new friend and said thank you. With a big smile on his face, he introduced himself only as Albert. For the first time in his life, he felt empowered. He loved every second of the adrenaline rush that had come from beating up on the bully and feeling his warm blood flow on his fists.

"One day I will become the most powerful man in the United States and maybe the world," he said with conviction.

His new young friend was expressionless, Fraiser's eyes were like big black pools of oil. His pupils were fully dilated. "Frasier Montgomery," he said, extending his hand. His half-hearted grin revealed a noticeable space between his two front teeth.

Dunham instantly liked him. He knew back then they would become the best of friends. "No one ever stood up for me before. Why'd you do it? You must have known you'd get expelled?"

"I don't like bullies. I had wanted to kick his ass for a long time. You were very brave doing what you did. I did not want to let those other boys hurt you. It would not have been fair," he said with a slight grin forming on his face. "Plus, I just love how it feels to let my fists pound on someone's face," he said, without any emotion.

Albert patted him on the shoulder, a satisfying smile growing on his face. "I think we will be great friends. My father will take care of this mess. You don't worry."

"I never worry. I've been tossed out of better schools than this," Fraiser said, his expression turning to sadness.

"Will your parents fix this?"

"This was my last chance. Now, I will be off to military school where this shit won't be tolerated."

Albert's mind was spinning, as a light bulb went off in his head. "I will get my father to let me join you. It might do us some good, but not in the way our parents might think." His cunning mind was at work, already looking toward the future. "I owe you for what you did today. I will never forget it."

Once again, his father and mother would not use their power to convince the Headmaster to keep their son at that school. While Frasier got sent to the strictest military school in upstate New York, Albert had to try two more private schools.

Albert's reputation would follow him from school to school, as well as his newfound temper. His final expulsion from school left his parents with no other option but to send him to the military school where Frasier attended. Little did they know their son would begin building very close bonds with other young rich boys that had the same ambition as he did.

The beautiful thing about the new military school was that it taught Albert how to use his power the way he wanted to, allowing his wealth to build a close-knit family of friends that would soon function like a well-oiled machine. His new friends would later be instrumental in making him the Emperor of the United States.

As he worked his way through college, he matured and learned to manipulate strangers and people in authority with his newly developed charm. He had grown up. He never got as tall as his father, but his 5'9" height did not hinder his ability to command his power over others. He had allowed his blonde hair to grow long, wearing it in a ponytail, losing almost seventy pounds.

When he started his junior year in college, his father gave him his outline of the family manifesto like the other Architects before him. He was instructed to follow the path set up by his Great Grandfather and not deviate. "We've all created our plan for our family's wealth accumulation, and you must begin and formulate your strategy now."

He kept his notes private, never sharing it with his father up until his father's death. As was the tradition with his family, the previous Architect manifesto was passed on to him. He had an excellent blueprint for ruling the United States and the world.

Albert was brought back to the present hearing Frasier call his name. His heart was beating fast, realizing for the first time since Brian Russell violated his trust, he had relapsed into a state of uncontrollable anger, like how he felt the day he almost killed the class bully in High School.

He saw Frasier shaking his head. He knew he was not pleased with what he was seeing. "You're losing yourself. We have to remain focused, or your plans will be exposed," he said, his tone serious.

"I had thought with Russell out of the way; we could move forward without any disruptions. Now, too many people are in our way. What I've planned for almost twenty-years could be in jeopardy," he protested. He liked everything in his life orderly and arranged neatly. While he knew anyone looking at this file would not be able to figure out what he had planned next, he did not want his encrypted folders opened before Stage Five got put in motion.

Montgomery could see Albert was becoming paranoid. "Stage One went off without a hitch. Iran has been set back almost forty-years, creating a new level of Islamic chaos the Middle East has not seen in its worst times. Stage Two, with the bombings of the subways and airports in the United States, those key states have the President distracted enough that he is unable to deal with the ongoing problems in Iran, Syria, Iraq, and Afghanistan," Frasier said with a grin. "Now you have to take a deep breath and proceed on with Stage Three. You cannot let up on ruining President Chesterfield's legacy and his bid for re-election."

"How can I with all of these unknowns lurking out there?"

Frasier smiled. A smile Albert hated. "I think you need to let me deal with those distractions my way now. Let the chips fall where they may. If we wait much longer to find out what they know, it might be too late."

"I don't like it, but maybe you're right. Let's wait for another few weeks and see if anything happens before Stage Three begins."

Frasier showed his disapproval. "I will let it go just three weeks. Then, Turner, the professor, and anyone else I think can hurt you will be dealt with swiftly and permanently. I will be monitoring everyone very closely. If I get any indication, they are close to hindering your plans; then they will be terminated," he said, his pupils were once again dark black pools of hate.

"What's the status of the FBI's investigation of Russell's murder?"

"Roberts has buried it on some desk that won't see the light of day until they're done investigating the recent bombings. No one will be looking into our connection to him," said Frasier.

Dunham was not happy with that answer. "I am not worried about the FBI. I'm worried about Paige Turner and now Dean Miller. You do know that he has new tagging software that can show every place a fly has been in the last week."

Montgomery had a puzzled look on his face. "So. They are not law enforcement. Do you believe Turner will have enough time or information to know we killed her friend?"

"I cannot afford to be associated with Russell or his murder investigation."

"Then, let me do what I do best to protect you."

"Fine. But only if Turner or the professor begins to build a trail back to me."

45

Bradley Stevens had briefed Paige about his interview with Dean Miller. "He's the real deal," Bradley said. "The professor's on the verge of revolutionizing tracking software. The NSA's programs he had sold them years ago do not even come close to what this guy's new software and state of the art codes can do. The great thing about it is that he's not violating anyone's privacy rights."

Paige opened her eyes wide, very interested in hearing more. "He can plug-in someone's photo, and or name, and have his software spit out a full detailed report of every place they've been, who they've met with, and what they've said publicly, as long as it's on the internet or surveillance cameras tapes?"

Bradley held his big hand up like a traffic cop wanting Paige to stop asking questions. "Let me finish. It does so much more. Imagine if he did a search on let's say Brian Russell, which he did for me. His printer spat out ten pages of details on who Brian Russell was, who he had met with recently..." he could not stop bouncing in his chair. "and, who he had contact with frequently. It gets even better. The damn printout not only had everyone who was in contact with Brian Russell, but all those contacts had their own detailed spreadsheet of who they were in contact with during that time frame. It spat out a remarkable circle of connections to Brian Russell." Bradley took a deep breath, allowing his boss to jump in with another question.

Paige was now at the edge of her chair. "Who else knows of this software? NSA? The President?"

Bradley just smiled. "Only the professor, his wife, and Seth Alexander and now us. That's it. I brought back the printout. You need to see the circles of influence that was surrounding your friend Brian. It's a who's who of the most powerful people in the US of A," he said, his voice had a nervous edge to it.

Paige slowly began digesting the data. She was biting her lip almost drawing blood. "You do know what all of this means...right?" she said.

Bradley just nodded, lost in thought.

"There are some of the most powerful and wealthiest men on this report. I can see how Dunham might be building his shadow government right under the nose of President Chesterfield. If what is in those files is going to happen soon, and these men are involved, we must do something to expose all of them, including Dunham, and expose the next event. They have to be stopped or slowed down so the president can put something into action."

Bradley looked at Paige, then looked at his watch. "I forgot to mention while I was with the Professor, someone followed us while we walked around UCLA."

"Are you sure?" she said, surprised. "Dean's been sensing it too."

"They were obvious and did not care when I made eye contact. I did not let Dean know. His anxiety levels are through the roof already. But, one of the men was a guy named Frasier Montgomery. Ex-British Special Forces. I had written a story fifteen years ago about him. He was drummed him out of the military for his brutal interrogation tactics. He's one mean motherfucker. My gut's telling me he could be the person behind the wheel that killed Seth and maybe the one who murdered Brian? His name popped up on Miller's printout numerous times."

Paige pointed to the report she was holding. "Shit, you're right. He's on the list. It looks like there is a lot of activity that revolves around Frederick Ellison, who it appears was Brian Russell's boss. Not sure what all of this means, but before we even think of exposing these people and tying them to the Architect's plan, we need all of our ducks lined up in a nice neat row."

"After seeing Frasier Montgomery, we might need to get a security team to protect the professor and his family. We cannot afford to lose him," Bradley said seriously. "Here's the copy of what professor's software spat out," said Bradley, handing Paige the thumb drive.

"I just hope we are not already late to stop his Stage Three," Paige said a worried edge in her voice.

Bradley had a worried expression on his face. "It is what it is. Maybe you figure out how to release some of what you already know on your show Sunday?"

Paige shrugged her shoulders. "I was thinking the same thing. Might have to run it by Clay first."

She took the initial printout and headed toward her boss's office. She wasn't sure what or how she was going to present this on her Sunday show. She knew that she had to release some of what she had uncovered. How her viewers would accept her comments is the big question.

"Thanks for meeting with me," Paige said, sitting down on the leather couch in Clay's office. He had numerous foreign dignitaries, the last four presidents, and some very wealthy people's pictures hanging on his walls, along with all the awards the TV show had received over the years. Clay was a great editor and chief, always airing newsworthy stories, without the partisan political bullshit the other networks did.

"Glad you wanted to talk. I have some ideas for Sunday's show I want to run by you," he said, his expression serious.

Paige felt the color drain from her face. "I'm all ears," she replied anxiously.

"With all that has gone on these last ten days, I would like you to focus on the attacks. I had some of our other reporters interviewing and digging into what's happening inside the Chesterfield Oval Office..." Paige interrupted him.

"I think you should report that, but not on my show. I've been working on the Brian Russell murder and the files he had sent me. I want to incorporate some of the data I've verified so far into my *'Corrupted Intelligence'* show. I have a good line up of guests that will make you proud. If you'd like, I can review some of it with you now?" she asked.

"Paige, I know by that look on your face you're thinking of exposing the Architect. You cannot bring up Albert Dunham in anything you've been doing. You are, I mean we have stolen property, and it could be a legal nightmare for us," he said.

"I know that. I was not going to use Dunham's name. But, instead, talk more about a shadow government that might be building inside the United States." Paige noticed that she had Clay's attention.

After fifteen minutes of reviewing the direction she wanted to go and showing her boss the printouts Dean Miller had given her, Clay Thomas was in full agreement with her. "I think you'll hit a home run with this segment," he said.

"I hope you watch the show?" she teased.

A few hours later, Paige had taped her show and was in the editing room reviewing it by herself. She was pleased with what she had said. She just hoped that Dunham would be watching on Sunday when it aired.

46

The Architect's directors, his chosen cabinet, were all there to monitor his mental fitness, as he navigated his way through his five stages. They had been called together by Frederick Ellison.

Like Ellison, they were concerned that their identities had been compromised. They were panicking that Paige Turner and professor Miller were getting close to exposing all of them.

This group of billionaires, unlike Dunham, were not so confident with a wait and see attitude, as it pertained to the individuals, they believed had access to the Architect's files. Ellison knew all too well what Turner and her band of reporters, could achieve with their current investigation. Now with Professor Dean Miller in the mix, their concern had gone nuclear.

They all knew Miller's reputation as a cyber expert. If he had copies of Dunham's files and were able to open the ones that are encrypted, it would be all over for them. He could bring the results to Turner or even the president. They were anxious the microchip Russell created for the NSA satellite would be overridden by professor Miller's cyber programs. They all voted unanimously to eliminate Dean Miller. He, in their opinion, was the only person other than Russell that could disable the satellite.

Ellison addressed the group, trying to reassure them that everything was under control, but his facial expression was unconvincing. "Gentlemen, this little setback is being controlled and monitored..." he said. He was interrupted by the president of Trident Communications.

"Frederick, please stop your bull-shit. We are all aware of the mess you and Dunham have created with the breach by Brian Russell. Your inability to stop Turner and Miller have given us pause to reassess yours and Dunham's leadership with our group's plan," Greg Radcliff said.

Ellison said calmly. "I know the simplest solution is to eliminate the risk, but it did not work that well with Russell. I do support Dunham's wait and see approach. We do not need more eyes on us if we do something rash."

Radcliff replied quickly, expressing his frustration. "The FBI has no leads on Russell's murder, so what makes you think killing Turner and Miller would be any different. We have the right people in place to bury their untimely deaths. You need to nip this in the bud. Let me be blunt. If there is any indication we could be exposed, I can assure you we will all pull our support for you and Dunham," he said harshly. "You need us to complete the remaining stages."

Ellison could see that Frasier was uncomfortable with what Radcliff was saying. "Frasier. You have something to add?"

Frasier was pacing the conference room, his impatience showing. "Yes, I do. I just got word from one of our moles at Turner's TV station that she's airing her show Sunday about a 'Shadow Government' led by some very wealthy individuals," he said, pointing his finger at everyone in the room. "She's supposed to tie the recent attacks in with this unknown group. We need to watch her show tomorrow. It might seal the deal on what we need to do to protect ourselves," he said.

FBI Director Chad Roberts, General Tucker Phillips, Gregory Wilbanks, Brian Russell's replacement, and Todd

Mathews, all were sitting in the back of the conference room, waiting for Ellison to respond.

"If everyone else could stop talking and calm down it would be appreciated, "Frederick chastised everyone in the room. His face showed his displeasure, especially with Radcliff's threat. "We do have a serious problem. I do not think to threaten our leader is a good idea," he said. "At first Dunham and I thought it might be nothing, but I for one cannot wait to see if we've been exposed by Brian Russell," his remarks had everyone sitting up straight in their chairs.

Frasier was eager to comment. "I know Albert wants to do a wait and see, but I should be allowed to eliminate Turner and Miller. I support Radcliff's idea. I can do it without it coming back to bite us," he said, his voice had an eerie tone to it.

Ellison was quick to interrupt him. "No. First, let's watch her show and then decide. She might be speculating, just to stir us up. We can't afford to act hastily," he said. "Then it would expose us."

Frederick tried to get control of his meeting. "The reason you are all here is to see if we can move up some of our plans. I believe we are in a good position, especially with the country still reeling from the attacks on the train stations and airports. It should be enough of a diversion to allow us to begin "Stage Three."

He looked at Todd Mathews, who had not lifted his head, and was staring blankly at his watch. "Do you have somewhere to be? I need to know where you're at on the microchip for the upcoming NASA launch next month?"

He slowly lifted his head. His eyes focused on Ellison. He shrugged his shoulders before he responded. "It will be tight. I was not planning on everything, getting moved up. I discovered a week ago that Brian Russell had not installed the software like he was told to do. It looks like we are behind by approximately three weeks," Mathews nervously said.

Ellison after hearing the news started to loosen his red and blue paisley silk tie. It was a bad sign when he began rolling up his sleeves. He was upset.

"That won't happen," he remarked, his voice rising. "If you want to tell that to Dunham, then, well, I can't begin to tell you what might happen."

Todd began to stammer. "I... I've been...I mean my team's been working on getting caught up twenty-four-seven, and correcting what Russell had done," he glanced at Gregory Wilbanks, the newest member of the inner circle.

"We will meet our deadline," Wilbanks nervously promised.

"Very good. I knew you'd not want to screw up at such a critical time," Ellison said sarcastically. "Now for our final piece of business. Dunham wants FBI Director Roberts, Montgomery, and General Tucker Phillips to stay back so we can have a video call with him. We are moving up some other parts of our plan due to some new information we have on Turner and Professor Miller.

47

Even though her show had already been taped and edited, she was overly anxious about what she was about to set loose on the airways. Paige had decided to wear a white tight knit dress that exposed her shoulders, as well as her well-toned figure. Sometimes she wore a red dress or a navy blue one, but for this show, she wanted to come across as soft and calm. What she was about to expose she hoped would become the main story on the evening news.

She wanted the Architect's files to become an explosive story, to slow down the remaining stages that were left. She had anticipated President Chesterfield would keep it from the American public.

After their recent White House meeting, she did not feel right putting herself and her news organization in a compromising position working with the president on this story. Especially since the president had close ties to this man, Paige knew what she was about to do would upset the President.

Now she was about to break the most significant news piece since her show started, exposing the men and women in power who fit her definition of *"Corrupted Intelligence."* Paige believed these powerful men continued to infest every aspect of the government and corporate America. Paige understood she would be pissing off her president and ruining her reputation if her show and what she had to say was not received well by her audience.

After talking with Bradley and reviewing what Dean Miller had given her, she knew the direction she needed to take. She sucked in a deep breath and leaned back on her couch to watch her show.

"*Good morning, afternoon, and evening to all of our followers around the world. I am Paige Turner, and this is "Corrupted Intelligence, The Secret Manipulation of the American People.*

"*My friend and college classmate, Brian Russell, his wife and son, were brutally murdered ten days ago. I had received a package from him, that I believe cost him his life. He had left me a disturbing voice mail message mentioning a group of billionaires who were leading a shadow government in our country, with hundreds of men and women working for or within the current administration. If what I've read so far is correct, our FBI and CIA are working with these traitors.*

In the package I received was a thumb drive that contained hundreds of files, some encrypted, that validates my theory that the person or persons who had created these files had some hand in the recent attacks on Iran and our homeland. What I've de-coded so far is that this person, this shadow government, has Five Stages planned. We have by my account experienced two of them already with the recent attacks at home and abroad.

The scary thing about all of this is that these people with their group of conspirators believe they are doing something that is in the best interests of America and its citizens. They are the perfect example of Corrupted Intelligence.

One man, the leader, goes by the title, The Architect. He wants to change our constitution and become the new leader of our country. He talks about becoming the Emperor of the United States, EOTUS. He wants power and will not stop until he achieves his goals, even if it means murdering thousands of

Americans. This group of billionaires had written in their manifesto that the Stock Exchanges around the world and here in the United States would be manipulated once the attacks took place. I beg someone at the FTC to investigate all stock sell-offs before each event. Hopefully, you can find a trail.

What Stage Three, Four, and Five will be, well, I am not sure. My team of investigative reporters is working on finding that out. President Chesterfield, I am sending you a copy of this thumb drive. Please have your best people you trust work on finding this person. I have a list of billionaires I will be calling to interview to see if they can shed some light on this problem. I want to invite Albert Dunham to come on our show and offer some help in finding these traitors."

The show went on for another thirty minutes. Paige, using a video slide show, broke out a web of people connected to Brian Russell, excluding Dunham for the time being. She did not accuse any specific person of being a traitor but left the suspicions to dangle out there for her listeners to digest. She also wanted the Architect and his followers to absorb what she had said.

Paige looked straight into the camera lens and made a plea. *"Mr. Dunham. America needs your help now."* And with that closing remark, she ended her show.

"That was one ballsy play you did Paige," Bradley said, a smile exploding on his face.

"Yeah, it was. I wasn't sure where I was going to go with this, but it just flew out of my mouth. It will be interesting where the shit lands and sticks. I hope Dunham will agree to an interview."

"We'll just have to see how big his ego is?" Bradley remarked.

"I am sure it's huge. Let's hope Dunham agrees to the interview before more bad news hits our country," Paige said worriedly.

As she stood, she saw Clay Thomas standing by the doorway. He did not look happy. She knew by his body language he was pissed and ready to read her the riot act.

Clay was in her face, his eyes on fire. "What the hell just happened? Didn't we agree to let the president handle the investigation?

Paige let a half-hearted smile crack on her face. "I had to do something to draw Dunham out of hiding. Bradley and I believe Dunham is the puppet master. The media is a powerful tool, and I wanted to use it to bring these traitors to the surface."

"That's bull-shit. Also, it's impossible. Why would Dunham even want to help you expose his movement? Do you believe the most liked and respected man in America would come on your show now?" Clay said, exasperated, throwing his hands in the air.

Paige was rolling her eyes at her boss. She knew when he was a drama queen. "Calm down. If I am wrong, then nothing will happen. If I am right, then this scumbag maybe will halt his other stages and give our country time to find all the men and women working for him. We have already lost good people because of these crazy files."

"You're a little shit, Paige Turner. You don't realize what you've done this time," Clay said, frustrated. "You might just have put our network at a big financial risk. I hate saying this, but your tenure here might be in jeopardy. I just got texted by the chairman of the board. They want to talk to me about your show," he said, turning around and storming out of her office.

Paige bit her lower lip, watching her friend leave her office. She had never seen him so angry at her. As soon as her office door slammed shut, her cellphone rang. It was POTUS.

48

Dunham and Ellison were drinking their Balvenie single malt, as they sat back to watch Paige Turner's show. "I hate that bitch. I thought after we eliminated her husband, she'd have crawled under some rock and faded away. But, no. She's now become my biggest pain-in-the-ass," Dunham said.

"Ellison slammed his elbow into the ribcage of his friend. "I told you then they both needed to go. But you wouldn't listen," he said cynically. "I saw this coming a long time ago."

"It's never too late," Dunham said coldly. "So, shut up and watch her fucking show."

When she got to the part about the Architect's plan and all the co-conspirators, both men sat up straight, their eyes wide with shock. "What did she just say?" screamed Albert.

Ellison was trying to calm him down, but nothing was working. "We need to slow down right now until we figure out what she knows," said Frederick.

"No. We must keep to our schedule with Stage Three and Four. The chip has to be installed without alerting the staff at the NSA. We cannot wait," Dunham said, his face twisted with concern. "Once the satellite is under my control, nothing she says, or the president says will make a difference. Control will all be mine."

"Turner, if she's as smart as I think she is, will soon figure out what's going on. I have to go on the assumption she has printed copies of your files, has made numerous copies of

Russell's thumb drive," Ellison said cautiously. He knew Albert's temper and did not want to be in the pathway of it.

"I thought you agreed with me on a watch, wait, and see on Turner? Do you still feel that way now?" Albert said, his drink ready to be launched across his den.

"Two things I see. Turner is trying to bait you to come on her show, which I think might be a good idea. But we might have a bigger problem. What if Professor Miller has copies of your files and is using his new software to dig into everyone on our team? What if he can decrypt the file that has the chip schematics in it? If that gets exposed, then the satellite launch would be scuttled by Chesterfield," Ellison stammered.

Dunham massaged his scalp with his fingernails, drawing blood. "Chesterfield won't stop the launch. It's his secret project. We can't let that bitch expose the chip," he said, his face turning beet red. "We need to stop her."

"I agree," Ellison replied. We could have a bigger problem first. What if Miller has a way to track our stock sell-offs? His intern did get close to us. If his software he created works like I think it does, things might be moving faster than we had expected."

"Shit. Stop all your fucking questions. It's simple. We have to move everything up and begin Stage Three and Four earlier and stop Turner and Miller." Albert was lost in thought and had seemed to calm down as he took a long sip of his drink.

Ellison shrugged his shoulders. "Frasier can handle that for us. He's itching to get started. I first need to check on a few things, but I believe the timing might be right. It just hinges on how fast Turner gets her team activated. We will have to monitor her and Miller very closely before Frasier does his thing."

"Why? Can't we cause an accident, like what happened to the intern?" Dunham asked.

"That might be difficult now. Frasier was outed by Bradley Stevens, Turner's reporter, who was talking to the professor. Our hotheaded friend might have just put Turner on high alert. If that's the case, we should use someone else to eliminate her from the equation."

Albert was rubbing his chin, deep in thought. "Maybe we should kill everyone?" he said sarcastically. "All you and Frasier want to do is murder, as your solution to everything. Don't you?"

Frederick nodded his head. "It's the easiest and most effective solution. It just needs to look like an accident. Then we can go back to our original timetable. So far, Albert, you haven't been exposed. Killing Turner and the professor could cause an investigation, but you are too far removed right now from it. Our people at the FBI and the Justice Department can slow an investigation down. You'll at least be happier, and no one will know about the chip."

Dunham was now laughing. "Let me think about your proposal. How well did it stop Turner after her husband was murdered because he got too close to what we were beginning to put into place?"

"It will work this time. We've learned our lesson with Russell."

"You're so full of shit Frederick. You've never learned, but this time, it better work. Now let's get our plan back on track. I want everything moving in the right direction without worrying about Turner or the professor."

Ellison just rolled his eyes, knowing when Dunham makes up his mind. Nothing can sway him. "I've been in contact with our European allies, and they're ready to get started. The Markets will again collapse on your word. Also, your plan for the Sinai region is set to go too."

Albert massaged his chin. "The Markets have made a slight bounce back since the Iranian attack and the bombings here. President Chesterfield has done a fine job assuring the country that we're safe. Now, any word from Todd Mathews? Has he started selling a portion of my portfolio again?" he asked.

Ellison nodded. "The last transaction was sold earlier today. Once the Europe deal moves forward, we'll give it a few days so that you can repurchase your investments. Then, with Stage Three and Four going live, it should gross you over seven-hundred and fifty billion dollars," he said confidently. "No regulatory board will even know what you've done."

"Then, let's get moving," Dunham said.

49

President Chesterfield did not curtail his anger with Paige. "What the fuck did you just do?" he asked, his voice at a fever pitch.

"My job, sir," she replied un-rattled.

"Didn't we have an agreement to keep each other in the loop on your investigation?"

"We did, but I am a reporter, you know, and did not feel I needed your permission to do my duty as a reporter or discuss what or how I do my show?"

"When it involves National Security you do," he bellowed.

Paige had become frustrated with Chesterfield. She wanted to tell him off but realized she needed to temper her arrogance. "Mr. President, need I remind you that at this point-in-time, you are the only person in your administration who knows the Architect's stolen property had come from the office of Frederick Ellison? In my opinion, these files have a close link to your friend Albert Dunham."

"Shit, not evidence, just your opinion? You can't slander a man like Dunham. He'll crush you in court, if not ruin your career," Chesterfield said.

"I can handle Dunham. Right now, I have evidence and files pointing to Dunham and Ellison. If it proves to be wrong, then I will re-track my accusations. But, right now, you need deniability, which is what I can do for you. I will give you the necessary leads so that you can have your Attorney General and anyone else in your administration pursuing legitimate avenues against Ellison and Dunham."

Chesterfield had become silent. "Ms. Turner, I don't like how you are talking to me. Sadly, you're right. Let's hope your little stunt works," he said in a calmer tone.

"Thank you, sir. I think you need first to find the right people inside your administration you can trust. You'll need them as my investigation begins to gain momentum," Paige said, her tone taking on a softer edge. "Maybe start draining your swamp. It will send a serious signal to Dunham and his secret shadow government he's trying to build that you're on to his scheme...or coup."

President Chesterfield let loose with a thundering laugh. "Maybe I should have you working for me. I do not have too many on my staff, who would speak to me the way you did. Let's check-in by the end of the week," he paused, "I mean if you need to speak to me, you know how to contact me."

Paige tried to contain her giggle, but it slipped out. "Thank you, sir. I will keep in touch."

* * * * *

Chesterfield had his Chief of Staff in his office listing all the items he needed put into motion. "I need a list of who at Justice we can trust. Next, I need some suggestions on who I can use behind the scenes to investigate and flush out all the men and women inside this shadow government Dunham seems to have created," he ordered.

Felix Wilson had always seemed to stay a few steps ahead of his friend and president. "Sir, I've made up a list for us to go over. It wasn't easy, but I feel everyone on this piece of paper we can trust."

"Good. Now let's begin to clean house. We have a re-election to win."

50

Frederick Ellison and Albert Dunham had just finished their meeting. They had agreed they needed to be more focused on all their goals.

"You're right. Even if Turner and Miller have copies of my files, it will take them too long to get through all the encrypted codes that matter," said Albert. "All the work and lobbying we've done, as well as a large number of campaign donations we've made, are about to pay off with dividends. The House's newly passed budget bill was pushed through the Senate and approved with sixty-four votes," he said happily. "This was the first legislation in a long time that was supported on both sides of the aisle. They were so pressured by the media and voters to get things done that they never figured out what they passed had benefited our group," Dunham said grinning. "Even the president will sign the bill if he wants to get re-elected."

Ellison said. "The money that's been allocated for infrastructure projects are going to most of our contractors. That's approximately fourteen billion dollars. It will be more as the projects go on stream as budgets get adjusted up," Ellison said, unable to contain his joy. "With this new budget, our drug companies are being subsidized by the Feds to help keep prescription drug costs down," said Ellison, unable to contain his laughter, he had started to gag.

Dunham, for the first time, was able to smile. "What about the tax dollars we're going to get for expanding the land we recently purchased for Fracking of Natural Gas and Oil?

Ellison took a deep breath, regaining his composure. "Getting our people elected last mid-term has been paying off tenfold."

While Dunham and his group of billionaires were about to increase their wealth ten-fold, only he and Ellison knew the real beauty of the newly passed budget. Hidden deep inside were strategic cuts in the Judicial System, Intelligence agencies, and Military. For Dunham, this was more important than the money he was gaining from this bill. These little, unnoticed provisions in the budget would be the grease that would make his remaining Stages move ahead smoothly.

"Are we done here?" Dunham asked.

"Yes. I need to meet with Montgomery at the Oasis Club. We have a lot to discuss. Turner and Professor Miller are still a problem, as we move ahead.

"Don't get careless with Frasier. You know how I feel about killing them at this time. It must be done without tying it to us," said Dunham. "We don't need any investigations right now that might put us under the looking glass."

"I understand fully. Montgomery's been briefed. He needs to have a little free rein to do what he does best. You do know what I mean?"

Dunham was scratching his scalp. "I do. But, if you don't feel he'll curtain his sick urges, then I'll have to get involved, and he won't like what I will do," he threatened.

* * * * *

Ellison was driving to the Oasis Club in George Town, a place where all men of influence met for some needed privacy away from nosey reporters. Frasier Montgomery was sitting next to him in his Bentley. They were discussing the new problem Turner was posing.

"Albert needs some way to knock Turner off our trail," said Frederick. "Frasier, tell me some of your ideas on how we can curtail Turner and her herd of reporters?"

"She needs to be killed. It's as simple as that," Fraiser said, grinning.

Ellison shook his head. "I want it to happen too. It can't happen now, but…soon. However, I need another idea from you that might slow her down."

"How about her two reporters having an accident. She's very close to this Bradley Stevens. It should knock the wind right out of her sails. Remember what happened to her after we eliminated her husband?" he said, a creepy smile on his face.

"That's not a bad idea. Go for it. Call me when it's done," Ellison said. "Make sure it looks like a random accident and not one of your brutal assassinations."

Ellison let Frasier out a block from the Oasis Club. He admired how his friend could be so calm planning to murder two reporters. He acted aloof, which scared him too.

"He's been like that since school," he muttered. He could still see the bloodstains at his school from beatings Frasier had inflicted on those classmates who irritated him or bothered him or Albert. They had become a tight-knit group, maturing into the men they were today, a far cry from the actions they all took while at their military academy.

The doorman opened the door on Ellison's Bentley. He was escorted swiftly into the club by a second doorman and taken to his private room where his meeting would begin. Inside the large conference room were the congressional dirty dozen, President Chesterfield's FBI Director and the Director of the CIA. General Tucker Phillips, was parading around the room like a caged lion.

Ellison did not waste any time. "Gentlemen, glad you could all make it on such short notice. Let's cut to the chase.

The time has come to move up our plans and begin Stage Four of the Playbook. For this piece of the puzzle to work, everyone must do their part within the timeframe we will discuss today. Every assignment you have will only work if all of you and your teams work together and in sync. Any misfiring or initiating your assignment too soon or too late will jeopardize our ability to take back our country we lost three years ago to a progressive Democratic president." Ellison panned the room. He did not see anyone with a bewildered expression, so he began laying out what everyone had to do.

"We have exactly one week to make this happen. I believe President Chesterfield is being fed a lot of crap from Paige Turner about our plans and all of us. If we miss our target date, some of you, or most likely all of you might be finding yourself behind bars for treason. There's no turning back now or dropping out. You've taken an oath to our group, and you're expected to honor your promise to the Architect."

The meeting went on for three hours. One by one, over the next two hours, each man filed out of the Club, so they would not be seen together. Little did Ellison know Professor Miller's software was tagging everyone at the club who passed in front of the security cameras inside and outside the building.

51

Dean Miller was nervous as he placed his worm inside the security software at the Oasis club. "Are you sure the president has approved this?" he asked Paige nervously.

She placed a reassuring hand on his shoulder. "It's been all approved. Just get us the data," she said, concealing her little white lie.

For the first time, she felt scared. Even with Bradley's assurances, something deep down in her soul told her something terrible was about to happen.

"Take a deep breath," Bradley said. "We're doing the right thing here. We've felt the change happening for years inside our government. We didn't know who to look at or even where to start until we got Russell's thumb drive. Now, thanks to Brian, we can do what we do best, expose a conspiracy we've known existed."

"Bradley, I don't know what my life would be today if it were not for you and Sean. You became the family, the brothers I never had after Rick was murdered. Words cannot express how I feel," Paige said, wiping a tear from her eye.

"We all never had any time to have a family. What we've committed to doing for our careers and now for you, has given us the family we so wish we had," Bradley said, squeezing Paige's shoulder.

Dean Miller craned his neck, staring at them. "Can you both take a break from this love fest and get back to work here?"

Paige pushed Bradley away and walked over to the computer screen Dean had in front of him. "Anything yet?"

Just as she said it, a spreadsheet popped up. On it was hundreds of names. Each name had been matched with the individual the professor tagged that attended Oasis Club meeting.

"Paige's jaw dropped open. "I don't believe it. Everyone on this list connects to Dunham. It goes deep inside Chesterfield's administration, as well as the justice system."

Bradley was jotting down some names in his notebook, pushing Paige off to the side so he could see the screen. "Fuck. Frasier Montgomery connects to everyone. He's the ass-hole who's been following Dean and me," he said upset. "Dean do something for me. Can your software bring up the cameras in Westwood where your intern was murdered?"

"I tried that, but that day the cameras had a glitch and either erased the footage or did not record anything. I was disappointed," he said.

Bradley was scratching his chin. "I know that after 9/11 every city installed all new cameras. Even if something were erased accidentally, a copy would get stored in a backup drive, separate from the main system. A new version of the cloud or as the conspiracy theorists say, government's eye in the sky."

Dean was typing in some codes which took up four lines of gibberish to Bradley. "Damn, you're right. I'm in the other backup drive. Let me type in the date and time of the hit and run...there we go, bam," he said, pressing the enter key.

Paige and Bradley were watching the screen intently. Then Dean began pointing his finger at a person walking across Gayley.

"That's Seth. It's him," he said his voice cracking because he knew what he would be witnessing next.

Paige saw it first. The black Chevy Suburban started to move. Then, they could see the driver, a big grin on his face, gripping the steering wheel tightly as he gunned the car toward Seth Alexander.

Dean looked away from the computer screen just as Seth had become airborne. He had seen it once and did not want to witness it again. Bradley hit the pause button on the keyboard.

"There," he said, pointing. "That's Frasier Montgomery. I'd know that space between his two front teeth anywhere. We got Seth's murderer."

"Yeah, but who do we show this to? Again, we've hacked into a government system we're not supposed to be in," Paige said, frustrated.

"We can send this tape anonymously to the FBI agent handling this case, and out on social media. I can also attach a breakdown of everyone Frasier Montgomery ever worked for and is currently working for. That should stir up some shit," Dean Miller said.

Paige was nodding her head, deep in thought. "That's a great idea. We might rattle the bushes and send everyone running for cover. Once on social media, I can use it on my next show," she said excitedly.

Bradley did not seem so thrilled with that idea. "I think we better digest what we have here. Let's give this a day and let it sink in. I want to send Sean up there. He has a detective friend at the Olympic Division. He might know how to use this tape in their ongoing investigation," he said. He can see him later today."

"Okay. But I am not going to let the FBI bury this evidence," said Paige. "I want to hear back from you and Sean tomorrow morning."

"Fine boss. Will do," replied Bradley with a salute, as he turned and left the computer room.

52

Later that day after the Oasis Club meeting had concluded one of Frasier's men intercepted Sean Adams's' phone call to an FBI agent in the San Diego field office. When presented with the voice message, Montgomery's mood had instantly changed. *Turner's people are moving way too fast. How the fuck did he get a video of the hit and run showing me behind the wheel?* He groaned.

He was immediately on his cell to Ellison. "We've got a big problem," he told Frederick. "Sean Adams, one of Turner's reporters, is on his way tomorrow to the FBI San Diego Field office with a video of me running down that fucking intern," he said, his anger exploding over the phone.

"What do you mean a video? I thought your contact at the LAPD Olympic Division erased all the footage on those cameras an hour before and an hour after the accident?" Ellison asked, his frustration oozing out of Montgomery's phone.

"He said he did, but it seems after 9/11 the Fed's created automatic backups of all footage so something like this could not happen. All I know is that Adams has one and taking it to an agent Roberts put in charge of the murder. I thought the FBI director was burying this case. I can't let the reporter or the video get released," Frasier said.

"Okay. This time get the evidence first before you kill Alexander," Ellison reminded Fraiser.

* * * * *

Sean was sitting at Union Station in Los Angeles, organizing his files on his computer, making sure everything was being backed up to the cloud. While he had enough evidence to put Montgomery away for life, he was even happier with the new evidence he had gotten about Dunham and his Chemical Company. He was excited the data had shown Dunham Industries was intentionally mixing toxic chemicals banned by the FDA, which were known to cause cancer, with their weed retardant. What was more incriminating Dunham sprayed the poison in specific geographical areas known for high wind conditions.

"This should bury Albert Dunham. I have to get the report to the CDC when I get back," he mumbled, as he uploaded the last file. *"Bradley will be so pleased with what I found."* Confirming all his evidence was backed up on the cloud and copies were sent to Bradley and Paige, he closed his laptop, slipping it in his knapsack. He looked at his watch and realized it was time to board the train.

* * * * *

Frasier had spotted Sean and followed him to the first-class section on the train. He was sitting by himself, on the right side of the car, his laptop resting on a dropdown tray from the seat in front of him. He was typing on his keyboard, unaware that Frasier had taken a position directly behind him. The car was almost empty, which gave Montgomery enough freedom to carry out his plan.

He pulled the slim plastic tray, which held the syringe out of his jacket pocket. Being ever so vigilant, he looked up and down the aisle to be sure his next action would go unnoticed. He opened the container and took out the syringe filled with a hefty dose of heroin. Once he injected into the carotid artery, in a matter of seconds, the reporter's heart would stop. He'd appear to be asleep for the two-and-half-hour ride to San Diego.

Frasier slowly stood, the hypodermic in his left hand. He gripped the back of Sean's headrest, which anchored his body, as he rose from his seat. He craned his neck one last time to see that no one was watching him. The train had not pulled out of the station. Passengers were still boarding, which made what he was about to do more urgent. If he were fast enough, he'd have time to gather up Sean's laptop and papers and be off the train before anyone noticed something was wrong.

His left hand had started inching its way toward the right side of Sean's neck. He readied his arm to plunge the needle deep into the reporter's artery. Frasier was startled when he heard a loud voice coming from the rear of the car. It was the conductor who had just entered the first-class compartment.

Frasier accidentally bumped Sean's seat startling him. The reporter turned and looked up. His eyes grew wide with fear the moment he recognized who was standing over him with a hypodermic needle. Sean screamed for help in the loudest voice he could muster, but it did not seem to matter to Montgomery.

Sean could hear the conductor shouting, "Hey, you. What's going on here?" When the first blow from Frasier's massive fist struck the young reporter across his jaw, he knew unless he fought back, he was about to die.

Sean's instincts took over, even though Frasier had rung his bell, he kept his balance. When the next fist came, he lifted his laptop, which deflected the next blow.

When Adams saw the needle coming at him like a missile, he slid his body across the double seat, banging hard against the window.

The conductor, a big muscular black man, grabbed Frasier by the collar and yanked him back, causing him to stumble backward. That gave Sean enough time to jump up and run toward the front of the car. He passed three other passengers that were now standing up, surprised expressions on their faces, as he ran by them. He did not see Frasier put a bullet into the middle of the conductor's heart.

Then, Sean heard a pop. Then, three more. As he got to the end of the car, he felt his spine explode from one blast, and then everything went dark when the last bullet entered the back of his head. The train had started its slow move out of the station.

"Shit, shit, shit," Frasier screamed, frustrated. He stepped over the conductor and reached across where Sean had been sitting and gathered up his belongings, including the cracked laptop.

Montgomery noticed three passengers were standing, frozen in time. He unloaded his gun and watched them fall back onto their chairs. He ran toward the back of the car just in time to jump onto the moving platform.

He watched the train move out of the terminal. There were no police or alarms sounding. "Damn, that worked better than I thought. Only five people dead. Not bad for a hard day's work," he bragged. He thought of dialing Ellison to tell him of his success, but he felt he better wait until he listened to the news when he got back to his hotel.

53

Dunham was outraged with what happened on the Amtrak train. He was not surprised it had turned out that way. Frasier had always been an arrogant son-of-a-bitch. Maturing did not temper him. It just made him a sociopathic killer. His irrational behavior had made the news. It was lighting up every channel.

Dunham dialed Ellison. They needed to talk. He was pissed that his number one in charge of his plan had given the go-ahead to kill the reporter without checking with him. The timing of this mess could not have been at a worse time. Stage Three was getting ready to be kicked off, and now he had to fix a problem that never should have happened. On the second ring, Frederick answered.

"I know why you're calling," said Ellison, his voice sounding nervous.

"What the fuck did you think would happen using Frasier? On a fucking train? In the middle of the morning? Five people dead?" Dunham could not control himself. "Frasier is becoming a god-damn liability. You've got to fix this thing."

"I know. The reporter had a video of Frasier driving the car that killed the professor's intern. We needed to stop him from giving it to the FBI," Ellison said, sucking in a deep breath.

"But how are we going to fix this mess?" Dunham asked.

"I think we should cut ties with Frasier and throw him under the bus. If he's dead, we can pin everything on him. It might make us look bad, but with what you've got planned with Stage Three, it would all be forgotten by the next news cycle."

Dunham let loose a loud sigh. "I'll miss him. He had saved me many times. I do owe him," he said. "But, not after this screwup. Just be quick and dispose of the body so it will be found by the local authorities."

"I'll get Tucker to do the job. He has always hated Frasier. Too undisciplined for his liking."

* * * * *

Ellison was sitting across from Tucker Phillips. "We have a problem that needs your professional touch. Frasier must be liquidated immediately. His body needs to be found by the LAPD by tonight. We need this mess resolved now before Dunham leaves on his mission. Just make sure whatever files or papers he took from that reporter are discovered near Montgomery's body."

Phillips allowed a big smile to form on his face. He never smiled, but hearing what his task was, gave him pleasure. "It's about time Frederick. I'm surprised Dunham waited this long to take the rabid dog out of his misery."

"Call me when it's done," Ellison said.

"Yes, sir. Copy that," he replied.

54

Paige had heard the news of Sean's murder from Bradley. He had heard about it on the police scanner he used to track down new stories that were breaking. He didn't think he would ever have to tell Paige again that someone she cared for had died for investigating a story.

Bradley was sitting with Paige on her deck overlooking the Pacific surf as it pounded the shore. The sun was about to set, but she could not see the beautiful orange glow through the waterfall of tears that had started cascading down both her cheeks.

"How the hell could this happen?" she cried. "Why, Sean? He was so young," she sobbed.

Bradley did not know what to say. So, he did what he did best; he remained quiet and wrapped Paige inside his big strong arms. "The initial reports are coming back that it was a lone shooter. You're not going to believe this. They identified the shooter. It was Frasier Montgomery."

"No," she screamed. "Damn you. You wanted me to hold the story that would have put Frasier's face on the news. Now he's murdered our friend and four more innocent people," she screamed at Bradley.

He bit his lower lip, unable to say a word. He was feeling more outrage than Paige for what he failed to do. "I blame myself for all of this," Bradley said, his voice raspy. "They have every LAPD police officer, and FBI agents looking for

Montgomery. I'm releasing our video and the links this bastard had to Dunham, as well as a whole bunch of people inside President Chesterfield's cabinet."

Paige, with a blank stare, signaled Bradley to leave her home. "Please go. I need to be alone. Do what you have to do," she said a sadness he had not heard from her in a long time.

Bradley got up and walked off the deck and out the front door. He knew she'd get over it, but how long it would take her this time would be the big question. Inside his car, he dialed a private detective he knew.

Blake Hunter was an ex-Navy SEAL with a security protection service. His partner, Aden Parker a retired Secret Service agent, knew Bradley when he covered the Gulf Wars. Paige and everyone around her needed protection, and these two guys were the only two people he felt he could trust right now.

* * * * *

It had been six hours since Bradley had left her beach home. Paige was exhausted from crying. Her emotions about Rick's murder had resurfaced. She had pulled out a banker box of her husband's notes, and files on the last story he had been working on that got him killed.

She had never read them. Why she picked today to look at Rick's file box, she did not know. She was shocked at what her husband had been investigating.

"Oh my God," she said. She could not believe what was inside his files and what names he had tied into his theory. It was two-thirty in the morning, but she knew he would not care. She dialed Bradley.

"Can you get here? We need to talk. You're not going to believe what Rick was working that got him killed," she said and hung up the phone.

55

The United States media had not let up on President Chesterfield and his inability to address the attacks against the United States. It had been almost two weeks since the Iran attack and the bombings on American soil, and still, there were no answers as to who or why this had happened.

The President's press secretary, Rachel Monroe, kept to her talking points that the recent bombings at the train stations and airports were not committed by any known terrorist group.

"I know every American wants answers to these horrific events and you can be assured that President Chesterfield has the CIA, FBI, and Homeland Security working on this situation twenty-four-seven..." Rachel was interrupted by a reporter.

"Is it true that the President believes these attacks were orchestrated by men inside his administration who are being controlled by a group of billionaires building a shadow government? Does the president believe one man going by the title The Architect, is behind all of these attacks?"

Rachel did not seem surprised by the two questions. She had expected it. "Yes, we all listened to Paige Turner's show last Sunday. President Chesterfield has been in contact with Ms. Turner and has his team looking into the documents she purported she had. At this time, since this is an ongoing investigation, that's all I can tell you."

Another reporter shouted out a question. "Does President Chesterfield feel the murder of Brian Russell and now Sean Adams, both friends of Paige Turner are related to this Architect and the files Ms. Turner says she has in her possession?"

Rachel was caught off-guard by the question. "I can't comment on those murders right now," she said defensively. With that last statement, the press secretary ended the press conference.

* * * * *

If things could not get worse, they just had. The news had been spewing out online and on televisions everywhere. *Usually*, one major event would have the world on edge, but today six devastating tragedies had occurred against the United States. President Chesterfield, with his Chief of Staff, could not believe what had happened. Like a dam breaking, the attacks were continuing to happen around the world and in the United States.

Kabul, Afghanistan, (AP) - A suicide bomber had crashed through a security gate that was hosting the American Ambassador, and 31 CIA employees and 5 American civilians at a Hotel in Kabul. All Americans were killed.

First report was a new faction had branched out from ISIS and had been planning this attack for weeks. Sources from the State Department acknowledged President Chesterfield had been briefed on the intelligence and refused requests to add more security to protect Americans.

Chesterfield looked at Felix, his eyes wide with disbelief. "Tell me I wasn't briefed on this?" he asked.

"It's bull-shit, Evan," Felix said. "I've had no intelligence whatsoever that there was a threat. No one from State has tried to contact you or me with anything regarding any potential threat."

Chesterfield seemed lost in thought. "Get Rachel in here immediately. We need to get our message out right away." Before he could finish his thought, another news flash came across his TV monitor:

Washington DC, (AP) - Two American Embassies were attacked today. First, in Bagdad, and the second Madrid, Spain. Both United States ambassadors were killed, as well as five people on their staff by what appears to be two teams of five terrorists acting with timed perfection. Once again, a breakdown in security has cost American lives.

Again, a spokesperson with the State Department and one confirmed by the CIA implied that President Chesterfield had been briefed about these pending attacks and refused to act to protect Americans.

Felix was immediately on the phone to Rachel Monroe, Trent Hall, the Secretary of Defense and the Commander of the Joint Chief's, Admiral Hollingsworth. Wilson was not very polite with his request to everyone.

The president then told Felix to call his FBI Director Chad Roberts and CIA Director Thomas Hood. He wanted to first listen to their take on what happened before he arrested their asses. Then, he wanted his Secretary of State, Carolyn Waterfall to explain herself about the press releases her team had made.

Once he was finished with them, he would begin to deal with the problem at hand. "Felix be sure everyone arrives fifteen minutes ago. I want no excuses or delays. If you need to send my US Marshalls to bring them to me in handcuffs do it," he commanded. He spun his chair around lost in thought, as he gazed at the White House lawn.

The president heard a loud groan from his Chief of Staff. He slowly spun around, and with his right hand, he signaled for Felix to speak. "Tell me," he said.

"It's all over the internet. Tomorrow Greece, Italy, and Spain are refusing to pay their next loan payment to their EU creditors. Our stock market in late trading has begun a large sell-off. The Fed is expecting tomorrow to be worse than the crash of 2008," he said, showing Chesterfield his cell phone screen.

The president was now cradling his head in his hands. He was frozen and sweating profusely. "Any suggestions?" He asked, sadly. He knew that everyone who was after his scalp would now have enough ammunition to begin impeachment proceedings.

* * * * *

Dunham was rubbing his hands together, a big smile on his face. He looked at Ellison and could see his joy too. "Well, it's finally begun. Stage Three has just started, and there is nothing Turner can do to ruin it for me. Soon I will be able to ride into the Capitol and save the day. This country will be begging me to help. Let's start moving on getting Chesterfield out. Vice-President Allan Preston has no backbone for any of this and will be easily manipulated."

As Ellison left Dunham's home office and closed the door, Dunham was on the phone calling the AP's reporter to confirm his news conference today. What he was about to do to put himself in the public eye was beyond anything his father, grandfather, and great grandfather ever did. The Dunham family had always stayed behind the scenes funneling their money to the men and women who could help their ambitions toward their goal...financial control of the United States. He knew that today was the day to come out of the shadows.

Albert Dunham knew Ellison would be surprised at this move. Like everything he did, he would not share his thoughts or ideas with any of his closest advisors.

Dunham more than ever needed Turner to do what she did best. He hoped she had the guts to try to expose him. Once he had started Stage Four, the reporter, if she's as good, as she claims to be, would release her story to try to soil his reputation. He was banking on that so he could ruin her character. Then, labeling her an alarmist would be the icing on the cake.

Albert knew if his plan worked there would be nothing anyone, including the president and Turner, could do to stop him. He just needed confirmation from his man at the NSA that everything was still on schedule. Once he knew everything was in place for the upcoming satellite launch, he could start Stage Five in three months.

56

Paige had laid out all of Rick's files and notes on her dining room table. She had them organized by date, then by subject matter. Bradley and Clay Thomas were reading some of the files. Both men had shocked expressions on their faces. They did not believe what he had been investigating.

"I don't believe in coincidences. Rick had stumbled upon a scary conspiracy. Why didn't he tell me what he was working on?" Paige wondered.

"I knew Rick very well. He's just like you. He wouldn't release a story or talk about one until he had gathered all the facts and evidence he needed," Clay said.

"I know. He could have run things by me."

"Yeah. And what would you have done?" asked Bradley.

"Nothing," she said sadly. "I didn't know Dunham had a story to tell back then." She took a deep breath straining to gather her energy and said. "Okay, now. What are we going to do with all of this?" she asked, pointing at the pile of files on the table.

Clay was keeping a close eye on Paige. He could see her emotions oozing out through her words every time she said or heard her husband's name. He had always remained silent when Paige was working on a story. He trusted her instincts, but on this one, he felt she might not be thinking clearly.

I want Bradley to deal with Rick's files and you to continue working on your current investigation. You're too close to this," he said. I'm not sure what PM10 is, but it seems to have Dunham's name all over it.

Paige screamed with her eyes. "That isn't going to happen. My current investigation, as far as I can see blends in perfectly with what Rick had started. If Dunham was somehow involved with my husband's death, Bradley and I will work together and sort it out. He'll know if I am unable to think clearly," she said.

Clay just shook his head. He knew better than to argue with her. "All right. But, the first sign you're making emotional decisions and not dealing with facts, I'm pulling you off this story. Is that clear?" he said sternly.

"Now that we've gotten that out of the way, here is what I'd like to do. I want to do a special show about the shadow government that is forming and how billionaires are infiltrating our political system. My focus will not be a complaint about the power of lobbyist money or getting rid of Citizens United. I want to show in detail how men like Dunham are controlling the most powerful members of Congress, especially in Chesterfield's administration."

Bradley interrupted. "We'll need to tread lightly here. What we have are reports that show a pattern of people that communicate together. What Rick has in his notes, need to be verified before we tie Dunham into something illegal. We still do not have proof that an actual conspiracy is happening..." he was interrupted when his cellphone pinged with a news alert. "Shit. Turn on the TV. You're going to be shocked at what's happening," he said.

57

Paige sat in disbelief as she watched the news explode on her TV screen. "Do you believe this will be worse than two-thousand eight?" she mumbled.

The stock market opened at 9:30 A.M. Eastern Standard Time, and as predicted, the Dow had dropped over fifteen hundred points. The European markets were set to close with their most significant drop since 2008. The tentative default from Greece, Italy, and Spain had everyone in a panic.

Forecasters had no answers as to what this might do to the world economy, especially the struggling United States economy. Every news organization had the panic button pressed. Every analyst interviewed all said the same thing. Everyone seemed distracted by the financial situation and had forgotten about the second attack against American interests in less than three weeks. Paige too was watching what the news media chose to report on:

"*We appear to be heading to another major depression, something worse than the 1929 stock market crash,"* One reporter said on CNN business watch. Another reporter attempted to show some humor, but it did not go over well with his audience. *"Look for people jumping off New York's skyscrapers, as the week progresses,"* he said, trying to force a smile on his face.

Paige could not stop staring at her TV monitor. "What just happened? Was this Stage Three in Dunham's playbook?" she moaned. "If so, he's a genius. We're going to have difficulty taking down this bastard," she said.

* * * * *

President Chesterfield was stunned. He did not need this today. He had called his Fed Chief hoping for some answers. Roslyn Chase, the Fed Chairman, her voice hoarse, tried to offer some assurance but was not too convincing. The president then began talking to his Chief of Staff, while his Secretary of State Carolyn Waterfall stayed glued to the TV monitor.

Then, Waterfall interrupted them. "Mr. President, I know we need to get the European markets stable, but we have to respond to the recent attacks.

Chesterfield drew in a deep breath before he responded. "I am at a loss. Who can I trust in my cabinet to help get a handle on all of this?"

"Sir, the attacks can be dealt with another day. Right now, we need to get Greece, Italy, and Spain to meet their debt obligation after the last bailout. We cannot allow Greece to do this again. The last restructuring of their debt was a disaster, and now Italy and Spain are trying to do the same. Europe needs to step up and solve their problems. We can no longer rescue that part of the world. We have our problems to deal with," Carter said, total exasperation stamped on her face.

Chesterfield massaged his scalp firmly, almost drawing blood. He looked at his Secretary of State. "I am assuming you do not feel up to the task. Right?"

The Secretary of State shrugged her shoulders. "I've burned that bridge once before. I have left messages with each of the respective presidents, but no callbacks. I'm being intentionally ignored," she replied, trying to mask her frustration, but unable to hide it from Chesterfield. "I believe they have lost confidence in us, especially with all the attacks we do not seem to have a clue about."

"Any suggestions, other than me, who might have some luck talking to these three idiots?" asked the president. Before the secretary could reply, a special news alert flashed on the president's TV monitor.

Chesterfield threw his arms in the air. "What else could go wrong now?" he grumbled.

Everyone in the Oval Office seemed surprised at who was appearing on the news.

A TV commentator was introducing Albert Dunham, as one of the world's wealthiest men, and America's real humanitarian. He was about to begin speaking for the first time to FOX News.

Chesterfield had met Dunham during his run for the presidency. He had a political relationship with him but did not have a close friendship with the man. The president was familiar with his philanthropy and what he seems to be doing with his wealth.

Chesterfield knew Paige Turner did not think the same way about the man and held his breath on what was about to happen. The president turned up the volume and leaned back, ready to listen.

"Mr. Dunham thank you for coming on our show to tell our viewers and the world what you want to do about what's happening in Europe," said Mark Todd, from Fox News.

"Thank you for having me," Dunham replied. "First, I want to tell everyone how appalled I am about the recent attacks on our wonderful country. I am sure President Chesterfield is doing everything within his power to find the scum who are behind these senseless murders of innocent Americans." Dunham paused to take a sip of water.

Chesterfield looked at his Chief of Staff and then his Secretary of State, a befuddled expression on his face. "Is he questioning my ability as president with his remarks?" he asked. He did not expect an answer, as he already knew what it was. He turned back to the TV to listen to Albert Dunham.

"Sorry for digressing. I am so upset about those terrorist monsters. Let me continue answering your question. What is happening in Europe is just the tip of the iceberg. If something's not done immediately, the rest of the Euro-Zone will collapse, triggering the collapse of the United States Economy. Then, China will collapse, and the financial world as we know it will no longer exist." Dunham spoke in a non-alarming tone, his appealing smile resonating well on the TV screen. *"I know the three European presidents, and have a fine relationship with each of them. I have been in communication a good part of my morning with those three leaders and will be flying out to meet with them jointly. I am confident by tomorrow this matter will resolve itself. I can assure every American I will not let our economy collapse, even if I have to inject my money and that of my closest friends, into those countries to stabilize them."*

Dunham continued with his interview for the next forty-five minutes. He talked, with specifics, about his vision for getting over twenty-five million unemployed Americans back to work, rebuilding inner-city schools, so the poor can receive the proper education that would take them out of poverty. He also told the reporter his ideas for restoring America's infrastructure with investments from the large corporations that have been reaping large profits at meager tax rates. He promised his plan would not cost the taxpayer anything.

Dunham's message was simple and easy to understand. Keep the government out of the picture and let the wealthy corporations re-invest to re-build America and make it once again the land of bountiful opportunity. He ended his interview with an enthusiastic finish.

"The United States is the greatest country on the planet, and with the help of some very wealthy corporate friends, me, and the support of every American we will finally see every American citizen working, educated, and earning a good living above the poverty line. Thank you for letting me speak today," Dunham said, waving to the camera, a big smile on his face.

Chesterfield looked at Carolyn and then at Felix. "Is he running for President? If so, I'd vote for him. What a speech. Can we let a private citizen negotiate with a foreign country, let alone three countries?"

Felix was not so confident. "I do not think there is anything in the constitution that prevents a businessman talking with and or making deals with a foreign country. But, let's not get too excited. I remember another billionaire who became President with a bunch of solutions that never materialized," said the Chief of Staff.

"That might have been so then, but Dunham sounds sincere and is willing to stick his neck out first before taking any credit. Can you get him on the phone for me? I want to talk to him before he flies out," Chesterfield asked. "Then, after that, get Paige Turner on the phone. I need her to stop whatever she's doing that involves Dunham."

* * * * *

Dunham slid into his Malbec. He immediately called Ellison. "What did you think?" he asked eagerly.

Ellison hesitated for a second, trying to gather his thoughts. "You sounded like you're running for President already. I'm confused. This move today is unlike you. What's up with that?"

"I saw an opportunity and took it. If my calculations are correct, this could make me...I mean us, over nine hundred and fifty billion dollars. Almost a twenty percent return on the investment I plan on making."

"I don't see it. How can you be so sure Europe and the United States will support what you want to do?" Ellison said skeptically.

"You never did understand how to make big money. You're a good loyal friend, but you would not have your billions of dollars if not for my vision. Don't sweat the small details. Wait until I return from Europe." Dunham saw on his cars TV screen that the Dow had stopped falling and was making a correction. His interview had worked. "Turn on CNBC and see for yourself. I just made two hundred billion dollars in just two hours. Remember, buy low and sell high," he said, laughing before he hung up on his friend. He was getting a call from the President and did not want to miss it.

"Hello, this is Albert Dunham," he answered, knowing full well it was the president calling.

"President Chesterfield here, Mr. Dunham. I just heard your interview and was intrigued by what you're proposing to ward-off the economic disaster in Europe."

Dunham tried to hold back the chuckle that was oozing out between his lips. "Just trying to be a good citizen, sir. If what I plan to do is acceptable to those countries, then I've done my job."

"I'd like my Secretary of State to attend your meeting," the president asked.

Dunham held back his response for almost fifteen seconds, which he knew would feel like a lifetime to the Chesterfield. "I don't know how to say this, but all three presidents do not want to deal with your administration on this matter. It's either me or default," he said smugly.

Chesterfield was caught off-guard. He was at a loss for words. "That makes no sense. The EU is unwilling to help, and they are refusing help from us?"

"I'm afraid so. I hope I can calm the three presidents down and work a good deal for all of us," Dunham said.

"I don't like it, but I will give you one-hundred percent of my support. However, I will be sending Secretary Waterfall to the meeting in an unofficial capacity, to show them, and the world that this president and our country will be there to support them."

Dunham was delighted. "That will be perfect Mr. president. I must go over a day earlier to set up all the small details of the deal I'm proposing. I will send your Chief of Staff the exact location and time of the meeting. It was a pleasure finally getting to talk with you," Dunham said.

58

Turner and Bradley had Dean Miller on Skype. All three of them did not know what to make of the Dunham interview. With all of Rick's files and what they already had from the thumb drive Russell had given them, nothing was making sense now. Paige was beginning to question her instincts about this man.

"My experience interviewing guys like him over the years has shown they have a harder shell to crack. On the outside, their public appearance, they appear credible, but when that external facade cracks with unrefutable evidence, you uncover a financial agenda lurking under the surface. Their good deed is a distraction," said Turner. "Pardon me for being skeptical. I don't believe anyone is that selfless.

"Well, I'm impressed with Dunham's vision and promises," said Miller. "He sounds like the perfect guy to get this crisis handled. You believe there's a catch to what he's saying?" Dean asked.

Paige shrugged her shoulders, doubt showing on her face. "All I know is this is the first time he's gone on TV for an interviewed," she said. "All we have are these files Russell stole, and nothing proving they came from Dunham or Ellison's computer. There are three murders associated with the Architect's Manifesto. We know Dunham is one of the wealthiest men in the world and had loved his privacy until now. The only thing we know for sure is he's a philanthropist. He supports worthy causes. His family goes back to the late eighteen-hundreds. A little too secretive for my liking, but he seems to use his family fortune for worthy purposes. And, now the current heir seems to be changing his family's original manifesto. It's not making sense."

Bradley was not so impressed. "Remember what we're doing. Paige, your friend, was murdered because of these dossiers, which were made to appear like diaries. We know for sure that Seth Alexander, Dean's intern, was killed by Frasier Montgomery who by all indications knew Dunham in high school, and we believe works for him now. And, our friend Sean Adams, is dead, murdered by fucking Frasier Montgomery. Another notch on his belt," Stevens said, noticeably upset. "This billionaire is the perfect example of your *Corrupted Intelligence* theory, and he needs to be exposed."

"So, what are you saying?" Paige asked.

"I'm saying let's not forget about our current investigation and not be distracted by Dunham's antics. If he's conspiring to create a shadow government and maybe become the next Julius Caesar, this meeting he has set up in Europe might be part of his overall scheme. It's the perfect way to win over the hearts and minds of every American and people around the world and cast doubt on president Chesterfield as a strong leader."

Professor Miller seemed more curious. "I wonder how the Dunham family got their fortune. I know the late eighteen-hundreds were filled with families building wealth on the backs of hard-working Americans. Some of the early stories are not so flattering on how they accumulated their money," he said. "Maybe I should run Dunham's family through my software and see what pops up. We've found everyone connected to him, but not who connects to his family. It could be an interesting read of an American dynasty. I'll try to see if find any trace of financial transactions before and after each of these jolts to the stock market."

Turner seemed lost in thought, processing what the professor just said. "Good idea. Maybe I should interview him?

One thing I know is that we need to wait on exposing him until we have more evidence."

Miller was already punching in some keywords when a thought popped into his head. "Turner can a private citizen act as a diplomat for our country without presidential approval?"

Turner, her eyebrows raised said. "That's a good question. I'm not sure.

Bradley was shaking his head. "If Dennis Rodman can go to North Korea and try to make nice with that crazy leader, then Dunham can do whatever he wants as long as he's not making deals for the USA."

"Dean run whatever search you can on the Dunham family and then see if Albert Dunham made some interesting profits in our fluctuating stock market," Paige said.

59

After Turner signed off on Skype, Professor Miller started his search. He did not know exactly how he wanted to trace the family history of the Dunhams. They had been a very secretive family, staying in the background for over a hundred years, hiding from public scrutiny. He knew one thing about the wealthy, they did at times hang out together, and maybe his software could find some meaningful data that would help explain who Albert Dunham was and who he wants to become.

Miller typed in three of the wealthiest families he knew of from previous searches he had done during the testing stages of his software. J.P Morgan, John D. Rockefeller, and Andrew Carnegie. He knew there were others but figured if he started small, it would make his search more manageable. If this worked, it would build a massive collection of people who had or currently have some connection to the above three men.

As the searches were spitting out information, one continuous piece of information kept showing up. From the late nineteenth century to the twenty-first century, the Dunham family had some connection to these three men and their business conglomerates.

The first Dunham appeared to have built his fortune following the path of J.P. Morgan, J.D. Rockefeller, and Andrew Carnegie but targeted his fortune creating business conglomerates in Europe, Asia, and the Middle East. The countries and leaders that had come aboard his plan gave him free rein to accumulate his wealth. Miller was not sure why he took that route outside of American interests; nevertheless, he now had something to search. He began entering more keywords to see what would be flowing out onto his computer screen. What started spewing out was getting him very excited. One strange item caught his eye. He had never heard the term PM10 before Paige mentioned she found it in her husband's last news piece.

"Why would the Dunham pharmaceutical company concern itself with PM10?" Dean typed in some more keywords and waiting for his software to do its job.

After about three hours, he had created a frightening picture of the Dunham family. His next job was to begin doing keyword searches using the encrypted keywords inside each of the files. He understood it would take longer and went searching for his wife and kids. He needed some quiet family time.

60

The meeting room at the American Embassy in Rome was filled with reporters, both international, and from the United States. President Chesterfield had had his Secretary of State reserve the embassy ahead of time to project to Europe and the world that POTUS was sponsoring the meeting.

Albert Dunham was not too happy with it being in the embassy, as he had to cancel his most desired location at the ancient Colosseum. His stage had been set so he'd appear like Julius Caesar, helping the citizens of the world. President Chesterfield had outplayed him after their phone call.

He had to settle for a large oval twelve-foot conference table instead. For him, it worked out perfectly once he had seen a photo of the conference room.

Inside the large hall was a carved mahogany king lion gothic throne chair, resting in the back corner of the room. *That will do nicely,* he told himself.

He demanded to be seated on it and at the head of the table, facing the cameras. The three presidents from Italy, Spain, and Greece were ideally placed to his left and right to provide maximum exposure from the cameras and reporters. The Secretary of State at her embassy had been seated at the far end of the conference table, away from Dunham and the others attending the meeting and out of camera view.

It was apparent to the Secretary of State that this was Dunham's show, and he did not want anyone from Chesterfield's cabinet to be part of what he wanted to accomplish. She was told ahead of time that she was not going to be part of the negotiations.

Dunham did not waste any time. With both arms resting on the carved padded arms, his fingers caressing the dark wood he was a man acting like he was about to have an orgasm.

He sucked in a deep breath, forcing himself to get control of his emotions. "Gentlemen and Lady," he said, acknowledging everyone cordially. "I am happy you've agreed to meet today to stem off an economic catastrophe." With the grace of a well-seasoned diplomat, he looked directly at the cameras and smiled. He repeated the greeting in Spanish, Italian, and Greek, his accent perfect.

He passed out three manila folders, excluding the Secretary of State intentionally. Earlier, he had been briefed by Todd Mathews and was thrilled at how much money he had made with the last two market crashes. It now was easy for him to make the deal he was about to tell the world.

Dunham started nodding his head as he stared into the cameras.

"What you have in front of you is an agreement signed by over fifty corporate CEOs doing business around the world, including your respective countries. Like me, they've all agreed to inject enough capital into each of your countries to help you pay off your existing debt. There will be enough money to help put almost every person wanting to work, back to work." The cameras were flashing madly, and the reporters were inching their way past the Secretary of State to make sure their mics could hear every word Dunham had to say.

Dunham shrugged his shoulders, his eyebrows raised, apologizing to the Secretary for being left out. Little did anyone know he was beaming on the inside, as he was accomplishing exactly what he wanted with this part of Stage Four. He watched the scowl on Waterfall's face grow. He held back his urge to clap. He was in charge and loving it.

He turned his attention back to the three men who were there to negotiate. They already understood their deal that was agreed to almost three weeks ago during his first trip to their countries. Nevertheless, he proceeded to talk to them, as if this was the first time they had met and read their country's contract.

Secretary Waterfall looked stunned. *"He's doing my job,"* she told herself.

Dunham looked at her as if he knew what she was thinking and gave her a wink. "There is one stipulation you all have to agree with, so this process will work for your new investors and the citizens of your respective countries. I have listed some simple austerity measures each of you will have to implement immediately. Most importantly, your new investors will have to be exempt from any corporate taxes until these new loans are fully paid back. Each of you will have one week to approve this deal, or it will be pulled. As a show of good faith, I have negotiated on your behalf a week's extension for your upcoming debt payments. If this works, you will no longer owe your European banks any money. Your new creditors will be working with you to make your economies prosperous."

Secretary Waterfall seemed shocked by Dunham's proposal, and at the same time impressed with his overall plan. She wanted to speak, maybe ask a question, but thought better of it. He was in full control. He had the attention of everyone. She understood that she was witnessing for the first time how large corporations were going to be able to control how a country lived day-to-day. *"Shit is this how he is going to take control of the United States as EOTUS,"* she mouthed silently. She continued talking to herself. *"This never would have been approved by congress without months, maybe years of speeches and partisan bickering."* She sat back and just watched what was to happen next.

The president of Greece was the first to stand and applaud. Next followed the president of Italy, and then the president of

Spain. The three men all shook hands. Italy's president hugged Dunham and kissed both his cheeks. Though the cameras were flashing, wanting to capture this historic moment, Dunham for the first time seemed uncomfortable. However, like any smart businessman, politician, and now diplomat, he, without missing a beat, allowed his charming smile to return.

If this part of his plan worked, he'd have more control over Europe than Germany. He would finally achieve what his great grandfather had wanted at the beginning of the twentieth century.

Except for the official signing of the agreements, the meeting ended with the four men leaving through the meeting room doors. Dunham had reserved a private villa for their celebratory lunch he had catered. Secretary Waterfall was left sitting by herself dazed by what had just happened.

* * * * *

The news media was all abuzz about what one wealthy man, Albert Dunham, was able to accomplish, what no other country, even the mighty United States, with President Chesterfield, as the leader of the free world, could do.

The world markets were making one of the most significant reversals in history. People on the streets of Greece, Italy, and Spain were dancing and hugging each other. For the first time in decades, unemployment would be almost non-existent for those countries that have seen upwards of twenty-five percent unemployment for years. While Dunham had accomplished a significant feat, only his closest advisors knew how much money he had made in one day that he would use to pay his portion of the deal.

While his portfolio was skyrocketing, the hedge funds his billionaire friends who were part of this deal, we about to make a fortune on top of the profits they'd be receiving from what these three countries were about to give them.

Back in the United States, Dunham, a man a few days ago who was unknown to the average American, was a national hero. The Fed Chairman was on the news claiming that working with big business to build up America's economy could become the new norm for doing business. People were calling for a ticker-tape parade for Dunham.

61

Paige and Bradley, with Professor Miller back on Skype, were not as happy as the rest of the world. They knew who he was and needed a sound plan to expose him. What had been uncovered by the professor's recent search told a very different story.

However, his money was going to be the one card that could keep him out of jail. They went back to review the most recent report Miller had prepared and found it shocking, as well as confusing. The close connections Dunham had with some very questionable political and business leaders around the world were alarming. The report also had Dunham weeks earlier meeting with Greece's, Italy's and Spain's presidents making it appear that this debt default was just a stunt to manipulate the markets, as well as elevate Dunham as a national hero.

"I am not sure how to present this to the president, but I think he needs to see this," Turner said, doubt floating in her voice. "First, I need to investigate if Dunham and these helpful billionaires profited from the recent crash of the international markets. I believe this could be the biggest shift of assets in modern history," she said.

Professor Miller replied. "I can run a detailed report of their connections with each other, but getting a line on their investments is above the capabilities of my software. Maybe Chesterfield can make it happen? He sees the bigger picture and can advise us what he wants us to do next."

"Fine. Right now, I must get ready for my Sunday show. I'm unsure of what or how I will present the Dunham that my viewers have seen."

"I heard you before. You're an honest and factual reporter. I am confident you'll do the right thing here," Miller said, his voice sounding grave as his Skype connection was having problems streaming.

"This is different. Dunham has won over the American public and the world in one single day. Proving he's connected to some bad people or even making him out to be this horrible madman who wants to be the next Julius Caesar will prove very difficult or make me appear crazy. It will make me seem like a conspiracy theorist. History has shown that money, good jobs, national security, will allow everyone to overlook the truth," Paige said.

Bradley interrupted. "I was able to get into Sean's cloud account. I'm still trying to interpret what he had uncovered about Dunham. It seems that his pharmaceutical company might be intentionally poisoning Americans and people around the world," he said, sucking in a deep breath. "The bastard has been for over two decades infecting innocent people with his poison pesticide and selling them the only drugs that can cure them or force them to keep using them. I need to keep digging. I hope this will be Dunham's downfall."

Paige for the first time since Dunham's international show, let a smile grow on her face. "Does this possible crime tie into what Rick was working on that got him shot?"

Bradley shrugged his shoulders. "I don't know yet, but I will be looking into it pronto."

"Please be careful."

62

Dunham wrapped up a heated conversation with Ellison. "You know that's unacceptable. There's too much at stake right now. Find Frasier and dispose of him," he yelled.

Frederick was irritable. "I'm doing the best I can. Frasier must have realized, after his last two fuckups, he needed to disappear. That's something he's very good at," said Ellison.

Dunham's voice got louder. "If Frasier is in survival mode, then none of us are safe. He might just be hiding, waiting for the right moment to finish his job and come after all of us," he said, his tone taking on a nervous edge. "Keep looking for the ass-hole. I will be home in two days."

Dunham knew he needed to have these loose ends put to rest before he moved on to Stage Five. Right now, he had one more meeting in the Middle East to handle. Then Stage Four would be finished.

His cellphone pinged. He was getting his reminder about Paige Turner's show. This time it was different. She was pre-empting another news shows with an urgent news alert. Dunham clicked on his TV in his hotel suite and leaned back on his couch to watch. "This should be interesting," he said. "What could this pain-in-the-ass reporter have to report?"

* * * * *

Paige had one minute before she aired and was facing a problem that could shatter the reputation she had built over the last ten years. After talking with Bradley and Dean, she knew the direction she needed to take. She expanded her lungs, letting in a deep calming breath and opened with the same introduction she did for every show.

"Good morning, afternoon, and evening to all of my loyal listeners in the United States and around the world. I am Paige Turner, and this is a special segment of 'Corrupted Intelligence, The Manipulation of the American People.

"Today, one of America's great men, did something that governments were unable to do. This one man was able to stem the economic catastrophe that was happening earlier this morning. Albert Dunham will soon become a household name that will be loved by hundreds of millions of Americans. Unlike many wealthy families who have helped make America great, the Dunham family goes back to the late eighteen hundred's, building a family legacy that should inspire every citizen that the American Dream is alive and well.

They built their fortune, helping the United States grow economically and providing tens of thousands of jobs for hardworking Americans. I, like most of you, want to know more about Albert Dunham and his family. So, over the next few weeks, I will have my investigative team trace this family's history, so we can rightfully see the role they've played in our young history. Paige took a moment to pause and released a deep sigh. She already knew the answer. She wanted to act like she was impressed with the man who she believes was responsible for all the recent attacks on American soil and the murder of two of her friends.

"But first, I need to report on some sad news. As I said a few days ago, my friend and college roommate, Brian Russell was brutally murdered because of a thumb drive containing files about a conspiracy within our country. Since my investigation started, two more friends were killed because of these files.

I believe that the person responsible for these murders is Frasier Montgomery," On the TV monitor a video showing him behind the wheel of his SUV the moment he killed Seth Alexander, and another video of him leaving the train car where Sean Adams and four innocent bystanders were shot.

Paige swiped a tear off her cheek and continued. *"With the help of Professor Dean Miller, the leading expert in cybersecurity, he has been able to build an interesting timeline of everyone that Frasier Montgomery has associated with over the last ten years. With some more verification, these reports will be given to the proper authorities to help in their investigations."* Paige bowed her head dramatically before she continued.

"My investigation is getting close to exposing this conspiracy. Today, I am convinced that there is one man, the remaining heir to his family's evil plan who is now well into completing his five Stages in his sick Manifesto. After what's already happened in our country and around the world, it is my estimation the Architect has completed four of his five stages.

As most of you know, my husband Rick Turner had been murdered five years ago. I have uncovered inside the paperwork of his last investigation, a story about a wealthy family and a Shadow Government conspiracy happening behind the back of our former president. After reading my husband's file notes, which included a detailed account of who he believed was the puppet master of this conspiracy..." Paige paused, taking in a calming breath and continued, *"I now believe that the man and family my husband was investigating is the the Architect, I am looking into currently.* Turner paused to clear her throat and take a sip of water before continuing.

"As I kept reading and researching the data in each of the files Brian Russell had sent me, it has become evident that this man is getting ready to finalize his plan that could forever change the United States as we now know it.

"I know I am getting close. I believe this same man authorized Frasier Montgomery to murder Seth Alexander, an intern at UCLA, who had been deep into his investigation of this Architect. I believe this man ordered the murder of one of my reporters, Sean Adams, along with four other people." she clicked a button, and Frasier Montgomery's face appeared on the screen again... *"and I believe this murderer works for this Architect,"* Paige stared into the camera and spoke.

"I wonder if Albert Dunham can shed some light on this conspiracy since Montgomery is a close friend of his. You're a great American and seem to have your hand in some notable events. Maybe you can shed some light on this family, and this Architect?

Paige kept staring into the camera lens and made a plea. *"Mr. Dunham. America needs your help now."*

She gathered up her notes and Dunham's files. She imagined the interview with him and how she would show him on National TV the records she had, and watch his reaction. Would he admit or deny the writings were his? Now it was a waiting game. She prayed that Bradley would add more to her file detailing this man's pharmaceutical illegal operations.

63

Dunham did not believe Turner could be so brash. He found it humorous. "She doesn't know what's going to happen. I'm going to enjoy watching her destroyed of everything she holds dear...especially her goody-two-shoes reputation."

He told his pilot his new flight plan. He had one ace up his sleeve just in case Turner was getting close. He had to use it. Dunham had set up this meeting a week ago with the Israeli and Palestinian Prime Ministers, as well as the leader of Hamas. Since he kept his promise to Israel to put Iran back to the stone-age, it was time for him to call in his chips and get the Jewish State to compromise and find peace in the region.

Dunham knew he needed to saturate the news cycle with his accomplishments. He wanted his actions to dilute Turner's breaking news, keeping Stage Five on target and out of everyone's radar. The satellite launch was more important than any of these external world events he had created and solved.

The press conference had been set up in Jerusalem for the world to see, the two long-time enemies sign a significant peace accord that would open the borders and allow for easy passage between the two countries. What made this even more poetic was a non-political figure, a mere businessman, a citizen of the world accomplishing this feat.

For Dunham, it was just another step toward his overall plan to become the most powerful man in the world. This media event would complete his Stage Four.

If Palestine and the Gaza Strip agreed, as well as Israel, everyone, especially the Palestinians would finally receive the infusion of funds they needed to help develop their infrastructure and give their citizens a life filled with hope, not bloodshed. What it would do for Dunham of course, would increase his wealth, as his companies and his inner circle, would be the first to benefit from the economic growth in that region.

Now he was getting closer to being worshiped as America's savior. Once the long-awaited satellite was in orbit, it would give him more power than he could ever imagine.

He knew he had some hurdles to jump over. The first one was named Paige Turner. He had to maneuver and position himself now, so nothing Turner would say or expose about his family's manifesto or his current files would come back to his family or himself in a negative way. His thoughts were interrupted as he felt the wheels of his plane touch ground in Jerusalem. His white limo was waiting to take him to his meeting, but not before a brief talk in front of the media.

Hamas was reluctant at first, but after Dunham promised them the financial aid they needed, and pressure from Russia to agree, they were slowly coming on board. All parties were skeptical and untrusting, but they made promises that needed to be kept...at least for the time being. They all needed capital to rebuild their countries, and this meeting would guarantee it.

Israel wanted a significant political change in the United States, and Palestine wanted an equal footing with Israel. Hamas just had to agree to stop fighting for a least two years. Dunham had the power to make all of this happen. If it worked, he would solidify the political position he wanted.

64

The breaking news about the Middle East summit in Jerusalem took every news organization by storm. The only reporters who were able to cover the impromptu meeting, where the embedded media staff that had been covering the news and the bloodshed for years in that region.

Dunham was slowly becoming a *Master of Media* manipulation. He had released his revised schedule to the journalists he knew were in Jerusalem, with the hope they would have their numerous camera crews filming his plane landing, recording his brief speech on the tarmac, and follow his motorcade to the meeting site. The only thing missing for him was the American flags waving on the front of his vehicle. He knew that this would be coming soon.

Waiting for him at the summit location were the three leaders from Israel, Palestine, and Hamas, all standing at the end of a red carpet, laid out for their new friend. Cameras were snapping this historic event. The current mortal enemies were shown shaking hands. They sat in three seats to the right of Dunham's podium, and once they were seated, he started his speech.

"Good afternoon. My name is Albert Dunham, a proud American businessman who wants to see our world achieve its potential. I want to infuse money into Israel and Palestine, as well as Gaza. Today will be a great first step toward an end to all the fighting and killing that has been going on in this region for decades. If these leaders cannot control the mistrust that goes back hundreds of years and create a new beginning, none of my efforts will work." Dunham, like a seasoned politician, paused long enough for the camera flashes to capture the moment and the applause to die down.

Dunham put his arms up, and with a big smile, signaled everyone to quiet down. "Since the nineteen-seventies, American presidents have tried to bring peace to this holy land without much success. Centuries of mistrust and the inability to forgive have kept this region at war," he paused to take a sip of his water. He did not want to choke on his words that he did not believe. "Today, after months of negotiations behind closed doors, and away from the news media, I am pleased to announce that Israel, Palestine, and the Gaza Strip with Hamas's support, will sign a five-year historic peace agreement that will finally bring lasting peace and economic growth to this region." Dunham turned to the three men to his right and asked them to come forward to join him at the podium.

"Let's join hands and show the world how when good people help good people peace can happen," Dunham shouted raising his arms, forcing the others to mimic him and stretch their arms high above their heads. To his surprise, the three leaders were smiling.

"Before I go, I want to express my thanks to these great men for taking a bold and brave step for their respective countries and citizens. I will say to all the news media and media pundits to find the silver lining to what you've witnessed today. Stop trying to find the angles, the reasons any of this won't work, and try to join in and share what just happened in front of your viewers. You have a big responsibility to show the world good news can happen," he said. Dunham in a surprising move looked at the cameras and said, "Paige Turner, I will call you when I return, and we can have the interview you want."

It took thirty minutes for the agreement to be signed. Each leader gave a speech. Dunham then allowed a few selected journalists to ask questions.

The first question came from an associated press reporter. "Mr. Dunham, did President Chesterfield approve of this summit? Did he even know you were in negotiations with these leaders?"

"President Chesterfield did not know about my meeting. I did not want to burden him with more problems after the recent bombings in Iran and the United States. I feel that as a businessman and citizen of the United States, it was my civic duty to try to bring a sense of lasting peace to the Middle East. A non-political person can get so much more done without all the bureaucratic bullshit that seems to be riddling our congress and executive office. I wanted to take the blame if this summit failed and that's why I kept everyone in the dark until the peace accord was signed," Dunham said, panning the shocked expressions on all the journalist's faces. After another forty-five minutes of taking questions, Dunham went back to his plane and headed back to the United States.

* * * * *

Paige and her team had been watching Dunham's speech. All of them were shocked at what just happened. Bradley looked at Turner, his eyes wide with disbelief. Dean Miller was applauding while on Skype. He was already on his laptop, plugging in some search options.

"Shit, the arrogant bastard just screwed us. I am damned if I do and damned if I don't. I haven't given Dunham enough credit. He's a masterful genius," Paige remarked, the color drained from her face. "He just might pull this off and become the next leader...shit Emperor of the United States."

Bradley stood and started to pace around the room, nodding his head, something he did when he was pissed and thinking. "What's our next move?" He asked.

Paige was slowly shaking her head. "I don't know. He's unlike any businessman I've ever encountered. What I do know is that he wants to come into my court for an interview. I must be ready. She looked at Bradley; her brain was on fire processing what she had to do to expose Dunham as the Architect.

65

President Chesterfield and Felix Wilson could not believe what they had just heard. Wilson was on the phone trying to track down the Secretary of State to see what her take was on all of this.

"How the fuck could he do what all recent presidents have attempted to do, and get it done just like that? Chesterfield asked, knowing no one had a logical answer. "Any luck tracking down Carolyn?"

"No one's seen or heard from her since she left Rome the other day. All the State Department knows is that she wasn't returning home first. She had one personal errand she wanted to make. I've tried to call her, but she's not answering her phone."

Chesterfield seemed surprised. "Is she hiding from me? She never deviates from her set itinerary. What about her security detail? They are never out of communication."

Felix had a puzzled look on his face. "There has been no communication from any of them, sir," he said, shrugging his shoulders. "They are always in contact with their home office on an hourly basis. I'm beginning to worry. It's not like her not to check-in," the president's Chief of Staff said, his concerned expression had Chesterfield anxious.

"Get everyone on this. I want Waterfall found today. I need her here with me to figure out what's going on inside her fucking State Department."

"Sir, we have a bigger problem. Today, the house judiciary committee voted to start a formal impeachment inquiry. They are getting underway as we speak. I need to go there and listen to what they believe they have that justifies tossing you out of office." Felix sensed the president wasn't too concerned, but he did not trust the dirty dozen who have been trying to ruin his presidency since the election.

"If I were on the other team, I'd impeach me for what's been going on. Now I look like an idiot with no control over foreign policy or my administration. Go do what will make you happy, but first, find my Secretary of State."

Chesterfield leaned back in his chair and swung it around to stare at the front White House lawn, something that was becoming a habit lately. He knew he was a shrewd politician and understood how to win over the public. However, the unprecedented actions that Dunham had been crafting and was continuing to massage were scaring the holy shit out of him. If this guy wasn't running for President, he needed to know what his real motives were. No one he knew did the type of things he just did without an angle.

Chesterfield buzzed his secretary. "Call Dunham. I need him here to brief me on what the hell he just did," he ordered.

The president knew that Albert Dunham was unlike any wealthy American he's ever known. He was on the surface, acting in the best interests of America, but something seemed a little too easy and organized. He knew that foreign diplomacy never worked this easy without the other countries wanting something in return.

Everyone wants something, and Dunham was not that different. He didn't know what angle he was promoting. Chesterfield thought it might not hurt to have this billionaire in his corner if the impeachment hearings get a footing inside the House.

* * * * *

Dunham was on his secured line while airborne back to the United States. "We did very well today. Once my country has its upcoming elections, and Chesterfield is either impeached before or not re-elected, then you will have your wish regarding Israel. Patience is a good Muslim virtue; something your people have forgotten.

Hassim Arwardi, the leader of Hamas, held his tongue. He hated Dunham for how he had turned his back on his men a few years back, a time when they worked so well together. He knew Dunham was a man who could not be trusted.

Arwardi said, his tone threatening. "I have just so much patience. No more than two years and you'll give me the missiles I need to destroy Israel...correct?"

"No. It's for five years. You must stick to our plan you've agreed to for the signed timeframe. You saw what I could do to a country like Iran. So, your little strip of land you call Gaza will be no problem for me to level to the ground. I have enough military support and weapons to wipe you and your people off the face of the earth. Just be a good little Muslim and follow my orders this time and all your wishes will come true." He disconnected the call before Hassim could say another word.

Dunham's last call was to his wife, Maggie. "Did you see me on the news?" he asked eagerly. Her approval meant the world to him.

"Yes, darling. I am so proud of you. When are you coming home to me?" she asked with the seductive voice that drove him crazy.

"Soon. I have one more stop before we're together. I've missed you so much. Thank you for supporting my work. I know it takes time away from us, but the world...our country needs me. All of this means so much to me."

He laid his head back on his seat; a big smile appeared on his face. What he had been planning was finally coming to fruition. He remembered he had to make another phone call. He had never felt so empowered before and was enjoying every minute of it.

He called the Israeli Prime Minister to thank him for his cooperation. "Saul, I am very pleased you kept your end of our deal. I know it took a lot of chutzpah, to go against your citizens," Dunham said. "I hope your upcoming election goes well for you."

The Prime Minister, a man with a short fuse for a temper, sucked in a deep breath and held back his hatred toward Dunham. "Let's not attempt to be friends. What you did for Israel to eliminate our worst threat on our existence is appreciated. I don't owe you anymore. Is that clear?" Saul Levin said. He was an American-born Jew.

"Saul, any idea you had that we might have been friends is ridiculous. You know how I feel about Israel and the Jewish people. If I had my way, it would have been your country's nuclear weapons I would have destroyed, not Iran's. Those hundred nuclear missiles you have are way too much for such a pain in the neck country that continues to milk the guilt from everyone for the Holocaust. It's been over for almost three-quarters of a century. Get over it and move on," he said sarcastically.

The Prime Minister would have shot him on the spot if he had said those things in person. "You're a bastard, and one day the world will know you for who you truly are," he replied sternly.

Dunham just laughed. "I'm a hero around the world and soon will have enough power to bring you to your knees, begging to kiss my ring. Now, the next time I need a favor, you'll say yes. Don't piss me off, Mr. Prime Minister." He ended the call before Saul could respond.

He pulled his manifesto from his briefcase and began writing. He had a few more ideas he wanted to work out on paper. Then a short nap.

66

President Chesterfield's press secretary, Rachel Monroe, was a family friend, and a retired political commentator who came on board because she believed he would be a great president. She hated how the press and everyone in the Senate and House treated him. After what had just happened in Europe and Jerusalem, she knew her president was going to get both barrels from the White House Press Corps and laid down some ground rules.

"Ladies and Gentlemen, President Chesterfield will be out here shortly to comment on the major event that happened today in the Middle East. He will also address the deal that took place with Italy, Spain, and Greece. The president will then open the floor to questions that you have regarding all the recent terrorist attacks. However, he will not take any questions regarding the recent bombings at our airports and train stations. It's an ongoing investigation, and until he has concrete answers for you and the American people, he will not address that issue. Be assured the attacks on our Homeland is our number one priority and every law enforcement agency we have is working twenty-four-seven on finding the terrorists who murdered so many Americans," she paused, taking in a deep breath, as she welcomed the president.

"So, if we can get started..." she turned to her right and announced the president's arrival. "The President of the United States."

The entire briefing room stood and immediately sat when the president was at the podium.

"Thank you all for being here on such short notice...oh, yes I forgot, you guys and gals are here as much as I am," he said awkwardly trying to make a joke. Only a few of the members of the press laughed.

"Today, we witnessed a historic event in the Middle East, something six presidents before me could not do. While I am happy that the region will work toward long-term, lasting peace, I am concerned that we do not know the details of their agreement with each other. While it is wonderful that a man like Albert Durham could accomplish such a feat without any other country's help. It concerns me that Israel is making secret agreements without our knowledge. Our long-standing treaties with Israel could be in jeopardy, as well as the structure of our other agreements within that region."

A reporter sitting in the back of the room yelled out a question. "Mr. President, do you find it strange that lately you've been left out of the loop on a whole host of major worldwide events?"

Rachel was rushing onto the stage to scold the reporter when Chesterfield raised his hand to stop her. "That's a valid question that I will try to answer." The president panned the small briefing room, closed his eyes, deep in thought.

"I recognize that our country has had numerous terrorist attacks over the past few weeks here and around the world. As president, I am trying to come to grips with it all." Chesterfield saw the shocked faces, as his words registered inside their minds. He watched a dozen arms rise wanting to ask the next of many questions. "I know you all are anxious to hear from me about these events, but I am not ready to answer any of them.

"First, here is what our country is dealing with right now. We have an FBI Director and CIA Director who are baffled about the bombings at our train stations and airports. That should not be happening. We have the best intelligence agencies in the world," he paused, knowing his statements were only making things worse.

He signaled all the raised arms down. "I know what I've been saying is shocking. I want to be transparent with the American public. We do, like Paige Turner reported the other day on her show, have too many people inside our government that have interests that are not benefitting every citizen. Today, I am beginning an internal investigation of my Cabinet and the entire administration. I will be announcing some big changes within my administration and will bring our government back to its constitutional checks and balances that our founders envisioned. My first order of business has been to replace Director Roberts and Director Hood." President Chesterfield did not want to mention that the two men had been arrested on treason charges yesterday. He pointed to a female reporter in the third row. "Hi, Stacy. It's your turn."

"As a reporter that's been covering presidents for the last sixteen years, I find all of this shocking and unbelievable that you, as our president, do not seem to have a good grip on what's happening in your administration, on our soil, and around the globe. How can you ask the citizens of this country to re-elect you as their president and commander and chief?" she asked.

"That's a very fair question. One that I have been asking myself for the last few weeks. I take full responsibility for everything that has happened under my watch as your president. However, like all presidents before me, trust in the people you pick to be in your cabinet and the men and women you pick to run the most powerful agencies in the world are not required to run every decision they make by me. I thought I had appointed people I could trust and who understood the direction I wanted for our country. That doesn't seem to be the case."

Another reporter jumped up and asked a question. "Mr. President, I have two questions, both related. First, have you spoken to Paige Turner about her ongoing investigation and the one her husband had been doing before he was murdered? Second, is there any credible connection to the Iranian bombings, and the attacks on our soil and embassies?"

President Chesterfield did not want to address any of those events, but the reporter's questions were valid for this briefing. "As far as we all know, no known terrorist organization has claimed responsibility for these attacks. Right now, we are focusing on a few known groups, American born groups, that could have possibly caused those bombings. Also, with the devastating attack on Iran, it is becoming clear that we have a new terrorist organization that is trying to start a major world conflict." One reporter interrupted Chesterfield, but the president kept his cool and continued talking, ignoring the question.

"I have created a special task force, using our US Marshalls, who are looking into these incidents on our soil, and their investigation is ongoing. Arrests will soon be happening, and you will all know within weeks who the real traitors are." He paused, looking at the reporters in front of him, noticing they all had puzzled expressions.

The president raised his hand, signaling them to wait on their questions. "I will have answers for all of you and the American public within a week or two. One thing I can say is that this terrorist organization appears to be homegrown and not associated with any Islamic Jihadist group based on the intelligence we have so far. I will end this press conference by answering the first question. I am not worried about any pending impeachment hearings. I will say that the *Dirty Dozen* should be careful about what they wish for," he was hoping the threat would resonate into their chambers. "Those who live in glass houses, should not throw stones," the president said. "My only concern right now is to win back the trust of the American citizens I took an oath to protect and defend." With that, he turned to his right and walked away from the podium.

* * * * *

President Chesterfield marched into the Oval Office immediately after his press conference. He was noticeably upset. His face had turned beet red. He knew he might have put his foot in his mouth, but he had decided to act tough and presidential. He knew he had nothing to lose.

A smile cracked on his face when he saw sitting on one of the two couches was Admiral Hollingsworth, Chairman of the Joint Chiefs, Trent Hall his Secretary of Defense, and his Attorney General Marilyn Sawyer. Sitting on the other couch were FBI Director Chad Roberts and CIA Director Thomas Hood in handcuffs. Standing over the two directors were four US Marshalls. Their orders were to escort Roberts and Hood to an undisclosed detention center for processing. They were traitors, and the president decided to treat them as such.

With a middle finger salute, he barked out a satisfying order. "Get these bastards out of my office. I just wanted to see the looks on their faces as they were marched out of here, disgraced and in handcuffs. Some of your other co-conspirators are in custody as we speak."

Roberts, with fire in his eyes, his upper lip quivering, spat at the president. "You'll regret doing this. I can promise you that," he threatened.

CIA Director Hood did not say a word. He hung his head, his chin resting on his chest as he walked out of the Oval Office.

President Chesterfield looked at Admiral Hollingsworth and then at Secretary Hall. "Who's next?"

The Attorney General did not look happy. "Mr. President, I am not sure what you're doing is lawful."

"If I believe these bastards have conspired to harm this country that I swore I would defend, then let them try to prove me wrong. There is enough evidence I will present if it comes to that," Chesterfield barked.

67

Paige was at her Malibu home, talking to Bradley, Clay Thomas, and Professor Miller. With all that had gone on with Dunham and the surprising move he had made, stress levels were very high.

She did not know where to go next with all the data she had accumulated from Dunham's files. There was so much circumstantial evidence, but nothing to connect him to any of the bombings or murders.

Frasier Montgomery was on the FBI's most-wanted list, but even though he had some connections to Albert Dunham, Frederick Ellison, and General Tucker Phillips, neither she or the FBI could find any evidence that those men had ordered the murder of Brian Russell, Seth Alexander, or Sean Adams.

"Any ideas where we should go from here?" she asked, frustrated. She could see the exasperation on all their faces. "Come on guys, think," she pleaded.

Dean was first to speak. "I am as irritated as you, but why can't we just release what we have and let public opinion be the judge on Dunham?" he asked.

Paige responded. "We can't. The man is a national hero right now. Soiling his reputation with innuendos and notes he made in his files could put all of us into a painful and expensive lawsuit. If that happens, we'd never be able to investigate what his next move is with Stage Five," she said. "We need to keep digging and turning over every rock to find the co-conspirators we believe are helping him with his manifesto."

Bradley jumped into the conversation. "I've been looking over Sean's notes on his Dunham investigation..." Paige interrupted him.

"What notes. I thought Frasier took his laptop and satchel?"

"The Cloud, Paige. Remember when I told you that we needed to have all of our work connected to one cloud account, so nothing would ever be lost...well our little Sean followed directions," Bradley said, grinning.

Paige smiled. "You mean we have his file notes?"

"Better than that. We have Sean's investigation into Dunham's chemical company and three pharmaceutical companies. His older brother, Theodore Dunham runs the chemical company as the CEO but, Albert Dunham is the president of all three of his drug companies and his chemical company."

Clay Thomas spoke. "What does that have to do with our investigation?" he asked puzzled.

"Nothing in particular. However, these are the only businesses that Albert Dunham is in full public view. Sean was working on a theory he had that Dunham's chemical company was intentionally poisoning certain geographical regions with their retardant spray to benefit their drug companies," Bradley said.

Paige could see Dean Miller taking notes and then typing on his keyboard. She re-focused. "Did Sean have proof of this?"

"Yes. Sean had hired a geotechnical engineering firm to do two-dozen subsurface surveys in three geographical areas where Dunham Chemical Company sprayed their banned retardant. Sean was then working with the CDC in those areas to see if there were any abnormalities with children or adults due to increased toxins," said Bradley.

Paige was combing her fingers with both hands through her long hair. "If Sean was here right now, I plant a wet juicy kiss on his lips..." she took in an emotional breath, "but I can't because of Frasier Montgomery. Well, if we can't get him on the bombings or murders of our friends right now, then maybe we can get him arrested for environmental reasons and maybe affecting the health of hundreds of thousands of Americans. Let's see how likable our little Julius Caesar will be then," she said.

"I've got something," Professor Miller said. "Did you know that the cancer rate in those three geographical areas has spiked over the last ten years. The number of cancer cases in children has jumped almost eighty percent, and among young adults, the cancer cases are up almost seventy-five percent."

"Paige let me work this case," Bradley said. "I owe it to Sean."

"It's yours. Whatever you need from me, you have it. I'll keep working on the current investigation. Maybe we'll bury Dunham from both angles."

Dean interrupted. "I can help too, but my time is limited now with my *We the People* movement that's ready to start picking its candidates. Bradley, I just sent you five files with enough data to keep you busy for a few weeks."

"Bradley be sure to interview Theodore Dunham. I'd love to hear his take on his brother and the recent events. Albert did have a notation in his manifesto that he had to keep his brother happy since he was not picked to be the next heir to the Dunham legacy. He made him the CEO of the chemical company, but Albert remained the Chairman of the Board. Maybe some bad blood inside the Dunham family?" Paige said mischievously.

Bradley was waving his hand at this screen. "I just got Miller's files. I need to go to work. Paige, be careful and Professor, good luck with your movement. It will have my vote," he said before disconnecting his monitor.

Paige was jotting down some notes before she spoke to the remaining members of her conference call. "I'm going to continue to pursue all avenues that lead to Dunham. He wants an interview, so I will give him one and see what he does when I show him what was on the thumb drive Russel sent me."

"You can't do that," Clay said. "Revealing stolen property right on national TV?"

"Why not. I did receive this from a source. Maybe if Dunham claims that the files are his, I will return them to him as a friendly gesture. I would be surprised if he will take full credit for what he's written. I want to hear him explain his way out of some of the things he's written and how they coincide with all the bombings and market crashes. That's all Clay," she said, smiling.

"Good move, Paige. I hope he agrees to come on your show now," Clay said.

"Yeah, me too. I bet Dunham will keep his promise he made on the world stage. His ego is too big to back off now. Well, let's all get back to work. Can we check in with each other in a week?" asked Paige.

Everyone said yes. Paige pressed the "red phone icon," and her Skype conference call ended. Then, her cellphone rang. It was POTUS. The request was short and unfriendly. Chesterfield wanted Paige in his office now.

Paige was in her car heading south down coast highway. First, she was going to go to the studio to gather up her files. Then, on to LAX. The president had transportation waiting for her again.

68

Frasier Montgomery watched as Paige came out her front door. Her red 650I BMW convertible, with its top-down, was welcoming her. She turned out of her driveway and headed south toward Santa Monica. He had been staking out her home and office for the last four days and could not determine any regular schedule she kept.

"It's either now or never," he said, slamming his fist on his steering wheel, jealous she had the car he loved. "four-forty-five horsepower, zero to sixty in four-point four seconds. He knew everything about it. The bitch is going off the road and down on the rocky cliff — such a waste of a great car. Die, die, die," he screamed as he peeled across coast highway, in a white Chevy Suburban he stole from a long-term parking lot at LAX. He made a sharp U-turn. He was going too fast to notice the two US Marshalls sitting in their vehicle in the adjacent driveway from Paige's house.

Frasier was already speeding down the coast at almost eighty miles per hour when he caught Turner. He was now just inches away from her rear bumper when he gave her a little nudge to get her attention.

Paige noticed the large vehicle speeding down on her and then slowing just inches from the rear of her car. She was pissed but just stuck her arm out of her car, waving him to go around. He bumped her again, this time harder. Now, she was in a frenzied panic. She pressed her foot hard against the accelerator and felt the torque of the engine kick in and pull her away from the crazy man trying to kill her. She pressed the SOS button on her rearview mirror, hoping she had enough time to call for help.

Frasier was now laughing as he sped up to catch Paige. "If she thinks she can outdrive me, that will never happen," he screamed. He put his forty-five in his left hand and held the gun out the window as he drove with one hand on the steering wheel.

Paige felt relieved when nine-one-one answered. "What is the emergency?" the woman asked, her voice calm and unemotional.

"I'm on Coast Highway approximately a mile from my home at four-six-zero Coast Highway. A White Chevy Suburban is trying to run me off the road. Please send help immediately. I am in a red BMW convertible. My name is Paige Turner..." before she could say another word, the Suburban was again on her tail, but this time she noticed his gun.

"Ms., are you sure? Maybe you should pull off the side of the road and let the vehicle pass you," she suggested.

"What part of running me off the road don't you understand. Now the crazy driver is waving a gun at me," Paige shouted as the first bullet just missed her left ear, shattering the front windshield. "Did you hear that, bitch?" she screamed.

"Was that a gunshot?" the nine-one-one operator asked. Then Paige's line went dead as the second bullet impacted the rearview mirror.

Now Paige was terrified. She had glass on her lap, and she could feel blood dripping down her cheek from her temple. She was now in survival mode. She craned her neck to see where the Suburban was, just in time to notice it was Frasier Montgomery grinning from ear-to-ear. "Not today, you son-of-a-bitch," she screamed. She could hear coming from the south police sirens. She pushed her foot on the accelerator as hard as she could, and her car seemed to kick into turbo drive.

As she gathered her wits and sped down the highway, something unexpected happened. Two surfers holding their big surfboards, covering their faces, stepped out in front of her car. She swerved to the left, heading straight toward a big green garbage truck. Its long metal lift spears were coming toward her. How she did it, she did not know, but she missed the surfers and the garbage truck.

Frasier wasn't so lucky. He missed the two young men, but not the garbage truck. The surfers dropped their boards, their eyes wide with disbelief, and grabbed for their cellphones. The impact Frasier's car had on the garbage truck was nothing compared to the crumbling metal sound his vehicle made.

One of the metal lifting spears impacted Frasier's face, ripping his head clean off. The surfers were running across the road. One was snapping pictures, and the other was videoing everything.

Paige had heard the crash, just as she came to the two police cars that were blocking the road.

The two US Marshalls, in their unmarked car, stopped and remained in their vehicle. They were just there to observe and protect Paige from Montgomery. The garbage truck had done their job for them.

"Mr.s President. Montgomery is dead. Impacted with a garbage truck. You were right. He was monitoring her. It looked like he had chosen today to try to kill her. I guess it's Karma, sir. A piece of garbage being taken out like this. Turner might be a little delayed, but we'll make sure she's on her way as soon as possible. We'll meet up with her at the plane and brief her on what we know," US Marshall Rogers, said.

"Scott, the Attorney General will be in contact with the local FBI office to coordinate this investigation with the local police. Please cooperate. Hopefully, we'll have whatever files that bastard had on him," the president said.

69

Paige was being attended to by the paramedics and at the same time being interviewed by a local detective at the LAPD. "Ms. Turner, do you have any idea why this man had such road rage against you? Did you do something to provoke him?" the detective asked.

Paige's eyes grew wide with disbelief by the detective's question. "You're kidding. I'm glad the SOB is dead. You do know he was shooting at me, while trying to run me off the side of the road, right?"

The male detective just shrugged his shoulders. "Was this a relationship that's gone bad?" he asked.

Paige was ready to jump up and punch him in the face when a tall, handsome man, flashing a US Marshall badge stepped in the middle of the heated interview. She was facing the bright sun and didn't at first recognize him.

"Are you alright, Paige?" Rogers asked. She squinted a puzzled look on her face, unable to see the man's face. "This incident is now under Federal Jurisdiction. Inside that crushed car is a man wanted for three other murders. Ms. Turner will not be answering any more of your questions," the US Marshall said.

Paige looked up at the man, trying to block the bright sun's rays from her eyes with her hand. She now recognized who had been speaking. "Why are you here, Scott?" she asked.

Rogers remained professional in front of the detective. "Ms. Turner, we can discuss that on our way to your plane. The president needs you right now," he replied, his tone serious. He looked at the medic that was attending to Paige. "Is she okay to leave now?"

The young fireman nodded his head. "Just a small cut. No stitches needed. She's okay to go," he said. "I recommend she be seen by a doctor to rule out a concussion.

The shocked detective, his hands on his hips, watched as Paige rushed into the government vehicle, and Scott Roger's partner got behind the wheel of Paige's car and drove south toward the airport.

* * * * *

Tucker Phillips was dialing Dunham. "Sir, Frasier's dead."

"So quickly. Good job," Dunham replied.

"Not by me, sir. He was attempting to kill Paige Turner on Coast Highway near her Malibu home. The crazy bastard was trying to run her off the road, speeding down the highway, shooting at her, when he slammed into a garbage truck. He was decapitated."

Dunham was silent, in shock from the news. He had never imagined his friend would die this way. "Well, it's over. We can get back to our plans now," he said.

Phillips sucked in a deep breath. "Sir, two US Marshalls were on the scene. It was Chief Deputy, Scott Rogers who took Paige into custody. I believe she's on her way to see the president," he said.

"Where have I heard that name before?" he asked.

"He's ex-special ops with the Navy. A real American hero and a loyal American and loyal to this president. If he's now helping Chesterfield, we might have bigger problems than Paige Turner and her investigation."

"Get your butt back here. We need to talk," Dunham said, his voice cracking. "I've got a meeting with my brother tomorrow. Let's meet up at my home, say around five. I'll have Maggie prepare some dinner."

"Copy that sir," Tucker replied, ending the call.

70

Dunham had made an unscheduled visit to his chemical company. He wanted to check up on his brother and be sure he had stopped using the toxins in their retardant spray. The Architect knew that Sean Adams had been working a story about him and PM10. He did not trust Theodore would follow through with his request.

He found his brother in his office, behind his large oak desk. He was working on his computer when he walked in.

"Teddy. How are you doing these days?" Albert said, sounding overly patronizing.

Theodore had a surprised look on his face. "What do I owe this honor of a visit from my world-famous brother?" he said, sarcastically. He clicked off his screen to hide the email he'd received from Bradley Stevens.

"I can't come to visit my older brother, unannounced?"

"You never come for a social visit or to find out how your niece and nephew are doing, or how my wife is doing, so this visit must have an ulterior motive."

Albert rolled his eyes and sat down in front of his brother. "You're right. I don't give a shit about you or your family. I only care if you're making money at my company and following my orders.

Teddy pressed his keyboard and turned his computer screen toward his brother, sliding his chair over to sit face-to-face with him. "So, what the fuck brings you to my company?" he said, emphasizing the word my.

Albert let go a laugh. "It's not you're company; it's mine. I am Chairman of the Board and major stockholder. Everything that goes on here only goes on here with my approval," he said, his voice rising.

"I know why father gave you reins over all Dunham businesses. You're a bigger asshole than he was. He liked seeing himself in you. I, on the other hand, was a disappointment. I was too much like our mother. So please tell me why you're here and then get the fuck out of my face," Theodore said, his face red with fire.

"Oh, I like that anger. Maybe if you'd have shown that to Father, you'd be in my shoes."

"Never. I like myself just the way I am. Now get on with why you're here."

"I want to know if you've stopped adding the toxins to our retardant spray. I can't afford the attention it might cause right now. My cancer drug sales are through the roof of what I had set up with my pharmaceutical companies. You did stop it when I told you?"

"It was done right after you ordered me to do it a few weeks ago. Let me ask you something. How do you live with yourself knowing you've given hundreds of thousands of people, young people, even children, cancer?"

"It's easy. I look at my bank account every day. I now have so many people that need my drugs that I can charge them whatever I want, and they can't do a thing about it. The government is in my back pocket and won't stop me either."

"Just don't come by anymore. You can email me or text me with your requests."

"You'll see me whenever I want. You still can be removed from this company and left with nothing. So, stop with the attitude and do your job. After the election, we can resume business as usual."

"Election? You're not still thinking of becoming the next Emperor, are you?" Teddy asked, allowing a bellowing laugh to explode out of his mouth.

Albert stood and did not reply. He marched out of the office without saying goodbye.

Teddy leaned back in his chair, clicked the stop key on the video recorder inside his computer, and smiled. "Who's the smart one now, little brother?"

71

Inside his limo, Dunham was on his cell calling the only man he knew he could trust now and one who was indebted to him. With Montgomery dead, he needed a new enforcer to keep his plan on schedule.

"Thomas, we need to talk. It's time to initiate the failsafe plan we discussed awhile ago," he said.

Thomas Hayes, an ex-Chicago PD Detective, owed Dunham his life. "I can be in Bethesda day after tomorrow, sir."

"Good. See you then."

Hayes was happy to hear from his new boss. Like it was yesterday, the day they first met had begun flashing in front of him like a movie.

Fifteen years ago, while at a fundraiser in Chicago, Hayes was providing onsite security for the event. He was still working for the Chicago PD and looking for a burglar who had been breaking into hotel suites while their wealthy occupants were at events at the hotels where they were staying.

He had been watching the elevator that serviced four penthouse suites. He did not know who was staying up there; nevertheless, he wanted to catch this person in the act.

Hayes believed that everyone staying upstairs was at the charity event and headed up the next elevator to catch the man red-handed.

Thomas Hayes did not know Albert Dunham had been walking back to his hotel suite. A man dressed in all black, wearing a ski mask was running down the hallway toward him from his room. Hayes noticed that the well-dressed man had his eyes staring at the carpet. Dunham was unaware of what was about to happen in the corridor.

Hayes saw the man, still with his ski mask on, bolt out of the Penthouse Suite. The detective noticed the man in the ski mask, pointing a gun as he ran toward the hotel guest.

Everything was happening so fast that Hayes quickly removed his revolver. He noticed that the well-dressed man was standing frozen in his tracks, staring at the approaching figure dressed in black.

What surprised Hayes next was what Dunham had done. Without thinking, and with no concern for his safety, the billionaire lowered his shoulder; his chin pressed to his chest. Then, like a linebacker, he laid into the approaching man and leveled him with a hard thud.

Within an instant, Hayes was rolling the fallen man on his stomach and bending his arms behind his back and cuffing him. Out of breath, the detective looked up and introduced himself.

"Detective Thomas Hayes, Chicago PD. Are you okay?" he asked, a puzzled look on his face. He noticed Dunham rubbing his right shoulder.

Albert, while massaging his shoulder, said, "Fine...really fine. Why are you here? Is my wife okay?"

Hayes extended his hand. "I was at the charity event and trying to catch a bugler who had been breaking into the penthouse suites at this hotel while the occupants were gone. We've had this guy on our radar for months. I got lucky when I saw him get into the penthouse elevator. He had a master key and had just entered your suite when I got up to your floor. Good thing I had my master key and I followed him in..."

"Is my wife okay? Stop talking and answer me!" Dunham shouted.

"Sorry," the detective said embarrassed. "Yes, sir, she's alright. Just a little shook up, but not hurt. When I heard her scream, I identified myself, and that's when this guy started to run. Your suite is almost three times the size of my one-bedroom apartment," Hayes commented.

"I've got to check on my wife. You can finish your story later. Do you know who I am?" Dunham asked.

I certainly do Mr. Dunham. I was listening to your speech tonight. You're a very generous man," Hayes said.

Dunham smiled. "And powerful. Before you lock up this bastard, I'd like to have a word with him in private? No one tries to rob me or tries to hurt my wife, my Maggie, without some punishment. Can you do me this one small favor? You won't regret it," he asked the detective.

That night after Albert dealt with the burglar, Hayes and Albert became excellent friends. "You ever need a favor, just call this number," he said, handing him his business card.

A year after that incident, a young boy Hayes had arrested had died while in his custody. The autopsy had shown numerous broken ribs and a brain embolism from multiple blows inflicted on the boy. It didn't help the detective's case that he had taken a very long route to the precinct after the boy received his beating. What made things worse was that the detective did not attempt to get the boy medical help before he died.

When Dunham heard what had happened, he sent his best lawyers. Hayes did not go to jail. The detective lost his job and pension. Albert never forgets a debt he owes. The detective was paid back handsomely for saving his wife. Now, the detective was forever indebted to his new employer. Over the years when Dunham needed some off-the-books problems resolved, he secretly let Hayes do the job.

72

Paige's meeting with President Chesterfield had begun late. After her long flight to the Capitol, she had been kept waiting in the Oval Office with Scott Rogers. The US Marshall wore a dark suit, his head buried in a tablet, never looking up once when she had entered the room. His aloof attitude was making no sense to her.

Paige could not stand the silence and said. "After your bull-shit introduction at the accident and the four-plus hours on the plane, your silence is driving me crazy," she said. "I thought we were friends. Has something changed?"

Scott slowly lifted his head and closed his tablet. He was now smiling. "I've been ordered to not speak to you until the president has a chance to brief you on our investigation. I'm not rude, just following orders Paige."

She was now sizing the man up who was once her husband's friend. By your mannerisms and appearance, I'd say you're ex-military. "What branch of the service were you in?"

"Navy Special Operations. Why ask?"

"Just curious. Why a US Marshall and not Secret Service?" she grilled him.

Scott could not contain his laughter. "President Chesterfield warned me about you. Charming, beautiful, and very curious. You've changed, for the better, I might say, since your wedding."

Paige was taken aback by his remarks. With all that had been happening over the past few weeks, she had forgotten that

Scott was supposed to be the best man at their wedding, but his work had gotten in the way. That part of her life had been blacked out since Rick's murder.

Rogers noticed he had made her uncomfortable. "Didn't mean to bring up those memories," he said, his tone softening. "Back to your question. I work at the pleasure of my president."

"Why go into the Marshalls office?" Paige asked.

"I feel the US Marshalls office match my personal beliefs about our country and keeping it safe. You do know it was established to be a unique and elite cadre of law enforcement professionals that swore an oath to be part of the continuum of our grand American experiment in self-government. Something I fought for with three tours in the Middle East," he said proudly.

Paige, for the first time, laughed. "Well-rehearsed, she said. "Thank you for your service and helping to keep our experiment in self-government moving forward," she said sarcastically.

He just looked at her, wanting to read her the riot act for disrespecting him, but thought better of it. Showing he was upset, he said, "Let's just sit here quietly and wait for President Chesterfield," his tone cold as ice as he went back to reading a file in his tablet. "Oh, the president didn't warn me about your rudeness."

Paige could see that she had hurt his feelings. *Turner, when will you learn to be nice?* She scolded herself. Fortunately, President Chesterfield entered the room; his mood serious. Now, Turner had become more anxious.

The president, without a hello, immediately began recapping his last few days since Dunham's antics on the other side of the world. Chesterfield took a seat in his favorite armchair. Paige was on his left sitting on the couch, and Scott Rogers was on his right on the second couch. "Have both of you exchanged introductions before we start our meeting?" the president asked.

Rogers was first to speak. "Yes."

Turner forced a smile. "Yes."

Chesterfield noticed the cold chill in the room. "Now, Paige, are you playing nice with my US Marshal?"

Her eyes had become little slits as she spoke. "Chief Deputy Rogers, can I call you Buck," she asked, letting a big smile explode on her face. Sorry for my rudeness. I must still be a little tense after what Frasier Montgomery tried to do to me." She stood and extended her hand to him.

Rogers stood and welcomed her handshake warmly. "Nothing to apologize for Ms. Turner," he replied. "We're all good here. I should have made talked with you while on the plane. When I see you, I see your husband, Rick. He was a great guy. He was embedded with my unit in Iraq. Everyone in my unit liked him."

Paige's face drained of color. She recalled in some of Rick's possessions, a picture of him and all the guys in Rogers unit. "I remember now. I have a picture of you and your men with my husband. He had written to me on how welcoming and protective you were toward him. Thank you very much for keeping him safe there," she said, wiping a tear from her cheek.

Chesterfield took control of the meeting. "Paige, you too can get caught up after our meeting. I wanted to speak to you face-to-face and bring you up-to-date on what we're going to do from this point forward regarding Dunham." He could see that Turner was ready to argue with him.

"Before you start with your Freedom of the Press crap, and other bull-shit you reporters like to spout, you will have to listen to what I have to say first," Chesterfield said, showing an aggressive that Paige had not seen before.

"I am not sure where all of this hostility is coming from Mr. President, but I am here at your request ready to listen to what you have to say. Please remember, I brought you Dunham's files. I did not have to do it. And, yes, I do take the

First Amendment very seriously. I hope you are not going to ask me to abandon it," Paige said.

"I know what you and your team are doing now, but we do need to talk about it and coordinate our investigations."

Paige could not remain quiet. "What my team has uncovered so far needs our attention without your input," Turner said, instantly regretting the threatening tone she had. "I don't want or need your help. You'll hamper what we can do."

Rogers pushed up from the couch and began pacing around the Oval Office. He looked like a caged tiger. He appeared ready to punch Turner in the face. "Patrick, I don't know why you allow this reporter to talk to you this way. As I told you, we do not need her. My team can investigate Dunham and eliminate his threat before he puts his fifth stage in motion."

"Rogers, sit your butt down and zip it so I can get on with this meeting. And address me as Mr. President," he ordered. "Let's start over," the president said, his voice taking on a calmer tone. "Paige, I asked you here today to hopefully get you to allow Scott to work with you and your team. He is the only person I trust. Besides stopping Dunham, if it is him doing all of this, I am fighting for my political life and need to have some wins right now." Chesterfield could see Paige ready to argue with him, raised his hand like a traffic cop to stop her from speaking.

"Dunham, by his recent actions has made me out to be an inept president, which has fueled the "Dirty Dozen" to begin impeachment hearings. I am going to be meeting with him tomorrow to see what he wants from all of his recent activities."

"I believe it will be complicated making Dunham out to be a villain," "Turner said. "After my last Show, the emails and twitter responses have been overwhelmingly positive. Once I bring in Dunham for his interview, I might be able to show another side of him."

Chesterfield coughed, trying to clear his throat. "That's why I asked you here. You cannot have that interview right now. Dunham is seen right now as a real American hero, and anything you might do to make him seem otherwise can hurt our country and my presidency. I see you want to speak, but let me finish my thought, and you might understand the importance of my request."

"I'm listening, but already I am not liking what I am hearing," Paige responded, her jaw clenching.

"What I am about to tell you has not been leaked to the media yet. As a favor to you and all that you've done so far, for our country, I want you to hold your Show here in the Oval Office to let your followers be the first to know that I am cleaning house. I have arrested FBI director Roberts and CIA director Hood for treason. I have asked the Secretary of State Waterfall for her resignation. As far as you're concerned, the Secretary of State has an undisclosed medical condition."

Paige was genuinely surprised. She was flattered that she would be getting such an exclusive. "I'm happy on the one hand and skeptical on the other," she said. "What do I have to do in return for this exclusive story?" she asked.

Chesterfield sucked in a deep breath before he replied. "I am getting to it. You first need to know that our priority right now is to stop Stage Five, whatever it might be?" Chesterfield said. "After careful review, I now believe that Dunham and the Architect are all the same person. You've been right and thank you for sharing the thumb drive with me."

Turner finally got it. The light bulb went off in her brain. "You're bringing in Dunham to see if he'll be your new Secretary of State?"

Chesterfield nodded his head. "I have no other choice. Even if he's the perpetrator of everything that's been happening, which I am sure of now, I need him by my side to help fend off this impeachment hearing. All of this is a political nightmare. Sometimes you need to keep your enemies closer. But, if he is the person responsible, having him inside my cabinet will help us monitor his actions."

Paige was stunned by the president's motives. She finally believed Chesterfield's motivation was to get re-elected, even at a high cost to the United States.

"I am sorry you feel this is your only alternative. It's a big mistake. You're playing into Dunham's game plan. Let me ask you this. Where is the FBI's investigation into the murder of one of my reporters or the murder of Brian Russell or Seth Alexander? All these killings happened because they were investigating this Architect, who I believe is Albert Dunham. Our values, maybe your values are being misplaced. Freedom of the Press has First Amendment protection under the constitution. Do you want the ignoring of the killing of reporters or any American citizen attempting to protect our country from a domestic terrorist to be part of your legacy?"

"I'm offended by your comments. There are ongoing investigations into those criminal acts by the FBI. We, correct me if I am wrong, have ended the life of Frasier Montgomery, who we believed was the perpetrator of those killings. What more do you want from me?" Chesterfield asked.

"You didn't have anything to do with his death. A garbage truck ended his life. Shit, I want the investigation looking into who hired Montgomery to murder these men. I am getting the impression you will bury this investigation with the appointment of Dunham as your Secretary of State," Paige lashed out.

"This decision is bigger than you or me at this time. If I don't get re-elected, then someone, maybe someone like Dunham, might be sitting in this Oval Office and then what will happen to your investigation," Chesterfield said, annoyed. "Now go and work with Rogers and get me more proof so I can lock Dunham up."

Paige did not know how to respond. "I won't cancel my interview with Dunham. Something is very fishy with everything he was able to accomplish without your intelligence team knowing anything about it." She watched the president swivel in his chair and stared out at the White House lawn.

Scott Rogers finally spoke. "You'll soon find out that Dunham has canceled his interview with you. You need to stay out of our way. My team will be handling the investigation regarding these attacks and the murder of your reporter and friends," Scott said sternly. "Just be thankful you have this exclusive press release and be satisfied."

Chesterfield spun around. "Paige, I do not want you to stop your investigation into Dunham and his Manifesto, but please be careful naming him before you have all your ducks lined up. I'm assigning Rogers and his team to work with you. You will have all the resources I can provide, as long as you keep sharing your progress with us," he said, not giving either of them any choice. "Can both of you play nice with each other?"

Turner did not look pleased. She nodded her head in agreement. Rogers just grunted out a yes.

"Paige, I know you have a lot of material to brief me on, but maybe you could do it with Rogers and begin working together? Now, Miss Turner, give us fifteen minutes, so we can get this press briefing set up. You can wait out in the waiting room. Rogers will call you when we're ready." The president shook Turner's hand and watched her leave.

73

The press briefing had started thirty minutes later, lasting for five minutes. After Paige Turner asked the president her questions, Chesterfield was going to meet with the White House Press Corps next and answer their questions, including why Turner had been given the exclusive story first.

During the press interview, Paige tried to wring more information from the president, but Chesterfield was not going to tell his listeners more than that the Secretary of State had resigned her position for health reasons. She did get to ask one question which seemed to unnerve the president.

"Mr. President. How long have you known about Secretary of State Waterfall's declining health?" Turner asked, her hand-held microphone extended, trying to capture the president's words.

Chesterfield's facial muscles tensed. He was noticeably caught off-guard and struggled to come up with a logical answer to her question. He did not want to come across, looking like he was lying. "It's a private matter. So, let's leave it at that," he replied, noticeably disturbed.

"Does her resignation have anything to do with the recent intelligence missteps at the State Department?" Paige could see that the president was pissed. She knew she stepped over the line. She couldn't get Dunham out of her head as the new Secretary of State.

Chesterfield stood and moved away from his desk. His comments were almost inaudible. She knew she had to turn off her microphone.

"Fuck you, Turner," he barked. "You were already briefed on this. Not very professional," he said and stormed off to the White House Briefing Room.

Paige did not like putting the president in an awkward position. She was happy she had turned off the mic. She now wanted to dig deeper into the State Department and the absent Secretary of State. She hoped that Dean Miller could see how deep Dunham's tentacles went inside Waterfall's State Department and if the Secretary had ties to any of this.

* * * * *

Rogers was walking briskly with the president, pissed at Turner for putting his friend on the spot. "You need to distance yourself from that journalist. She's going to link you to her investigation of Dunham, and it might come back to bite you in the ass if you appoint Dunham as your Secretary of State," he said.

74

Paige was in her suite at the Mayflower Hotel in Washington D.C., Bradley sitting next to her on the couch. She kept switching back between CNN, FOX, and MSNBC. The only news coverage was about Dunham and the unbelievable accomplishment he had achieved in a matter of eight days. Nothing about her interview with Chesterfield. While she made an enemy with the president, she also irritated the major news channels with her exclusive. The three major news organizations remained focused on Dunham and very little time to the resignation of the Secretary of State.

Dunham's economic plan for Spain, Italy, and Greece was genius each newscaster said. A clip of a Dunham interview went viral.

"*What I brokered was nothing spe*cial," Dunham said, shrugging his shoulders. *"Governments have too many layers of bureaucratic BS,"* he said. *"Too many factions and too many sides to satisfy. I have been fortunate to have made a comfortable life for myself and my wonderful wife, Maggie. My parents taught me to give back to the world that helped make me successful. That is what I did. I hope that my actions will motivate more people in my position to step up and help."*

"Do you believe this crap?" Paige moaned.

Bradley squeezed Paige's shoulder. "Does that man look like the monster we are making him out to be? If I didn't know better, I would have faith in him too, like everyone else," he said.

"Me too," Paige said, shaking her head.

Bradley leaned forward and grabbed some trail mix and washed it down with his beer. "He sounds too good to be true if you want my opinion. Men like Dunham do not do what he did without getting something in return. I want to wait to see how his deals begin to unfold. We need to monitor what corporations begin to fill in the void in Europe and Palestine. I will bet that most, if not all of them have some connection to Dunham," he said.

Paige was nodding her head in agreement. "Actions speak louder than words. And, the actions that will begin to transpire over the next few months will tell the real story. I hope Dunham is the real deal. Our world could use a person like him. But, right now, the jury is out."

"Now we have to wait and see how every American accepts Dunham as the new Secretary of State," said Bradley.

Paige seemed lost in thought. She bounced out of her seat and was at her laptop. "I think we need to get Dean Miller to run a search of where Dunham has been since Brian Russell's death. Maybe everything that's happened lately was all pre-arranged."

* * * * *

Thomas Hayes went to the computer monitor at his headquarters, looking over the shoulder of his tech assistant. "Sir, I just got a hit on Turner and her reporter Bradley Stevens. They are at the Mayflower Hotel in an elevator coming from the top floor. They must be in a penthouse suite," the tech assistant said.

"Good work," Hayes said. "They will have to wait. Our other targets take priority. Turner and Stevens go last, as well as that ass-hole professor. Let me know when you find our other targets," No, on second thought, send two of our men to the hotel to monitor them. Let's begin to figure out their schedule and if the president has given them a security detail. If so, they will be a challenge, but not impossible to eliminate."

75

Maggie had surprised Albert after his long flight home by preparing dinner for him. She had given their chef the night off, as well as their kitchen staff.

Maggie had made his favorite meal: Veal Marsala, with roasted red potatoes, and Brussel Sprouts. Before they sat down, she poured two Gin Martinis, with a light spray of Vermouth.

She motioned him to follow her to the living room. The fireplace was blazing, and some Sinatra was playing through their ceiling speakers. She had a sheepish expression on her face; he knew it meant she wanted to talk about something important.

Albert pursed his lips, his heart beating fast, knowing the woman in front of him, was the only person who truly loved him and believed that he was a great man. She knew about him being the Architect and his family's history.

Maggie so far did not know the specifics inside his Manifesto. He worried that once she found out what he was doing his relationship with his wife would be destroyed.

He knew he had to distance himself from his alter ego-*The Architec*t, so he could enjoy what Maggie had planned. He was planning on erasing all connections to him and the Architect and hoped that Thomas Hayes would have some excellent news for him soon.

Maggie plopped herself down on the couch, her slender legs curling up under her sundress. "Come sit next to me," she said, patting the cushions with her hand. "I have something I want to discuss. It might require a few more Martinis."

Albert had been trapped before by Maggie and smiled, waiting for her request. He sat down and put her hand in his. He leaned in and gave her a warm, loving kiss. "I am ready. Should I have my wallet out too?" he smiled.

Maggie blushed. "No nothing like that. It's more personal," she said, taking in a nervous breath. "I hope you'll agree with me," she said, her voice showing a sign of nervousness.

"Relax sweetheart. You know I would do anything for you, especially if it makes you happy."

A big sigh of relief escaped from her lips. "I am so glad you said that. I love you so much. You are the most loving person I have ever known." She inhaled and continued. "I know how disappointed you were when we lost our son at birth, and I could never have any more children," she saw him wanting to interrupt, but she raised her hand signaling him to wait and let her finish.

"I know you saved my life over our son's. I know how much you love me and are not upset we cannot have children. I have been talking to this adoption agency, and they have a newborn boy that needs a good home like ours. I want to be a mother. I know how wonderful you'd be as a father," she said, wiping a tear from her cheek.

Albert was shocked. He tried to hide it. He loved Maggie and could see how much this meant to her. "Are you sure you want to be a mother? It will change both of our lives. Our privacy, our alone time will be hindered," he saw her beginning to cry. "Sweetheart, I am not saying no. I want you to be a hundred percent sure you want to become a mother. It's a big responsibility," he said, bringing her into his arms and hugging her tightly.

Maggie pushed off from his embrace and looked him in the eyes. She could see the glassy expression that told her his answer. "That's a yes?" she said, bouncing wildly on the couch.

"Yes. I would love to be a father and start a family with you."

Dinner was fast and delicious, but not as pleasant as the dessert Maggie had planned for him in their bedroom.

* * * * *

While Maggie was in a night of deep sleep after their lovemaking, he was on the phone in his den. "You have to move up the plans I gave you. Something has come up, and I cannot afford to have any loose ends right now. Turner, Stevens, and Professor Miller need to be dealt with ASAP," he told Hayes. "It just can't wait any longer.

"That's a tall order right now. I will need some help," Hayes told Dunham.

"Whatever you need. Money is no object," he said before hanging up the phone.

* * * * *

Maggie had woken up, rolling over to cuddle up with her husband, finding only his pillow. Curious and thirsty, she staggered downstairs to the kitchen. She noticed the light was on in the den and heard Albert talking on the phone.

Not wanting to disturb him, she waited outside the partially opened door for him to finish his call. She did not find it unusual for him to be working early in the morning. What she found disturbing were the words he was saying to Thomas Hayes, the detective who saved her life. When she heard the call end, she listened to her husband curse, something he had never done around her.

She had never seen this side of him before and was scared. Cursing did not bother her. It was the murderous tone in his voice. Her heart was pounding as she rushed to the kitchen to get a glass of water. Trying to gulp down the cold liquid to calm her nerves was not working. She was startled when her husband burst into the kitchen.

He immediately noticed her hands shaking. "Maggie, are you alright?" he asked sweetly.

She turned to face him, trying to hold back her fear, but couldn't. She could see that he noticed it too and prayed she could say something convincing.

"I had a bad dream. When you were not in bed, I went downstairs looking for you," Maggie said, noticing the sweet smile begin to evaporate from her husband's face.

"I remembered I had to make an important call to Europe and with the time zones, this was the only time I had."

"Yes, I understand. I saw your light on in the den. I did not want to disturb you with my dream, so I got a glass of water to calm me down," she was surprised how well she could lie when scared.

"Tell me about your dream," he asked.

"Maybe later. Let's go back to bed."

For the first time, Dunham could see his wife was lying to him. Had she heard anything he had said to Hayes? He could not allow his feelings for his wife change, but as his father had taught him, Maggie was disposable if she came between him and his dream. He prayed that he did not have to make that choice. But first, he needed to get ready for the adoption interview tomorrow.

76

Maggie and Albert had been home no longer than thirty minutes from a business function when she asked him to sit down on their couch to talk.

"I have something to say," Maggie said, her tone serious.

Dunham had never seen his wife so distraught. He sensed it was from the other night when he was speaking to Thomas Hayes. He hoped it wasn't that.

"Maggie, sweetheart. I've never seen you like this. You can talk to me about anything. Is it your health?" he said, forcing a worried expression.

"No, nothing like that," she said curtly.

"Then what has you so worried?"

"Albert, I don't know where to begin. I think I will get right to the point. I heard you talking to Thomas Hayes the other night. You spoke of eliminating your closest friends and that reporter, as well as other people I don't know. Is that true?" she asked as tears rolled down her cheek.

Dunham thought he could twist the conversation she'd heard. He realized lying to her would only make the situation worse. "What you heard was correct," he replied emotionless. "But not the way you are interpreting it."

Maggie cupped her hand to her mouth, gasping for air. "Murder? Who are you?" she screamed. "What type of man have I been living with all these years? I've trusted you. I believed in you, as well as your dreams; our dreams," she screamed.

He thought hard about what he would say. "The life we have did not come to us by luck. Business is a ruthless game, and sometimes you need to do things that by some standards are immoral. What you heard were expressions of anger. They were business terms reflecting my anger. I am not a murderer. The word *eliminates* or *gets rid of* are terms businessmen like me use to curtail my competition," he said, his voice controlled. "or put to rest anyone who is trying to soil my name."

Maggie was shaking her head. "I don't believe you. The phrase '*Get rid of*' or the word '*Eliminate*' to me means one thing, murder. They say something more, mainly when directed at your closest friends. Explain how Paige Turner fits into your explanation. Is she competition with you and your businesses?" she scolded.

Dunham sucked in a deep breath before he replied. He was thinking of the right answer and had none. "We've been married twenty-five years. I fell in love with you when I turned twenty-five and promised to give you the best life I could. I think I've done a great job. Yes, I have hurt people along the way. Yes, I've done things I regret, but everything I did was for you, for us," he said, his eyes looking at their carpet. "Your question about Turner is true, but not in the sense, you think. What I want to do is destroy her career or as I said, kill it. It's an emotional expression maybe not politically correct, but it's just what it is," he said.

Maggie patted her eyes with a tissue. "I do appreciate the life you've given me. I also love a man I believed was this kind, gentle, and giving soul. Who are you really?" she asked calmly.

"I am that to you and only you. My business partners and friends need to respect me. If not, then I don't need them anymore. If I need to be ruthless, then so be it. Congenial people in business finish last. I have plans that have been passed down from my great grandfather, and now I have an opportunity to accomplish something my great grandfather never dreamed could happen. If I need to be tough, then so be it. If I need to be ruthless, I will be that person. I've had this dream since I was given the reins to the Dunham legacy, and nothing is going to stop me from reaching my goal."

Maggie's face contorted with disbelief. She had never heard her husband talk that way to her. "Even murdering people to achieve your goals? Don't we have more money than we could ever use?" she asked.

"It is no longer about the money. It is about power and control. We are a few steps away from becoming the most powerful family in America and the world. I won't let anyone, either friend or foe, stop me now," he said, his veins on his face ready to explode.

"Do I fit into that last scene?" Maggie said nervously.

Albert reached across the couch and put both his hands on her shoulders. "Look at me, my dear. Are you with me or against me?" His words had her shaking.

She shook off his hands from her shoulders and slid to the farthest part of the couch. Then Maggie surprised him with her response.

"I took an oath when we got married. For better or worse, till death do we part. I have always taken that oath seriously. I am your wife. I love you with all my heart. If a friend or foe wants to hurt you, then they are trying to hurt us. You now need to include me in everything you're going to do from this point on. I am the only one you can or will ever be able to trust," she said, reaching over and pulling him into her arms. "Albert, promise me that you will never lie or keep anything from me again. I need the truth, so I will be able to protect you...us from this point on."

For the next three hours, Albert told Maggie everything in his Manifesto. He gave her a brief overview of what was created by his great grandfather and everything inside all the files. He also told her his ultimate plan and why some people needed to go.

He was surprised that she was on board with everything. He was surprised she had some great ideas as to how to move into the final stage with a minimum of collateral damage. That night they made the most passionate love ever. He was feeling great now and could see his dream fulfilled with Maggie's help.

* * * * *

Dunham was back in his home office; his door locked. He needed to have a conference call with Frederick Ellison and Gregory Wilbanks. The launch of NASA's new telecommunications satellite was on schedule to launch within ten days, and he needed to know if his new computer chip was finished and ready to be installed before the launch.

"Gentlemen, I need an update on our software?"

Gregory spoke first, his voice sounding very anxious. "Sir, I've been working day and night on this and almost done. Russell left me a mess, but we should meet our target date," he said.

Dunham hated uncertainty. "What the fuck do you mean should meet our target date? You fail, we fail, shit, I fuckin fail. I never fail," he shouted. "Do you know how big this chip is to my overall plan? Without it, Stage Five will not happen. I do not have to tell you how I deal with failure, Mr. Wilbanks. You do remember the man you replaced, right?"

Now Wilbanks was sweating profusely. "Sir, I won't fail. I didn't explain myself well. "I had to make some modifications to what Russell had first created. If you had used his chip as it was, you would not get control of the satellite. Sir, I promise you the modification I've made will give you full control of the satellite when it reaches its full orbit," he said with confidence.

Ellison jumped in. "Albert, let Gregory get back to work so we can get caught up on a few other items."

"Okay. Gregory, you'll be rewarded handsomely after the launch and our first test," Dunham said.

After Wilbanks signed off from Skype, Ellison started briefing Dunham on all that had happened with Montgomery.

"Albert, as you know, Frasier is dead. Such a horrible accident on Coast Highway. The bastard was going to kill Turner in broad daylight and try to get back on your good side."

"So, what's the good news?" Dunham asked.

"Yes, he's out of our hair, but he's been linked to us, especially me and Tucker Phillips. We have the US Marshalls office, FBI and the Justice Department wanting to interview us. Also, they seem to have a list of all our members who were on our bus a few weeks back and looking to interview them too," Ellison said, sounding nervous.

Albert pounded his fist on his desk. "What the fuck is Chesterfield doing using the US Marshalls? Don't we have anyone inside that agency that can help us?

"He only trusts his special team of US Marshalls right now. The one in charge is a real son-of-a-bitch. Very loyal American. Loves his country and all that bull-shit," said Ellison.

"I'm meeting with Chesterfield tomorrow about the Secretary of State position. I was not sure I wanted it, but maybe now, what the hell. I'd be just four spots away from the presidency," he grinned.

"It could make it easier if you decide to run for president," said Ellison.

"What do you mean decide. I've already decided. I don't know how I'm going to move into the White House when the time comes. If this computer chip works, I will have full control over everything here in this country and around the world. Shit, I could build my own White House anywhere I wanted," he laughed.

Ellison just rolled his eyes. "I gotta go. My meeting with Scott Rogers is in two hours. I need our attorney there and fully briefed. Let me know how it goes tomorrow with the president?"

77

Paige was sipping a beer and munching on some pretzels, gazing at the pounding surf from her patio deck. Bradley was off interviewing Dunham's brother while professor Miller was deep into his *"We the People*" movement. She had four manila folders on the side table next to her beer, unable to concentrate on Dunham and all she had to do with her investigation.

"Close your eyes, girl," she whispered. "Everything can wait." With that, she instantly fell asleep. Paige could nap anywhere and go into a deep dream sleep immediately. Out on her deck, the light cool breeze was massaging her face, and the warm rays from the sun caressed her body. For the first time, her dream, which always included her husband, found him talking to her about her investigation.

"*You're missing the real link to Dunham and what he wants to accomplish,"* Rick was saying. *"You have the answers inside his files. Don't keep focusing on what he's letting you read. Narrow your parameters to the encrypted data only. It has all the answers.*

Paige was reaching to touch Rick, unable to feel his warm skin. *"Honey,"* she said, her voice sad. *"What's inside those files? I don't understand,"* She whimpered.

Like most of her dreams, when she wanted to talk to Rick, his image would start to fade and then she'd wake up crying. But, not this time. Rick had more to say.

"*I can't keep meeting you this way. You have to let me go,"* he begged. *"Look deeper into my last investigation, you have more answers you need right in front of you there,"* he said, and with a wave of his hand, vanished.

Paige was moaning loudly, still deep into her dream, when her cellphone snapped her awake. Rubbing her eyes and blotting them with her tee-shirt, she answered.

"Professor?" she said, her voice was annoyed. "I thought you were not going to call for a while?"

"I know, but I think I figured out how to decrypt Dunham's encrypted files."

She was startled by his remarks. "That's a coincidence," she replied, feeling a creepy chill come over her body. "Let's meet face-to-face at UCLA. I need to get away from here right now. I can be there tomorrow. Will that work?"

Dean was confused about her remarks. "I think we can do this by Skype, but if you want to come to visit, you're welcome."

"See you tomorrow," she said and ended the call. She needed to layout all of Rick's files on his last investigation to determine if what he had told her in her dream had any merit. Already, the professor had piqued her curiosity.

An hour into her work, her phone rang. It was POTUS. "Shit, what does he want now? Hello Mr. President," she answered, sounding a little annoyed.

"Well, hello to you too, Ms. Turner. Is this a bad time?"

She realized she had come across too rude. "No, no. Just up to my eyeballs in this investigation into Dunham. What can I do for you?"

Chesterfield exhaled loudly. "I need to see you tomorrow at the Oval Office. Please stop your investigation until you hear what I have to say to you. It's a matter of National Security," he said.

"Tomorrow? What time. I was meeting with Professor Miller tomorrow-he believes he can open Dunham's encrypted files," she said. "Can it wait a day?"

"No. Be here by nine in the morning. I will have a plane ready to pick you up at four-thirty in the morning at the same location as before. Then, I will, on the taxpayer's dime get you back to California so you can meet with Miller later that afternoon. Is that fair?" he said.

Paige wanted to ask what this was all about but knew if he had tried to tell her over the phone, he would have done it already. "Sure. See you tomorrow. Anything you need me to bring?"

"No. Just want you to be part of an announcement I am going to make." And, with that, the line went dead.

Paige was thinking. "What announcement?" she muttered, then realized what Chesterfield was going to do. "Damn. He's going to make Dunham his new Secretary of State."

78

Dunham was waiting inside the Oval Office for the president. He was sure he knew what Chesterfield wanted. He just needed to hear him beg him to become the next Secretary of State. His plan was now falling perfectly into place. Then, Stage Five would commence, and it would be too late to stop him.

President Chesterfield, Paige Turner, Scott Rogers, and Felix Wilson entered the Oval Office at the same time. Dunham seemed surprised. He was hoping for a one-on-one with the president.

Dunham was shocked to see Paige Turner friendly with the president. He was now getting nervous about what this meeting was about, speculating if Turner had figured out what his Stage Five was going to be?

Paige sat down on the couch across from Dunham. They both had icy stares that could have frozen them right where they sat. Chesterfield could see the tension on their faces. It didn't matter. He needed to get on with his meeting and his announcement.

"Thank all of you for being here on such short notice. I've brought both of you here today because of how well respected both of you are as American patriots, as well as the respect you have from all of us. And, with that in mind, let me get to the point of this meeting. I want to announce two things today. First, I initiated a special investigation into a group of citizens who have been meeting secretly over the last few years. I suspect this group has links to what Ms. Turner has uncovered in her Shadow Government Scandal. Twenty men and women have been singled out and being interview by the FBI as we speak. If this investigation does confirm that these individuals were responsible for the attacks on American soil and at our embassies, I have ordered the FBI and the Attorney General to arrest them for domestic terrorism and treason," Chesterfield said.

Paige was first to respond. She looked over at Dunham; his face drained of color. "Sir, that's wonderful. I am happy I could help."

"Secondly, after Secretary Waterfall's resignation, I need to fill her position in my cabinet immediately. Mr. Dunham, I would like you to be my acting Secretary of State," Chesterfield asked. "With the election less than two years away, I have the authority to make a temporary appointment and by-pass congress. If I can get your answer by the end of today, it would be appreciated."

Dunham did not seem surprised. He did not expect it after hearing about the investigation the president was conducting. "Sir, I am honored to have your confidence. I want to serve at the pleasure of my president," he replied. "I am not sure I am qualified," he said modestly. He was looking at Turner and back at the president, trying to size them up. Was this going to be a distraction to slow him down with his Stage Five?

Chesterfield, without hesitation, responded. "You're more than qualified. What you've done with Spain, Greece and Italy saved our country's economy. Then, what you accomplished with Palestine and Israel, is nothing short of a miracle."

Paige almost passed out. She could not believe Chesterfield would put this man in one of the most potent and vital jobs in the country, especially hearing the investigation he was doing with the Architect's group of conspirators. She was at a loss for words.

Chesterfield again could see that Turner was not happy with his decision. He ignored it and went behind his desk and sat down. Mr. Dunham, I still need your answer by the end of today. Okay?"

Dunham carefully thought about his response. "As of this moment, with my current business dealings, I need to check with my advisors about potential conflicts of interests, and what this job would do to my personal and business life. Don't get me wrong. I am extremely honored. I need some time to weigh all the factors that would come into play with me accepting. Can I have forty-eight hours, Mr. President?" he said, sincerely.

The president, noticeably disappointed, asked his Chief of Staff, Felix Wilson, to walk Dunham out. Chesterfield very politely asked Turner to stay back so they could talk.

Dunham turned and gave Chesterfield a stare that brought chills to his entire body. The president's potential new Secretary of State did not look happy that he would not be privy to what he said to Paige Turner. The president hated how he could read body language and wonder if he had just made a horrible mistake.

Paige was pacing around the Oval Office, noticeably agitated. Once the door had sealed shut and Dunham was out of earshot, she spoke. "Mr. President, I respect you and this office, but you've made a horrible mistake about placing Albert Dunham in such an important position. I am sure you hadn't vetted him, because if you had, you would have already learned that he's the individual who organized the meeting you are investigating at his ranch," Turner said, her tone reflected her anger. "I now have the proof we've been looking for to nail Dunham to the cross," she said.

Chesterfield motioned for Turner to sit. "I did vet Dunham. His family history, his philanthropy, and if you remember, his bold actions these last few weeks show he's a proud American. I am not sure you've seen the most recent polls, but his approval rating is higher than mine at the moment."

"Sir, you can't be serious? He's been deceiving everyone," Paige argued.

Chesterfield ignored her remarks. "We do know that the group was at his ranch for their meeting. However, Frederick Ellison organized it. Dunham's family hasn't been at that ranch in over a decade. You don't understand politics, except as a journalist. Our country needs a win right now, and the polls are saying Dunham is a win for everyone. I am running for re-election and accusing a great American like Dunham of the heinous acts you say he's committed would be political suicide. So, unless you have proof beyond any reasonable doubt, you need to stand down on your investigation into Albert Dunham. That's an order. You understand me?" the president said sternly.

"I understand you perfectly, sir. You want to get re-elected at any cost. What should I do with all the evidence I've been giving Rogers? Is he done with this investigation too?" Paige's frustration was coming across loud and clear.

"I'll give you a pass on your insolence. Scott will be working on the investigation with his team only. I included you today, because of what you've done for us so far. Now you'll have to back away, so I can heal my administration and get re-elected. You can go now. I have work to do," Chesterfield said, noticeably upset.

79

Maggie Dunham was astonished, as well as thrilled, for her husband. The Secretary of State position she knew was one of the most critical cabinet posts. It would give her husband the credentials he'd need to one day become the leader of the free world.

"Albert, sweetheart, I am so proud of you. We have a lot to talk about, so we can make all of this work," she said, planting a big wet kiss on his lips. "I love you so much. You'll see that from this day forward your past as this Architect will not matter to you or the world."

Dunham leaned back and looked into Maggie's eyes. "After Secretary Waterfall resigned, I had a feeling that her vacancy would open up to me. Chesterfield has no one at this time he can trust. He seems to trust me, which will make what I have planned to do go even smoother," he said without emotion. "I told him I needed forty-eight hours to make my decision."

Maggie stepped away, noticeably concerned with what her husband had just said. "Albert. What are you planning? You promised me that side of you was over," she said, sounding worried.

"I did make a promise to you, but there are a few more things that have to fall into place, so that our future, my future as America's leader, will happen. My business is very fragile now. I have to tidy up a few loose ends," he said, his voice resonating with a coldness that frightened her.

"You promised me," she said, with tears cascading down her cheek.

Dunham tightly took hold of both her arms, squeezing them firmly. "Look, you have everything any woman would ever want. Please, don't get in my way right now," he said, raising his voice. "I've come this close to my dream, and I'm feeling a little stressed now." he said, holding up his right hand, his index finger and thumb just a quarter-inch apart, "so stop questioning me and let me do what I do best."

Maggie's eyes were wide with fear. She didn't recognize her husband, and it scared her.

He noticed her trembling and shrugged his shoulders. Not wanting to address her fears and went back to his ranting. "Then, we can talk about cleaning up my act," he said caustically. "Thinning out of political leaders by men of wealth has been going on for centuries. My granddad hated Joseph Kennedy. Joseph Kennedy built his family's legacy by breaking federal laws. He was a god-damn bootlegger. Then he had the nerve to clean up his act and go legit, so his sons could run for political office. My father loved his father and helped him rid our country of President Kennedy and his pain-in-the-ass attorney general brother. For our kind to survive, sometimes political change is inevitable," he said coldly. "Political change is coming. I need a little more time, so my Stage Five will work perfectly, and our experiment with democracy can evolve to where it was always meant to be."

Maggie did not know how to react; her words stuck in her throat. She could not believe what she had heard from the man she loved. "Just call me when your done doing what you do," she replied and stormed out of their hotel room.

Dunham did not react to her tantrum and immediately called Hayes. He had more orders to give him.

80

Chesterfield and Felix Wilson were deep in a heated conversation about his idea to appoint Dunham as Secretary of State. His chief of staff was not unhappy with the choice, just the timing of it.

"You should have waited a few weeks, maybe a month before you announced this appointment to the world. Carolyn needs time to adjust to her stage four cervical cancer and mourn the end of her political career. The country is still shocked about her health and losing one of the best Secretary of State our country has ever seen. She was on track to be your successor."

"It's politics, Felix. Optics are everything. I need to show the country I am still in charge, even during these impeachment hearings that are going on. We just arrested the FBI and CIA directors and maybe a few more traitors before the election. What we're doing is a good thing for the country and me. Do you know that we have an on-going investigation into the bombings on our homeland and the destruction of the Iranian weapons and nuclear facilities? I need to find the perpetrators. I need to have this part of my cabinet running smoothly. I need someone out there that can deal with all the shit going on around the world, and Dunham fits the bill."

Felix took a deep breath and looked Chesterfield directly in the eyes. "We've trusted each other for over fifteen years. I am your friend, and you need to step back and see what your about to do will come across as poor judgment. Appoint Dunham if you must, but please wait a few weeks to announce it. Let this time be about Secretary Waterfall. Then, in a week or two, you can have your press conference," he said.

Chesterfield had a blank stare, deep in thought before he responded. "Felix, you are my most trusted friend. I value your counsel. Maybe you're right about waiting. Dunham wanted forty-eight hours, so I guess I am waiting."

"Also, won't you need Congressional approval first?" Felix asked.

"No, the attorney general said since this will be an emergency appointment, I had the authority. And, even if I don't, it's done. Let them find another reason to impeach me," he said sarcastically.

Felix's eyes were wide with disbelief. He shrugged his shoulders, shaking his head. "You're the boss, Mr. President, but I am glad you're going to wait a while," he said relieved.

"Glad you're on board. I thought by keeping Dunham close will allow us to keep a better eye on him. Just in case Turner is right that he's this Architect."

"Shit, Patrick," Wilson said. "If you suspect he might be the Architect, then he's closer to achieving the plan we've deciphered inside his files. You think to grant him this much power is a wise move before we've properly vetted him?"

"This move might guarantee my re-election. Dunham is very popular now and can give us a broader base of voters. I am still the president," he barked. "He'll have as much or as little power as I want to give him. Don't worry so much. I know what I'm doing. By the way, with the new communications satellite launch in three weeks, the NSA will be able to track Dunham's whereabouts better than Professor Miller's software."

"I hope you're right. Dunham might be too close for comfort, Mr. President.

President Chesterfield always knew when Felix was worried. "Okay, let's take another look at the report professor Miller had created. Maybe with a new perspective, we might be able to figure if Dunham is this Architect."

"Will do sir."

"Can you have it to me yesterday?" he asked.

"Even better. I can have it ready for us to review later today," Felix said, acting relieved.

81

Paige had checked into her hotel suite at the Plaza Hotel in Manhattan a few blocks from Columbus Circle. Dean Miller would be available with Bradley on Skype to bring her up to date on their investigation into Dunham's chemical and pharmaceutical companies.

She had put the do not disturb sign on her door and was about to bury herself into all the printouts she had gotten from Miller. The timeline about the Dunham family still had her fascinated.

Just as she was about to dig into her files, her cellphone rang. She looked at the display. It was US Marshall Rogers.

"I cannot hide from you, can I?" she said, sounding annoyed.

"Well, thanks for not calling me Buck. But it's easy to follow you. Dulles had you listed on an early flight to Manhattan, and a simple search of hotel guest registries and well, that's my investigation secrets. You do know that the bad guys can do the same if you're worried?" he said, in a more serious tone.

Paige knew this was not a social call or to find out how she was doing. "What can I do for you today?"

"I am downstairs and would like to meet with you to go over my investigation into Dunham and Frederick Ellison. I think you'll be fascinated by what I've found so far."

"Fine," Paige replied.

“See you in five minutes. Just having my men survey the perimeter and lobby to be sure it’s secure," he said a worried concern in his voice.

Scott Rogers rang the suite's doorbell. When Paige opened the door, she was surprised he was carrying a large file box. He marched in and dropped it on the coffee table in front of a large couch. He then sat down in a club chair across from the table.

"No polite greeting from my favorite bodyguard," she said sarcastically.

Rogers did not look up as he started to spread out the files he had brought. He just waved his hand and mumbled a quick good morning to her. "We need to get started on what I have brought you," he said, a rushed tone to his voice.

Paige had a curious look on her face. "Is this how president Chesterfield makes his apologies?" she asked smirking.

Scott seemed confused. "Not sure what you mean. The president doesn't know I am here. Before I speak with him on what I've uncovered, I needed to talk with you and Professor Miller first. I need a favor I cannot get from the NSA or FBI. We still don't know who we can truly trust at this time, and I don't want to spook the Architect or his people."

"I am not sure what I can give you. I am running into brick walls when it comes to Dunham and Ellison. These files are proving to be nothing more than one man's writings. We have not been able to decrypt the other files inside the thumb drive. I've run into a dead end with this guy," she said.

Scott released a warm, charming smile that made his chiseled facial features even more handsome. "One of my cyber experts on my team has cracked open all of those files. They’re filled with so much shit I felt I needed your expertise as an investigative journalist to interpret them. I am not sure President Chesterfield will want to do anything about these files until after the election," Rogers said, combing his fingers through his thick wavy hair.

"I have that same sense. We had a little fight before I left DC. That's why I am here. The professor should be here in about an hour and a half. Let's see what you've got. You show me yours, and I will show you mine," she said, sending him a warm, friendly smile.

For the next hour and a half, Rogers showed her a scary list of terrorist groups around the world that appear to be supported by the Architect and his inner circle. General Tucker Phillips is the commander of all these groups. There were terrorist groups in Columbia, Pakistan, India, Iraq, Saudi Arabia, Lebanon, Germany, France, North Korea, China, South Africa, Egypt, and believe it or not, even in Israel."

"This is nothing new," she said.

"It is if these groups have no links to any of the top ten terrorist groups around the globe. These are new groups that have been doing small missions, testing the waters, and laying low. They seem to be waiting for orders to launch a major attack," he said, frustrated.

"Let's just hope that they've used any portion of the internet or cellphone networks, so the Professor can run a search against any of our suspects we already know about."

Scott, for the first time, looked worried. "The last file we opened, had information on NASA's new communication satellite, which is President Chesterfields pet project. There are no records on such a satellite either at the CIA or NSA. NASA denies knowing about it. There are at least a dozen names in the file that have all been working on this secret government weapon. Here is where I need your help. Why would this Architect have a file like this and murder to keep it hidden?"

Just then there was a loud knock on the door. Scott drew his weapon. "I'm not expecting anyone," Paige said.

Dean was surprised and shocked to see a gun pointing at his head. "Nice way to greet a friend, Paige," the professor said, terrified. Scott slipped his gun back in his holster. "Sorry about that. I'm a little edgy lately."

Paige jumped in. "Dean, I thought we were going to speak via skype?

“Chesterfield needed me back in D.C., and I thought I’d see you first. My wife and kids haven’t been to Manhattan in a long time.”

Paige pointed to the couch for him to sit. “We have a lot to discuss, and I hope you're prepared to work most of today?"

"All of today? I have meetings all day and need to be at the White House at five-thirty. You do know that my *'We the People'* PAC is getting into high gear this month?"

"It can wait. When you see what Scott brought us, you'll not want to leave," she said.

83

Dunham was livid. Ellison had just brought him up to date on Tucker Phillips briefing he had. "What do you mean they're looking into our army of fighters?" he barked.

"Tucker got word from five of our groups. This Scott Rogers seems to have a lot of connections around the world for a fucking US Marshall. One other concern, he's been asking about the upcoming NASA launch. Could he know we're connected?" Ellison said.

Dunham thought for a while, then said. "Impossible. Those files on Russell's thumb drive had a new encryption code that even the best at the NSA or Homeland Security couldn't crack," he replied. Then, his face turned bedsheet white. "Shit if they even suspect a compromise with the satellite and this Scott Rogers guy gets Chesterfield to delay the launch, I'm screwed."

"I know what Frasier would be saying right now," Ellison remarked.

"Me too. Maybe it's time to begin eliminating at least three of the biggest pain-in-the-asses? Let's ruin Turner's reputation first and neutralize her popularity. Rogers and Professor Miller can be dealt with severely at another time," Dunham said coldly. "Maybe I should accept the Secretary of State position? I'd only be four steps away from the presidency then," he laughed.

Ellison had a shocked look on his face. "Let's not get carried away right now. You can't keep murdering everyone that's getting in your way."

"I wasn't thinking of assassinating Chesterfield, only speeding up the process to get him impeached. The vice-president has no backbone for any of what it takes to be president, especially with his health. You know he's not running with the president for re-election."

"Really. Who's going to be Chesterfield's new running mate?" asked Ellison.

"Not sure now, with Waterfall resigning. It really won't matter if he gets impeached. If the house does it, we have enough votes in the Senate to execute it. Then, if something tragic happens to the speaker of the house, I'm next in line," Dunham said, a big grin exploding on his face.

"Albert, can we get back on point. What are we going to do about Scott Rogers' investigation, as well as the one Paige Turner is doing? They are getting close and could tie you and the Architect together."

"Again, Frederick stop worrying. No one in this country would ever believe I am the big bad Architect, especially after I do my upcoming interview with Turner. I relish her accusing me. With what I've done recently for this country, whatever she implies or suggests will make her out to be a crackpot...which I pray happens.

"Call Tucker and tell him he needs to figure out how to eliminate Rogers and Miller. Once that's done, they need to lie low for the next few weeks. Once the satellite goes up, then I will give the General the signal to begin his part of Stage Five. Now, I need to call Ms. Turner and have that interview."

84

Paige's muted cell pinged. She palmed it and noticed it was Dunham calling. "I need to take this," she said to Rogers and Miller. Her finger on her lips for them to be quiet.

"Mr. Dunham. So nice to hear from you," she said in her charming voice.

"It's my pleasure, Ms. Turner," he said, forcing himself to not choke on his words.

"What can I do for you?" she asked.

Dunham sucked in a deep breath before he replied. "I'd like to take you up on your offer of an interview. I really would like to help you find this Architect character," he said.

Paige had put Dunham on speaker so that everyone could hear. "What day did you have in mind?"

"How about the day after president Chesterfield announces that I am his new Secretary of State pick," he said, wishing he could see Paige's face.

Paige was not surprised, but curious as to why he'd be telling her this in a bragging tone. "Sorry I didn't congratulate you in the Oval Office, but better late than never. Based on what you've done recently, President Chesterfield is making the right choice before his re-election bid," she replied, her voice even and well-controlled.

"Does next Tuesday, at my home in Bethesda work for you. I will have everything you'd need set up for your Show."

Now, Paige was surprised. "That will work just fine for me, Mr. Dunham," she said.

"Then, it's done. See you next Tuesday," he replied, and the line went dead.

Paige looked at Scott and the Professor, disbelief on her face. "What was that all about?' she said.

Scott was checking his calendar. "That's the day of the satellite launch."

"Then, we need to find out what this might mean to him. I need to call Bradley and get him here with us. His part of this investigation can wait for now."

Scott was immediately on his phone. "Morgan, it's Scott. I need everyone together for a conference call. We need to shift our direction on the Dunham and Ellison investigation," he said.

Professor Miller seemed confused since just getting to Paige's suite. "I'm not sure what's going on, but it sounds like you need me here all day."

Paige responded. "We believe that the Architect's Fifth Stage has something to do with the upcoming NASA launch of their new communication satellite. Scott's team was able to break the encryption code on those additional files we saw in the thumb drive. We now have specifics. We have the names of terrorist groups around the globe who have their allegiance to the Architect. It's this new satellite that has us stumped," she told him.

Miller was quick to respond. "I know all about the satellite. While they might describe it as a communication satellite, it has many more uses than that. It has the software programs the NSA bought from me when I retired from my business. On the surface, its functionality is to have improved counterterrorist tracking. It has the best facial tracking software ever created if I do say so myself," he said, patting himself on his back. "Unfortunately, what NSA wanted me to do, in good conscience, forced me to retire and teach."

"Are you going to tell us what they wanted you to do? And, if they can do it?

"I can. I need to get to a lab I'm using at Columbia and bring you some of my old files from the original satellite project. It might have all the clues you'll need to know why anyone would want to highjack this launch," Miller said. "Oh, by the way, Russell inserted a file on the thumb drive that was for my eyes only."

"Do you have any idea why he did this?" Paige asked.

"He was paranoid when he added this file. Russell wrote that he appreciated how I taught him how to break a code. That's all he said. I'll have to review some of my lectures and try to remember what he was trying to say. But, first on to Columbia." Miller was out the door without a goodbye.

Paige looked at Scott; they both were shrugging their shoulders mystified about what he had just said.

Scott said. "I guess we wait. I'm hungry. Want to order in or go downstairs?"

"Downstairs sounds great. I've been cooped up in this room too long and need some fresh air."

85

The Architect had just finished his briefing with Gregory Wilbanks. "You're sure there is no connection to you and your friends at the NSA?"

"Yes, sir," he said. "There is no trail to me or us. We're all set for launch on Tuesday. Once the satellite achieves orbit, there are a few items needed for it to adjust and activate its systems. Once I get word this has happened, we will have full control of it whenever we want," he said nervously. He wanted to say more, catching himself and realizing less is better when it came to this man.

"Good job, Gregory. We'll talk soon."

With that, he was back talking with Thomas Hayes. "Where are we at with Dean Miller?" Dunham asked.

"He's was at Columbia early this morning working on his *We the People* movement until he got an urgent call from an excited Paige Turner. He's now at the Plaza Hotel in Manhattan near Columbus Circle, and agent Rogers is there as well. I did not know ahead of time that Turner was going to be there, so we do not have any listening devices inside her suite. I do have four men in the lobby having some coffee waiting on my orders."

"Any fucking idea what the three of them are up to?" Dunham said anxiously. Then, he remembered his phone call with her. *"Did that bitch put me on speaker?"*

"What I do know is Rogers, and his team have been working non-stop on decrypting the rest of your files. He left

DC in a rush to see Turner in Manhattan. My gut tells me he's had a breakthrough."

Dunham jumped out of his chair behind his desk. "This can't be happening right now. If they find out about the satellite and the army I have around the globe, they'll put two and two together and ruin my plans," he screamed. The veins on his face looked like they would explode, as he tossed a glass paperweight across his office. It hit a bookshelf with numerous photos of himself accepting awards for his philanthropy and charity work, and then it crashed into tiny pieces on the floor.

"Sir, one thing I do know is that president Chesterfield does not have any clue about what Turner and Scott are doing. If we create a few distractions, like terrorist attacks, we could slip under their radar and take control of the satellite before anyone knows what hit them?" Hayes suggested.

"I like the way you're thinking. How soon can we get something going?"

"Today if you'd like. General Phillips has a hard time keeping his troops calm for now. They could use a little action to keep them occupied. You should then have enough time to get the NSA business handled."

"Okay. But, make it something big that will have every network and news organization talking about for weeks. I want Chesterfield looking lost as Commander and Chief. I want him relying on me as his Secretary of State," Dunham said an evil smile on his face.

86

Bradley had just arrived at Paige's suite when all their cellphones went off with pulsating siren blasts. They all looked at their screens and saw what was happening. Paige yelled to Scott to turn on the TV. The four of them sat down and watched the live feed in shock.

At least ten well-coordinated attacks were happening in London, Paris, Japan, Jordon, Israel, Iraq, and South Africa. They were all happening in populated shopping districts.

Men in unmarked vans were stopping in the middle of the streets, stopping traffic and shooting anyone that was near them. Innocent men and women having lunch were mowed down. Mother's strolling with their babies did not have a chance as the bullets tore their bodies apart. Each attack lasted only minutes. Then the unmarked vans, with precision and planning, drove off and disappeared.

Reports were coming in estimating the death toll at over a thousand, with at least another thousand wounded or in critical condition. Before they could catch their breath, three additional well-timed attacks took place, but this time in the United States.

Paige was cupping her head with her hands. "What is happening?" she moaned. "This Dunham's Fifth Stage?"

Before anyone could respond, reports were coming across the TV.

"Rodeo Drive in Beverly Hills was attacked by four men wielding automatic rifles. Seventy-five affluent residents, in

what has always been a safe community, have been touched by terror," the reporter said, tears flowing down her cheek.

Paige flipped channels. Another report was airing.

"Three more attacks just happened in Boston, Chicago, and Dallas. It was similar to the attack in Beverly Hills. The United States is under attack. Where is our president?" the reporter begged, his eyes staring into the camera.

Scott was thumbing through his print outs from the decrypted files. "Shit. The Architect has contingencies laid out in Stage Five if he needs a distraction," he said.

"One hell of a distraction," Paige said. She was deep in thought, trying to come up with a logical reason for Dunham to do this right now. He's agreed to an interview with me. He must know by now that I have his files. Could he assume we've decrypted some of them and we know about the satellite, and he's in panic mode?"

Bradley responded. "After talking with Dunham's brother, there is more to this Architect than we can imagine. Theodore Dunham knows nothing of this Architect. He told me that the Dunham legacy was a club for heirs only, which he, even though he is the oldest brother, was excluded. He's a nice guy, with a nice family," Bradley said.

Paige gave him a look that told him to move on with his story. "You sound like Sean. Please get to your point," she said irritably. She regretted what she had just said. "Sorry. I'm a little stressed right now. Not fair bringing up Sean today."

Bradley nodded. "Yeah, I miss that little shit too. He could ramble. Well, Teddy told me that he does not like his brother. Feels he's a dishonest man and harming the Dunham name. He does remember once hearing his father and a few of his associates talking, and the name Architect came up. That's all he knows. But, one thing he does have with proof of, is his brother, Albert Dunham, is intentionally poisoning large geographical areas so his cancer drug sales will go through the roof."

"That's all well and good, but what does that have to do with proving Dunham is the Architect?" Paige asked.

"Nothing, but Teddy does have a video of his brother talking to him about what he's doing with his chemical factory and how it affects his drug sales."

"Do you have these tapes?" Paige asked.

"Teddy will give them to us, if his brother gets too close to achieving his dream, EOTUS," Bradley said. "If not, then the tapes remain a family secret."

"As bad as this is today, we can't let it distract us from our investigation," Paige said.

"Oh, but it will. I just got texted. POTUS wants me back to the Capitol ASAP," Rogers said. "I'll leave you with my files so that you can work on this shit. My team will be here working with you, as well as protecting the two of you. Stay put. It's not safe right now."

Paige waved goodbye. She was looking frazzled and out of sorts. She was dialing her boss Clay. She needed his counsel.

87

President Chesterfield was standing on the White House lawn. To his left was Albert Dunham, to his right was his Secretary of Defense, Homeland Security Secretary, and the new FBI Director, Mathew Gentry.

Reporters and cameras littered the White House lawn. Behind them were hundreds of citizens all shouting profanities at their president. Some were holding up placards with unflattering words: *Impeach Chesterfield. Throw the Bum Out,* and one very painful sign: *Hang the Mother Fucker.*

Chesterfield could see the angry crowds. He was upset too. It was not just in DC that people were outraged. Riots had broken out all over the country, as anger toward him, and his presidency grew to a fever pitch. He raised his arms, signaling everyone he was about to speak. A hush came over the crowd.

"My fellow Americans. Today is another sad day for our country. We've witnessed how cowards can, without any conscience, murder innocent men, women, and children. It's been a war zone for the last two months in our country and an assault on our beliefs as an open democracy. I have been wanting to avoid taking severe actions that would impair the constitutional freedoms we enjoy, but right now, with all the uncontrollable rioting going on in our streets, I will be initiating martial law. There will be a curfew on every American until we get a good handle on what's happening with our national security." He paused and sipped from a bottle of water. "I have activated our National Guard, and they are on high threat alert.

They will be patrolling our streets, and they will need your cooperation with our temporary curfew."

The crowds that were quiet a moment ago were screaming profanities and throwing rocks, bottles, or whatever they could get their hands on at the White House and where the president was giving his speech.

Chesterfield ignored their reaction. He expected it. "As everyone knows, I have been cleaning house within my administration. I am pleased to announce that Albert Dunham has accepted my offer to be our next Secretary of State effective immediately," he said. He was pleased that the rioting crowds had stopped and where now cheering his decision. He spoke for just five more minutes to introduce his new FBI director. He would not take any questions from the press.

* * * * *

Inside the situation room Chesterfield had gathered his joint chiefs, Homeland Security Secretary, the Secretary of Defense and new Secretary of State. Felix Wilson looked drained. The last twenty-four hours was taking its toll on him.

"Gentlemen, our world has a serious problem that now seems to have spread to our shores. For the first time in our history, there seems to be a coup happening within our government," he said, his voice cracking.

Admiral Hollingsworth interrupted his Commander and Chief. "Sir, we've been addressing your concerns and making the necessary changes. It's only been three weeks since we initiated *Operation Clean Sweep*," he said. "What's happened now could be the work of this fucking Architect. Could he be in the Fifth Stage that he mentioned in his manifesto?

"What are you trying to say?" Admiral. "Are you questioning my decision today?" he said, his voice rising with frustration.

Hollingsworth stood and paced around the room. "Martial Law is the wrong message. We're playing into the Architect's hands. If he wants to be the next Emperor, then we've handed him a big spotlight to win over the American people." When he said that, he looked Dunham straight in the eye. "Have you even vetted your new Secretary of State?" he asked, his voice showing his disgust for Dunham.

Felix could see the president getting rattled by the Admiral's remarks. "Let's calm down and figure out what we're going to do about these attacks. We need to find these murderers first before we start turning on each other," he said, pointing his finger at Hollingsworth.

Scott Rogers entered the situation room. All heads, including Dunham's, turned toward him. Chesterfield was finally smiling.

Chesterfield stood and said. "Gentlemen, you all know US Marshall Scott Rogers. He and his team are heading up the investigation into finding and locking up the Architect. I've asked him here to brief all of us on his progress. He does feel the attacks around the globe and on our soil was a distraction by the Architect, not his Stage Five plan."

Scott was surprised that Chesterfield would blurt out what he had briefed him on during his flight from New York. "Mr. President. Before I speak to this group, I need a few minutes of your time, privately," he asked.

"Shit. Okay. Let's take a short break," Chesterfield said, showing his frustration.

Inside the Oval Office were Rogers and Wilson. They both remained standing while Chesterfield plopped down behind his desk.

"What's the big deal that we had to interrupt the meeting?" the president asked pissed.

"I don't like talking in front of Dunham. I still believe, like Paige Turner, he's the Architect. You've fallen into his little trap," Rogers said.

"What the fuck? You can't question my decision. This country needs stability right now, and Dunham was my best choice. He has higher favorability ratings than me," the president barked.

Scott looked at Felix for help, but all he got was a shrug of his shoulders. "If you're going to let him be your Secretary of State, you have to delay Tuesday's NASA launch," he said.

"That's crazy. I need it so I can find all those fucking terrorist cells that are attacking our allies and our citizens. It's the best defense we have right now."

Rogers was not sure if he should reveal what he found in the Architect's files, but knew he'd regret it if he didn't. "Sir, my team was able to decrypt the other files inside the thumb drive, and we found out that the Architect was very interested in your new communications satellite..." Chesterfield interrupted.

"Interested? How the fuck did he even know about it?" he shouted. "I thought it was classified?"

Felix stepped in. "Maybe the Architect's reach went deep into the NSA?"

"I can't believe we've been compromised there too," Chesterfield wailed.

Rogers said. "It is still too soon to know, but a delay of a few weeks will give my team and me enough time to figure it out."

Chesterfield looked at Felix, then back at Rogers. "You do know that Tuesday has the perfect window for a sound and successful launch. If we delay it even one day, it could put our schedule back at least nine months, even a year, and that's unacceptable. Even if the Architect knows of our satellite, what will he do with that information?"

"I'm not sure, sir. I want more time to figure it out. We're digging into the entire NSA department to see if there are any connections to Dunham, Ellison or any of his cast of characters. I need some more time," he pleaded.

Chesterfield was rubbing his chin, deep in thought. "We don't have more time. I've spent billions of taxpayer dollars on this project and need it working so I can get re-elected. If I am not the president, then, shit, let the next guy deal with this," he said.

They were back in the situation room. Rogers had been instructed to omit everything he had on the satellite from his report. He was ordered to brief everyone about the other files on the thumb drive and the army of terrorist cells mentioned inside the Architect's encrypted folders.

As he briefed everyone, he watched Dunham react to his words. It disturbed him that the man he believed to be the Architect was smiling, lost in thought somewhere. *What the hell has president Chesterfield just done to our country?* Rogers asked himself.

88

Inside Paige's suite, the three of them were stunned at what President Chesterfield had said. While the rioting across the nation was subsiding, angry citizens roamed the streets ready to test the National Guard.

The three major news channels were non-stop about Dunham's appointment as Secretary of State. Most of the reporting was positive, which only made Paige sick to her stomach. It had gotten worse when Scott called and told her about his meeting with Chesterfield and that he would not delay the launch.

"What the hell's wrong with this guy?" she complained.

Scott sounded stressed. "He's only focused on getting re-elected at the moment. Nothing else matters, even if it means putting himself ahead of what's best for our country. We should find a better place to meet. I am not comfortable with Dunham having Chesterfield's ear. I don't think we're safe right now."

Paige's voice had a nervous edge to it. "What do you have in mind. I need to get back for my Sunday Show. Then I have to prepare for Dunham's interview at his home. Shit, this changes everything. He's the god-damn Secretary of State," she said.

"Admiral Hollingsworth has some ideas for us. He's pissed at his Commander and Chief also, but being the dedicated military man he is, won't criticize his Commander and Chief. He's comfortable helping us on the QT," Rogers said.

Paige told Scott that Professor Miller was working on a broad search, now that he has all the names of the leaders of those terrorist groups. He is hopeful that their faces, even parts of their faces, can be tagged. It's a reach, but what else can we do right now. The fox is in the henhouse, and Dunham's ready to have us for dinner," she said.

Paige ended her call with Rogers and looked at Bradley and Dean. "We've got a big problem that I am not sure we can handle. I think the Architect, Dunham, has started his Stage Five. I worried we're too late and will have to watch from the sidelines," she said dejectedly.

Bradley shook his head. "Never say die. We've got a lot of ammunition. So, let's begin using it like good journalists and start attacking Dunham and if needed, Chesterfield."

Professor Miller acted skeptically. "Are you guys crazy? Do you really want to start a fight with the president and his new Secretary of State? What if the data you've accumulated has been interpreted wrong? Could it possibly be that Dunham is a victim here and Ellison is setting him up?"

Paige looked at Bradley and grinned. "Not a chance. Everything you've been giving us these last few weeks points to Dunham as the Architect. Ellison is just the face, not the brains of the Architect's plans."

"I hope you're right. If not, our careers are over," the professor said, biting his lower lip.

Paige patted him on the back. "Keep searching. We'll turn up something useful. I'm sure of it."

89

Dunham was back in the Oval Office. He had just finished another briefing on the attacks around the world with the joint chiefs, the FBI, CIA, and the Secretary of Defense. It amused him that the president's current intelligence agency had no clue as to what or who committed these acts. He was pleased there was no mention of the satellite launch, which he prayed meant it was going off on schedule.

"Secretary Dunham," the president said, a smile on his face. "How do you feel about jumping into the fire immediately. I need you to visit a group of our embassies at or near these recent attacks. You'll have a full Marine unit to protect you."

"Mr. President, it sounds just perfect. I am a little in shock about all of this, but ready to help our country be safe again," Dunham said, trying to contain his joy that his final stage was getting closer to completion. "I assume you need me to find some answers and assure our allies we still have their backs?" Secretary Dunham said.

"Exactly. I am confident with your connections and contacts you'll be able to rebuild our alliances. I need it for my re-election. You'll need it too if you want to remain Secretary of State after the election."

"I can leave on Tuesday. I have some minor housekeeping chores that need to be taken care of with my businesses and an interview I promised Paige Turner I would give her," he said.

"Sir, one thing that concerns me. How were you able to push my appointment through without going to the House first?"

"That's easy. When Congress goes on so many recesses that if I need to fill any vacancy in my cabinet that requires their approval while they are not in session, then the constitution allows me to keep our government working while they are closed down for business," Chesterfield said, allowing an evil grin to crack on his face. "Those bastards want to impeach me. So, while I am still president, I will fulfill my oath of office to the best of my ability."

Dunham was almost ready to burst out laughing. Chesterfield did not even know he's the one pushing for his impeachment. It was an integral part of Stage Five. "Sir, if you do not need me, I need to go home and talk to my wife, Maggie. She's just over the top happy about all of this."

"One thing I need to warn you about Ms. Turner and this interview. I asked her not to bring up the Architect, but she's determined to complete her fake news investigation into this imaginary man. Don't let her rattle you. I need you sharp for this mission," the president said.

"Don't worry. What could Paige Turner ask me about the Architect? I do not have a clue who this man or his family is. Does she think all billionaires know what we all do day-to-day? I'll be fine, sir." Dunham said, holding back a belly laugh.

90

Paige understood that she had just three days to prepare for the Dunham interview at his Bethesda home. She would have loved it on her turf, but it would have to do.

"We need to figure out what this new satellite is all about. Why would Dunham be so interested in it?" Paige asked her team.

Scott was the first to answer. "As Secretary of State, Dunham would not have any access to NSA and any of its departments. The satellite would be of no use to him unless he were the president," Rogers said.

Professor Miller raised his hand. "Maybe I have an idea. A little reach if you ask me, but it is something." He passed out copies of one of his printouts. "Look here," he pointed at a line on the first page. "Gregory Wilbanks, one of Ellison's computer geeks and the person who replaced Brian Russell, has been in contact with at least a dozen NSA personnel who have been working on the satellite."

"Why are we just now finding this out?" she asked. "Anything linking Dunham too?"

"Nothing about Dunham. For your next question. We never thought about NSA or this satellite until Scott broke into that file on the Architect's thumb drive. I just had finished my search of every member of that team and Wilbanks's name popped up when he took over his Russell's job. So now we have to figure out what Wilbanks was doing talking to these people who were supposed to be working on a highly classified project?" Paige interrupted Miller. She was staring at the professor, digesting his words.

"Maybe Mr. Wilbanks should be interviewed on my Sunday Show?"

Professor Miller shook his head. "You did not let me finish. He was in a horrible car accident on the turnpike yesterday. He's on life support. It doesn't look good," he said.

"That's a bunch of crap," Paige said. "Can you get me the police report?"

Professor Miller had anticipated her request and handed her the report. "Here. I guess I am beginning to know you too well," he smiled.

Paige read over the report. It was just what she suspected. "A Black Suburban, no license plates, no witnesses, and no leads," she said.

Scott said. "Why not try to interview some of the NSA personnel who met with Wilbanks. I bet they are scared now after his accident. It doesn't take a rocket scientist to know what's happening. Put the story out there so they can begin to worry," he said.

"Great idea. I have just the reporter who can and would love to break the story," she said. "Maybe something like this?"

"*Upcoming NSA satellite launch might have been compromised. At least a dozen members of the launch team are suspected of having connections with one of Frederick Ellison's employees, who's clinging for his life after a mysterious car accident. A preliminary investigation is pointing toward murder. Will there be an FBI investigation before the launch on Tuesday?"*

"How does that sound?" Paige asked.

"That should rock the boat a bit. It might even rattle Secretary Dunham for your interview," Scott said.

"I sure hope so. I want to lay into that bastard with both barrels," Paige said. "I've got a phone call to make."

* * * * *

The AP, most major newspapers around the country, and every TV news media station reported Paige's information word for word. President Chesterfield's press secretary, Rachel Monroe was immediately out in front of the story, debunking it and trying to assure the White House press corps the story was just a rumor and not based on facts.

Paige Turner had been interviewed on her station's morning newscast, promoting her Sunday show and hinting she will be able to explain the questionable links between one of Frederick Ellison's employees and the dozen NSA employees who have been working on the Tuesday scheduled launch. When asked for more details, she just responded with *"Watch my show Sunday."*

* * * * *

Paige looked at her team and asked. "What do you think? Did I do enough to delay the launch?

Dean Miller shrugged his shoulders. "I think you just stirred up a whole bunch of shit for yourself."

Scott Rogers did not pull any punches. "If I know the president, he's going to be pissed about what you just pulled. Chesterfield's trying to salvage his political career and legacy. Your actions just made an enemy you don't need right now," he said.

Paige seemed puzzled. "How so? Did I lie or fabricate the truth? Did I release anything I cannot back up with facts?"

Dean Miller responded quickly. "Your facts are circumstantial, not real evidence. I've told you what I printed up for you were just connections each of these players has with each other. It could be innocent. Maybe with all of them being computer geeks, they have an informal group where they go to meet to discuss new technologies. I'm just saying you're jumping to a serious conclusion without more facts."

Paige bounced up from her chair and started pacing around the room. "We all agreed that the launch needed to be delayed. We all concluded that inside the Architect's manifesto and his Stage Five plan, were detailed facts about the communications satellite and how he needed it in orbit by a certain date. Even if I'm proven wrong, but get NASA to delay the launch, we've won the first battle."

"The way I understand how this works, NASA or NSA will not delay anything without the president's approval. They will proceed on with the launch no matter what everyone in the news media is saying. They do not work on rumors but clear and precise facts. So, you've not accomplished anything with this stunt, but put your reputation at risk," Scott said, his tone more angry than usual.

Paige did not seem moved by his little scolding. "Then we have two days to get the facts I need before my show airs Sunday," she said.

91

President Chesterfield was furious with Paige Turner. He wanted to arrest her, lock her up, and throw away the key. "How the hell could she do this to me?" the president screamed. He looked at Felix. "I want agent Rogers in my office an hour ago," he snapped. "He's got some explaining to do."

"Will do sir. But we have bigger problems than that. I've completed some internal research, and it seems that Turner might be correct on what she's reported. "Gregory Wilbanks, an employee of Frederick Ellison, who by the initial reports we had from professor Miller, was close to at least a half dozen of our NSA team members working on your satellite."

Chesterfield did not seem concerned about Wilson's comments. "So. What does that have to do with the launch on Tuesday?"

"He was killed in a car accident that appears to be suspicious. It has the same signature as the murder of Dean Miller's intern. It does not by all appearances look like an accident, but possibly a murder. He's the young man who replaced Brian Russell, you know, Ellison's employee who brought the Architect and his plans to the surface. I'm just suggesting we should think about delaying the launch until we get a better handle on all of this?"

Chesterfield, his anger boiling over, said. "I don't give a shit about any of this. I need this satellite up and functioning. Just get me, Rogers, now," he shouted.

Felix shook his head in frustration. "Sir, even if your weapon is compromised?"

"I don't believe there's a problem. Everyone is chasing ghosts right now," the president said.

* * * * *

"Scott, Felix here. The president wants you back in DC immediately. Drop everything you're doing. A plane is waiting for you at JFK," he said, his voice resonated with stress.

Rogers had his cell on speaker, so Paige and professor Miller could hear the conversation. "You sound frazzled. What's the big rush?"

Felix was talking fast. "Chesterfield is having a major meltdown because of Turner and what she's about to expose on national TV. The media blast I bet had her signature on it, right?"

Scott gave Paige a harsh look, shaking his head in disgust. "Can't say. I'm on my way to the White House. We should be at the Oval Office in less than two hours. See you then."

Paige bit her lower lip, noticeably upset. "Do you think you're in trouble over my little stunt?"

"I've been in worse over the years. I'm just concerned not briefing the president on my findings first," he replied, shaking his head.

"Remember, Chesterfield brought you into the picture because he did not have anyone in his intelligence community he could trust. He put us together to find the Architect and expose him and his plans. Might I remind you? That's precisely what we've done here," she said.

"Yeah, I know all too well what we've done. But, as US Marshall, my loyalty to my country comes first. I don't know what I'm going to say to him about any of this and why I kept him out of the loop. He did order us to keep him up-to-date, remember?"

Paige bowed her head, deep in thought. "Are you asking me to delay my report on Sunday?"

"Maybe. I'm not sure just yet. Let me see what's on the president's mind first. I don't know how Dunham might be figuring into all of this right now."

92

Paige was on the phone with her boss, Clay Thomas. "I need help. I'm spread too thin and cannot investigate everything I need to get ready for Sunday's show," she said.

Clay was slow to respond. She could hear him breathing heavy through the phone. "I just received a scathing phone call from the president, as well as Secretary of State Dunham," he said. "You cannot do the show you want to do on Sunday. Figure something else out about your investigation, and don't mention anything about the satellite or those NSA employees connected to Ellison's employee, Gregory Wilbanks."

"You can't ask me to do that. I've already told my listeners and the world about this," she argued. "I won't."

Clay drew in a deep breath, realizing he was going to have a stubborn fight on his hands. "I can, and I will. If you even come close to bringing up this shit storm of problems, well, shit Paige, be reasonable. The president told me if we cause him to delay this launch, our National Security will be at risk."

"You know that's bull-shit. This story is real. It's the closest I've come to the Architect and his Fifth Stage. There must be something extremely critical to his plans for him to murder Gregory Wilbanks, so we cannot question him," she said.

"You do not have proof Wilbanks was murdered," Clay argued back. "The police report shows he had a fatal accident."

"Everyone connected to the Architect's Manifesto is dying...no let me correct myself...murdered. Brian Russell, Sean Adams, Seth Alexander, Gregory Wilbanks, need I go on?

Have you forgotten Frasier Montgomery tried to kill me? Who will be next?" she asked.

"Unless you have concrete proof there is something wrong with this satellite, then you will not expose our station to the wrath from the president or possible justice department investigation you might trigger," Clay said.

"Give me some more journalists so I can get us the proof I need," she begged.

"Fine. I can give you five. But, if you don't uncover more than what you have now, you will not include the satellite story in your show? Right?"

Paige shook her head, rolling her eyes as she looked at Professor Miller. "Okay."

* * * * *

Scott Rogers was sitting inside the Oval Office with Secretary of State Dunham, Admiral Hollingsworth, and NSA Director, Douglas Babcock. Felix Wilson was walking around the room, a nervous stride in his pace.

"Sit down Felix," the president ordered. "You're making me uneasy. Now, let's get right down to why I called this meeting. I wanted director Babcock to brief us on the potential of any scandal at NSA. Douglas, you've got the floor."

The NSA director cleared his throat. "Gentlemen, I was shocked about the irresponsible reporting that's been going on, especially from Ms. Turner. The FBI vetted every member of my launch team. I am confident they have not violated their security status regarding this secret project," he said. I have not found, after questioning my team members and those at NASA, any problems that would warrant delaying this launch on Tuesday. It's important to know that Tuesday is the ideal time to put this satellite in orbit. Severe weather patterns are heading toward Houston, making it imperative that everything goes off as scheduled."

"Thank you, Douglas," Chesterfield said. "Agent Rogers, let's have your briefing on the work you've been doing in locating this Architect and its bearing on my satellite launch?"

Scott was caught off-guard. "I seem to be in an awkward position here. I wasn't expecting to brief all of you. Mr. President, are you sure you want me to talk about my entire investigation here?" he asked, looking at Felix for help. He was wondering if Chesterfield wanted to expose himself and his office to be working with Paige Turner in front of Dunham and Babcock?

Felix stepped in, realizing the three of them needed to talk first. "Maybe a short recess, sir?"

Chesterfield seemed confused. "I don't think we need a recess. Everyone here has the necessary security level clearance for what we have to discuss," he said.

Felix walked over and whispered in his ear. "Sir, we do need a recess." The president asked Dunham, Babcock, and Hollingsworth to step out of the Oval Office. "Gentlemen give us five minutes."

Chesterfield seemed pissed at his Chief of Staff, as well as Scott Rogers. "This better be good," he threatened.

"Sir, are you sure you want everyone in the room to know you've been working with Paige Turner? What logical reason could you spin to the press? Remember, she's helping you because you didn't have anyone in the FBI or CIA that you could trust when this all started," Felix said.

"Why do you we have to include her in this?"

Rogers responded. "How do I explain I have, or we have anything from the thumb drive, without including Turner in the conversation?"

"You do it. Turner's about to ruin everything, and I cannot afford another loss in my column of fuck-ups," Chesterfield said.

Scott would have liked to have briefed Felix first, but Chesterfield seemed to be out of sorts. "I was able to decrypt the remaining files on the thumb drive. Professor Miller was able to run his search and came up with an impressive list of characters that are involved with your launch. They had definite connections to Gregory Wilbanks and Brian Russell who were employees of Frederick Ellison. Those two men also had a connection to your new Secretary of State, sir."

The president was now combing his fingers roughly through his hair. "What the fuck do you mean this Wilbanks 'had' or 'was'?

"Sir, he was involved in a suspicious car accident. He's dead. Again, another person associated with the Architect's Manifesto is dead."

Chesterfield let out a long breath. "So, based on this, you want me to delay the satellite launch? Do you even know if or what this Architect wants with our satellite?"

"No, sir. That's why I need more time."

"Well, you don't have it. This satellite was built with impenetrable firewalls and is hack-proof. It has software that would detect any intrusion and destroy it before it made it to the next firewall," Chesterfield said smugly.

Felix jumped into the conversation. "Maybe you should look into this. What if this was the Architect's only objective for his Fifth Stage? What if he had a mole inside NASA or the NSA?"

Chesterfield's face was fire red. "I don't want to hear any more about this. The launch will go off on schedule. And, Scott, you're not needed back in the Oval Office. I want you to remove yourself and your team from this Architect investigation and go back to your real job," he said rudely.

Felix was in shock at what just happened. He walked Scott outside, passing Dunham and Babcock in the reception area. By the elevator, Wilson said. "Call me later. Keep working on the investigation. Find out who this Architect is pronto? Or this country and Chesterfield's presidency is over."

"How can I find out more about this satellite and why it's so important to the president. It's just a communication satellite, right?" He could see the color drain from Felix's face.

93

Dunham was back at the State Department behind closed doors. He was on a secured line talking to Ellison. "Frederick, the launch will go off on schedule. Now, is Wilbanks replacement up-to-speed on everything?

"Yes. We've got the serial numbers on the Speaker of the House's pacemaker. Once the launch achieves orbit and the satellite is fully operational, we'll have full control of it, and can test the weapon on the Speaker's pacemaker," Frederick said. "Also, the FBI has buried their investigation on what happened at your ranch. I guess your distractions are working.

"Good. We also need to figure out the timing for the Vice President to resign," he told Frederick.

"We still haven't figured that out yet. We shouldn't be talking on the phone, even if it's secure. Let's meet up, and then we can digest what's left to do. First thing is to get the satellite in orbit, and our software chip activated."

"Be at my home on Monday. I want to run a few things by you before my interview with Turner."

"You know how I feel about this. You should cancel it. Turner could hurt you. She's a tricky bitch when it comes to face-to-face interviews."

"There is nothing she can do to me. I'm untouchable. Plus, I am smarter than her. Once I have control of the satellite, every citizen in America will be cheering for me to be their next ruler," Dunham said.

"I hope you're right," Frederick answered.

"I'm going to be gone with Maggie this weekend enjoying myself. I cannot believe I'm so close to becoming the next president, no, no, I keep forgetting, the Emperor of the United States."

* * * * *

Dunham was on the phone with Thomas Hayes. "I need you to eliminate Dean Miller this weekend. If his family gets in the way, then include them. He's the most dangerous person who can wreck my plans."

"What about the US Marshalls who are guarding his family?" Hayes asked.

"Handle them too if necessary. Just get it done before Monday," ordered Dunham. "War has collateral damage."

"What about Turner and her other journalists. You do know she now has at least five additional reporters digging into everything on your thumb drive?"

"Shit. When did that happen?"

"Today. Turner begged her boss to let her continue her investigation and said that if she could not come up with concrete evidence on who the Architect is and why the satellite is so important to him, she would not be able to run her story on her Sunday show."

"Do you have enough men in place to slow them down?" Dunham asked.

"I have a better idea. Let me deal with the NSA team they will be interviewing. If they can't find them, then the probe won't get any momentum."

"Okay. But, I don't want them dead. They are needed, so all of this will work smoothly."

"Got it, boss."

94

It was Saturday, and Paige had prepared lunch for Bradley on her deck at her Malibu home. The sky was a deep blue, with scattered puffy white clouds. They were preparing for her upcoming show on Sunday. She had a difficult choice ahead of her. Should she go ahead with her existing evidence and expose the potential scandal at the NSA and NASA? Or talk about the Architect and the four Stages completed over the last two months.

Then it hit her. She knew she could not reverse what the Architect had done with the first four stages of the manifesto, but maybe stop or delay what was planned with the satellite launch.

"What if I'm wrong about this?" she asked Bradley.

"While we don't have clear and definitive evidence, we still have some improprieties that need addressing. The fact is that President Chesterfield does not have a strong grip on his administration. His handling of foreign affairs sucks. All he's worried about is getting re-elected. The worst thing is that he appointed an unknown quantity, Albert Dunham, to the fourth most important position in the United States that could have a tragic and lasting effect on our democracy," Bradley said. "If the Architect, Dunham, wants to be the Emperor, we need to figure out what the satellite has to do with it?"

"Good point. We'll focus on Chesterfield. He's broken his promise to me about his desire to expose the Architect. I think we have enough to show that he is not looking out for the country or the Constitution he has sworn to protect. I think I can tell an interesting story about *Corrupted Intelligence* and how much it's embedded in every fiber of his administration. You need to dig deeper and find out exactly what this satellite was built to do?"

Bradley was shaking his head. "Go easy. The impeachment committee doesn't need your help here. If he gets impeached, that leaves the door open for this Architect or Dunham to be even closer to the presidency or being Emperor of our United States. It's terrifying right now. We have a shadow government controlled by a madman that appears to be growing, and Dunham is leading the movement," he said, his voice cracking. "I'll try to speak with my contacts at the NSA and see if I can get some answers on what this communications satellite is capable of doing."

"Let's wait and see what the reporters Clay gave us come up with too. I think Sunday will be an eye-opening show, no matter how it turns out."

Bradley was massaging his neck. He seemed noticeably stressed. "One thing I still can't get my head around is the abrupt resignation by Secretary Waterfall. I cannot believe she part of this shadow government plot, and it was her time to step aside for Dunham. Especially after his little stunt in Europe and the Middle East? I'd like to have a one-on-one with her."

Paige wrinkled her brow, deep in thought. "There are a lot of questions that have gone unanswered. We don't have enough time or people to dig into everything. It's frustrating. The Architect's done an outstanding job getting us to chase our tails and missing signs inside his most important Stage. It's been a well-oiled plan that has been in the making for almost a hundred and fifty years," she said, exhaustion showing. "Every time we think we're getting close to exposing this man, the Architect keeps completing everything in his manifesto before we can stop him."

Bradley shrugged his shoulders and said. "Let's throw both barrels at this satellite launch and try to force the president to delay it until the American public understands what Frederick Ellison's employee's role was with those twelve NSA analysts. What's the worst that could happen to us?"

Paige grinned. "I know President Chesterfield no matter what I do now won't make him like me anymore or any less than he does right now. I need to have Miller's latest search on those NSA employees to be ready for my show," she said. "Have you seen or heard from him since yesterday's meeting?"

Bradley shook his head. "No. I've left him three messages today."

95

Hayes had his men in position. Professor Miller did not suspect he was being followed back to his temporary office at Columbia. His wife Allison and his children were heading down the Henry Hudson Parkway for some needed shopping in SOHO. They too did not see the two black Suburban's following them.

"Are we good to go, sir? We have them in our sights, and this is the perfect spot for the accident," Hayes' man said.

"If you have an opening, then execute your orders," he replied.

The two Suburbans sped up trying to box Allison's Red E-Class Mercedes into the middle lane. What they didn't know was that Joshua Gomez, one of Scott Rogers' Marshalls was behind the wheel. He had been in this same situation many times in Central America when apprehending criminals for extradition back to the United States.

"Mrs. Miller, kids, we're going to be in for a rough ride. Don't worry I've got this handled, as he immediately slammed on his brakes, turning his steering wheel sharply clockwise until his vehicle skidded hundred-eighty degrees.

The two drivers of the Suburbans were surprised as the Red Mercedes stopped and was facing them. Joshua opened his driver side door, using it as a shield as he aimed his revolver at the drivers. They panicked, sideswiping each other. The Suburban in the fast lane bounced off the other Suburban and spun out of control, hitting the guard rail. The other Vehicle lost control rolling three times until it came to a stop on a grassy area off the parkway.

Joshua immediately jumped back into the car, his right foot pressing on the accelerator, and his left foot pushed hard on the brake. This action spun the Mercedes around, as Allison and her two children, their noses pressed to their door windows watched in amazement as the cars that wanted to harm them were disabled. They were now speeding down the Henry Hudson Parkway at ninety miles per hour. The agent was talking into his wrist mic. "Do you have them?" he asked.

Beau Brown and Everett Harrison were in the backup vehicles Rogers had assigned to protect the professor's wife and children. "We have them cuffed and ready for transport," Brown confirmed.

Once Joshua felt they were safe, he alerted the team that was protecting the professor. "Heads up. You might be getting some company," he told Morgan Jenkins. He was another ex-SEAL that was heading up a team of seventy-five US Marshalls around the country trained to counter any domestic terrorists.

"We spotted the three men fifteen minutes ago. What took you so long, Gomez, on a siesta?" he razzed him.

"Just out for a little drive, checking out the scenery," he replied. "Be careful. We need these guys alive," he said.

* * * * *

Walking back to his temporary lab at Columbia, Dean Miller was oblivious to the danger he was facing. He knew he had security protection, that was not visible to him, and he felt safe. He was getting tired of all of this and wanted to get back to his *"We the People"* movement. He had one last thing he needed to give Paige.

He was reading some emails on his phone when he saw a text pop up on his screen from his wife. He stopped abruptly, in shock from what she had written. *We are all fine. We were attacked on the turnpike. Joshua was a real hero. Be careful!*

His heart was now beating rapidly. A cold sweat blanketed his body, as he remembered the day Seth got hit by an SUV. He started to dial Allison, when he saw two men running toward him, both wearing ski masks, with their guns pointed at him. Miller quickly spun around and noticed a third man, about fifty yards away. All he saw was the red laser beam on his chest. He was paralyzed with fear. He did not want to die, but as the three men boxed him in with nowhere to run, he was resolved to expect the worst.

The first shot echoed, bounced loudly against the college buildings. The masked man pointing his gun at him went down like a rag doll on the campus lawn. A bullet perfectly placed between his eyes. The other two men were tackled to the ground by four Marshalls. Each masked man found one knee pressed hard on the back of their neck, while their arms were pinned behind their backs and handcuffed.

Professor Miller, dropped to his knees, his hands cupped against this mouth. He had never seen a person shot before, let alone between the eyes.

Deputy Morgan Jenkins was first to reach the professor. "Sir. Are you, all right?" he asked.

"Just need to change my underwear," he said. "What just happened. I had gotten a text from my wife. Are they, all right?"

"Mrs. Miller and your two children are safe. Just a little rattled. We need to get you and your family to a safe location until we sort out what just happened."

Dean looked at the agent, shaking his head. "I need my computer and some other items from my office for Paige Turner."

"Okay. Just five minutes. We need to secure the campus and can't have you exposed right now," Morgan said a nervous edge to his voice.

As the professor and U.S. Marshal, Jenkins reached the top of the front stairs by the entry doors to the computer lab building a powerful explosion blew them back off the steps and onto the hard cement walkway. Dean felt the hot burning air thrust him backward. He was airborne off the steps and landed on his back hard, knocking the wind out of him. Then, when his head hit the hard cement, everything went dark.

Seconds before the explosion, Morgan was panning the area and noticed someone who seemed out of place. About two hundred yards from his position was a man, in a New York Yankee jacket and matching baseball cap, holding what seemed like a detonator. He saw the red button. He instantly grabbed the back of the professor's shirt collar and was yanking him back when the blast knocked them both off the steps. If they had opened the doors, the explosion would have consumed them. Instead, the door took the brunt of the hot burning flames.

Morgan had the wind knocked out of him from the Professor landing on his body. Dean bounced off of him and was laying on the walkway motionless. He checked he had all his body parts and then felt the professor's neck and found a pulse. He was being pulled from the area by one of his men, while two others from his team dragged Miller to safe ground.

"Did you see the ass-hole who set off the bomb?" Morgan asked, his voice raspy.

"Yes, sir. We were distracted by the blast. When we turned around, he was gone. He did not know we'd be around."

"Columbia has excellent security cameras. Get with campus security and get me those tapes. I want everything from the entrance on Broadway and every camera inside this courtyard. Also, get the feeds on the last five days inside this building," he ordered, pointing toward the building that had a large hole where the door had been. "There must be something on that footage we can use."

* * * * *

Thomas Hayes was pissed about failing to kill the professor and his family. He was angrier at himself for missing the signs that the professor had a security team watching his back. "Shit. US Marshalls are protecting civilians?" he grumbled. He was immediately on his cell calling Dunham on his burner phone, as he walked down Broadway to the one-hundredth and tenth street subway to catch the number one train to forty-second street to Times Square Station.

"Sir, I fucked up. I lost one man, and four were captured and in custody," he said, his voice resonating with anger.

Dunham was silent for ten seconds before he spoke. "Will this come back to you?"

"No. These were freelance killers I've used before. No allegiance to any one group. Just in it for the money."

"Then, I should not have anything to worry about?"

"No. I don't think so. I made sure the professor's lab and everything he uses for his searches, were destroyed with the explosion. He should be slowed down enough so the Tuesday launch will not be affected."

"What about his lab at UCLA? He must have back up software and programs. It's not over just yet. Now I want you to monitor Scott Rogers and report what he's doing with Paige Turner," Dunham ordered. Then the line went dead.

96

Paige had gotten the phone call from Rogers about the attack on the professor and his family. She was in shock. She had put her friend and his family in danger with her investigation.

"Do we have any idea who did this?" she asked.

"We have four of the attackers. We're interrogating them as we speak. One was an ex-Chicago detective who got terminated for corruption. Dunham's new head of security, Thomas Hayes, had been arrested by the Chicago PD around the same time. Dunham pulled some strings and got him released. We're checking to see if he has any current connection to Dunham's security chief."

"Can I interview them?" Paige asked.

"That's a big no. It's an ongoing criminal investigation that now involves Homeland Security and the FBI. They are being turned over to them as we speak," Scott said.

"Do you trust Homeland Security and the new FBI director to do their job?" she said, doubt resonating in her voice.

Scott blew out a big sigh. "Don't go there. I am an officer of our judicial system and still have a lot of faith with the people who are in place to protect us. These guys are not going anywhere but to a holding cell where we put terrorists and people who want to bring harm to Americans. Now, I'm on my way to you. I should be there after your show on Sunday. Something you and the professor are doing has someone very scared. I've increased your security detail. Cooperate and let them help you."

"Sorry for doubting you following the law. Thank you for protecting me. I'm a little shook up after what just happened.

"That's my job, Paige," Scott said. "I'd never forgive myself if something happened to you," he said, squeezing her arm.

"I'll see you later? Dinner after my show?" she asked sweetly. "When was the last time you had a home-cooked meal?" she asked, trying to cool down the tension she sensed in his voice.

Scott finally allowed himself to smile. "Home-cooked meal sounds great right now."

After Rogers left, Paige read over what she was going to say on her show. She was confident she had enough evidence to tell her viewers and have a successful show on Sunday.

The attack on the professor and his family confirmed for Paige that the direction she was going with her investigation was rattling some cages. She was now more determined to put everything she had out there about the satellite launch and let every media outlet make it the big news story of the day and maybe for the next few weeks.

Paige was making up a grocery list when her phone rang. It was Clay Thomas. "Shit, what does he want now?" she muttered. She thought of not answering it; however, she knew better. "Hello Clay."

"Working on your Sunday show?" he asked meekly.

"It almost finished," Paige said cautiously.

"Then, we need to talk. The satellite is off-limits, as well as the Architect. Further, Dunham is off-limits too," he barked, his tone turning abrasive.

"That's not going to happen, Clay," she shouted back at him. "What I have is a good story that needs airing. Something has been going on at the NSA, and it involves this satellite launch and the Architect. Shit, you know it's connected to this fifth and final stage," she lashed back.

"I just got off the phone with the president. He's pissed that you, shit, that our station, would jeopardize an important part of his war on terrorism. He's assured me he's investigated your rumors and found nothing out of the ordinary. Ellison's employee did know those twelve NSA analysts. His relationship to them was nothing more than the other fifty other men and women who belong to a cybersecurity group which periodically meets around the country for classes on the latest and greatest things that geeks do for their jobs. Unless you have definitive proof that Dunham is the Architect, you need to err on the side of caution before you slander a great man like Albert Dunham."

Paige held her breath, trying to calm herself. She was ready to explode. "That's bull-shit, and you know it. My show goes on as scheduled, or you can fire my ass," she threatened. "We're a news media station that reports the news. We never bow to pressure from lawyers or presidents. Just by Chesterfield talking to you, and by the sound of it, threatening you, it tells me we have a big story that has to be exposed. If I am right and the satellite gets launched, and something happens that affects our countries safety…I'll never forgive myself. If I am wrong, then what harm does a brief delay do to Chesterfield? Oh, yes, it's all about his re-election. I forgot."

"Paige, I know you're right, but this could be the end of both our careers and our station," he said.

"If so, then I will accept it. I would feel worse if we did not do anything."

97

Paige had just gotten off the phone with Dean Miller. He was noticeably upset, but not swayed from helping her. While his Columbia lab currently is a crime scene, all of his backups he downloaded onto the cloud were not.

Professor Miller was able to get Paige all the recent search printouts that connected all twelve NSA employees working on the new satellite, with Frederick Ellison's cybersecurity company, Albert Dunham, who sat on its board of directors and Gregory Wilbanks.

What Paige found interesting is the close connection every analyst had to Brian Russell. It went back for almost four years. "It's amazing how long this Architect has been working on his little plan. It seems that all of his Stages revolved around this NSA project," she said to Bradley.

"The real question is, what does it have to do with anything the Architect would want? It's a communications satellite?" Bradley said doubt in his voice.

"We'll never know. I believe Dunham's first four stages were to elevate him to the front of the line to lead our country. Let's hope my show can delay the launch so we can have enough time to dig a little deeper?" she said. She glanced at the large digital clock on her wall right in front of her desk she used for her show. "It's almost time. Wish me luck."

Bradley, with two fingers, crossed blew a kiss to her, something he did before each show. "Knock their socks off."

Paige sucked in a deep breath as she watched her director, his hand held up counting down to alert her she had seconds before she was live on the air.

"Hello, I am Paige Turner, and you are listening to my Sunday show: Corrupted Intelligence, The Manipulation of America. Over the last two months, I have been reporting on a man known to us as the Architect. I've told you that a dear friend of mine, Brian Russell had copied this Architect's secret files, his manifesto, exposing his entire scheme. Since then, we've learned this individual had five stages he had planned for our country that would make him the wealthiest and most powerful man in America." She paused and took a sip of water from a glass on her desk.

"We've witnessed the total devastation of our train stations, airports, and embassies, over the last two months, as well as a major shakeup within President Chesterfield's cabinet and administration. From all these events, some billionaires have made a killing in the stock market. These recent events are referenced inside the Architect's manifesto. Since investigating this story, three people I have known who were working to expose this Architect are dead. Yesterday, Professor Dean Miller and his family almost lost their lives because they were helping me with my investigation. Let us all remember, because I do remember, the attack on me by a man known to be friends with Frederick Ellison and Albert Dunham, a Frasier Montgomery. He tried to kill me. Again, I find all this very disturbing and in need of more investigation by our president and his justice department," she paused, sipping on her glass of water.

"We now know that four out of the five stages the Architect mentions in his manifesto have been completed. My investigation has uncovered direct links to those attacks inside his files. We have yet to feel the impact of Stage Five," she said, pausing to look straight into the cameras. *"I think I know what*

the Architect's Stage Five might be..." she said. "More to follow after a brief commercial break.

The commercial break went longer than scheduled. Clay was screaming at her. He had just gotten off the phone with the President. "Chesterfield is pissed. He's ordering you, me to cancel the show. He's sending down the FBI to put padlocks on our station," her boss said nervously.

Paige just looked at him in disbelief. "Is he nuts? The government can't shut down our station. We're not a third world country. The show continues. He's bluffing. He should know me better than that. I take the freedom of the press seriously. I must be hitting a nerve, which tells me I'm on the right track," she said, her anger building. "Let his FBI show their face here. I'll put them on national TV."

Paige was back behind her desk on the set, ready to continue. "Sorry for the delay, but we've had some technical difficulties, but I am back." She saw Clay holding his head in his hands, looking at her with desperation etched on his face.

"As I mentioned before, our break that Stage Five seems to be the final piece of the Architect's plan, his missing piece to his complicated, but well thought out plan. Tuesday, a new communication's satellite created by the NSA is scheduled to be launched by NASA," Paige paused, taking another long nervous sip from her glass of water. She noticed five men, in black suits approach Clay. They were lifting him by both his arms. One of the men signaled her, his hand slicing across his throat, to stop her show. She could not believe what she was witnessing.

Her hand had started to tremble, but she knew she had to finish what she had started. *"Inside one of the Architect's files was a folder labeled NSA Satellite. It had a dozen NSA analysts, who have some connection to Frederick Ellison and a Gregory Wilbanks who by coincidence was Brian Russell's replacement. I believe that this upcoming communications satellite launch might be compromised. I am not so sure this communications satellite is what the NSA has told all of us."*

She noticed two men in black suits coming toward her desk on her set.

"I think my show is being shut down by the FBI or should I say President Chesterfield?" she said, looking straight into the cameras. *"President Chesterfield, what are you hiding form all of us?"* she yelled into the camera.

Bradley pushed the cameraman to the side and pulled the camera back away from the set. He was able to capture Paige grabbed by two husky FBI agents and lifted off her chair. Then, like the excellent reporter Stevens was, he was walking over toward the two agents, with a microphone shoved in their faces.

"What are you two guys doing here? Do you have a warrant to close down this show?" he barked out his questions.

Both agents seemed noticeably confused and unprepared for his questions. "We are here at the orders of the FBI director."

"What has Paige Turner done to warrant being arrested?" he accused.

The one FBI agent stammered for a logical answer. "She's not being arrested. She's needed by the FBI to answer some questions."

Bradley gave Paige a wink. "Does she need a lawyer for these questions? Look you goons, if she's not being arrested then get your god-damn hands off her," he demanded.

Paige turned her head and mouthed to Bradley, *"Thank you."* As she was escorted off the set.

* * * * *

President Chesterfield was looking at Felix and then at his new FBI director Mathew Gentry. His new NSA director, Lawrence Elliott's color drained from his face as he bowed his head.

"Fuck. That went well," Chesterfield said. "Now I look like a total inept leader of the Free World, who just arrested a journalist on national TV."

Felix was noticeably upset but tried to control his temper. "Gentry what were your fucking orders?" Wilson asked. His face beet red.

The FBI director took in a deep breath. "Get Paige Turner to stop her show," he stammered. "I guess my men got a little carried away," he said his voice almost inaudible.

Chesterfield stood and began pacing the room. "Wasn't there a plug they could have pulled, an off switch they could have touched, instead of arresting a reporter that was reporting the news, on her fucking weekly TV show that is viewed by over two hundred million people around the world," he screamed. "Is everyone here against me?"

The new NSA director finally spoke. "Mr. President maybe a delay with the launch is warranted. Our next good window, weather-wise, is in four months. I'd rather know that the satellite wasn't compromised before we put it in orbit," he suggested.

Chesterfield knew the real reason he needed the satellite launch and in place. His re-election bid rested on it now. "No. I want everything to go ahead as planned," he ordered. "I am not going to let a little piss-ant journalist dictate how I protect this country."

Felix was listening to a call that was coming into his cellphone. "Sir, I have the Attorney General on the line. She's not very happy," he said, handing his phone to the president.

98

It was Monday, and the shit had hit the fan about what Chesterfield and his FBI had done to Paige Turner. She was already back to her home in Malibu holding a press conference in her driveway.

"Yes, I am very pleased that president Chesterfield has postponed his new communications satellite launch. I think four months is enough time for the president and the NSA to be certain the satellite wasn't compromised or is part of the Architect's final stage," she said, a charming smile on her face.

One reporter asked the question she knew was coming. "Ms. Turner, why did the president remove you from your show yesterday? Was there any formal charges made against you or your station?"

"Why? That's something you need to ask the president, his FBI director, and Attorney General. As for formal or not so formal charges against my station or me, I am still waiting to find out the reason President Chesterfield on national...no worldwide news, made America look like it had become a third world dictator country. That's all the questions I want to answer today. I have a show to prepare for with our new Secretary of State, Albert Dunham," she said with a wave goodbye.

One reporter shouted out a question to her that made her stop and turn toward the cameras. "You mentioned our new Secretary of State on your show yesterday. Do you feel he's connected to any of these horrible events or the Architect?"

Paige was thinking, trying to choose her words carefully. "I am not saying that. I find it too much of a coincidence that Ellison, Dunham, Frasier Montgomery and now Gregory Wilbanks are all connected in some way. I only want answers. I hope Secretary Dunham tomorrow can shed some meaningful light on this subject," she said and briskly walked back to her front door.

* * * * *

Sitting in her living room was Scott Rogers, sipping on a beer, as she came through her front door. "Sorry for the interruption, but the shit is beginning to hit the fan. I don't believe Chesterfield will make it through the impeachment hearings."

Scott looked at her and handed her a beer. "Sit down and talk about something other than the Architect, the president and what happened to you yesterday," he said, putting her hand gently in his and guiding her toward her couch. "Now, tell me about my long-delayed, dinner." Rogers had just gotten off the phone with the president, and it was not a very pleasant conversation after Chesterfield found out he was still protecting Paige. He did his best to hide his frustration with his job.

Paige was caught off-guard by his touch. It had been a long time since a man was alone with her in her home for reasons other than business. "You're right, no business tonight. Can we start with you telling me something about yourself? Your life, relationships, how you went from Special Forces to the US Marshalls office..." she saw Scott put up his hand like a traffic cop.

"Wow. Is this an interview, or are you interested in learning about me?" Scott said.

"Sorry. Old habits. Let me start over again," Paige replied, holding back a laugh.

Scott smiled and said. "I'm a widower. I lost my wife to cancer eight years ago. No children. I left my career with the military after my wife died and found a perfect home with the Justice Department and the Marshalls office. No current relationships, but could be ready," he said, releasing his hand from hers.

Paige blushed as his warm hand gently caressed her arm. "Sorry about your loss. I didn't know," she said, patting his hand awkwardly. "As you know, I lost Rick five years ago. Still not over it I guess, or not wanting to be over it. He was a journalist, murdered for doing his job. That's how we met. The case is now cold. No leads," she said, her tone turning sad.

Scott pursed his lips; his eyes focused on hers. "Tell me about it?"

"Are you sure? You said no business."

"This is not business. I want to know more about you. It seems that Rick's death is a big part of who you are and how you go about doing your job."

Paige was flattered he was genuinely interested. It's been a long time since she'd talked about her husband. It felt good. "I've always believed it was about his shadow government investigation. I recently looked at his old case files and believed he was getting very close to uncovering the conspiracy. I don't want to believe the Architect, Dunham might be connected to his death," she said, wiping a tear from her cheek.

"Can you let me look over Rick's files. Maybe a fresh pair of eyes, since I've been working on the Architect's case too?"

Paige nodded and got up, walking toward the den, which was her office. For the next four hours, they drank two bottles of a tasty red blend and ate lasagna, while picking apart all of Rick's files.

Paige, for the first time, noticed a side of Scott she liked very much. She felt a sense of relief that maybe she would not be alone in solving her husband's murder.

99

After a full day of demands for comments from the president, his press secretary entered the Oval Office. She looked stressed and exhausted.

"That was brutal, sir," she said unsmiling. "I can't keep the press at bay. They want comments from you, and the opportunity to ask you questions."

"What questions do they have that you did not answer on my behalf?" Chesterfield asked half-heartedly.

Rachel Monroe just rolled her eyes. Her irritation with her boss was beginning to show. "Mr. President, please, you know the answer to that question. You must hold a press conference and clear up what happened the other day. Your Secretary of State is going to give Ms. Turner her interview before he leaves for Europe and the Middle East. If he comments first about the stunt the FBI pulled at Turner's studio, you might not be able to walk back your actions and will have to live with it during your re-election campaign," she said sternly.

"Okay. Set it up in thirty minutes. I know what I want to say. It might not be pretty, but it will be honest," Chesterfield responded shakily.

* * * * *

The briefing room packed with the White House Press Corps was not given any rules and requirements from Press Secretary

Monroe. President Chesterfield walked onto the podium and without any greeting began to speak.

"Ladies and gentlemen of the White House Press corp, I am here today to speak about the unfortunate incident involving Paige Turner and my FBI. I know every American and people around the world witnessed a major misstep on my part and that of the FBI on Sunday," he said, his voice showing signs of stress.

"First, I want to apologize to Ms. Turner for the actions she had to endure, and the humiliation my office inflicted upon her. While I stand by my decision to protect our national security and highly classified, top-secret information from leaking to the public, I was unable to have the FBI meet with Ms. Turner before her show. I did not know what she was going to say until it aired. One thing I need to make clear to everyone is that when someone receives information that might affect our national security, it needs to be reported to the FBI," he paused, noticing all the reporter's hands waving for his attention.

"I will open this up for questions in just a moment. I have more to add. I was aware of the thumb drive Ms. Turner had had in her possession. I have had my intelligence community working diligently to try to find this Architect and decrypt some of the files that she had received. Ms. Turner had assured me, while she conducted her investigation, to keep me in the loop on her progress, especially when she discovered material that fell under our national security. Ms. Turner, I believe, wanted the headlines more than what was good for our country. So, I do apologize for my actions on Sunday. But, I do not regret trying to protect the United States from its enemies," he said and started pointing at his favorite journalists in the room. "Shelly, you're first."

"Thank you, Mr. President. This a two-part question: first, why was Paige Turner allowed to keep the thumb drive and investigate something you are now saying is a national security issue? And, my second question, what is so secretive about this satellite launch that you felt compelled to have your FBI, like Stormtroopers, swoop in and arrest a journalist?" she said and sat down.

Chesterfield started rubbing his neck. He appeared he was struggling to answer her question. "When Ms. Turner gave me the copy of the thumb drive, I had been given the impression she would no longer pursue or interfere with our investigation. And, to your second question, I felt our national security outweighed any bad PR I might receive from my actions." He saw Shelly jump up again.

"Mr. President, you did not answer my question regarding the satellite launch and its significance to our national security?"

"I won't because it does fall under our national security. Next question," Chesterfield said curtly. He was trying to figure out how many lies he had told during his answers.

"Mr. President do you now feel, after Paige Turner connected your new Secretary of State to Frederick Ellison, Frasier Montgomery, and Gregory Wilbanks, as well as implying that these men are connected in some way to this Architect, are you regretting appointing Mr. Dunham to one of your most important cabinet posts?"

Chesterfield was mopping his sweaty forehead with a handkerchief handed to him by Rachel Monroe. "First of all, it is in the public record that Frederick Ellison and Albert Dunham have been friends since high school. Further, it was not hidden that Gregory Wilbanks worked for Ellison. As far as Frasier Montgomery goes, that is something new to me. I am looking into that connection. But, as far as my choice for Secretary of State, I believe that Albert Dunham was the best choice for our country and the world at this time." Rachel Monroe walked onto the podium and whispered in the president's ear.

"Something that needs my immediate attention has come up. This press conference is over," the president said, briskly walking off the stage.

* * * * *

Back at the Oval Office, the Sargent at Arms from the House was standing with an envelope firmly pressed under his armpit.

"Mr. President, you are now formally requested to appear before the House Judicial committee that has started your impeachment hearings," he said nervously. He handed the envelope to Chesterfield and turned, marching out of the Oval Office.

"Do you believe this shit?" Chesterfield said.

Felix Wilson was not surprised. "Sir, you've brought this upon yourself. I told you to leave Turner alone and let her show run its course. But, no. Your paranoia that everyone is out to get you clouded your judgment," he said harshly. "This last incident has given the House committee, your enemies, enough fuel to move your impeachment through the House swiftly.

"Now you are against me?" he moaned.

"No. I wish you'd take my council occasionally. It is my job, you know?"

Chesterfield slumped back in his chair, totally depressed. "Now what?"

"Go to the House and speak from your heart. Answer their questions and tell them the truth. You've not committed any crimes. Your favorability ratings suck. We can get that back once the satellite has been in place and you keep your promise to make America safe from terrorism," Felix said, hoping he was convincing. He didn't believe his friend had a chance in hell of not getting impeached.

* * * * *

Dunham was sipping brandy with Ellison in his office at his Bethesda home. "I think the delay of the satellite will turn out better than I thought," he said.

"How?" Ellison asked.

"What Chesterfield just did with Paige Turner has shown every American what a failed leader he is. I couldn't have done it any better myself. Now, if I can get him to re-launch the satellite, and he then loses control of it, it will be easy to convince him to resign. Then, it would make what I have planned easier."

Ellison had a puzzled look on his face. "You do know that before Chesterfield announces his resignation, the Vice-President will be sworn in? How is that going to help you?"

"Simple. We all know Vice-President Preston is not in the best of health and has already told Chesterfield he will not be running with him for re-election. Right after I have control of the satellite, it will be so sad that the VP suffers a massive stroke and the Speaker of the House has a severe malfunction of his pacemaker. Then, who is next in line to be president?" Dunham said.

"Albert, you forget about the President Pro-Tempore of the Senate?"

"No, I didn't. I've got that handled too. The Senator has the same pacemaker as the Speaker. The manufacturer is going to have one big lawsuit and investigation by the Justice department diverting all the attention away from the satellite that I control."

"It's going to look like a coup," Ellison said.

"Maybe, but during these next four months with what I am going to accomplish as Secretary of State as well as activating my army of supporters here and around the world, the American people will be begging me to be their president...oh I mean their emperor," he laughed.

Frederick just shook his head. "Albert, if anyone can pull this off, it's you," he grinned.

100

Paige was incensed with the president's statements at his press conference. "That ass-hole. That's the thanks I've gotten for even telling him about the thumb drive and the Architect's files."

Bradley tried to calm her down. "He's trying to save his political career. It's not working, so he needs a scapegoat, and you're it."

"How the hell can I do my interview with Secretary Dunham?"

"The same way you've done every interview. Ask questions and press him for truthful answers. We know he's connected, even if Dunham turns out to not be the Architect. The good news for you is that he agreed to the interview by telecast with you at your studio," said Bradley. "It's as close to being on your home turf."

"Maybe I should first figure out why the president is so secretive about the satellite? That's a stupid question. Like he'd ever talk to me again?" Paige mocked herself.

"We reporters know how to speculate. So maybe I should stir the waters with some of my other media contacts and get them to begin a deeper investigation. We do have four months to dig into this," Bradley said.

"Good idea. I've got some choice questions for Dunham. I wish we were not doing it via a telecast. I prefer an in the flesh, face-to-face, but he's leaving for Europe right after our interview."

"Maybe you can convince Dean to use his tracking software to monitor Dunham on his first official international trip?" Bradley suggested.

"Not sure we should be doing any surveillance of the Secretary of State. I'm sure the NSA and Secret Service will be monitoring everything that has to do with his trip. I'd hate for the professor to get caught. Maybe we can do it like we've done before, after the fact?" Paige looked at her watch. "Shit, I've got one hour before my interview. Talk to you after it," she said, rushing off.

101

Dunham had just finished his mock interview with his handpicked staff. They had grilled him on what he should say and not say during his talk with Paige Turner.

"Sir, Turner is a crafty journalist. She's going to ask you questions that will seem simple and non-threatening. It's at those times you need to be cautious. Then, she'll throw out a question from left field that will surprise you."

He looked at his new team of support the State Department provided him and was laughing inside. "I'm perfectly capable of handling any questions Turner will toss at me. Now, clear my office. I have some phone calls I need to make," he said, waving his hand for them to leave.

"Frederick, has everyone been mobilized in Europe?"

"Yes. There will be attacks staged near each of your locations. Once they happen, the Secret Service will get you to one of their safe zones, most likely an embassy. I will have the media in place for you to make your statement," he said.

"Perfect. Stage Five will resume shortly. It's frustrating that we have to wait until the satellite launch for everything to be in place," Dunham said.

"Albert...I mean Mr. Secretary, remember, this delay is working out to our advantage. These small events will only bury Chesterfield even further in the hole you've dug for him.

"Okay. I've got to go. The telecast for my interview with Turner is about to start. Wish me luck."

Frederick felt a pain in his stomach just thinking about Turner. "We should have killed her when we had the chance. Be careful. Don't let your ego get the best of you." He told Dunham.

102

Paige sat behind her desk that was on her studio stage. The same place where two days ago, the FBI maltreated her and dragged her off her show. Today, with Dunham at the State Department, and on a split-screen, she was confident the FBI would not show up.

She had gotten her signal from her producer that they will be going live in one minute. She could now see on her monitor the large mahogany desk that Secretary Dunham planned to sit behind. Behind him were two American flags bookending a large world map with large colored pins reflecting all the Embassies the United States had around the world. *"Impressive,"* she told herself. She now realized he was going to be a showman, as well as a difficult person to interview.

She was startled to see Dunham walk into his office, dressed in a black pinstriped suit, white shirt, and an American flag tie. He sat down, placed his hands flat on his desk, and smiled directly into the camera. "Hello, Ms. Turner. I am glad we're going to do this interview finally," he said politely.

"I am glad we're going to do it too," she replied, smiling back at him. She saw her producer start his finger countdown. "I guess we're about to go live," she said.

"Hello, I am Paige Turner with an exclusive interview with our new Secretary of State, Albert Dunham," she paused, taking in a deep breath. "Mr. Secretary, thank you for agreeing to this interview. I know with your new job and all the responsibilities it brings, I am honored you could make time to speak with me and my worldwide audience," she said.

"Ms. Turner, it is my pleasure to speak to you and your large following. I have always been a big fan of what you're doing to uncover the *Corrupted Intelligence* that continues to plague our government as well as the leaders of large corporations around the world."

Paige was surprised he would open the door so early about all the topics she wanted to ask him. "I am glad you brought that subject up," she said. "I'd like to first go to the promise you made a little over a month ago about helping me find this Architect, who I believe has perpetrated all the attacks here in our country and around the world. The files that Brian Russell had sent me portrays a terrifying picture of a man who wants to rule our country, like an Emperor."

Dunham did not seem fazed by her comments, but quite relaxed. "I too am glad you brought up this Architect. I first need to explain something to you and your listeners. I've had some of my investigators look into your allegations...actually conspiracy theories, about one man who would or could rule our great country," he said, his voice calm and reserved.

Paige interrupted him. "I want to get to that, but a little further into our interview..."

Dunham shot back, "No. I want to finish my answer first, Ms. Turner," he said, his tone biting. "My investigators have looked into Brian Russel, something you should have done, and his connection or motive for releasing these stolen files. Your judgment was clouded by your friendship. What I found will surprise you," he said, leaning into the camera.

Paige was caught off-guard and did not know how to respond. "Brian Russell was a dear friend, and any suggestion that he did something wrong is not going to fly on my show," she said defensively.

Dunham very dramatically sat straight up with both his hands raised in front of him. "Whoa, Ms. Turner. Now, don't get ahead of yourself until you hear all of what I have to say," he replied defiantly. "Your friend did steal those files from a computer at Frederick Ellison's office. The courts frown on that kind of behavior."

Paige was now on the defensive. "Are you saying that Frederick Ellison is the Architect?"

Dunham was now shaking his head, showing his disapproval with this line of questioning. "No, I am not. I am saying that my files that were stolen are not what they appear to be."

"Then, please enlighten all of us what those files are," she said sarcastically.

"It is known that Frederick Ellison and I have been friends since High School. That friendship has stayed strong all these years as our families and business interests have grown."

Paige did not like that she had lost control of her interview. "It seems that those businesses have prospered very well during our most recent attacks," she shot back.

"Are you blaming me for being a smart businessman? I have experts that analyze all market conditions, and sometimes we get it right, and sometimes we get it wrong. It's called speculation. If you'd broadened your investigation, you would have seen that I had made a ton of money during the 2001 and 2008 market crashes."

"Didn't the Architect have notes that predicted those events? How can one man be so lucky if he's not the person who is orchestrating those events?"

"Maybe because of your zeal for a meaty story you've interpreted the notations in those files incorrectly? I am the Architect depicted in those diaries," Dunham said, bowing his head.

"You're the Architect?" Paige replied, surprised.

"Yes, but not the Architect you've invented or gleaned from what you've read from my notes and my family's writings."

Paige could not stop herself from stammering for a response. "The notations about the Architect wanting to be the next Julius Caesar are not accurate? You, as the Architect, wanted to become the wealthiest and most powerful man in the world. You've put those notations into your files," she said, realizing she was opening herself up to ridicule. She recalled Professor Miller's caution about everything inside the files being circumstantial.

Dunham forced an embarrassed smile. His body language gave a picture of a man ashamed. "If you must know. The reason Frederick had my files was that he was helping me digitalize the old writings from my Great Grand Father, his son, and his grandson, my father. I've been wanting to write about the Dunham family and explain to the world about my Great Grandfather's vision for our family and our country. Unfortunately, Brian Russell stole those files, deleted them from Ellison's computer, and now I am back at square one with my dream," he said, swiping a well-positioned tear from his cheek.

"What about the other encrypted files on Russell's thumb drive? Aren't those yours?" she asked nervously. She knew he'd have an answer to that question too.

"I am not sure what files your referring to? Those must have been Russell's. My investigation, which I have already turned over to the FBI is looking into Russell's connection to Gregory Milbank and a secret cyber hacker group that has been disrupting networks around the United States and the world. I believe they were trying to, with help from Russell and Wilbanks, disrupt the NSA's upcoming launch. Something about it scared them."

"You're saying that a cyber hacker group is responsible for all of the attacks worldwide and here in the United States?" she asked.

"Ms. Turner, you do know there is a war going on worldwide that involves terrorists? What your sloppy reporting has done has encouraged those terrorists to keep attacking our country and our allies because they believe our president and our intelligence community is working for a Shadow Government that you and Professor Miller have invented from what you misinterpreted in Russell's stolen files."

"What about the brutal murders of Brian Russell, Seth Alexander, professor Miller's intern, my reporter Sean Adams, and the attempt on my life by your close friend Frasier Montgomery?"

"If you're insinuating that I had anything to do with those murders or the attempt on your life or the professors, it is unfounded and insulting. Frasier Montgomery was a friend. And, I do mean a friend. I haven't seen or heard from him in years. He was always a loose cannon, and I am sad that his life went in a horrible direction."

"You're saying Montgomery was not working for you or Ellison during those attacks?"

"I won't dignify that accusation with an answer. I've been supporting our country, like my family before me, with charitable groups that have helped build up needy communities. I've helped turn around an economic crisis in Europe and help get Israel and Palestine to sign a peace treaty. Why would I want to kill anyone or have a man like Frasier Montgomery kill anyone over what was written in my diary or the files of Brian Russell?"

The color had finally drained from Paige's face. She was at a loss for words. "I don't know what to say right now," she said, her voice cracking from the stress of the moment.

Dunham tried to contain his laugh at how he had destroyed her on national TV, but he just kept nodding, his lips pursed. "On a happy note," he said, smiling. "As Secretary of State, this country owes you a debt of gratitude for alerting us about a possible satellite breach. However, I would like you to please return all my files. You've already embarrassed me enough. My written dreams and ambitions are personal and have very intimate feelings you've exposed to the world about my family and me," he said sternly.

Paige could not speak. "Secretary Dunham, again, I don't know what to say. I will have those files back to you immediately."

"Thank you. I know how you, as a journalist, want to report the facts as accurately as possible, but in this case, you did not do your homework and should be ashamed of yourself."

"I would like to talk to you some more about..."

Dunham interrupted her. "Our interview is over. I have more important things to do than talk to a reporter that is a sensationalist and only out to make a name for herself." With that, he stood and walked away from the cameras.

Paige was stunned at what just happened. After being harassed by the FBI and put in her place by Dunham, she was sure her career was over.

103

Paige walked off her studio stage, briskly trotting back to her office when Clay Thomas signaled her to see him first. By the look on his face, she knew this was not going to be congratulation on an excellent interview moment.

"I know I fucked up," she said. "I'm still spinning from what just happened."

Clay had a sober face. "I just got off the phone with our Chairman of the Board. She's furious with me. She wants your head on a stick and put out in front of the studio for everyone to see what happens when a reporter steps over the line," he said, shrugging his shoulders. "While she wants you terminated, I convinced her to place you on a leave of absence for the next six months, with pay."

Paige was noticeably pissed. "That's bull-shit. For all, I've done for this station with my show, and great investigations...one mistake, and one, I am not convinced was a blunder, but a misstep, I get placed on leave. You're not giving me any other alternative, except to resign."

Clay put both his hands up. "Cool off and get your head on straight. You're too close to his investigation. Ever since you discovered Rick's case files, you've been, well, way off message," he said.

"Don't bring Rick into this. It's Dunham. He has something else up his sleeve. I can promise you he will screw all of us. If I am right, which I hope to God I am not, our country might never recover from what he has planned," she said, her voice so loud everyone outside of Clay's office turned their heads.

"You've been ordered to back down from investigating Dunham. Don't make me fire you over this."

"I'll make it easy on you. I quit. I won't stop pursuing Dunham," she said, storming out of his office.

She walked by Bradley without saying a word. Inside her office, she started filling up a bankers box of her items and files she had on Dunham. All it took was five minutes, and she was out the front door heading to her home in Malibu.

*****

Sitting out on her deck, watching the sunset on the horizon, she felt relief blanket her body. "Now I can do what I do best...investigate the news," she muttered to herself.

She took a long sip of her wine when her cellphone rang. It was from Scott Rogers, and she didn't need more criticism. She tried not answering but thought better of it.

"Hi. I guess you heard?" Paige said, slurring her words.

"I watched the show. You took a big beating from Dunham. He's an arrogant son-of-a-bitch. I just got done telling Chesterfield that too," he said.

Paige sat up at attention. "You did what? What did he say?"

"To go fuck myself and not ruin his re-election bid."

"What did you say then?"

"I told him it was time for me to retire. I told him I couldn't work for a president who is only motivated by getting re-elected when our country is being taken over by a homegrown terrorist like Dunham," he said, sounding like he had been drinking for a while too.

"I quit my job today too," she said, gulping down her wine. "Want to join me for a drink on my deck and contemplate our futures?" There was a long pause, an unexpected silence from Scott. Then, she heard a loud banging on her front door.

"Hold on a minute," she said, staggering off her deck. Her fourth glass of wine had given her a good buzz.

When she opened the door, standing there was Scott holding a bottle of wine. "Yes, I would like to join you," he said with a sheepish smile while talking into his phone.

Paige did not know what was happening to her, but she put her arms around him and gave him a big kiss. She then dragged him into the house, leading him back to her bedroom.

As she began to pull her oversized tee-shirt up and over her head, she revealed she was not wearing anything underneath. Scott was surprised by how gorgeous she looked at that moment.

"You're beautiful," he stuttered as he removed his shirt and let his jeans fall to the floor.

Now they were both staring at each other, both naked and both noticeable aroused. Scott lifted her in his arms and carried back to her bed. It was like they had done this before. It seemed natural, the intimacy they both were feeling.

After two hours of passionate lovemaking, mixed with small talk, they both passed out from exhaustion. Before Paige fell asleep, she looked at Scott, and snuggled close to him, feeling safe once again.

104

Secretary Dunham had just landed in London to meet with the American ambassador to Great Britain. He had finished a conversation with president Chesterfield who could not get over him being the Architect Paige Turner had been talking about these last few months.

Dunham was pleased the president believed his bullshit and did not care. The president's preoccupation with getting re-elected had him losing focus on national security matters.

"Are the attacks ready to proceed?" he asked Tucker Phillips.

"All ready. My only concern is I am still a person of interest in the last attacks. What if Dean Miller and Turner investigate again?"

"After how I handled myself at my interview with Turner, she'd be lucky if a tabloid will even run a story from her. Don't worry. I've got your back," Dunham said.

* * * * *

The international Press Corp was out in force covering Secretary of State Dunham's first diplomatic mission since being appointed. All the media had from the White House was that Dunham was in Europe to strengthen America's coalition to fight and put out of business every terrorist group inside Europe, the Middle East, and Africa. There were fifteen nations from Europe attending, plus ambassadors from Russia, Saudi Arabia, Jordan, Egypt, and Iran.

Dunham's diplomatic mission was going to be huge for President Chesterfield. He was expecting his favorable ratings to turn around with the help of his new Secretary of State. What he did not know was that Dunham had other plans for Europe and his Commander and Chief.

Dunham looked at his watch. It was all going to start in one hour. He just had to keep all the foreign diplomats inside the American embassy, while the world watches with horror as the Architect's next plan moves forward.

Dunham's speech was laying out what the United States and president Chesterfield needed from each country. "Terrorism is our world's number one priority. Economies won't grow or prosper unless these animals are removed from the face of the earth. America is committed to putting them all out of their misery," he said, his voice resonating with confidence.

Without warning the large room shook from the bomb blast outside of the embassy. Then came the staccato sounds from automatic rifles. The windows inside the conference hall shattered. The room resonated with screams and everyone diving for cover. Dunham did not. He looked at a couple of camera operators and made sure their attention was on what he did next.

"Everyone remain calm. We have a safe room that will protect us until the Marines get control of whatever is happening outside." Showing the calm of a leader, Dunham led the large group toward a large metal door. As the last ambassador entered the room, he turned toward the cameramen and signaled them to follow him inside. "Over here, gentlemen. I'll protect you," he said in a loud voice that resonated over the constant and never-ending machine gun sounds exploding inside the conference room. Once the large door closed, Dunham was able to see all the world leaders scared and huddled together in the corner of the safe room.

"This room will withstand any assault or bomb. Everyone remain calm." He held up a communications device. "I will be able to communicate with our security in just a moment. I am not sure what just happened, but my guess is the terrorists we want to destroy just made a statement that the fight won't be easy," he said, looking straight into the cameras that were pointing at him.

There had been four more powerful blasts that rocked the saferoom. Moments later, the gunfire had subsided. Dunham's Stat Phone beeped. "Great job," he said into the mouthpiece." He looked at all the nervous faces the cameraman had captured on video and said. "We're all clear to leave."

Everyone inside the room began hugging each other. The Russian ambassador kissed Dunham on both cheeks as everyone paraded out of the safe-room.

A Marine detail, in full battle gear, guided everyone to safety. Dunham held back his smile as he surveyed the conference room that was in shambles. Five men, all wearing masks were lying on the floor, pools of blood spewing out of their bodies. Outside was another story. The front gate to the embassy was a sculpture of tangled metal.

Waiting for each ambassador was their own Press Corp begging for answers. Dunham, as if staged ahead of time, walked over to a group of reporters with camera operators by their side, making himself ready to brief them on what had happened.

At first glance, Dunham noticed a few Marines and embassy security on the ground, not moving. He appeared disinterested. The Secretary of State had just finished briefing President Chesterfield about the attack.

"Before I attempt to answer your questions, I first want to send my condolences to all the families who lost loved ones today. They were doing their job to protect everyone at the American Embassy. They are all heroes," he said, his hands shaking as he spoke.

One reporter asked the first question. "Were there any warnings that an attack would happen today?" she asked.

Dunham looked at her, pensive. "We always have suspicions of a pending attack. With this being a meeting to form a coalition to end this form of barbaric, murderous acts, has only reinforced our resolve to declare war on all terrorist groups around the globe."

Another reporter asked. "The other ambassadors are saying you're a hero for keeping yourself calm and collected and getting everyone inside the embassy's fortified safe room."

"We have lockdown procedures for attacks like this. I was following our embassy protocols. Being new to all of this and for the first time being front and center to an attack of this magnitude...well I was just happy that my embassy staff had told me about the safe room or we might all have been dead right now," Dunham said somberly.

105

President Chesterfield had convened his security council looking for their intelligence analysis about the devastating attack at the American embassy in London. The death toll of American and British citizens was staggering. The crowds outside the embassy were huge and took the most significant impact from the car bomb blast. On the large TV monitor, he could see inside the courtyard to the embassy five embassy security personnel lying face down, their bodies twisted and motionless from the first explosion.

A reporter from CNN was reporting what had happened. "I am at a loss for words," the reporter said. *"The Marine detail that had been guarding the front entrance and side entrance to the embassy must have been stunned by the first explosion. What we now know there were four men, all with suicide vests who had rushed through the mangled entrance gate. It seems from all observations that the Marines momentary hesitation allowed the terrorists enough time to get close enough to the building detonate their suicide vests. Four Marines were stunned. Their training and bravery prevailed as they were able to get their bearings and opened fire on three more terrorists who had rushed the front entryway,"* he said his voice quivering. He was noticeably shaken by what he was reporting.

"Please bear with me. I have never seen anything like this before, especially at an American embassy. It appears the Marine detail inside the embassy immediately secured all the ambassadors and Secretary of State Dunham. I have just been informed that they had taken defensive positions, waiting for

the attack to breach the front door. Then, another explosion created a large opening for four additional men, holding AK-47's, in typical black terrorist uniforms, their faces masked, to rush into the embassy. Before they could murder more civilians, the waiting Marines greeted them with a barrage of bullets. It was over in a matter of seconds. I am happy to report all embassy personnel, Ambassadors, and our Secretary of State are all safe and unharmed. I have one question for President Chesterfield: How in God's name could this happen, in an American embassy and on British soil? Where were your intelligence agencies this time?" he said, ending his new report noticeably frustrated.

Chesterfield looked at his new CIA and FBI directors. "Do you two have any fucking answers? I don't seem to have any!"

Mathew Gentry, the new FBI director, spoke first. "What my people are telling me is that this attack was well orchestrated and must have been in the planning stages for months. These terrorists were using weapons that went missing from a shipment three months ago under your previous FBI and CIA directors," he said.

Chesterfield combed his fingers through his hair, showing signs of his exasperation. "Are you telling me that Roberts still has traitors inside your agency?"

"I've been trying to quietly clean-house since you locked up that traitor. I'm close to connecting some dots. You might not like who I've connected to these people."

The president looked at his new CIA director, Chesterfield's stare could have set him on fire. "What do you have to say for yourself?"

Lawrence Berry was a man of few words. "Our operatives in Europe heard the chatter on the internet and cellphone communications. We were aware that an attack was imminent. We did not know where or when. With all the shake-ups inside your administration and your new Secretary of State coming on board, we were focused on keeping him abreast of the most current intelligence. I had what I believed were enough men on the ground to curtail any terrorist attack, but the leads we got, had us going on wild goose chases."

Chesterfield looked drained, his face the color of a white bedsheet. "Are you suggesting this shadow government conspiracy is real. If we cannot get accurate intelligence from the two most professional agencies in the world, then something must be brewing inside our borders? We need to start looking at who might best benefit from ousting me from the presidency."

FBI director Gentry spoke. "I have some scenarios I've been playing with, and it doesn't fall that far from what Paige Turner and Scott Rogers tried to bring to your attention. I need a few more days, maybe a week and I can have a detailed report on your desk," he said.

The president looked at Felix. "Call Secretary Dunham. I want to ask him a few questions."

Before the president could continue with the rest of his meeting, the United States Attorney General Marilyn Sawyer walked into the Oval Office. Chesterfield immediately noticed her somber expression.

"I can see you do not have good news to report. So, pile it on. This day cannot get any worse for me," he said sarcastically.

Sawyer did not waste time with her report. "Mr. President, your case against your ex-FBI director Chad Roberts for treason does not fit the criteria you've given my office. Also, as for CIA director Hood, his actions or lack thereof do not fall under the guidelines of treason. All you're able to do is terminate them. I cannot lock them up or hold them any longer," she said.

"Perfect. I am beginning to think that running for re-election will put me in the grave," Chesterfield said, cupping his head in his hands. "Now everyone, leave my office. I need to process this shit you've thrown at me.

106

Paige had woken up, her head on top of Scott's muscular arm. She turned to face him, one eye peeking at him while he slept. For the first time in a very long time, she was happy. She tried to lift her head gently.

"Going somewhere?" he asked, his voice sounding like it was still asleep.

"Not too far. Going to make some coffee and catch up on the news. You want some?"

Scott scooted his body up against the padded headboard supporting himself by his elbows. He let the bedsheet drop to his lap, exposing his muscular chest and six-pack. "Would love some. Black, no sugar, please. She noticed him staring, realizing she was naked.

"Sorry if I am making you uncomfortable," she said, coyly covering up some of her private parts with her hands.

"Not at all. You're a beautiful woman and a pleasure to look at, with or without your clothes on," he replied, smiling. When he tossed off the blanket he was under, Paige noticed how excited he had gotten.

"Maybe coffee can wait for a few minutes," she giggled. She was on top of him, slowing slipping him inside her. She loved how he felt. Her husband had been a great lover, but there was something special about Scott, and how he did not rush her.

He was staring, enjoying watching the slow rise of her emotions, her body quivering multiple times, and when he felt she was ready, he helped her bring her orgasm to its climax at the right moment. She began kissing him all over his face, ending with his lips. Forty-five minutes later, they were done and exhausted.

"Now, I need some strong coffee," she said, caressing his hair as she jumped out of bed.

Paige was in her usual routine in her kitchen, except she had an overnight guest that did not let her get a lot of sleep. She flipped on the small flat-screen TV on her counter and began filling the coffee pot with water when she heard the news about the embassy bombings in London and the coordinated attack by an unknown terrorist group.

"Scott, she shouted. "You need to come here now," she said, alarm in her voice.

He looked at the video stream of the devastation at the American Embassy in London. "How the hell could something like this happen? A car bombing, I would understand, but a well-coordinated attack? Shit, I'd bet my life it was an inside job," Scott said without hesitation.

"If I did not know better, I'd agree with you. No way embassy security, let alone the Brits, would be caught so flat-footed. It's Stage Five and the Architect, no it's fucking Dunham, who has his fingers in this," she said, her anger spilling out from her lips.

Scott said. "Call Dean Miller. Get him to run a search on everyone on our list of people connected to Ellison, General Tucker Phillips, and Dunham. I'm going to call a few of my guys from my old team. They owe me and would love to help us figure this out. I don't think the CIA or FBI will accomplish too much based on their previous record," he said irritated. I want to know where Tucker Phillips has been before and after this attack.

Paige was already on her cell, dialing the professor. "Hi, Dean. Have you seen the news?"

"Yes. I can't believe what just happened. Are we, our country that vulnerable around the world?" the professor asked a deep sadness in his voice.

"I'm not sure. I need a favor," Paige asked.

"Anything."

"I need you to do one of your searches on the following names," she said. She read Miller the list. He told her he'd have the results in a couple of hours. "Focus most of your efforts on Tucker Phillips and Dunham."

"I guess my retirement can wait?" she said, looking at Scott who had just finished his phone call.

"Well, they do say you need to keep busy after leaving a career. I had always wanted to start up an investigative agency. Maybe this is a good time to do it?"

Paige smiled. "Could you use a good investigative reporter?" she asked.

Scott grinned. "I was hoping you'd apply."

"I am not sure if my old boss will have anything to do with me. I'm confident that Bradley will help. Let's get over there and see if he'll talk to us."

Scott could not stop smiling, as he watched Paige get excited about doing something about Dunham. "Once we're done talking with Bradley, we will be meeting with a few of the men and women I know would be perfect for our new team."

107

Every news station in the United States and around the world was covering the attack. Some were speculating it was a new terrorist group that had formed in Great Brittan, and other reporters were saying it was an off-shoot of ISIS and Al-Qaeda.

Inside the United States, the House Committee to Impeach President Chesterfield kept screaming for his removal immediately. This event was what they needed to build a majority, bipartisan coalition to move the hearing out of committee and into the House chamber.

One interesting side news story was that Secretary Dunham had become a national hero. He had given a press conference after the incident. For the first time since accepting his new position, he was able to project to all Americans and the world how he was going to be a pro-active foreign affairs leader.

While president Chesterfield was being bombarded with questions about yet again another security deficiency within his intelligence organization, Secretary Dunham was holding a second press conference.

"Ladies and gentlemen of the press. The international meeting that got disrupted a few days ago has not deterred the countries in our coalition to back away from finding and putting an end to all forms of terrorism. Today, I have good news to report. The leader of the group responsible for the attack on my American embassy," he said, emphasizing *MY,* "has been found and killed in a heated gun battle in Paris, along with thirty of his followers."

For almost fifteen minutes, the Secretary answered question after question, never mentioning President Chesterfield. He kept the conversation all about himself and what he had done to protect every ambassador under his care and custody.

"Let me finish with this thought," he said, his tone had become somber. "Terrorism is a pandemic I promise you will be dealt with whatever means possible. As Secretary of State for the United States, it will be my mission over the next few weeks to build a strong coalition with our allies and non-allies to work together to fight terrorism in every corner of our world. Everyone, traveling to countries within our coalition need to feel safe when they are outdoors enjoying what life has to offer," Dunham said. "I will, and can, make you this promise: that terrorism, as we know it today, will be something we will see in our rearview mirrors as we move forward toward a new and prosperous world." He finished with a wave of his hand and walked away from the podium.

* * * * *

President Chesterfield seemed dumbfounded by Dunham's comments. "Those were my words...my instructions for him to convey from the President of the United States," he growled.

Felix Wilson did not seem that surprised. "You knew from the start that Dunham had an ego as big as a truck. What did you expect when you turned over the press conference that you should have done, to your Secretary of State?" his Chief of Staff said, caustically.

It was as if Chesterfield did not hear Wilson. "He did not even mention my name?" he shouted. "It's as if I don't exist?"

"Unless you get out in front of this, you can kiss your presidency and your re-election bid goodbye."

"Great. How do you suggest I get through this impeachment hearing?"

"You need to do something bold and brash — no more political safe calculations. You need to win back the trust of the American people," Felix said.

"Get my NASA director on the phone. I want my satellite back on schedule." He could see Felix shaking his head as he waved his hand, shooing him to leave his office.

108

It had been thirty days since the bombing at the London embassy. Secretary Dunham had been winning over the American people and the rest of the world with what he had accomplished. And, during this period, President Chesterfield had been subpoenaed to appear before his impeachment committee twice.

At Paige's Malibu house, sitting on her deck overlooking the blue Pacific Ocean, she and Scott were reviewing what they believed Dunham was up to from the reports that Professor Miller had researched for them. Added to their data was all the research, Scott's team of ex-law enforcement personnel had accumulated. It was clear to them that all the countries within Dunham's coalition were the same countries that harbored the terrorists that were led by General Tucker Phillips.

"We've got so much proof..." she said frustrated... "but nowhere to go with it. No one wants to hear from me or mess with Secretary Dunham right now. His favorability ratings are through the roof. Anyone connected to him is getting a pass by the press. Tucker Phillips, that murderous bastard, is laughing at all of us as he keeps killing off all of Dunham's adversaries," Paige said.

Scott was unsmiling. "My team does have something we can use on the General and maybe connect it to Dunham and Ellison. I don't know yet how we're going to use it."

Paige seemed to perk up a bit. "Tell me," she said, yanking on his shirt sleeve.

"On these dates over the last four months," he said, pointing to dates on a spreadsheet he pushed in front of her, "General Tucker Phillips has been seen meeting with every known terrorist group leader. During the last thirty days, Ellison and Tucker Phillips were seen with each of the jihadi leaders. The best part is we have surveillance showing Secretary Dunham on one occasion meeting with those same three Jihadi terrorists along with Phillips and Ellison right by his side."

Paige was at the edge of her seat. "So, why can't we use this now?"

"We haven't been able to locate or find from satellite images any of those Jihadi leaders. I believe they are all dead now. The General is our leading suspect in their murders."

"That's a good thing, right?"

"Yes, that they are dead, but no for helping us. The spin that Dunham can make from what we suspect is that he alone has rid the world of the worst of the worst. Something I believe he wants everyone in America to believe. He wants to be the next EOTUS," Scott said, his frustration showing. "Remember his favorite quote from Caesar:

"*I am-no, I want to be like Caesar. I want to give little trouble to my opponents, then, after they have been overpowered and had accepted it, they will see that my tyranny was only in name and appearance and that my first acts were not so cruel, but the requirement that was needed for my monarchy to work smoothly as a gentle physician. That my acts of cruelty would seem to be assigned by Heaven itself. Then and only then will the Roman citizens have a terrible yearning for me and accept everything I have done to rule them."*

Scott shrugged his shoulder. "It's scary that he believes this shit?"

"The scarier thing is a majority of Americans are buying into his bull-shit every time he does something good for them."

Paige slumped back in her chair. The color had drained from her face. Before she could say more, a "Special News Alert" exploded on her muted TV screen. She turned the sound up.

What they were both witnessing was the launch of President Chesterfield's communication satellite. The reporter was saying:

"President Chesterfield, after an extensive investigation into reports that America's new communications satellite had been compromised, the president gave the go-ahead to launch it today. While we do not know what this satellite will do for our national security, reports say that it could be a game-changer for President Chesterfield."

"Game-changer for Chesterfield? How will this satellite help the president?" Paige asked. "I am more concerned about what it will do for Dunham."

Scott did not hesitate with his response. "My sources at the NSA have told me it's not a communications satellite, but a cyber weapon to help stop all the recruiting the Jihadi extremists are doing online. It also can create or prevent cyber-attacks. What I could not find out is how powerful it is. President Chesterfield could become very powerful and able to dictate the type of foreign diplomacy he's been wanting to achieve since taking office," Scott said.

"What if someone like Dunham, the Architect, gets control of this satellite?" Paige asked.

"You mean if Caesar, the new Emperor, was able to use it?"

"Yes."

"He'd have full control of every missile defense system, all banking transactions, power grids...shit you name it; he'd control everything."

"This scenario was inside one of his encrypted files. But, how would he get to control it?" Paige asked. "He's not president yet?"

"Good question. I guess we are going to have to wait and see?"

"No, we have to begin getting this plausible alternative out there. The world has to begin to question Chesterfield and Dunham before it's too late."

"Once the satellite is activated, it will be too late. Chesterfield won't get re-elected. He's more likely going to resign before he's impeached. If Dunham runs for president, he's a shoo-in. No one from either party, even professor Miller's new *We the People* movement will have a chance."

Paige turned off the TV and was getting dressed. "You coming?"

"Where?"

"No questions right now. Just trust me," Paige said, kissing Scott on the cheek.

109

Paige had her home office set up for a teleconference with some of her international friends, most of them journalists, with a small contingency from the intelligence community in Europe. Scott seemed impressed by the resume of the people she had listed on a yellow pad she had in front of her.

Paige told Scott that these men and women were all willing to work on uncovering the worldwide conspiracy that had begun to rear its ugly head around the world. She had so much support from everyone on her list; they did not hesitate to look into all the associations that Dunham, Ellison and Tucker Phillips had in common with two dozen terrorist groups around the globe.

Paige began the confidential conference call on time. "Thank you for all agreeing to listen to me, as well as, to help put into the open everything Secretary Dunham, as the Architect, is currently doing. I am convinced more than ever that the answers he gave me about his role as this Architect was not just a family title given to him. Something is about to happen with his Stage Five, and I think it will be devastating to my country as well as the rest of the Free World," she said, her tone somber.

A reporter for the AP was first to speak. "We all know that this investigation will not be easy. We've been looking into the Architect for a while, ever since you exposed that he existed.

It's not been easy. We do know that Dunham and Ellison are in bed with governments and intelligence agencies around all of Europe. Our problem is that we have been having too many doors slammed in our faces. Some of my colleagues have gone missing. Every step we take forward, we go back five steps," he said his voice resonating his frustration.

A female investigator with Interpol stood. "I'm not supposed to be here. However, I cannot sit back while my superiors kiss Dunham's ring. They like all the monetary benefits he throws at them. I have some material proof from professor Miller's research. I believe it could end the reign of terror that the Dunham family has perpetuated.

The teleconference went on for almost two hours. Paige seemed a lot more relaxed after listening to everyone brief her on what they've uncovered.

"Great work, everyone. I believe I have enough to go live with our collaborative investigation. It will seem more real to my listeners with all of you validating the findings," she said. "What I need is a venue to broadcast."

Her friend from British Network News, the BNN, offered her studio to Paige. "My Editor and Chief is very excited about this story and would love to have you on our network."

"Scott Rogers, my partner, will be joining us. See you tomorrow. I want to air my report as soon as possible," Paige asked.

110

President Chesterfield, his eyes glued on the digital as it ticked down to the launch sequence of his satellite. The NSA Director was calling out the countdown…three, two, one. Everyone inside in the Situation Room had their eyes glued on the large monitor. When it turned black for a few seconds, they gasped. Babcock informed them it was a regular occurrence while the weather satellite's cameras stopped recording, and the new communications satellite attempted to boot up and become operational.

Babcock was pressing his earbud, listening for a response from Houston. His face turned bedsheet white. He looked at the president and shook his head.

Chesterfield did not know what to make of NSA Director's reaction. "Speak up. What's happening?"

Babcock's words sputtered out of his mouth. "Sir, we've lost our communication signal to the satellite. NASA has tried rebooting, but we're still unable to connect. At the moment we have a satellite spinning around the earth, and we do not have any control over it," he said, blotting his forehead with a napkin.

"What the fuck does this mean? What just happened? If we don't have control, who does?" He was rubbing his temples, his chin resting on his chest, staring blankly at the monitor. His thoughts were spinning, hearing bits and pieces of Paige Turner's words: *"Stage-Five, the Architect has compromised your satellite."*

"Sir, I checked and doubled checked our systems. I doubt anyone could have hacked into this system. It was top secret-with firewalls. It's impenetrable. Only the people in this room knew about what this satellite could do. We'd be in a whole lot of trouble if our enemies got a hold of this weapon," Babcock said, slapping his forehead. "Sir, I misspoke. Roberts and Hood also knew of this weapon and could have been working with Wilbanks."

Chesterfield leaned back in his high-back leather chair, his hands squeezing his cheeks. "Shit. I'm thinking the same thing. If we've lost control, then it needs to be destroyed," he ordered.

Babcock bit his lips, drawing blood. "Sir that might be a problem. We have no communication with the satellite to change its orbit and allow it to burn up in our atmosphere. Our back up code to get back control is not working. Whoever did this must have changed our log-in sequences.

"Can we blow it out of the sky," Chesterfield asked.

"No, sir. It's in a high orbit. If you remember, it was your fail-safe scenario."

President Chesterfield dismissed everyone and slumped in his chair, staring at the White House lawn. "What have I just done?" he whispered.

* * * * * *

Dunham was anxiously waiting for the briefing from his men at his compound. He sat in his office with Frederick Ellison and General Tucker Phillips. He was acting nervous. Everything he'd accomplished to this point with his first four stages would have been all in vain if he couldn't get control of the satellite. He looked at Frederick.

"You sure this will work?"

"The chip was specifically made to turn control over to you after our code sequence is downloaded. If the satellite achieves its correct orbit and becomes activated, there is nothing for you to fret over. It will be all over for Chesterfield and the United States as we now know it," said Ellison rubbing his hands.

Dunham needed to create more distractions for the president today. "How fast can we initiate three or four small bombing incidents in California, Chicago, and Virginia?"

Ellison seemed dumbfounded by his request. "You want to do what today? Isn't it enough the president will lose full control of his satellite?"

"No. I need Chesterfield to start thinking about resigning. I want him out of office immediately, so I can begin finalizing my Stage Five.

"Okay. We have all our cells on alert. It can happen within two hours."

"Then, give the orders. Now, let me watch history in the making," said Dunham, with no emotion showing on his face, knowing that he was about to be responsible for killing hundreds of Americans.

Ellison snapped his fingers signaling Dunham he had good news. He read the text and smiled. It was from their team in a bunker on a small island in the Caribbean. "Albert, you just got ownership of Chesterfield's satellite," he said.

Dunham was deep in thought. "Now, we wait. We will begin using this weapon and begin to change history within a week. First, I need to talk to the president and see how his satellite launch had gone." he said, unable to stop grinning.

“Let’s not get too overconfident,” Ellison cautioned. “We still have to relocate our laptop that controls the satellite back to your bunker at your ranch in Pennsylvania.”

“At this point, no one in Chesterfield’s cabinet knows I have control. So, keep to our plan and transport the computer to my ranch, ASAP,” Dunham ordered.

111

Like everything in the Beltway, a new presidential scandal had surfaced again and was plastered on every newspaper around the country. The national network news stations were interrupting their current news coverage to begin their speculation about the president's billion-dollar bungle of losing control of his new communications satellite. The media guesswork had already started, theorizing what this new event would do to his re-election bid, as well as his impeachment hearings.

One morning talk show host was interviewing a spokesperson from NASA. "What can you tell us about this satellite and if you'll be able to get control of it?"

The NASA representative said. "Right now, all I can say is that we had a successful launch and executed orbit of the NSA's new communications satellite," he said, nervously.

"So, was this a successful launch and orbit?" the commentator asked.

"That's a question that should be addressed to the NSA. It was their satellite that President Chesterfield was anxious to have operational weeks before we completed our investigation into the charges about a potential problem," he said nervously. "Once we had achieved orbit, all NASA personnel were asked to leave their computer monitors, as the president's team tried to activate the communications satellite. I found that very strange."

The reporter took the bait. "What did you find strange about that request?"

"At NASA, everyone in the room has high-security clearance and in all situations up until then, has never been asked to leave while completion of a launch takes place."

"Can you guess why they asked all of your team to leave?"

"Only two reasons. First, this was not a communications satellite, or after putting in their codes to activate this satellite, they could not get control of it. I think it's a little of both. I don't have more to say in this matter. You need to be having this conversation with the director of the NSA or President Chesterfield."

The rest of the morning and throughout the day, that interview occupied the airways and talk shows. President Chesterfield and his NSA director were not available for comment. The administration not addressing the issue only kept the rumors flying and the reasons for impeachment becoming more dominant within the House and Senate.

Secretary Dunham was not hiding from the press and was holding another non-sanctioned press conference in Saudi Arabia while he was still on his mission to build a strong coalition with America's allies.

His hands firmly gripping his podium on the tarmac, his plane in the background, started answering questions. "Before I take some of your questions, I want to comment about this satellite situation," he paused, panning his audience, their microphones stretched out trying to get as close to him as possible. "First, I want to assure everyone we did have a successful launch and orbit of our new communications satellite. We have temporarily lost contact with it, but our experts at the NSA have assured the president that it will be up and running within a few days." He looked at the two-dozen reporters and pointed to one he knew very well.

"Thank you, Mr. Secretary. "Why all the secrecy behind this communications satellite? Is it because it's not what the president or the NSA said it was?"

"That's an excellent question. While I cannot talk about anything that has top-secret status, I can say that this satellite was going to help our country with the fight against terrorism," Dunham said, hoping he had them all curious. He pointed at another reporter.

"Secretary Dunham, what does this mean that the NSA has lost contact with their satellite? Had it been hacked by one of our enemies? If so, could it be now used against us?"

"Wow, that's a mouthful. "I think those questions should be addressed to the White House and the NSA," he replied, trying to contain his enjoyment that more speculation would be hitting the airways.

After another fifteen minutes, Secretary Dunham ended the press conference, but not before having the last word. He first glanced at his watch, realizing that the next series of distractions for President Chesterfield was about to happen.

"Understand that our enemies, all terrorists, want to destroy the very foundation of our democracy. They also want to disrupt the economies of our Western Allies. They want a war against the West. I hope we get full control of this satellite very soon," he said, turning and walking back toward his plane.

112

A week had passed since the satellite went off-line. Complicating this mess for President Chesterfield was another series of attacks on American soil. The president was looking worn out and flustered. The firestorm of the satellite and recent terrorist attacks had become a war of words, between the White House and the media. President Chesterfield had just finished his final impeachment testimony in the House Chambers, and it did not go well for him.

It had been televised on C-SPAN for over eight hours. The president as hard as he tried to explain himself about everything that had happened under his watch was coming across as a defeated man. With no commercial breaks and no make-up staff, he looked worse than Nixon after one of his sweating attacks.

* * * * *

Paige could not believe what was happening to the president. She still felt Dunham had his fingerprints all over the bombings. She was desperately trying to figure out the details about this communications satellite, and what could the Architect do with it? Her associates in Europe and the Middle East could not find any known terrorist group that had recently set off bombs on US soil. The only saving grace was that there were no deaths associated with the recent explosions. No group had taken credit for them, but it seemed to have General Tucker Phillips's signature all over it. She couldn't prove it.

113

Dunham could not believe how well the new chip was able to modify the software on the satellite, allowing it to perform without any complications.

"It's easier than I had imagined," he told Ellison. "Now for some more tests," he rubbed his hands, a big smile on his face.

Ellison had a worried expression. "Shouldn't you wait a while. What's the rush?"

Dunham, with contempt in his eyes, replied. "I have the power now to do as I please. I need to see if we can interrupt the monetary highway of money transfers and divert the flow of funds to my accounts. Our enemies, those who are not in our alliance, who want to foil my plans, are now floating their funds from country to country. If I can snag all of it and bank it in my offshore accounts, it will be a grand day for all of us. The terrorists will see their money dwindle to zero and have no idea who did it."

"Don't you think the treasury department with their sophisticated cyber team will know you did it?" Ellison complained. "Why expose yourself so early?"

"That's the beauty of what Chesterfield created. The satellite hides these transactions behind firewalls that cannot be penetrated. It was the president's ace in the hole, as he put it. He was going to do what I will do, but I will get rich doing it. Now it's my time to take control of everything."

* * * * *

Eight hours later, Dunham was sitting inside his war room twenty feet down in his bunker below his ranch house in Pennsylvania. "I want their transactions diverted over the next ten hours. I want it to be a slow drip, as I drain the financial blood from Syria, North Korea, and Iran," a cold-blooded calmness resonated from his lips. "I have a meeting set up with Chesterfield tomorrow. Text me on my burner phone when all transactions are completed and with the exact numbers."

"Copy that," Thomas Hayes said. "What about Ellison and Tucker. Isn't it time yet?" he asked.

Dunham was shaking his head. He knew the time was coming to cut all ties from his past. He needed a little more time to put it into action. "After my meeting with Chesterfield. Then we can discuss it. I want to let him know first that I am running against him for president. He's going to feel so betrayed."

114

Paige was with Bradley and Professor Miller at her home in Malibu. They were arguing about the direction their investigation was going against Dunham. The frustration for each of them was that after Dunham had eviscerated Turner on National TV, they were at a loss as to how to proceed to expose Dunham and show him to be a traitor.

Bradley Stevens began pacing around the living room. "Teddy Dunham is reluctant to testify against his brother. He'd rather give us his videotapes of their conversations and see what we can do with them first."

Paige was shaking her head. She was not ready to give up on the real story about Dunham. "Everything we've read in his files and those encrypted files all match up with what's been going on. Even the compromised satellite. Why no one will believe us and instead believe Dunham, is beyond logic."

"Everyone running for re-election, even the president won't rock the boat Dunham is Captain of," Dean said.

"I know our little Caesar has control of the goddamn satellite. He must have tested it on North Korea," she said. "Having him arrested just for the violations at his chemical company would not punish him enough for what he's done. He could easily handle any fines imposed on him."

Dean seemed uncomfortable. "The president called me the other day. He wants me working for him temporarily. He believes that I can hack into the satellite and give him back control of it," Miller told them.

"You're kidding? He hung us out to dry the moment he made Dunham the Secretary of State."

"I know. But I truly believe the president needs, I mean my country needs my help right now. Whether we like what he's done, we cannot allow Dunham or whoever to keep control of this weapon. I love my country too much to allow my hurt feelings to prevent me from doing the right thing," Dean was letting his frustrated emotions show.

"When is this happening?"

"Tomorrow."

Bradley interrupted. "We still need to do something with what Dunham's brother, gave us. It will at least distract the Architect. Maybe even rattle him a bit?"

Paige threw her arms in the air. "I give up. Release the first two tapes to the networks who are supporting us. Let's see what happens."

115

President Chesterfield glared at his Secretary of State as he entered the Oval Office. Dunham appeared cheerful and upbeat. Unlike the president, who looked depressed and exhausted.

"How can you be so cheerful when my administration is falling apart around me?" Chesterfield asked.

Dunham did not react to the comment, keeping the big smile on his face. "My trip abroad went better than expected. To top it all off, North Korea had a spectacular fuck up with their missile tests. That little piss ant for a leader is in hiding, more paranoid than ever," he replied.

Chesterfield was in no mood for Dunham and his bubbly attitude. "Tell me something good about what you've been doing with our allies."

Dunham's smile evaporated from his face. "Sir, we have a shit load of problems with the EU and in the Middle East. They don't trust us anymore. Well, it's you that they don't trust," he said sarcastically. With all that's going on with your pending impeachment hearings, our allies are turning their backs on you."

Chesterfield, could not believe what he was hearing from his Secretary of State. "I had just spoken with six of our major allies, and they promised me their support. What happened while you were over there?"

Dunham's smile had evaporated. His confidence was growing, knowing what he was capable of doing with the satellite. He decided to hit the president with both barrels of what he wanted to tell him. "Our allies, after my meetings, decided to throw their support behind me," he said. He slipped his hand inside his suit jacket and handed the president an envelope. "This is my resignation. I submitted my application to run for president this morning. I don't think I can work for you. It would be too much of a conflict of interest," he said.

Chesterfield flushed with rage. "What kind of bull-shit is this? I appointed you to the most powerful position in my administration, and this is how you repay me?"

Dunham finally let a bellowing laugh consume the Oval Office. "Becoming the Secretary of State was all part of my plan, even though it was only going to be temporary. You were a desperate fool to put me in such a key position. I am the Architect, describe by Paige Turner. Everything has been spelled out in my Manifesto. You only wanted to get re-elected and became blind with ambition putting your country last," he said mockingly.

Chesterfield jumped up out of his chair, ready to strangle Dunham. "So, everything inside those files is true? All the attacks, the bombings, the innocent Americans dead, all for your sick dream to be the next Emperor of the United States?"

Dunham was texting while Chesterfield screamed at him. He raised his index finger, signaling the president to hold his thought. "Um...yes to everything you've just said. I am the one who created the mess you're drowning in right now. Impeachment was my idea. I've made you look incompetent and will continue to do so until you resign. I have all the power now. Your satellite is under my full control. Like what just happened to North Korea, is happening to Israel right now," he bragged, lifting the control device on the president's desk and turning on the TV. "Now sit down and watch."

Every news channel broadcasted a shocking event happening in Israel. Their missile defense system had been turned off, and hundreds of rockets were striking three highly populated cities.

As pictures of the devastation exploded on the screen, Dunham was again punching in a text. Within seconds, Israel's dome defense system turned back on.

"Now, Mr. President, do you want me to give you another display of my power?" Dunham boasted.

Chesterfield was lifting his phone to call his secret service detail. "I'm having you arrested for treason," he said, as Dunham raised his palm at the president.

"I wouldn't do that if I was you. My team has specific instructions in case I get arrested. They have my specific orders to start a war you cannot win. You don't want to test my resolve and see me destroy a few of your Navy ships. I'm just getting started learning my new capabilities with the weapon you built. I suggest you think of resigning before I make matters worse for you." Dunham stood and turned his back. He was out the door before Chesterfield could say another word.

116

Chesterfield had called an emergency meeting with his Attorney General and Admiral Hollingsworth. He needed help from people he believed were still loyal Americans to handle the Dunham blackmail threat. He was not going to let his Secretary of State become the next president of the United States.

Felix Wilson was livid. "I told you not to make him your Secretary of State," he screamed at the president. "We need a plan to take back control of that fucking satellite you felt would be your re-election ace-in-hole," his eyes were screaming at his friend.

Hollingsworth exhaled loudly. "Let's not begin to point fingers. Dunham was going to get control of the satellite no matter what position you'd have given him. He's having some sick fun at your expense and murdering our citizens at the same time. I know you've asked Professor Dean Miller to help you. Will he cooperate?"

Chesterfield was staring, his eyes glassy. "He should be here tomorrow. I have my Secret Service detail escorting him to Camp David. I want him in the most secure spot I have at my disposal."

"I'm not sure that's a good idea," the admiral said. "If Dunham has learned the capabilities of this weapon, then Camp David...not even the White House is secure."

"Do you or..." he pointed at his attorney general, "you have any idea what we should do?

Both men had blank expressions.

Chesterfield was noticeably upset. "We know the fucking Architect, Dunham, is laughing at all of us, and by the look on your faces...do I need to surrender?"

Admiral Hollingsworth responded. "I think we need to go back to using Paige Turner. She's the only one that's got this guy pegged. She can destroy him in the press. It might slow him down during his run for President. I bet she has evidence that would bury this guy."

"After what I did to her on national TV, she might not even answer a call from me?"

"Let me call her. I've always gotten along with her. I knew her husband Rick, while he was with our troops in Iraq. I know he'd want her to help her country," Hollingsworth said.

Chesterfield, for the first time in his presidency, felt defeated. "Go ahead and ask her."

117

Paige had just finished her phone call with Admiral Hollingsworth. She was dismayed at what she heard about Dunham, but not surprised. Her dislike for Chesterfield paled in comparison to her hate for the Architect.

She trusted Admiral Hollingsworth and agreed to help her country. "I'll be in D.C. tomorrow," she said. "I just have to tidy up some loose ends here."

Paige seemed perplexed. "Bradley, should I trust Chesterfield again? He's stabbed me once in the back."

"I've known him for a long time. He sounds genuinely worried. If he needs our help, we need to put our personal feelings aside and go help him and our country."

"We're reporters. What can we do to help him? What if he's going to use us again for his political gain?"

"I don't believe it. Chesterfield wants all the investigative material we have on Dunham and the Architect. He said he's at war with this man. If what he says is true about the satellite and what it's capable of doing, shit, we're all in a shitstorm of trouble if our country cannot get control back and destroy it," Bradley said.

"I'm still not sure how I can help. I don't have a show anymore," Paige said.

"I've been talking to Clay, and he's offered his full support. You'll have every resource you need to help bring down this animal."

Paige looked at Scott for some assurances. "Any thoughts about all of this?"

Scott was calm and unnerved by the president's comments to Paige. "Country first over our personal feelings right now. Our president needs us. So, let's pack our bags and go destroy Dunham once and for all."

Paige was about to turn off the TV when another News Alert appeared on her screen.

"*Over ten billion dollars of banking transactions flowing from four countries who support terrorism, have gone missing. Iran, Syria, North Korea, and Russia are blaming the United States. They have all threatened to retaliate.*

Paige flopped down on her couch, feeling the wind knocked out of her, "Could this be another power move by Dunham?"

"If Chesterfield's weapon is as powerful as he said, then yes. Dunham seems to be testing his new toy," Bradley said.

"Then, we have to expose him to the American public and the world. Put him in the court of public opinion and see how Caesar likes that."

While Paige talked, a thought came into her head. It was something a month and a half ago that Dean Miller had said about Brian Russell's thumb drive. She was texting him as she ran to her bedroom to pack some clothes.

* * * * *

Dean Miller had already left with his family to DC, eager to help his country. He had some ideas as to what he might be able to do to take away control of the satellite from Dunham. He asked his last remaining intern Kyle Devlin who, like Seth Alexander, worked for the professor at his software company and was a real geek when it came to coding and deciphering codes.

President Chesterfield, during his phone call with Miller, came across as a defeated leader of the free world and that scared the professor. Dean realized, for the first time, that Dunham had become the arrogant Architect.

What made professor Miller furious was how Dunham had begun flaunting his newfound power to the president and at the same time projecting an image of himself as a benevolent philanthropist.

"Mr. President, sir, I do not like what Secretary Dunham is doing to our country. However, I am not sure I can give you control of the satellite without being able to get into the NSA computers. I need a security clearance. Then, I have to find the new control board Dunham is using that is controlling the satellite. If you can do that for me, then I feel I can help."

"Whatever you need Mr. Miller, you've got it," Chesterfield said and ended the call.

118

Dunham had called a press conference to officially announce his candidacy for President, as well as his resignation as Secretary of State.

"*Members of the press, I want to thank you for all of your support these last few weeks. Your reporting of the many accomplishments I was able to do, first as a loyal and patriotic citizen of this great country, and for a short time as your Secretary of State,"* he paused, panning his audience, pleased with all the smiles he was seeing.

"*A few hours ago, I gave President Chesterfield my resignation letter and informed him I was planning on defeating him in the upcoming presidential election. I will be running as an Independent since I cannot in good conscience support any of the policies by Republicans or Democrats. Our great country needs fresh ideas and a non-political approach to helping our country keep its rightful place in the world as the greatest empire,"* he said, realizing he chose the wrong words. He quickly went back to his speech.

"In the next few days and weeks, I will be announcing my presidential platform. I promise to put every American back to work and be able to achieve the American Dream that has escaped many of our hard-working citizens for the last decade or more. I will not be bad-mouthing my opponents like previous presidents unless they start attacking me with lies and false

facts..." Dunham fell silent, looking at all the arms raised, wanting to ask him questions.

"I will be opening this press conference to questions in just a moment. However, I have one more item I need to address," Dunham said, smiling. *"Up until election day, you will be hearing more false rumors and accusations about me as the Architect. All I ask of you is to ignore them and judge me based on what I've accomplished and promise to accomplish as your president. Thank you for your time. Now for some questions."*

The press conference went on for another hour. Dunham answered questions that ranged from foreign affairs to the economy. He answered all of them with promises of what he would do once he was elected president. He made predictions that only he knew how he'd accomplish them. One question he did not answer was about the lost communications satellite. He cited that it was a top-secret project with an ongoing investigation, and as the former Secretary of State, he would not address it.

Two days later, a national poll showed Dunham had a seventy-five percent approval rating, compared to Chesterfield's twenty-five percent.

119

It had been thirty days since Dunham had his press conference. Paige Turner, Scott Rogers, and Dean Miller were going to have another briefing on Dunham and his role as the Architect inside the situation room. President Chesterfield remained seated as they entered the room. He looked like he hadn't slept in a week. The polls, state by state, predicted an embarrassing loss for the president on election day. He was running in third, ten points behind the *We the People* candidate, a Hispanic woman.

Before they flopped down in their chairs, the president started the meeting. "Please sit. I need to get this meeting underway. I am sure all of you watched Dunham's news conference an hour ago. The asshole has started putting the nails in my coffin."

Paige kept her serious face on and chimed in. "We're here to help. My country comes first," she said, handing Chesterfield a thick folder of documents. "We've uncovered a myriad of evidence to bury Dunham with a shit-pile of lawsuits, as well as criminal charges if your Attorney General has the guts to arrest him."

Chesterfield started shaking his head. "We can't. He's threatened to use my weapon against my military, as well as our banking systems. He needs to be outed by you, using the media as our weapon."

"Really? Now you want me to do my job while Dunham has his foot on your neck?" Paige said rudely. "I remember how he twisted his story to make me sound like an alarmist. What's to stop him from doing it again?"

Scott grabbed her arm. "Let's calm down and figure out how we're going to destroy Dunham."

President Chesterfield jumped in. "I understand your concern, but rest assured I will be making a statement very shortly outing Dunham as the true evil Architect."

Miller was calculating something on his smartphone, his finger raised in the air. "I think I know how to get control of the satellite," he said, a big grin on his face. "It was something Russell had sent me inside my copy of his thumb drive. It didn't mean anything to me then, but now it might be our only hope.

For the first time in weeks, Chesterfield smiled. "What do you need from me?"

"I need to have access to the NSA computers like you promised...not where the problem happened. It has to be from a secure hidden location so that I can work uninterrupted."

Paige looked at Scott, hoping he had an idea. "Johnny B. Goode. He's the best I've known that can figure out this communications problem, or at the least, help professor Miller. I have a very secure location they can work at," Scott said, confidently.

Chesterfield looked at Admiral Hollingsworth. "Can you coordinate getting the professor what he needs?"

"Sir, that won't be a problem."

"Now Ms. Turner, what do you have for us that will bury this bastard six feet under?"

Paige opened her thick file and began spreading her papers out on the oval conference table in the Situation Room. "Mr. President, there is so much material I don't know where to begin."

Chesterfield released a smile as he watched the reporter sort through her material. "Start with the easy stuff first."

Paige raised her head, her eyes focusing on the president. "Dunham's pharmaceutical company. I have company records, and numerous videos between Dunham and his brother Theodore showing him ordering the poisoning of millions of American's so that his drug manufacturing plants could sell lifesaving medications, at inflated prices."

Felix Wilson leaned forward, his elbows resting on the conference table noticeably excited at what Turner was telling them. "Even if this is what Dunham wanted to do, how did he transmit the poison that infected all these Americans?"

"A very subtle and unknown way. He let nature do it for him with PM10, particle matter ten. Every time a specific region has high winds, finite particles are pushed in the air and breathed in by innocent citizens. Dunham knew that by spraying his banned chemical retardant on vacant land, he'd have a natural way to spread his poison," Paige said.

"Do the videotapes you have show Dunham's criminal intent? The Attorney General asked.

"Yes, in my opinion. That's going to be your job after you view videos. Just know that Dunham's chemical company knew what type of safe chemical he could have used as the retardant," Paige said.

President Chesterfield seemed intrigued. "Aren't there agencies that monitor chemical companies and the products they use?"

Paige shuffled more papers around until she found what Dunham's brother gave Bradley. "Here are dozens of inspection reports from your director of CDC, who in another video that Dunham's brother took, shows Dunham paying him off. I could keep going on, but suggest you begin an investigation and get your justice department to subpoena Albert Dunham and bring him before a Grand Jury. Let's see how he weasels his way out of this. I expect, once this gets out, there will be hundreds, maybe thousands of class action suits against Dunham and his companies for what they have done," Paige said, slumping back in her chair looking exhausted. "There goes his hero image."

"Very good. I assume you have more to tell me?" Chesterfield asked.

Paige nodded. "I do. Unfortunately, I need a way to broadcast my investigation without Dunham being able to stop me."

Felix stood up and leaned over to the president, whispering in his ear. After Chesterfield nodded, he returned to his chair. "I think we have the perfect location for you to broadcast your new *White House* show," he said.

Paige had a bewildered expression on her face. "I'm all ears."

120

Dunham had summoned his council to his ranch. It had been a glorious time testing his new toy while building trillions of dollars for his war chest as he solidified his lead in the polls. Chesterfield's satellite, with the Architect's modifications, were working correctly.

He had become bolder and more aggressive with his presidential campaign showing his newfound power. He needed to have his surrogates in the United States Congress and around the world keyed into his current plan with only one hundred-eight days before the presidential election. In attendance, today, at his spur of the moment meeting, were the remaining members of the Architect Council.

In the room sitting around a fifteen-foot oval oak table was Greg Radcliff from Trident Communications, a German-based conglomerate. On his left was Stuart Mays CEO of AMB Bank, based in Switzerland, one of the vehicles he was using to shelter his newfound money chest of stolen funds. To his right was Rebecca Lowry from Great Britain, CEO of Apollo Virtual Solutions, the first company to create a hack-proof software. Rounding out the group was Martin Thornburg, founder of Thornburg Financial Services, the brains behind Dunham's genius investment strategies. Sitting across from the council was General Tucker Phillips, Thomas Hayes, Todd Mathews, and Frederick Ellison.

Dunham noticed that his Council, the descendants from the first Council his Great Grandfather created, appeared edgy and nervous. The Architect panned the room, his eyes like laser beams targeting everyone in the room. He was enjoying seeing them squirm in their chairs.

"I'm happy everyone could be here on such short notice. Today marks a new beginning for America, our world, and our new manifesto. Our dreams are finally coming to fruition. Over the next hundred and eighty days, with all of your help and the assistance from our new satellite, we will see a change within the United States and our current constitution that will give me all the power I need to make our country the most powerful nation on the face of the earth. What I can now do will make all of us wealthier than we had ever imagined," said Dunham, pausing to catch his breath. "Nothing can stop us. No military. No country, no law enforcement agency or the judicial system. I am ready to become the next Emperor of the United States," he boasted. He noticed all the shocked faces staring back at him.

While Dunham believed he had all the power, it was this council, of descendants from the creator who organized the Architect's original manifesto. Today, they did not appear pleased with Dunham.

Greg Radcliff from Trident Communications was first to speak up. "Albert, you're taking yourself too seriously. This power you believe you have only came to you because we allowed it."

Radcliff continued. "I can see that you're getting upset with what I am saying. You have forgotten the most important part of our manifesto was to remain in the background and out of the public's purview. You've become too big for your britches. Our manifesto was designed to get everything we're getting while staying out of the limelight. What you've got planned to make you this Emperor of the United States cannot continue..." Dunham jumped up and was ready to strangle this man.

Albert's face turned red with fury. "Let me make myself clear. The manifesto, my manifesto, is changed. You will now take orders from me and me alone," he shouted. "Everyone of you will either follow my path or be dealt with severely."

Radcliff signaled the others on the council to get up and ready themselves to leave. He did not see Dunham signal, Tucker Phillips and Thomas Hayes, to block the door to the conference room, their guns pointed at the council.

"I am not finished with all of you. So, sit the hell down. I have more to say," Dunham ordered.

Radcliff was nervously fiddling with his watch, as he listened to a crazed man shouting out orders to everyone in the room. Dunham did not know his watch had an emergency distress button he had pressed alerting the council's security team that they were all in danger. He sat down, assured he and the other members would be rescued.

Dunham glanced at his phone, reading a text he had just gotten. He typed in a short reply and smiled at Radcliff. Within seconds everyone in the conference room heard the explosions of gunfire coming from outside the complex. Dunham was smirking. He glanced at Tucker Phillips and was pleased he had gotten the okay sign that the council's security team was neutralized.

"That was a very ill-conceived attempt to show force against me. I hope you'll learn from this and support the changes I've made to the manifesto? Don't force me to terminate our relationship. It won't be a pleasant experience," Dunham threatened.

After another hour of laying out what was going to happen during his race to become the leader of the United States, all the council members were marched out of the conference room and escorted to their limos. They were forced to step over the twisted bloodied bodies of their security detail.

Dunham retreated to the conference room with Ellison, Hayes, and Phillips. He told Todd Mathews to go to his office and get ready for his orders. He had a lot to discuss with them about his next move with the satellite.

121

Chesterfield had summoned to the Oval Office his Attorney General, Marilyn Sawyer, the new directors of the FBI and CIA Mathew Gentry and Lawrence Berry. Paige Turner, Dean Miller, and Scott Rogers were there as well. He needed an update on all their progress to capture Dunham and ruin his image and get back control of the satellite.

The first to speak was Marilyn Sawyer, the Attorney General. "Mr. President, after conferring with my best legal minds at Justice, I am confident that I can charge Albert Dunham for treason and brand him a domestic terrorist. Here is a simple definition of a domestic terrorist: *The committing of terrorist acts in the perpetrator's own country against their fellow citizens.* It matches up with the U.S. Code of Federal Regulations. I won't bore you with all the legalize at this time," she said, with an air of confidence. "I am ready to proceed when you give me the orders."

Chesterfield was scratching his head. "I am not sure I want to do that at this time. I'm having second thoughts that he'd take fatal action against all of us."

Paige raised her hand. "Sir, I have an idea. Let me expose his chemical plant scandal. Knowing Dunham as I do, I think he'll use the satellite to show his power and then Dean can sneak into the satellite and give you back control. Once you've disabled the weapon, then you can arrest him and bring him to justice," she said, smiling.

"That I like," Chesterfield said. "I have something else I can give you to put a stake into his heart and get him to act irrationally." He signaled Felix to hand her a thumb drive with a recent video he had taped of Dunham admitting being the Architect responsible for all the recent attacks and his threat against the president and the United States. "I think you'll find this very interesting."

After Paige left the Oval Office, Chesterfield told his Attorney General that he wanted to have him hold a press conference while Turner is broadcasting and announce that Dunham is a domestic terrorist.

"This should scare the holy shit out of that bastard," Chesterfield said.

122

Paige was impressed with the make-shift studio the president had created for her. She wondered if Dunham would be able to find their location and cut her off before she could complete her broadcast.

Turner was seated behind a large teak desk, the background was of the White House, with a live feed of all the protesters outside the gates on Pennsylvania Avenue. She had gotten her alert that she had two-minutes before the broadcast would start.

Paige checked her notes and understood that a simulcast press briefing would be happening by the attorney general, who would be accusing Dunham of being a domestic terrorist. Professor Dean Miller's cue to hack into the satellite and disable it would be when he heard the two broadcasts.

Everything they were attempting to do was risky, as they did not know if it would even work or what retribution Dunham would unleash on the United States. She understood that they were out of options.

Paige watched her cameraman, who had started counting down...three, two, one. "Hello, this is Paige Turner coming to you from an undisclosed location with critical information for every American."

Turner jumped into her announcement with everything she had at her disposal. "What I am about to say has the full support of our President and Justice Department. First, I want to air a series of videos that will give you an accurate picture of who Albert Dunham, the admitted Architect, has been and continues to be over the last thirty days. Then, I will explain them to you."

The first three videos were of Albert Dunham talking with his brother, Teddy and confessing he knowingly poisoned millions of innocent Americans. The video also showed him paying off an official from CDC so his criminal act would be buried, hiding the evidence he used a banned chemical. Paige then explained how, through PM10, Particle Matter Ten, Dunham was able to transmit his poison to the most vulnerable Americans.

"Particle Matter 10 is a speck of finite dust that is transported by heavy winds. The CDC has banned certain chemical retardants that are proven causes of upper respiratory conditions, including cancer," Paige paused to take a sip of her water, a sad expression on her face. "What Albert Dunham had done knowingly, and in his own words, has intentionally poisoned hundreds of thousands of Americans, for the sake of profits." Paige looked straight into the camera, wagging her finger. "Mr. Dunham, how much money do you need? Was it worth all the lives you took with your greed?

Thirty minutes into her broadcast, Paige made another bold announcement. "Albert Dunham, at this moment you're being indicted by the United States Attorney General for your crimes against the United States. She is branding you and everyone working for you as domestic terrorists, not just for this PM 10 crime, but for the recent bombings on American soil and around the world."

After her damaging comments, another video streamed showing Dunham in the Oval Office bragging to president Chesterfield that he was the Architect that Paige Turner had accused him of being. The entire country and world would hear, from Dunham's lips, that he was responsible for all the recent attacks that had killed thousands of innocent people around the world. Her audience would listen to how he methodically affected the stock exchanges around the world so he could build his wealth.

After one hour, Paige signed off and breathed a sigh of relief. She looked at Bradley Stevens and smiled. He signaled her that her show had not been cut off. They had approximately five hundred million viewers. The count should be much higher as her broadcast had been streamed on every social media network. She knew she had to wait to see how the Attorney General and Dean Miller had done.

* * * * * *

Ten minutes after Paige Turner broadcasted her show, the Attorney General, Marilyn Sawyer, held a press briefing at the White House. She was inside the Oval Office standing behind a podium with the presidential seal. Chesterfield was standing to her right smiling at a dozen cameras and three hand-picked White House journalists who cover the White House.

Attorney General Sawyer looked down at her notes and began speaking. "My fellow Americans and our loyal allies. Today marks a solemn time in the United States and around the world. Our societies are under attack. Not by a terrorist group, but one man, an American, Albert Dunham. He has taken our country hostage. He has threatened our President with more attacks, more bombings, more disruption to our economy, and more interruptions to our power grids."

All the cameras were now pointing at President Chesterfield while Sawyer spoke. The president stared back at the cameras, an air of confidence on his face.

The Attorney General did not pause, while the cameras turned toward Chesterfield. "The Architect, Albert Dunham has threatened to destroy our military if we do not bow down to him. I was shocked at his arrogance and lack of love for our country. After watching the video made in the Oval Office, and the threats to our President and country by this American,

I wanted every US Citizen and everyone around the world to hear what their national hero has done and will continue to do if not stopped. As you will hear from his own words, he is unstable and wants to destroy our democracy. His delusion to be the next Emperor of the United States only shows us that he is crazy." Sawyer took a well-needed sip of water.

After fifteen more minutes, the Attorney General finalized her briefing. "The president and the Justice Department, along with the FBI and Homeland Security have branded Albert Dunham, a domestic terrorist. Warrants have been issued for his arrest and that of Frederick Ellison, General Tucker Phillips, and twelve members of Congress known as the dirty dozen. I will hold another briefing once I have these traitors in handcuffs.

The attorney general picked up her notes and ended the press conference without taking any questions.

* * * * * *

Dean Miller had gotten his signal and was working feverishly at his laptop, entering a series of codes to dismantle Dunham's control of the satellite. As the professor opened one firewall, another one popped up, blocking erasing his codes.

After an hour of trying, Miller threw his hands up in the air, frustrated that he had failed.

123

Dunham was furious. "How the fuck could the president allow that pissant of an attorney general do this to me? Doesn't he believe my threats?"

His wife Maggie huddled on her corner of the couch, her legs curled under her body. She was appalled from what she had just listened to on the news. "Albert, tell me this is not true. Could you murder so many people to accomplish your life-long dream? "Are you this monster that was shown on TV tonight?" She couldn't stop sobbing.

Dunham scowled at his wife. "Everything I've done I've done for us. We have power, and respect...now everyone will fear me and what I can do," he yelled. "I am at war and will not allow anyone, even the president, to try to take away what I've worked so hard to accomplish. Leaders have to be strong, and sometimes brutal, to achieve their goals."

Maggie jumped up from the couch and tried to leave the den. "I can't be in the same room as you. I don't know you anymore," she screamed.

Dunham grabbed her arm roughly and dragged her back to the couch. "You sit there and behave. I need you in my corner. Be the good wife I expect you to be," he yelled, his eyes wide with rage.

His cellphone rang. He waggled his finger at this wife, signally her not to move. He glanced at the screen on his phone. It was from Thomas Hayes. "What do you want?" he barked.

"Sir, someone tried to hack into the satellite's mainframe. We were able to thwart off the first attack, but I am not sure if we will be able to stop them for much longer," Hayes said nervously.

Dunham sucked in a breath before he replied. "I thought the new chip prevented that from happening?"

"I believe Professor Dean Miller is assisting the president on this. You do remember that he created most of the software that allows the satellite to function. Maybe he knows what Russell created since he was his teacher for a few years," Hayes said.

There was a long silence at the other end of the phone. "I've anticipated this. We'll go to plan B and give the president a kick in the ass for his disobedience. Everyone is going to have to respect my power, or they will be dealt with severely," Dunham muttered into his phone's mouthpiece. "Have Tucker get his men mobilized and ready to defend me at my ranch. I think we're going to war."

Maggie was biting the back of her hand, trembling with fear. "Albert, what's happened to you," she cried. "God will punish you for what you've done and plan to do."

"God? I am God now. You better get used to it if you know what's good for you," he threatened. "I don't care if it's you or the government trying to stop me. All of you will be dealt with harshly." He stormed out of the den and into his office. He was instantly at this computer typing in some codes for his satellite.

124

Dean Miller was surprised his attempt to break into the satellite's motherboard did not work. He looked at his intern Kyle Devlin. "Any thoughts," he asked a puzzled expression on his face.

"I read again what Russell had given you. I believe the override code he gave you was not to get control back but to change the orbit of the satellite. There are two motherboards, one to control the weapon, which we cannot break into, and the other is the stabilizing motherboard that is separate from the other systems on the satellite."

Dean re-read the message again and smiled at Kyle. "I think you're right. What if we insert a code that will go unnoticed and slowly begin to lower the orbit of the satellite until gravity brings it back down to earth?"

"Do we need to run this by President Chesterfield?"

"I don't want to, but I do not want the responsibility of destroying a multi-billion-dollar tax-payer asset on my hands either."

* * * * *

"Mr. President, Dean Miller here. I've misinterpreted the code Russell gave me. It's not to get us control, but to adjust the orbit of your satellite and slowly allow it to fall to earth, burning up on re-entry," Miller said. He held his breath, waiting for the president's response.

"Are you positive we can't get control of the satellite?" Chesterfield asked. "Can I send you more experts from NASA to help you? I cannot afford to lose this weapon."

"Sir, I understand your frustration. I am not sure anyone can do any better than I am doing right now. I am concerned if we wait too long, especially after what you just did with your Attorney General and Paige's broadcast, Dunham will retaliate."

Chesterfield's shook his head and gave Miller a direct order into his phone. "I do not want to give up just yet. Keep working on getting full control." Immediately after the president ended the call, a news alert popped up on his TV monitor.

125

Seeing Dunham's face on his TV monitor Chesterfield felt his heart pounding against his ribcage. "What's he going to say this time?" Dunham did not waste any time.

"I am Albert Dunham, and I am disturbed with your president. He's lying to distract Congress from moving on with his impeachment inquiry. Your president cannot protect the United States from foreign enemies. What might happen next will not be my fault," he said, wiping a tear from his cheek.

His camera was now focusing on him at a laptop computer. He wanted every viewer to watch him type on the keyboard.

"If anyone doubts, I love my country, this example is just the tip of the iceberg of what I am willing to do for every citizen who will support me. President Chesterfield, you should resign and save our country the trauma of seeing you impeached. Every citizen, within five hours, verify your balance in your checking accounts. Just a little thank you for backing my run for President."

During the next five hours, every American with a checking account had ten thousand dollars transferred in from the treasury department.

Dunham's telecast disappeared from the president's monitor.

Chesterfield slumped back into his chair behind his desk. He was staring blankly at the wall in the Oval Office. He glanced at Felix Wilson, then panned to Admiral Hollingsworth. What got his attention was Scott Rogers on his stat phone talking rapidly.

"Scott, what's got you so animated?" Chesterfield asked.

"Sir, I think we figure out how we can stop this madman. His ego might have given away a little weakness in his plan," said Rogers. "I need to discuss something with my team first. I can have some ideas that might save your satellite and arrest Dunham and his cohorts."

"What about what he just said. Is he going to harm us or give away more money to buy voter approval?"

Rogers was deep in thought, trying to find the words to say. "Sir, your satellite is being controlled on his laptop. My men have been watching his ranch in Pennsylvania, which we believe is his command center. If I can organize an assault, I am sure I can recover the laptop and give you back control of your satellite."

"I'd like to have something positive coming my way. How much time do you need?" the president asked.

"Maybe two hours. No more than three, sir."

Before Scott could leave the White House, the TV monitor was once again streaming a major *News Alert*.

"*The entire Eastern Seaboard and West Coast power grids have been shut down,*" the hysterical reporter said. Then he pressed his earbud, the color draining from his face. "*Five ballistic missiles have been launched from our NORAD missile facility and heading toward Hawaii. The estimated time of impact is in ninety minutes. Shit, shit, shit,*" the reporter said, losing all sense of control. *"One of our nuclear submarines just launched three missiles heading toward Saudi Arabia and Israel. Detonation in fifty-eight minutes."*

Chesterfield looked at Scott Rogers, and he could only shrug his shoulders in defeat. "I'm not so sure we have that much time to figure out a plan."

"Mr. President, in my years of experience as a Navy SEAL and US Marshall, I believe Dunham is bluffing right now. If he does this, he'll lose his leverage over us."

"I hope you're..." Before Chesterfield could finish his sentence, his monitor came back on. It was Dunham again.

"Mr. President, I hope you're impressed with what I can do with your weapon? I am just beginning to learn all its functions. So, here are my demands: First, you will resign as president before the week is over. Second, you will cancel your Attorney Generals actions she is taking against my men and me immediately, and third, you will tell all Americans that you support Albert Dunham as their next president. This part needs to coordinate with your resignation. If you do not do what I demand, what I did today will happen, but with more power grids going down and more of your missiles launched against your allies."

The monitor went black again, not allowing Chesterfield to address his demands.

Another News Alert came back up. All the power grids were back and functioning smoothly, and all the missiles have crashed into the Pacific and Atlantic Oceans. Also, Dunham made an announcement via Skype that got broadcasted on National TV. He told everyone that he was injecting two-hundred billion dollars into California, Texas, Florida, New York, and Michigan to put every citizen in those states back to work and adding fifty thousand dollars to their bank accounts to get them back on their feet.

One reporter was clapping. "We have just witnessed an unselfish act from a great American. I've never seen anything like this in our short history as a democracy. Mr. Dunham, you have my vote," the reporter said.

Everyone in the Oval Office sat in shock at what was happening. Thousands of people were taking to the streets with placards reading Dunham for President. Some were carrying signs that read President Chesterfield Resign.

The President stood up in his chair, which abruptly slid back and crashed into the window behind his desk. "Are most Americans selfish and only thinking of their pocketbooks? Will they truly support this traitor that has murdered thousands of citizens?"

"Throughout history, leaders who could put food on the table and make people feel safe always won over the masses," Rogers said. "We still have to stop this madman. He's a threat to our country's existence."

Chesterfield slumped down in his chair, his chin resting on his chest. "Scott, whatever you need to make your plan happen, do it. I need it done an hour ago.

"Copy that, Mr. President."

126

Scott Rogers was in a massive military tent four-hundred yards away from Dunham's front gate, protected by a forest of trees. He was in full combat gear. He had begun briefing his team on how their mission to capture Albert Dunham, Frederick Ellison, and General Tucker Phillips should go. Projected on a large screen was a layout of the Architect's compound.

"Today will be no different than most days with our job. Serve our warrants and arrest a criminal. Except for one thing. Albert Dunham not just the run of the mill bad guy. He's a domestic terrorist, controlling a weapon capable of inflicting mass casualties. He is hiding inside a fortress with enough safeguards to make penetrating and capturing him the most challenging arrest of our careers as US Marshalls." He glanced at his team, happy that all of them appeared ready to go.

Morgan Sullivan, nickname, Sully, was first to speak. "Scott, why not use some assault helicopters, breach the front and rear barriers and neutralize his men on the perimeter?"

"I'd love to do it. However, we are not sure how much control Dunham has with the satellite. We've watched him breach our power grids, launch our ballistic missiles without launch codes, and tap into the internet at his whim. Our helicopters are all computer operated. It too risky. We will have to do this mission old school, with the help of the National Guard and local SWAT. We will also use STAT phones, to communicate with our entire team," Rogers replied. "I will give you the frequency band we'll be using right before we have a go."

Everett Harrison, the team's tactical expert and ex-Navy SEAL who was with Rogers in Afghanistan and Iraq raised his arm. "Scotty, this shouldn't be any different than what we did capturing Taliban leaders and eliminating ISIS. So why all the concern for this civilian?"

"He's an American, a hero to a large part of the population. Plus, he has a powerful weapon with this new satellite. We've seen what he can do with his little games he's been playing. He made one mistake that should give us the window we need to breach his compound," he said. "Further, we need to go by the book on this one."

Beau Brown, the Emergency Operations Expert, chimed in. "Scotty, why don't we knock on the door and serve the warrant. We'll have our body cams on, and if he resists, we respond with equal force. Simple. Case closed," he said, wiping his hands together.

Rogers smiled at Beau. "I like that. K.I.S.S, keep it simple stupid," he answered, slapping his palm on his forehead.

Joshua Gomez, the team's weapons expert and jack of all trades was at their field laptop. "I think our choices have just gotten complicated. Two tactical vehicles and military buses just entered the complex. My first count shows he's got over a hundred well-armed soldiers, who look like us, taking positions around the perimeter of the ranch. I think they want a fight," he said.

Scott checked in with Admiral Hollingsworth to let him know what just happened at Dunham's ranch. He confirmed that the assault would happen in thirty-minutes. "Copy that Marshall Rogers. We'll be monitoring your progress from the situation room."

127

Hayes had finished briefing Dunham about what was happening outside the gates of his compound. He did not seem concerned that law enforcement was approaching his ranch.

"They look like they are ready for a war?" Hayes said. He looked at Tucker Phillips and heard him give some orders to his men outside.

Dunham signaled Phillips to rescind his orders. "I have a better idea that will make Chesterfield and his Attorney General look like fools. I'm leaving through my underground tunnel for an interview with CNN. I'll signal you when I am outside the ranch and safely on the road." He handed him a piece of paper that included specific keywords to signal his General to initiate his final solution for Washington, D.C.

"Keep your eyes and ears glued to my interview. When you hear me repeat these words on this piece of paper, you can initiate my final solution," Dunham said, laughing.

* * * * *

Thirty minutes after Dunham had left the ranch undetected, Scott Rogers and his team had reached the front gate. Before they could press the visitor intercom button, the hydraulics kicked in, and the twelve-foot high brass gate squeaked open.

"Be alert," Rogers said, "Somethings not right. It could be a trap."

The large brass gate opened, exposing a large circular driveway that bordered a lush green lawn the size of two football fields. Waiting for them were two dozen of Dunham's security detail, their weapons at their feet, hands raised above their heads, showing no resistance.

Rogers was puzzled. His gut was telling him something was not right. "I have these warrants," he said, waving them in the air. "I need Albert Dunham, Frederick Ellison and General Tucker Phillips brought to me immediately," he ordered. He could sense something was wrong. He didn't know what.

Then, walking out from the ranch's ornate oak door, was Frederick Ellison, Tucker Phillips, and Thomas Hayes. Big smiles on their faces, welcoming Rogers and his men to come into the house.

While Roger's men gathered up all the weapons, he handed the warrants for their arrests to Ellison. "All of you put your hands behind your back." He watched Beau Brown handcuff the three men.

128

Theodore Dunham was surprised to be getting a phone call from his sister-in-law. "Maggie? It's been a long time since we talked. What's up?" he said cautiously.

Maggie was whispering. "It's your brother. He's crazy. He's murdered so many innocent people so he could fulfill his lifelong dream of being the Emperor of the United States," she said, her voice trembling.

"I've seen everything on TV. He's had this crazy dream of being the Emperor of the United States since he was a young boy. He was a terrifying child growing up, especially after he hooked up with Frasier Montgomery and Frederick Ellison. He changed so much that it killed our father. When he was named the heir to the Architect's Manifesto, I had to leave and make my own life," Teddy said. "So why are you calling me now?"

"You know what Albert is capable of doing. Since he's taken control of president Chesterfield's new satellite, he's gone mad."

"So, what do you want me to do? Albert threatened me too, but I still gave the authorities the videos I had taken. I am waiting for him to punish my family and me in some way," Teddy said, his voice cracking. "Maggie, you need to step up and make a choice. Support or not support your husband."

"There are SWAT teams, US Marshalls and the National Guard inside my house. They are looking for Albert. He's escaped. Ellison and Phillips are in handcuffs, along with Thomas Hayes."

"That's a good thing, right?"

"No, Albert is going to be interviewed on National TV, and Todd Mathews is alone with his laptop in the bunker fifty feet under the main house. No that's not a good sign," she said. "If Mathews has orders from Albert to use the satellite for another attack, then something he will say during the interview will trigger it. His man has a computer that controls the satellite. There is no telling what instructions Albert gave him before he left."

"Again, Maggie, what do you want me to do?" Teddy was getting frustrated with her ranting.

"I need to know if I turn against Albert, will you hide me from him?"

"What are you planning on doing?"

"I can't say right now, as one of his security guards is coming into my bedroom. Goodbye. I will be in touch as soon as I can get away from here." She abruptly ended the call.

Teddy stared at his phone, confused about what his sister-in-law had told him. "Laptop. In a bunker under the ranch?" He immediately dialed Paige Turner.

"Ms. Turner, Theodore Dunham, Albert's brother. I just received a disturbing phone call from my sister-in-law. She's scared for her life. She said something about a laptop inside a bunker?"

Paige placed her phone with the speaker on so everyone in the Oval Office could listen. "Where was she calling you from?"

"Our family ranch, in Pennsylvania. She says the authorities are already there. She wants to give you some information but is frightened for her life. She doesn't know who to trust," he said.

"Thanks for calling. I will alert our team and try to help your sister-in-law. Can I call you back if I have more questions?" she asked.

"No problem. My brother, I must sadly say has lost his mind."

* * * * *

Admiral Hollingsworth was on his phone talking with Scott Rogers. "We just received a call from Maggie Dunham. She's fearing for her life and wants to cooperate with you. We now believe that Dunham's controlling the satellite from a laptop in a bunker at the ranch. Get his wife to cooperate and help you get inside and secure that computer. It's time to stop being politically correct and get that laptop back at any cost," the Admiral said.

"Sir, we are already inside the compound without incident. Dunham is not on the premises. I will put his wife in protective custody and find out what she is talking about," Rogers told him.

129

Albert Dunham was sitting across from a reporter from CNN in his study at his home in Bethesda, Maryland. He was cracking his knuckles, acting agitated.

"Mr. Dunham, you've asked for this interview, but haven't told me what you expect from me? You are a wanted man. You're American who is about to get arrested as a domestic terrorist. Is that what we are going to talk about today?" the reporter asked.

Dunham just smiled at the cameras. "Yes. However, first, I am going to talk about my country, our president, and how our experiment with democracy has failed all of the American people." He took a sip of water from a glass in front of him. "My recent actions have been misinterpreted by the media, the president, and the justice system. The attacks I directed was to wake up all our citizens to the corrupt administration that does not have your best interests at heart. I had to make sacrifices to show everyone how corrupted our government has been. I took control of President Chesterfield's new satellite weapon to protect everyone," he said, wiping the sweat from his forehead.

"I have used my new power to help all Americans achieve the American dream and live a happy life protected from all of our enemies..." the reporter interrupted him.

"Mr. Dunham, are you confessing to all the bombings and attacks on American soil, as well as in the Middle-East that cost almost five-thousand lives? Are you saying that all of these heinous, murderous acts were for the good of all Americans?"

He was nodding his head. "Change, positive change requires sacrifice by all of us. If a small number of people had to die to make my point, then so be it. There has never been a bloodless revolution. Now I can take care of everyone with the money I have appropriated from our known enemies around the world. I am committed to helping, no sharing this new wealth with every American if they will throw their support my way..." the reporter was noticeably upset.

"Mr. Dunham, you're not a well man. Coldblooded murder is a sin against God and this country. You will one day get your just reward." Before the reporter could leave, Dunham lashed out at her.

"Within a couple of hours, you and everyone will know the power I possess. Either be part of my new empire, bow to me as your Emperor or you'll perish.

The interview was over, and the reporter and her cameraman rushed out of Dunham's Bethesda house noticeably frightened.

* * * * *

Dunham was on the phone calling Ellison. His phone went to voice mail. He then tried Tucker Phillips and got the same result. When he attempted to call Thomas Hayes and heard his message, he knew something had happened at the compound.

He turned on the news and sat back, excited to hear what everyone was saying about his interview. He was looking forward to watching the president panic and shit his pants with the upcoming attack the Capitol and having no way to stop it.

130

Maggie Dunham was watching in horror as her husband threatened everyone in the United States. When he had finished, and the interview was over another news alert flashed on her monitor. Three ballistic missiles were heading toward the White House, the Capitol building and the Supreme Court. The commentator was wondering why evacuations had not started. Then a message flashed on her screen that all exits were in lockdown. The tunnel system under the capital was closed down too.

With Congress in full session and the Supreme Court hearing cases, the entire government, including the President and Vice-President, were about to be vaporized.

"No," Maggie screamed. No more dying." She bolted past her security guard running down her stairs and into the arms of Scott Rogers.

"Mrs. Dunham, what's happening?"

"Downstairs in the bunker," she gasped, unable to catch her breath. "Todd Mathews has the computer controlling those missiles," she screamed, pointing at the TV monitor.

Scott grabbed her by her shoulders and looked her in the eye. "Where's the bunker? Is your husband there too?" She shook her head. He signaled his team to follow them as he dragged Maggie Dunham with him.

They took an elevator down four floors. When the door slid open, they saw a steel door, like the one you'd see at a bank vault. A retina scan and keypad were on the wall to the right of the door.

Maggie didn't waste any time. She leaned in and placed her left eye on the scan, and simultaneously typed in a numeric code. Within seconds the door unlocked and swung open. Inside was Todd Mathews typing at his laptop.

He looked back over his shoulder and shouted. "Stay back. Once I press the enter key, there is nothing you can do now to stop us," he said. Before he could finish his threat, a loud explosion splattered his brains on the computer screen.

Joshua Gomez holstered his weapon. Beau Brown threw Mathew's limp body to the floor and began wiping the blood from the laptop's surface.

"Shit, there's a count down to impact. We have ten-minutes before these missiles wipe out our government," he said. "It's going to take me longer than that to counter these commands."

Scott didn't waste any time. He was calling Professor Miller at the White House. Before he reached the professor, he asked Mrs. Dunham where her husband was hiding?

Without any hesitation, she said, "At our home in Bethesda."

131

President Chesterfield high-fived Admiral Hollingsworth after hearing they had possession of the laptop. He did not seem to care that Todd Mathews was dead. The President just wanted to get control of the satellite and stop the missiles from destroying the capital and all of its occupants. He looked at professor Miller, desperation in his voice. "Are we screwed?"

Miller was already sitting behind the president's desk, madly typing into his laptop. "Sir, we're not dead yet. I need to get inside the laptops setting and pray," he said calmly. "I got it. I'm inside the laptop. It's going to be a big reach, with only one try to get it right," he looked at the president who was now on the phone with Scott. "Sir, if I can get you control, where should I re-direct the missiles?"

Chesterfield shrugged his shoulders. Miller started addressing the problem at hand. "Beau, type in these codes in precisely the order I am giving them to you. Be sure all dots and underscores are in place, or this won't work in the timeframe we have left."

Beau tried to take his eyes off the clock on the computer screen. He tried listening intently to Miller, but his eyes kept focusing on the digital numbers getting closer to zero and the missiles impacting the capital.

"Brown, focus. It's up to you right now. I know you can do this," Rogers shouted. Once we have control, use these three coordinates to re-direct those fucking missiles."

Scott was looking at a TV monitor in the bunker. It was showing a video of the three missiles shooting toward their targets. His only thoughts at that moment were of Paige. "Beau, you're running out of time," Rogers shouted.

Beau started typing in the codes Miller had given him. His fingers were shaking, trying not to hit the wrong keys or characters the professor had said for him to input. He finished and held his breath as he hit the enter key. Within thirty seconds, he had full control of the laptop and the satellite. He began entering the new coordinates for the three missiles. He prayed he wasn't too late.

132

Dunham was watching his TV, excited that soon he would be marching into the destruction he caused in the Capital. He fantasized how he would quickly announce he would be proclaiming himself the Emperor and re-writing the constitution with the help of his loyal congressmen and senators. He would hold a State of the Union type of address to all the American citizens who would be cheering him as their new leader.

He spread out his blueprint of how the new Capital of the United States would look and how it would embody him as Caesar of modern times. The Lincoln monument would be refitted with a statue of him sitting on his throne.

"*The Emperor will soon be sitting on his throne,*" he muttered. He kept watching and checking his watch.

"*Just five more minutes and everything will finally be mine,*" he told himself. He decided to call Maggie and tell her his good news.

"Maggie, it's finally going to happen. You will be my queen and help me rule over America and most of the free world," he bragged.

Maggie was weeping as she tried to talk. "I gave the Marshalls the laptop. They are going to stop you and this crazy idea you have. I don't know what's happened to you. I won't be your queen or your wife any longer," she said. "They know you're at our home in Bethesda. They should be there very shortly," she told him and ended the call.

He was pounding the couch cushions, yelling at an empty house. "Nothing can stop me. Mathews made my laptop hack-proof," he screamed.

Then, a breaking news report flashed on his screen.

"The three missiles heading toward Washington D.C. have changed course and were heading out to an undisclosed location in the Atlantic Ocean."

The reporter was pressing her earbud; a shock expression cracked on her face. "One of the missiles has changed directions again and heading toward Bethesda, Maryland, toward a densely wooded area. God have mercy on all of us," she said.

Dunham, dazed and confused, squeezed his eyes tight. "Damn you, Chesterfield. You haven't won yet." He jumped up and ran toward his bomb shelter below his home. Before he was able to close the large steel door, he was thrown back into his bomb shelter by a red hot flash. The pain engulfing his body was unbearable. Then everything went dark.

133

"It worked," Chesterfield shouted. "We're safe, and I have control of the satellite."

Attorney General Sawyer seemed confused. "Where did the third missile end up?"

"Just a little present for Albert Dunham, The Architect. Karma is a sweet bitch," The President said.

General Hollingsworth, Professor Miller, and Paige Turner knew exactly what Chesterfield had authorized. Paige had raised her objections, even though Dunham had murdered her friend and co-worker Sean Adams and tried to kill her on two occasions. She wanted to see him convicted of treason first and then executed for his crimes. She felt the president was letting him off too easy.

She had told president Chesterfield out of earshot from the Attorney General that he did not have the authority to execute an American citizen without a trial for treason. "Sir, what you're doing here will only empower the House to impeach you and give the Senate no choice than to find you guilty of murdering an American citizen," she said, her voice just above a whisper.

"Don't tell me what I can do when I am protecting this country from a terrorist attack. If one of Dunham's missiles, unfortunately, hits the wrong target, then so be it."

They all gathered by the large monitor in the Oval Office and watched two of the missiles explode two-hundred miles off the Eastern Seaboard. It was the lone missile that got their attention. Like a drone fixing on a target, the screen focused on a large estate secluded in the woods of Bethesda, Maryland. Within seconds they all witnessed a large blast flash on the screen. When their picture came back into focus, what was once Albert Dunham's family estate, was vaporized.

Marilyn Sawyer looked at the president, her eyes wide with disbelief. "Mr. President, what did you just do?"

"I saved this country from the pain of a bitter trial of a domestic terrorist. We will still have a trial for Frederick Ellison, General Tucker Phillips, and Thomas Hayes. Besides, you'll be kept busy rounding up the dirty dozen who helped and supported Dunham in his attempt to overthrow our democracy," Chesterfield said smugly.

"What you've done here will only add more fuel to your impeachment trial. You've overstepped your authority. Like the president before you, your legacy will be one of disgrace." Sawyer stormed out of the Oval Office.

134

It had been the most nerve-racking week for Paige. She was relieved she was home but was unable to erase the Architect from her thoughts. The good news was that Dunham was presumed dead. The bad news was that President Chesterfield had his weapon back in his possession. She understood how desperate he was to win his second term as President and believed he'd do anything to win.

She was meeting up with Scott that evening. When she had spoken to him after he secured the laptop, he too sounded exhausted.

Scott arrived at Paige's Malibu home around seven that evening. He had cleaned up, but his shower had not cleansed the emotions from that day.

Paige looked deep into his eyes. She saw the man she was falling in love with who struggled with his pain. "Can I ask how you're doing?" she said, giving him a big hug and gentle kiss.

"Better than I thought I'd be," she could tell he was lying. "I am grappling with the kill order I gave before reading Todd Mathews his rights. I'm upset that I allowed a conflict of interest, *your safety*, cloud my judgment, and force me to make a split-second decision."

Paige squeezed his hand. "If you hadn't acted quickly, we might not have gotten control of the satellite before the missiles reached the White House."

Scott put Paige in his arms and squeezed her tight. "I don't want to think about what may have happened to you. I'm happy Dunham got his just reward for his treasonous behavior," he said.

Paige stood up, breaking away from Scott's tight swaddle. "I'm happy he's dead too. I just wanted to watch him be destroyed in our Federal Courts and convicted of treason. Then, he could have been executed," she said.

Scott was shaking his head. "You know he still had a seventy-five percent approval rating as of yesterday? It's crazy that so many Americans still supported him. It would have been a crapshoot trying him for treason. He could have gone free with the way our justice system works."

"It's now Chesterfield's problem he's going to have to defend. I'm worried about him having control of this weapon. He's a desperate man who wants to get re-elected. We all witnessed what it can do," she said.

"Paige, I'm sure you're going to hold him accountable and put him under your watchful eye up to and after the election. You're a great investigative reporter," he said. "But we might have a bigger problem now. It doesn't appear Chesterfield will get re-elected from recent polls. The Attorney General was threatening to bring murder charges against the president for ordering the killing of an American Citizen, even that it was Dunham."

Paige did not seem too concerned with what Scott had said. "First, Marilyn Sawyer needs to find Dunham's body. Without it, it's going to be hard proving he perished at his Bethesda home. Does she have proof he was even there at the time the missile landed?"

"That's what President Chesterfield wants to know too. He asked my team to investigate, but I told him I'm retired," Scott said.

"You do you remember that we're going to start our new investigation agency? Together we'll keep everyone on their toes," Paige said, plopping down on the couch and putting Scott into her arms.

"Let's forget about business for now. I want to work on our relationship first," Scott said, kissing her lips.

Before they could get comfortable, Paige's phone rang. She looked at the display screen. It was Bradley. "I need to take this," she said.

Scott nodded. "Make it quick. I'm starving."

Paige's face had drained of color as she was listening to what Bradley was telling her. "Are they sure?"

"Satellite images recorded a man entering a tunnel that ran under Dunham's Bethesda house two hours after the missile leveled his home. Thirty minutes later, two men are seen leaving the area, heading toward a small private airfield five miles away. The FBI is out there as we speak searching for any evidence that someone survived the blast," Bradley said. "What would you like me to do?"

"I think we should let the FBI and President Chestfield handle this. We need a break for a while," she said.

* * * * *

Thirty Days Later

Maggie Dunham had been allowed to keep the ranch property and one of the family's bank accounts valued at over five-hundred million dollars. Attorney General Marilyn Sawyer felt it was a good reward for the help she had given the government.

However, Mrs. Dunham did not have time to enjoy her new life, as she was found hanging from her banister with a typed note pinned to her robe. It read: *I could not live with myself after turning against my husband.* It was unsigned. Her bank accounts had been mysteriously drained.

Walking on Pennsylvania Avenue, pushing a broken-down shopping cart, a man with a scruffy beard was staring at the White House. He was mumbling to himself. *"I'll be back to claim my rightful throne. The Emperor will fight again once I have my satellite back in my possession.*